Dreams Bigger Than the Night

Other Books by Paul M. Levitt

The Denouncer: A Novel
Stalin's Barber: A Novel

Dreams Bigger Than the Night

A Novel

Paul M. Levitt

TAYLOR TRADE PUBLISHING
Lanham • Boulder • New York • London

Published by Taylor Trade Publishing
An imprint of The Rowman & Littlefield Publishing Group, Inc.
4501 Forbes Boulevard, Suite 200, Lanham, Maryland 20706
www.rowman.com

Unit A, Whitacre Mews, 26-34 Stannary Street, London SE11 4AB, United Kingdom

Distributed by NATIONAL BOOK NETWORK

British Library Cataloguing in Publication Information Available

Library of Congress Cataloging-in-Publication Data
Levitt, Paul M.
  Dreams bigger than the night : a novel / Paul M. Levitt.
    pages ; cm
  ISBN 978-1-63076-078-6 (hardcover : acid-free paper) — ISBN 978-1-63076-079-3
(electronic)
  1. Organized crime—Fiction. 2. United States—History—20th century—Fiction. I.
Title.
  PS3612.E935D74 2015
  813'.6—dc23

                                                                            2015008483

Printed in the United States of America

For my wife, Nancy

Acknowledgments

John Donne reminds us that no man is an island entire of itself. My book emerges from a community, without which I would be the less.

First and foremost I am indebted to Henriette von Trapp for allowing me to edit and use parts of her memoir. A remarkable woman, she was the wife of the first von Trapp child, Rupert. Though stricken with crippling polio shortly after her wedding, she led an active life that included raising six children. My indebtedness extends to her sister Françoise, who first brought the memoir to my attention.

Warren Garfield, a longtime school friend, kindly found and reproduced the old newspaper reports of the Mary Astor trial. His own screenplay, based on the novel, gave me numerous ideas for revision.

Mitchell Waters, a first-rate literary agent, read the manuscript with a discerning eye, pointing out numerous stylistic misadventures.

My two editors, Gene Margaritondo and Janice Braunstein, artfully showed me the errors of my ways and, in so doing, saved me from subsequent despair. Kalen Landow tirelessly promoted the book, and Karie Simpson never failed to remind me of a deadline or an omission.

The distinguished people who have lent their names to the cover jacket reside in my pantheon of heroes: Frank Delaney, the brilliant novelist of Irish themes and the inspiration for chapter 2; H. Bruce Franklin, a Rutgers (Newark) professor and champion of justice, whom I tried unsuccessfully to hire several years ago but was rebuffed by the University of Colorado Regents; Berel Lang, professor emeritus, philosopher, aesthetician, holocaust scholar, and former colleague; and Alan Wald, an eminent historian of 1930s left-wing literature, now retired from the University of Michigan.

Warren Grover's book, *Nazis in Newark*, provided invaluable background information, as did the numerous unnamed reference and history books that I consulted.

As always, I remain indebted to my family for their moral support and for their patience with my absences, when I frequently retreated to my office.

Financial assistance came from the University of Colorado, and in particular the generosity of Philip DiStefano.

And, once again, I thank Rick Rinehart for his encouragement and friendship.

1

"May bananas grow in their throat; my God, I am passing . . . out!" the young man anguished in Yiddish after the emcee applied "heat" in the form of twenty dynamite sprints around the dance floor, causing the Yid's girl to go squirrelly and imagine that she had been assumed into heaven and stood before the throne of the Almighty. The heat also drove several other dancers to quit, even though the clock showed less than five minutes to go until the fifteen-minute rest period. Margie Smith, his part-time dance-marathon partner, mostly earned her living as a whore. "When my ass gets tired," she liked to say, "I enter a contest, but only for the specialty events." During breakout numbers, the audience "sprayed" the best dancers with coins and gifts. They had made it through nine days, picking up a fair amount of change from specialty events, particularly the fast ones in 4/4 time, like the Charleston, until the emcee weeded out the weak with a series of "sprints." As he dragged her dead feet around the floor, waiting for the bell, she fell asleep standing up. A pretty girl with a splash of red across her lips and mascara running down her cheeks, she wore a tired plaid bathrobe, dingy white socks rolled at the ankles, and open-toe terry-cloth slippers. Her waist-length brown ringlets, only nine days ago light and airy, hung like attenuated chewing gum, and her lifeless arms rested limply on his shoulders. Suddenly she awoke, groaning that her gut had exploded. Usually, she could sleep on her feet for three hours at a stretch, all the while moving. Not him. He never had the knack; besides, he weighed 160 pounds and Margie 110, so how could he have leaned against her? But on that sweaty Saturday night in early March 1934, just as the contestants began to drop out, Margie burst an appendix. When they took her to the hospital, she said she'd soon be back, but she must have meant on her back, because he later learned she'd quickly returned to Madame Polly's house on High Street. Meanwhile, he hoped the fifteen minutes of solo dancing allotted by marathon rules would not expire before some guy quit and he could take that gal for his own. The more-than-two-hundred hours of hoofing had left most everyone bedraggled. With the clock almost expired, a short, dark-haired fellow, whose tattooed arms exhibited, among other symbols, a winged eagle and Maltese Cross, and who danced like a cement mixer, threw in the trowel. His companion, who could still strut her stuff, looked crest-fallen. As she danced solo, her shapely legs moved smoothly and seamlessly, slipping from one step to another. Shimmering like a preening bird, she seemed to be saying, "Do you have the stamina and footwork to keep up with me in the specialties?" He knew then that she would rather call it a day than settle for a klutz who could do no more than shuffle his feet and sway weakly in time with the music. Breaking into several fast steps, he signaled to her that he was her man.

The event had begun just like the dozens of contests that Margie and Jay had entered before. The Dreamland Amusement Park in Newark, on Frelinghuysen Avenue across the street from Weequa-hic Park, regularly sponsored dance marathons, billing itself as the site of America's first such pageant. No piker, Victor J. "Buddy" Brown, the builder, owner, and manager, attracted name bands, major entertainers, and well-known vaudevillians to entertain the evening customers, who paid from twenty-five to forty cents for admission, sometimes more for a special guest performance. Mr. Brown hung the hall in patriotic bunting and always catered to the welfare of his dancers as well as his audiences. The layout exuded class: a polished dance floor circled by a low wooden wall, blue lights, a stage at the far end of the floor, rest quarters with cots in red-and-white tents, one marked "Girls" and one "Boys," a hospital area in larger tents to accommodate doctors, nurses, Swedish masseurs and masseuses, trainers, and beauticians. A row of booths along the wooden wall housed vendors touting foot eases, shoes, and hosiery. Refreshment stands sold hot dogs, Cracker Jacks, popcorn, and soda. Every advertisement reinforced the dream that fame and fortune would follow steadfastness. All of America seemed to have fallen for Horatio Alger's hokum: persist and you shall succeed. Hardly a week passed when a new endurance record wasn't set—for dancing, walking, piano playing, poetry reading, roller-skating, pole sitting, perambulator pushing, pie eating, oyster swallowing. Thousands of Americans, especially those out of work or underemployed, wanted to earn a check for $5,000 given to the last person standing—or prove themselves capable of shooting Niagara Falls in a barrel. Fame—it could even lead to a screen test in Hollywood, in which case, you could join the Okies flooding Highway 66, headed for golden California.

Her name, Arietta Magliocco, suggested dark operatic songs. Thin and limber as an eel, she had the staying power of an elephant. No sooner had they teamed up than the emcee called for another heat, a footrace through rubber pylons spaced at sharp angles around the floor. The added burden drove one fellow to quit for his cot, even though his partner kicked him in the shins, screaming that he had to continue. Another woman pleaded with her beau that she needed to sleep. "I'll be all right if I can just take a short trip to dreamland." Two more couples earned the audience's displeasure, and a disqualification from the floor judge, for fighting. In the first rhubarb, the man repeatedly slapped his partner's face; in the second, the woman punched her fellow's nose, drawing a rush of blood. One cute girl, with Marcelled hair bleached nearly white, kept her partner upright by dancing with her right pinky stuffed in his left nostril. At this point, they all danced as if they wore snowshoes, but any thoughts of his quitting were dispelled by Arietta's steely look.

Besides, he wanted to impress this demure elf with the bewitching widely spaced enormous green eyes. Strikingly fetching in her beautiful bones, she became his cynosure. Like a rash that itches all the more when scratched, she progressively invaded his skin. He felt like Odysseus encountering Nausicaa in a strange land—beached, bleached, and naked. The Mediterranean coloring, swan neck, Roman nose, and the sculpted line that ran from her high cheeks to the corners of her full lips, turned up slightly, brought to mind an odyssey of sin. Her brown hair, cut in a bob, made her look childlike, and yet, her constantly changing expression and penetrating eyes dispelled any idea of innocence. Within five minutes he loved her.

How could he not? Although they both laughed at the idiocy of marathons with their vaudeville routines and saccharine tunes that supplied the afternoon music—even the live musicians at night rolled their eyes when the emcee said that the "enduring American spirit" was on trial here—they joined hands to work the rail for a shower of coins and tokens of appreciation from the ringside ladies. Inspired by the mock weddings staged at marathons, he glibly told the applauding audience that he and Arietta had just met and would shortly be married, well aware that many a word spoken in jest is not without earnest.

A young woman with leg braces, sitting in a wheelchair, seemed particularly thrilled by the marital announcement and tossed nearly a dollar in coins. As they kneeled to gather them, Arietta whispered, "Another epidemic victim. Poor girl."

During one of the rest breaks, after they had wowed the crowd with their turkey trot and Texas Tommy, the emcee introduced a vaudeville team, Ed and Florrie Lowry. Arietta retired to the rest area. As the couple performed, a man entered wearing a salt-and-pepper *benny*, the rim of his black fedora shading his eyes. Instead of taking a seat in the stands, the man paused at the women's tent and then took up a position at the rail to watch the skit.

SHE: Say, Ed, don't you think clothes give one confidence?

HE: I certainly do. I go lots of places with them on. I wouldn't go with them off.

SHE: How do you like these stockings? I got them in Paris. They cost only two dollars over there, and here you couldn't touch them for less than fifteen dollars.

HE: Say, how did you know what I was thinking?

At the end of the routine, the audience enthusiastically applauded, and the emcee led the orchestra through a tired rendition of "Let Me Call You Sweetheart." Then the gong tolled. As Arietta came from the women's tent, he glanced over her shoulder and counted the couples left in the contest: fifteen. Even more frenetic than before, Arietta seemed intent on picking up the pace, though neither the music nor the rules required a quickened step. Breaking away from him, she swept into a rumba, danced solo for a few moments, and then extended a hand to a man dancing with another woman. Flattered, the stubble-cheeked fellow, stocky and light-footed, said "*Mit vergnügung*," and joined Arietta for a few turns of the Lindy Hop, dancing stylishly and beaming. His partner did not smile. In fact, her lips were so thin and hard, she could brand you with a kiss. Jay watched them spin away and hardly saw the man in the benny and fedora vault over the low wall, run onto the dance floor, pull a gun from his coat, and pump two shots into the chest of Arietta's new partner. The thin-lipped woman screamed; dancers dove for cover. The orchestra and emcee stumbled off the bandstand, and the ushers and attendants ran. The audience, suddenly realizing that the action was not staged, rushed screaming for the exits. In the commotion, the shooter escaped out the front door. The ticket taker subsequently testified that a car came to a screeching stop. A rear door opened, the murderer jumped in, and then the sedan roared off. She was too stunned to note the license plate numbers, but she thought the car resembled a Buick, or a Packard, or maybe even a LaSalle. It held two men wearing black homburgs. The driver, she noted, was wearing black gauntlet motorcycle gloves.

Bleeding from two large holes in his chest, the stricken man gasped for air and uttered some unintelligible German words. His partner sank to his side and took his hand. While trying to whisper in her ear, the victim expired. The dead man, according to his partner, was Heinz Diebel, the notoriously camera-shy American Nazi leader who'd been urging his followers "to drive the parasitic, Marxist Jewish race from America."

That someone had plugged him was no surprise, since every Jew in Jersey wanted to see him dead, though probably not many knew what he looked like. Besides, his own National Socialist party, the Friends of the New Germany, frequently quarreled among themselves, threatening each other with dire consequences for failing to show enough passion for the Nazi line or too much for the softer one of the Teutonia Society. But as Jay quickly learned, wanting in the abstract to see a guy dead and seeing him shot before your eyes are two different things. Diebel choked and gurgled as blood issued from his mouth.

Arietta shook uncontrollably and kept repeating incredulously, "I just danced with him!" Jay's sphincter and nausea told him to find a bathroom as soon as possible. If the coinage of life is blood, Diebel, owing to the holes in his chest, was now bankrupt. When the cops questioned Arietta, she said that she had never seen the man before the marathon and that she singled him out because she'd noticed his Lindy Hop. Diebel's companion, Gretchen Kunz, who wore her flaxen hair in a long, intricately woven braid, insisted with trembling lips that "the Jews killed him." Even days later, when the cops presented her with evidence that Mr. Diebel's fervor for Hitler had alienated the more-moderate members of his own party and that his womanizing had prompted death threats from numerous outraged husbands, she still held fast to the view that his killer must have been a Jew.

The local newspaper opined that the killing had the marks of a gangland rubout. Several days later, the pistol, a Browning model 1910, was found in a deserted lot with its serial number filed off. Other theories soon made the paper. This particular model had been used by the Serb student Gavrilo Princip, who had assassinated the Archduke Ferdinand at Sarajevo in June 1914. Perhaps the killer or killers intended to make some sort of political statement; after all, Diebel was attached to the extreme wing of his political party. But what was the statement?

When the *Newark Star-Eagle* ran the story, printing the names Arietta Magliocco and Jay Klug, Mrs. Klug mourned her son's low associations since completing college; and his father, called "Honest Ike," regretted "young Mr. Klug's dissolute life" and his frequent absences from work at the Jeanette Powder Puff Company, named after his wife. In their place, he might have come to the same conclusion: Jay is a bum. Having to live at home meant that his guilt never took a holiday, and his likeness to his father—lanky, lithe, and lean-faced, with full lips, thick lashes, and Levantine skin and eyes—made him feel joined at the hip. An only child, he had no siblings to diffuse his father's expectations. He was the hope of the family, the hope that the powder puff company had a future. But he had no desire to spend his life in a factory overseeing cutters and sewing-machine operators. Powder puffs! Frankly, he found the product frivolous, even if it did pay the bills.

"Jay, I feel you are lost. Aimless. A college graduate without purpose. I sometimes wonder if you'll ever find yourself."

His father then lectured him on the value of hard work and self-discipline. With the admonishment over, Jay hoofed it toward the Tavern. As he walked past the tidy houses with their postage-stamp lawns, he wished he could share the certitude of those who inhabited them. Notwithstanding the country's economic woes, the occupants seemed to know who they were and their function in life. Whether or not that assurance came from religion or self-regard or selflessness, he envied their certainty. He had seen many of these people in shul, which he and his mother occasionally attended on Friday night. As his coreligionists davened, he did as well, all the while remembering Turgenev's definition of prayer: the hope that two and two will equal five. In light of the current state of the world, like his father, he asked, "Where is God?" Mr. Miller, his Hebrew teacher who prepared him for his bar mitzvah, had said enigmatically, "You come to God through helping others, not yourself."

Jay's ruminations continued until he reached his destination. Although just a simple neighborhood restaurant at Meeker and Elizabeth Avenues, the Tavern attracted Newark's political bosses, business leaders, Bears baseball players, and even mobsters, whom Sam Teiger, the owner, founder, and manager, treated like everyone else. That particular evening, Ben Unterman, a journalist, lamented, "No matter how hard I try to beat the crowd, I lose."

Jay didn't mind waiting in line because Sam always supplied hors d'oeuvres, which Jews knew as *forshpiesers*. His wait, however, was brief because Puddy Hinkes and Willie Moretti invited him to join their table. He'd seen Moretti around and had heard about his involvement with "Longie" Zwillman, whose connections extended from the New York syndicate down to the cops on the beat and local ladies of the night.

Puddy, a small-time hood and boxer, could juggle debits and credits as well as Abbadabba Berman, Dutch Schultz's bookkeeper. A bagman, Puddy brought the payoffs to the mayor, the state senators, and even the governor. The guy knew the inside of federal buildings as well as a con knows the pen, and his loyalty to his employers stamped him as a comer. Four years Jay's senior, Puddy had taken a shine to him a year before, during a pickup basketball game at the B'nai Abraham shul, when Jay sank the winning basket in a game of twenty-one. At the time, Puddy had said that Jay's skinny legs reminded him of a spider and told him that if he ever wanted to make some extra cash, he should see him. But as the son of Honest Ike Klug, he had avoided the rackets.

Willie Moretti kept busy overseeing the widespread New Jersey wire system and numerous plush casinos, as well as the many "sawdust" or dice barns that ran from the Garden State into Pennsylvania. A stocky, round-faced, puffy-cheeked loyalist, who talked out of the left side of his mouth, Willie had an edgy sense of humor. From the vestibule Jay had seen him bending Puddy's ear. At the table, Puddy introduced them, and Willie cracked:

"Been grinding it at Dreamland lately?"

"I guess you read the papers."

Willie immediately began to occupy himself with the salt and pepper shakers. "Yeah, I seen them. I hear the gunsel was all bundled up. No one got a good look at him."

"That's true."

"Except for them spats, the cops probably woulda' never gone nosing around the Friends of the New Germany. Lucky they did."

Moretti was right. The killer had spats. But to that moment, Jay had forgotten, and the newspapers had never mentioned, the fact. So how did Moretti know?

"Whoever remembered that krauts like to wear spats was no fool," Jay said, hoping to elicit more information.

"Yeah," replied Willie, spilling some salt into his right hand and tossing it over his left shoulder. "Just for luck. I like to ward off any evil spirits. You know, it's a Catholic thing."

"What do you do when there's no salt around?"

Willie guffawed. "Smart kid. I make the sign of the *figa*, like this." Willie held up his fist with his thumb tucked under his fingers.

The two men had just finished dinner. Puddy and Jay ordered coconut cream pie. Willie paused.

"If I down another one of them cream pies, I'll never fit into my new suit. Better I should just have cherry pie a la mode."

"That'll keep you slim," said Puddy. "So, Spider, you still working for your old man?"

"Yeah, but a depression's not a good time for powder puffs. And nothing else seems available."

"If he needs a loan . . ."

"He would never ask."

"Money's money."

"Not according to Honest Ike."

Moretti continued to play with the salt and pepper cellars. "What about you?"

Before Jay could answer, Puddy said, "We could use a smart *lansman*."

"Why not?" thought Jay. His college degree had not brought him work commensurate with his education. Until now, the love he felt for his parents had kept him on the right side of the law. If his family learned that he palled around with Puddy . . . a *shanda*! It was rumored that even Zwillman made sure his mother never found out where his *gelt* came from. The bribe of bread had corrupted entire nations. Just look at Germany. "What's the deal?" he asked.

"Tell you what," said Puddy. "We'll drive over to my place. We can talk there."

Through the dessert, Moretti kept up a running commentary on Newark's nightspots, especially the Kinney Club at Arlington and Augusta streets, which offered a racially mixed clientele a taste of the forbidden in the heart of Newark's Barbary Coast. The Kinney Club was more than Jay's pocket could afford. Hoping for a return to the spats, he listened.

Finally, they put on their overcoats. Sam Teiger clapped him on the shoulder and said, "Say hello to your parents, Jay, and always do the right thing." Following Puddy into the gray street, he saw a new 1934 black Packard at the curb. A former schoolmate, Irv Sugarman, who'd left in the eleventh grade, opened the door. Irv apparently now worked for Puddy and Moretti.

"Hello, Jay. Hop in."

The sound of the door closing behind him, as he slid into the backseat, gave him a sense of importance. He was a capable boy with connections to people who actually ran the city. Still, he couldn't help wondering whether he would find himself in the underworld or in the respectable one, in crime or commerce? How would his family feel if his name appeared on a police blotter?

They drove to Puddy's office, a small room over a delicatessen, with spindle-backed chairs and a battered rolltop desk, which depended on a deck of cards under one leg to offset the sloping floor. From downstairs rose the mingled smells of pickles in brine, chopped liver and onions, Liederkranz and Limburger cheeses. Through the one window he could see in the lamplight the push-carts lining the curbs and the canvas awnings of the sidewalk stores.

"Sit down, Spider." Puddy plopped down with his feet on the desk. "You don't smoke, right?" Jay nodded without looking at him, his attention drawn to Moretti, who gravitated toward the window. Puddy removed the paper band from a cheap cigar, slipped it on his pinky, and struck a match on the side of the desk. "This stuff ain't good for me. I'm supposed to be in trainin'."

Moretti stared at the street below. "You're a born canvasback, Puddy. I don't know why you keep fighting."

"Hey, I like it. Besides, it gives me a reputation."

"What, as a punching bag?"

"No, a guy you don't lean on."

Moretti said nothing.

"We may have a job for you," said Puddy. "But before I give you my spiel, you give me yours. What do you like doin' most?"

"Writing."

"Huh?"

"Yeah, I like to write. Stories and essays . . . that sort of thing."

Moretti turned and stared as if in disbelief, and then returned his gaze to the window.

"Dutch Schultz . . ."

Puddy's pregnant pause was calculated. Well aware of the Dutchman's murderous reputation, Jay asked cautiously, "Yeah, what about him?"

"He has contacts in this part of town and we want to know more about 'em," Moretti said casually.

"We own office space across the street from one of the Dutchman's drops," Puddy added. "All you gotta do is sit and watch—and keep an accurate record. The days and times cars arrive and leave. Also license plate numbers."

"You might even get a glimpse of the Dutchman himself," Moretti chuckled.

"The papers say Tom Dewey is after him for tax evasion. I wonder where he keeps all his dough?"

Moretti's mood strangely changed. "Wise up, kid. If you don't want your fuckin' head handed to you on a platter, don't ask questions that ain't none of your business. Understand?"

"Absolutely!" Jay replied far too emphatically, feeling a trickle of urine escape from his pecker.

Puddy tried to play the peacemaker. "Hey, we're all friends here. We ain't gonna have a fallin' out just 'cause the kid asks a question."

"I don't like snoops," Moretti said morosely and began to pace. With each step his displeasure seemed to increase.

"Puddy, maybe I'm not your guy. I got too many things on my mind."

"Like?"

"Who's in charge? You never said."

"Does it matter? Those times you ain't watchin', you can write. We'll get you a nice desk, and a typewriter, too."

"When my old man asks where I work and the name of my employer, I got to have a story. Because sure as hell he'll ask."

Moretti cracked his knuckles. "I'm fed up with your whining, kid. I thought you wanted a job with real money. Come on, Puddy, let's go. He's all jitters, no balls."

Puddy tried to mollify his companion. "He's still wet behind the ears."

"So wet he's drowning. Just remember, if anything goes wrong, he's *your* guy." Turning to Jay, Moretti snapped, "Tell your old man the Canadian-American Liquor Company."

"I don't know anything about Canada. If he starts asking me questions, I'll be in the soup."

A furious Moretti said, "Then try the New Jersey Vending Machine Company . . . 1464 North Broad Street in Hillside."

"Doing what?"

"You talk to him, Puddy, I'm finished."

"Tell Honest Ike publicity. You said you wanted to write."

"And who's my boss?"

"Shit," said Puddy, now showing his annoyance, "you're the ink-slinger, not me. Make up what you fuckin' want."

"Does the company have a . . . phone?"

Moretti had shifted his bulky body in anticipation of starting for the door. "Look it up!" the enforcer growled. "And lock the door after you."

On their way out, Puddy paused, "Waverly 3-3165. Maybe instead of calling you 'Spider,' I oughta call you Jitters."

A week later, Jay found himself working from a shabby room, with a new desk and typewriter, three chairs, and a battered chintz sofa, between Spruce and Market on Prince Street over Lowitz's grocery. From his window he could see Sam Tubeman's Radio Repairs, across the street. The Dutchman's gang used Tubeman's as a drop for their Third Ward drug money. The dough then left Sam's place stuffed in the shell of a radio console, collected by one of Dutch's lieutenants.

Outside, he could hear the shoppers' Yiddish banter: "You can't dance at two weddings with one *tuchis*," and "Poverty is no disgrace, but no great honor either." The immigrants' dreams could be gleaned from their proverbs, and the condition of their purses read in their lined faces and frayed clothes. The merchants whom they patronized offered services like tailoring and dry cleaning and sold everything from barreled pickles and herring to fruits and vegetables, bread, clothing, and paper goods, all at bargain prices. The busiest block, Jay's, housed Kaplan's Delicatessen, with its dull white, hexagonal tile floor. It served fat corned beef sandwiches and pickles to patrons seated on wire chairs at rectangular tables with bowls of cube sugar for the tea drinkers. A few doors away stood Moishe Hupert's Fish Market, with "Moishe Fisher" painted on the double-glass windows. Inside, a large sheetmetal tank contained live fish—pike, carp, and perch for gefilte fish—which Mr. Hupert, as the housewives pointed into the tank, netted, killed on a butcher block with a single blow from a wooden club, scaled, and cleaned.

Telling his father that he had found a job for twenty dollars a week—five more than his father paid—he quit the family business. Asked for details, he prevaricated, saying he was hired by a vending machine company—and passed along the phone number. He mentioned no names.

"Jay," his father sighed, "I hope you know what you're doing."

"Does anyone—really?" Jay asked defensively.

His father reflected for a moment and kindly answered, "I guess not. To know is to know something, but what? That's the mystery. Good luck with it."

Late one afternoon, Jay ducked into Kaplan's Delicatessen for a chopped liver on pumpernickel, heard the clack-clack of checkers, and saw at one of the rectangular tables a group of the synagogue faithful with their yarmulkes. On the white tile top rested a board with black and red pieces. A fire-engine-red alarm clock stood on the table set for fifteen seconds. Rabbi Silverman, wearing a fedora, and a well-known Negro, sporting a derby, hunched over a game of lightning-fast checkers. A lot of the *schvarzes* played, also Eastern

Europeans. After a day of trying to grind out a living or looking for work, the men in the Third Ward migrated to Kaplan's. When the deli closed, players continued the game on the sidewalk, even in the rain. Standing behind a Polish tailor sucking on a sugar cube, he stood with the kibitzers watching the colored fellow, who spoke perfect Yiddish and called himself "T," short for "T-Bone Searle," rag the rabbi. *"Es vet dir gornisht helfen."*

"T, I always tell my parishioners that win or lose if they play checkers, their wives have nothing to worry about, because they're not drinking, gambling, or running around with women."

"Yeah, but checkers can't do for them what their wives can."

The kibitzers chortled, as Silverman lost track of the clock and forfeited his turn.

T-Bone, in his mid-thirties, had arms forged in brawny labor, having wielded a shovel for one of the government projects. The rabbi got beat badly. Jay waited until the next player likewise took a shellacking, which gave him just enough time to finish his sandwich and offer T-Bone a challenge. The two stacked up pretty evenly. Toward the end of the game, Jay ran off a sequence of captures but neglected to take the last piece and had to retract his moves, allowing his opponent to win.

"You're leavin', Jay bird? If you want lessons . . ." T-Bone laughed.

"I have an office just down the street. Why not meet me there for lunch tomorrow, if you're working in the neighborhood." Having bent a wire hanger into the shape of a miniature basketball rim and taped it to the wall, he added, "We can shoot buckets with a stuffed sock."

T-Bone showed up the next day, carrying two Negro newspapers, the *New York Age* and the *New York Amsterdam News*, which were featuring stories about whether or not colored athletes should boycott the 1936 Olympics to be held in Berlin. Naturally, most Jews opposed participation because it would serve as a showcase for Nazism, a subject and problem that all of America seemed to be talking about.

"Shall we have a friendly game?" Jay asked, pointing to the board.

Until his work project ended several weeks later, T-Bone never missed a lunch hour. Jay looked forward to his legends and laughter. T usually found a way to win at checkers, though not at B-ball, which admittedly was not his game.

"You ever play baseball?" asked T-Bone.

"Just stickball in the streets with a Spaldeen."

Slowly, T-Bone shook his head and positioned his checkers. "Great game. I'd still be playin' if I hadn't hurt my ankle slidin' into second base 'gainst the Pittsburgh Crawfords."

"You played pro?"

"Yeah, for the Kansas City Monarchs. The hot corner. I had an arm like a rifle and could one hop the ball better than any white boy in the majors."

Having started in 1920, the Monarchs were the New York Yankees of the Negro leagues.

"How old are you, T-Bone?"

"Thirty-six . . . twenty-eight when I got injured and started swingin' a pick and a shovel. If the Man upstairs had made me white, maybe my name would be right up there with Ruth and Gehrig and Lefty Gomez. But that can be said about a lotta black ballplayers, 'specially Satchel Paige and James 'Cool Papa' Bell."

One evening, Jay accompanied T back to his digs at the Douglas-Harrison Apartments, a long row of redbrick buildings, and sat next to him on the couch leafing through his scrapbook. The living room had few amenities: a wooden cable spool that held a radio topped with a lace doily and a porcelain figurine of Mary cradling Jesus, a rocker, some chairs missing spindles, a couch that had given up the fight to support any weight, and a framed needlepoint expressing the hopes of an oppressed people: "When all is done, there is God."

T-Bone's mother, bedridden with emphysema, asked to meet her son's newfound friend. A white-haired handsome woman, she shook Jay's hand and apologized for not getting out of bed.

"Too many cigarettes," she wheezed.

"You gonna be all right, Mamma, you just wait and see."

"In heaven, maybe, but not here."

"Everything happens for the best, Mamma. Trust in God."

She took her son's hand and beamed. "I do. And you also."

Shortly after T-Bone's work crew transferred to another ward, she died. Jay attended the funeral out of respect, the only white person present. Held in the basement of a church, the funeral took place in a room that had about twenty folding chairs, a table with crackers and cheese, and two pitchers of nonalcoholic punch. The mourners, in their frayed Sunday best, sat with hands folded through the service. Then two brass players—trombone and trumpet—played "Amazing Grace" as T-Bone, whose real name was Randall, wiped the tears from his cheeks.

On Saturday, March 17, 1934, around eight p.m., Puddy and Jay drove to a party in West Orange. It was a date Jay would never forget. Puddy had said a pal of his wanted friends to join him for a festive occasion.

"Who is this guy?"

"You'll meet him, just hold your horses."

"He doesn't know me from Adam."

"Relax, Spider. He said to bring friends. You're a friend, ain't you?"

"Yeah."

They drove down Beverly Road, and pulled up at a Tudor mansion with decorated half timbering, tall narrow windows, massive chimneys, and a roof pitched steeper than a ski jump. Dozens of cars had spilled over from the street onto the expansive lawn. Just outside the front door stood two Cadillacs, one red and the other an all-weather black phaeton.

A butler led them into the house, which was overflowing with raucous guests and booze. A rainbow of balloons floated overhead;

three musicians on piano, trombone, and sax played swing. Ladies wore fur stoles and beaded evening gowns that reflected the lamps glowing like golden apples, their necks and wrists dripping diamonds and pearls and rubies, with gents in dark English suits and silk shirts—white on white, black, silver, blue—sporting bloated pinky rings and smoking foot-long Habana cigars that they lit from platinum Ronson lighters. Two priests and a man wearing a white satin yarmulke moved easily through the room, stopping at the sideboards stocked with roast beef, cold lamb chops, pastrami, chopped chicken liver, smoked salmon, and whitefish. One table held just fresh fruits and desserts: lemon meringue pies, cheese cakes, cherry, apple, and blackberry pies, chocolates, Danish pastry, custards, cream puffs, and vats of ice cream standing in iced tubs. Amused to see three men of faith at this shindig, Jay moved close enough to listen. The Jewish man was talking.

"We really must stand together and rally public opinion. From our Berlin sources, I understand the Nazis so fear a boycott that they have dispatched undercover agents to different countries to suppress dissent—any way they can."

The younger of the two priests, a wispy fellow, agreed on the importance of unity. "With Jeremiah Mahoney behind the boycott, other Catholics will follow."

"Brundage," said the Jewish man, "is immune to reason and dogmatically insists the games must go on. I do begin to wonder whether his scheduled trip to Germany is to promote the glory of sport or himself."

The older priest, completely bald, laid a hand on his shoulder and said, "Rabbi Wise, the Olympic Committee may follow Avery Brundage, but the Amateur Athletic Union will have the final say. And Mahoney is the president of the AAU."

Of course: Rabbi Stephen Wise! His face had looked familiar. But here in this house . . . unbelievable! In his early sixties and Hungarian by birth, the good man was strikingly handsome with sharp features and dark hair. Shortly after Hitler took power in

January 1933, Wise had denounced the National Socialists and had organized an anti-Nazi protest in Madison Square Garden. Calling for a boycott of the Berlin Olympics, he was meeting with resistance from Brundage and his ilk.

The older priest continued. "Catholics stand with Mahoney, who is, after all, a former New York State supreme court justice and the head of the Committee on Fair Play."

To which his colleague added, "And Jeremiah has started a letter-writing campaign in support of the boycott."

"For the life of me," said Rabbi Wise, "I can't understand why Brundage would want to hold the games. They will only glorify the Nazi regime. The man's a college graduate, an engineer, rich. What does he stand to gain?"

The older priest replied softly, "Avery regards the opposition as Communists and, pardon the slander, self-serving Jews."

A bar with a brass foot rail held a prominent place in the living room, manned by three Negroes dressed in white jackets and shirts, black trousers, and red bow ties. Every conceivable drink from ginger ale and beer to Bols could be had for the ordering. Half a dozen waiters, all in black tuxes, appeared, evaporated, and then materialized at a guest's elbow with a tray bearing a drink. Glancing around the room, Jay had the impression of exotically colored cocktails floating through the smoky light. Puddy identified the famous gangsters in attendance. Awed by the company, Jay was all ears.

Charles Luciano's drooping right eye was a souvenir of knife-wielding kidnappers who'd severed his cheek muscles. Having survived that "ride" five years before had earned him the nickname "Lucky." Puddy said the guy could barely read a newspaper, but had had the moxie to arrange the deaths of Joe the Boss Masseria and Salvatore Maranzano, the Mustache Petes. Lucky stood listening to Meyer Lansky or, as Puddy respectfully called him, "the little man," who was saying:

"They never learn, do they? Traditions are fine, but what holds men together is money, not rituals."

The third member of this trio, Benjamin "Bugsy" Siegel, agreed. "That *omerta* stuff's old world. Come out to California and see the future. Los Angeles . . . that's where it's being made. Palms and pineapples and pinochle."

A handsome guy with slicked-down hair, Bugsy was reputed to have a ferocious temper and was regarded as a cold-blooded killer. Frankly, Jay thought the man looked more like a movie star than a hit man.

Gerry Catena, said to be a business associate of Abner Zwillman, slapped Puddy's shoulder and paused just long enough for Jay to be introduced, then vanished in the crowd.

A short, round-faced, cigar-chomping spark plug held up his dukes as Puddy approached. Jay recognized him immediately from the newspapers, where his mug had appeared more than once for his involvement in fights, in and out of the ring. A retired prizefighter, Nat Arno now worked for Longie Zwillman's Third Ward Gang as an enforcer and as the head of a group of toughs, the Minutemen, dedicated to breaking up pro-Nazi meetings and busting heads. Nat whispered in Puddy's ear and shook Jay's hand like a vise.

"Arno's the name. Nat. Ever see me fight?"

"'Fraid not."

"Nat does his best fighting on the street," Puddy chuckled.

"You know my motto, Pud, persuasion when possible, violence when necessary."

Nat shifted the cigar in his mouth and moved off.

A fellow in his early thirties walked up and shoved his paw in Puddy's. A moment later Jay met Morris "Moe" Dalitz, who led the Cleveland mob. Conservatively dressed in a blue suit and tie, Moe seemed interested mostly in criticizing the house owner's collection of paintings.

"Run of the mill stuff."

"What do you like?" asked Puddy.

"The real, not the idealized."

Dalitz, despite his cruel eyes, extended lower lip, and small, hard body, could have passed for a cultured art collector. Apparently, a few days before, Moe had been in the Village trying to persuade the painter Edward Hopper to part with an oil, *Room in New York*.

"On the left side of the canvas," Moe explained, gesturing with manicured hands, "a man in a dark vest and tie slumps in a parlor chair reading a newspaper. On the right, a woman in a spiffy red dress sits at a piano with one hand on the keys. The lower part of her body is turned toward the man, the upper faces the piano. A table stands between them. His interest in the paper and her posture suggest that he's indifferent and she's sad. The haunting loneliness . . ."

Moe would undoubtedly have continued had all the revelers not been interrupted by Luciano calling for everyone's attention.

"You ain't seen your host yet and that's 'cause he's been tied up with a surprise. Ladies and gents, Abe Zwillman *and* Jean Harlow!"

As the crowd applauded, Jean Harlow appeared in a sheer white dress that reminded Jay of a joke making the rounds: "I'm dying to see what the well-dressed girl will leave off this season." Clearly visible were her breasts and nipples and more. The movie critics said that she had a perfect body and never wore underwear, observations any fool could have arrived at; the critics also said that she used peroxide, ammonia, Clorox, and Lux Flakes to bleach not only her famous platinum tresses but also her pubic hair. Though Jay couldn't attest to the formula, he could to the color. Equally eye-catching was her creamy complexion, which resembled pink ivory and shone with a mysterious luminosity. On her left wrist she wore a jeweled charm bracelet featuring a pig, and on her left ankle a chain. She spoke like a guttersnipe and referred to herself in the third person, but her fans could never tell whether they were hearing her movie voice or her real one.

"You wouldn't mind, would ya, if Jean had a carrot?"

The guests all roared because the rich repast did not include vegetables. "Miss Harlow," she joshed, "has to keep her figure."

One of the Negro bartenders made a beeline for the kitchen and returned a minute later with a plate of tomatoes, carrots, celery, mushrooms, and asparagus spears.

People immediately surrounded her, leaving Zwillman, called *Der Langer*, Yiddish for "The Tall One," peering over the heads of her admirers. Though handsome, with black curly hair and bright observant eyes, Zwillman was no Clark Gable. A few years before, he and Harlow had been lovers. The columnists said Longie had paid movie directors to cast her and even invested in a film company for the sole purpose of advancing her career.

"How did you meet?" a breathless woman asked Harlow. The inquisitor, wearing a yellow dress with spaghetti straps, leaned so close to Jean they nearly bumped heads.

"In Chicago. I was appearing at the Oriental Theater. My host, Al Capone, took Abe backstage to meet me."

"*The* Al Capone?" a strawberry blonde said with such longing that she looked as though she'd embrace Harlow.

"None other."

The mention of Capone had elicited knowing looks and vacuous bursts of laughter, but before her fans could ask any further questions, she held up a hand.

"Jean is not the attraction tonight, someone else is." All eyes shifted to Zwillman. But Abe shook his head no. "We have with us a man who has been called the world's greatest entertainer. It gives me great pleasure to introduce Al Jolson!"

Materializing from one of the numerous rooms, a dapper Jolson, wearing an ascot, bounded into the crowd, shook hands with dozens, rolled out a repertoire of jokes and patter, puffed on a cigarette, strutted some dance steps, snuffed out the weed, called to the pianist, and, with the kind of Jack Diamond emotion that stamps a person as original, sang Fred Ahlert's "Who Played Poker with Pocahontas when John Smith Went Away?"

Looking through my history,
I found a little mystery,

About a certain dame—
How did little Pocahontas,
Take John Smith for all his wampus?
I bet I know her game.
He taught her how to play poker;
She sent him home without his dough.
Every time that he came back,
He found her with a larger stack.
Now here's what I'd like to know:
Who played poker with Pocahontas when John Smith went away?

As Joli performed, holding nothing back, revealing his feelings in the tenor of his voice, Longie and Jean retreated to the back of the room and disappeared. Puddy and Jay stood tapping their feet and clapping hands to the rhythm of the song. When Joli had finished, a woman nearly expelled a lung yelling "More, more!" By the time Joli launched into his third song, the thundering in the house could have been heard in Newark. One of the waiters touched Jay's shoulder. "Mr. Zwillman would like to have a word with you." Puddy's open mouth spoke for them both.

A small fireplace cast a golden glow that filled the paneled room and reflected softly in the leaded windowpanes. Zwillman was stirring the embers to resurrect a flame. A phonograph, perched on a radio console, played Puccini arias. The record jackets were lying on a felt-top table, next to chips and a deck of cards.

"Forget it, Abe, the flame ain't comin' back," said Jean in the same voice she had used in the living room.

Abe rested the poker against the bricks and contemplated her longingly, as he sat in a burgundy leather chair across from the matching couch on which she lounged. Her dress revealed more leg than one could see in a girlie show. However many hearts she had broken in Hollywood, she had definitely left one yearning in New Jersey.

"Make yourself at home," said Zwillman.

Jay looked around at the substantial furniture and decided he hadn't earned the right to sit as an equal. So he drew up a hassock, told himself not to slouch, and said nervously, "Nice house you got."

"Someday it'll be mine," Abe replied enigmatically.

Incredulous that he could be in the company of a movie star, Jay enthused, "I've seen all your pictures, Miss Harlow."

"Jean's here on a visit."

"Is one of those Cadillacs yours? I noticed the California plates."

"The red one. A gift from Abe."

"The black one," said Zwillman, "belongs to Jolson. But he's never driven it. He has a chauffeur."

"Maybe, kid, there's a caddy in your future. Right, Abe?"

The big man chuckled and, resting his elbows on his knees, cradled his chin in his hands. "Let's talk."

"If I can be of service . . ." Jay replied cautiously, breaking off because he knew that some of Zwillman's unsavory enterprises took a stronger stomach than his.

"Your reports on Dutch's boys are good stuff."

So he had finally determined his real employer.

"Thank you, sir."

"You have a way with words. When I read your accounts it's like reading a story. I'm impressed."

"I like to write."

"That's what Puddy says." Abe lit a cigar and tossed the match into the fireplace. "You're probably wondering why I wanted this information. Well, I'll tell you. I don't want to see any drugs in the Third Ward. Call it religious scruples. The Ten Commandments may not forbid it, but Jews shouldn't be using dope. I've warned Dutch before, several times. We're still friends, but . . ."

What, Jay wondered, was Longie's real beef, the drugs, or the calculated slight of Dutch's ignoring repeated threats? Maybe there was even another reason. Jay repositioned the book lying on the coffee table next to the couch: *The Great Gatsby.*

"Jean loves to read," she said indolently, reaching for her hand-bag and removing a box of Chiclets. Shaking a few directly into her mouth, she cracked her gum, inviting Zwillman's displeasure.

"Sorry, Jean thought she was with her own kind," she murmured and laughed mischievously.

Zwillman, who couldn't keep his peepers from her puss, responded with an affectionate smile that seemed like a secret code, and then turned to Jay. "The name's Klug, right?"

"That's what my parents tell me," Jay quipped, trying to appear snappy.

"Curse or clever?" Abe asked playing on the Yiddish double meaning.

"Clever, I hope."

"Me, too."

"He looks real smart . . . cute, too," said Jean, flashing a smile that promised she was prejudiced in Jay's favor—and that made him her faithful fan.

"You used to work for your father. How was that?"

"Awful. He believes in the sanctity of labor, no matter how dreary the job."

Longie huffed sympathetically. "Some jobs ennoble, most don't. As a kid I peddled door-to-door. It brutalized me. I swore that I would never grovel again. Let me give you some advice, son, whatever you do, do for money, a lot of it. There's nothing worse than a bad job *and* a flat bank account. Better to be a pimp than a pauper."

"I'd just like a job that doesn't turn my mind to rabbit droppings—and pays well."

"Since you want to write, what would you say to reporting for the *Newark Evening News*, in the arts section?"

"I . . . you mean . . . just like that . . . me?"

"You, Jay Klug. The editor owes me a favor."

At that moment, Jay could have used a drink. His mouth felt like feathers, and his dry throat brought forth only a croak.

"Did you say what's the deal?" said Zwillman.

Jay nodded emphatically. Longie briefly glanced at Jean.

"You'll be the movie theater critic for the paper, and you'll get paid twenty-five dollars a week. In return, I expect to see rave reviews for Jean's work." Longie fixed Jay with his gaze. "Understood?"

Finding his voice, Jay said too loudly, "Hell, yes!"

"One other thing. I got you a room at the Riviera Hotel. I keep one there myself. In return, I'll want some favors, including your writing newspaper articles critical of the Olympics, and letters for the American Jewish Congress, which is leading the charge to boycott the events in Berlin. I'll give you a list of names and addresses, letterhead stationery, and stamped envelopes. Dutch Schultz is on the address list. Be sure he gets a letter."

Jay desperately searched through his mind for an explanation that he could give his parents. They would undoubtedly ask how he could be earning enough money to pay rent in the Riviera, known for housing well-heeled businessmen, artists, politicians, and, yes, even some mobsters. His father would say that cub reporters make *bupkis* and live in boardinghouses in which you can't tell the bed from the board. Did he dare tell him the paper was footing the bill because he was on a secret assignment? No, his old man would reply that papers don't assign fledgling pencil pushers to undercover work, and then fold his arms across his chest and silently skewer him with that gaze Honest Ike always assumed when Jay lied.

Gerry Catena materialized at the door. "A telephone call for you, Abe. Important."

Longie reached into his vest pocket for a small leather case that held business cards, removed one, and wrote on the back his personal telephone number. "If you're ever in a tight spot, this may help."

No sooner had Longie gone than Jean asked if he knew how to play poker; when he said yes, they sat down at the felt-top table and stacked the record jackets on the floor. She dealt the cards and declared:

"Aces wild."

"Sure."

She regarded her hand, muttered "Shit," discarded three cards, and took three more.

Jay took two and asked, "How do you like being in the movies?"

"It's a living . . . for everyone in the family."

The gossip pages had often noted that Jean supported her parents and that her father had an insatiable appetite for luxury.

"Do you have any favorite actresses?" he asked.

"Yeah, Mary Astor. She's a peach."

Studying her hand, she grimaced and rearranged her cards.

"I can understand the rabbi, but why the priests?"

"Longie's tutors."

"Huh?"

"Yeah, they befriended him when he gave a few bucks to some Catholic charity. They suggest books he should read and talk to him about philosophy."

"You gotta be kidding!"

She put her hand down and gave him a soulful look. "What's wrong with a guy improvin' himself? If you wanna get ahead, Jay . . ."

Her unfinished sentence struck him less than the fact she had used his first name. He measured their difference in age: three years. "I'm trying. To tell you the truth, I promised myself that in the next few years I'd read all of Dickens."

"Hey, don't go overboard. You gotta leave time for other things."

"Like?"

Without replying, she tossed away one card, took another, and spread her hand on the table. "A straight flush: ace, two, three, four, five."

He tossed his cards on the table in a gesture of defeat.

"What's my winnings?"

"I thought it was just a friendly game."

"Jean takes her poker seriously."

"All right," Jay said, throwing up his arms, feigning a mock surrender. "Name your price."

"You take me to dinner in Hollywood."

"And if I don't get out there?"

"Miss Harlow's astrologer predicted a young man would come west and dine with her." She paused, appearing abstracted, as if she were actually giving credence to the forecast of some stargazer. "If you ain't got the dough, Jean will pay. Then after dinner we can go to her place and play poker."

"Tell me, Jean . . ." he hazarded her first name and she didn't object, "who do you play with at home?"

"You're the reporter. Why don't ya come to Hollywood and find out for yourself?"

On their drive back to Newark, while Puddy kept up a running commentary on the evening's events, Jay's thoughts were elsewhere. As an English major in college, he had become interested in dialects. This evening he had heard English conveyed in unfamiliar accents and tones. The words and idioms brought to mind a conversation with a linguistics professor. Jay had observed that on entering college he spoke one way, and was now leaving speaking another.

"I've gone from street slang to academic diction."

His professor had replied, "Look at it this way, you are now bilingual, which will enable you to fit right in. With your neighborhood friends, you can speak in jargon, and in polite circles, you can use the King's English. Call it protective coloration or adaptation. It's all very Darwinian."

2

Magda Hahne had nearly died in childbirth. Her one child, Rolf, had earned the enmity of his father because Magda could no longer conceive. Rolf, born in 1886, was the darling of his mother. She not only doted on him but also kept him safe from his father's wrath. As a youngster, Rolf excelled in school, proving himself adept at languages; he was also a gifted singer. Erik Hahne, barely literate, hated his son all the more for his achievements—and for his fear of dogs. Although an immigrant by choice, the father loved all things German and had come to despise the freewheeling life in America. Ignoring the pleas of his wife and son, he moved his family from Philadelphia to Umfel, Germany, his place of birth. On Rolf's tenth birthday, his father took him mushroom picking in the woods near the village. A German shepherd came bounding through the woods, his master out of sight. The dog, sensing Rolf's unease, growled at the boy, who retreated and cowered. Erik Hahne drove off the dog, removed his belt, and beat his son into unconsciousness. His explanation to Magda was that the boy had been cowardly. Magda moved out of the house and into another, taking Rolf with her. To keep Erik from being arrested, she never reported the crime. Rolf's back had been savagely striped and his left ear mangled. When he recovered, he barely spoke, and his father, having taken seriously to drink, rarely saw his wife and son again.

At the start of World War I, Rolf enlisted. He trained with a purpose and hardened his body into a killing machine. By the end of the war, he had acquitted himself bravely and, miraculously, escaped injury. When his mother asked him had he killed any enemy soldiers, he replied, "I did what I was ordered to do." Having no taste for village life, he remained in the army and, with his superior's recommendation, applied to the SS Intelligence Service, where he was interviewed by Ernst Eicke, whose first question was:

"Is there anything good that can be said about Jews?"

Misunderstanding, Rolf replied, "A Jewish doctor in Philadelphia delivered me and saved my mother's life."

Eicke flew into a fury. "Do you want to work for the SS or not? The Jews are vermin! If not for your knowledge of America and English, I would send you to a camp for reeducation."

Rolf Hahne apologized for his weakness and swore to uphold SS standards. Eicke, not entirely sure of this new man, assigned him to kill a "hymie."

"If he's an intellectual, all the better."

"The means?"

"Use your imagination and report back here when it's done." Making his way to a local medical center that employed Jewish doctors, Rolf waited in the lobby for one of the physicians to exit. But each time a chance presented itself, his resolve weakened and his hands trembled. To one side of the lobby stood a pharmacy. A young boy, perhaps five or six, clung to his mother filling a prescription for a pain killer. The boy had just come from a dentist's office. He was complaining about his jaw hurting. Reflexively, Rolf approached one of the pharmacists, a pretty young woman, and asked to buy a dentist's pick.

"A pick or a scaler? They're different, you know. The first removes stains and the second dislodges food."

"Pick."

"They come in sets of four and twelve."

"Four."

"We have stainless steel picks with nonslip grooved shafts. They're the best."

"I'll take them."

She wrapped up the package, and Rolf left. On the street, he slipped one of the picks up his sleeve and pocketed the other three. He then made his way to a small neighborhood synagogue that he had often passed. It seemed as though every lamppost was flying a Nazi flag, and some stores had painted on the glass front the word "Juden." The synagogue, perched between a bakery and a fish store, serviced a poor Jewish area of Berlin. The doors to both shops were open, and the customers' voices carried into the street. Women in shawls were buying rolls and challahs. An older woman was haggling with the fish merchant over the price of a river trout. The mingled scents of fresh bread and herring followed Rolf into the shul. Unlike the churches of his youth, this building smelled of prayer and parchment. He knew enough to take a yarmulke from a basket at the front door. The rabbi, a slight, sad-faced man, no doubt made sadder by recent events, was addressing a congregation of three, all silver-haired elderly men. Rolf seated himself at the back of the small sanctuary and rocked in unison with the others. Waiting until the other congregants had left, Rolf asked the rabbi if he could have a word with him in private.

The rabbi gestured toward a side door. "Please . . . in my office."

Rolf feared that a secretary might be present, but to his relief the room, with its battered rolltop desk and swivel chair, was empty. On one wall, a large white oval ceramic displayed in black lettering the Ten Commandments. The rabbi removed his tallith, folded it neatly, and turned his back to store it in a small wooden chest. Rolf took that moment to noiselessly come up behind the rabbi and drive the pick into the side of his neck. As the rabbi lay gasping, Rolf removed the tallith and placed it over the dying man's face and suffocated him. Leaving the pick in the rabbi's neck, Rolf slowly strolled to a streetcar and found his way back to his barracks.

The next morning, he reported to Ernst Eicke on his previous day's work. "I suspect it will make all the papers."

Eicke sneered. "A fifth of them are owned by the swine."

Indeed, the *Berliner Morgenpost*, a Jewish-owned newspaper, reported the story in headlines, and the writer emphasized the cruelty of the crime and the barbarism of leaving the dental pick lodged in the rabbi's neck.

The SS authorities, pleased by Rolf's cold-bloodedness, took Ernst Eicke's advice and assigned Rolf to work with Hans von Tschammer und Osten, the leader of the Reich Sports Office, which was planning, with the SS, to assassinate a few key U.S. figures who supported boycotting the Berlin Olympics. Although Rabbi Stephen S. Wise was high on their list, as were Jeremiah Mahoney and Ernest Lee Jahncke (one of only three U.S. members of the International Olympic Committee), these men were unassailable; a second list had the names of "traitors" who could hurt the German-American cause. Among them appeared the names of Americans sympathetic to the boycott, as well as Abner Zwillman and Arietta Ewerhardt.

"I can understand the first list," said Rolf, "but where does the second come from?"

"Wiretaps. One of our agents works in the New Jersey telephone exchange and has been keeping tabs on Fräulein Ewerhardt."

Rolf Hahne was taking coffee with Hans von Tschammer in the latter's office and reviewing his orders, which included passing for von Halt's aide-de-camp and joining the German delegation that would meet Avery Brundage, the head of the American Olympic Committee, in Sweden, and that would then return with him to Berlin.

"I see from your notes," said Rolf, "that in 1930 Brundage initially opposed the choice of Berlin for the 1936 Olympics. He wanted Barcelona."

Hans's smile bore a disconcerting resemblance to the one exhibited by Hitler, whose portrait looked down imperiously from the wall. "It took some doing. At the time, Rome and Barcelona were in the running. But that buffoon Mussolini ruined Rome's chances. Fortunately, the International Olympic Committee (IOC) met in Barcelona to decide. I say fortunately because by April 1931, Spain was descending into chaos. Some of the delegates couldn't even make it to the meeting. So the IOC decided on Berlin, which they praised for its orderliness. And that," he said proudly, "was even before the Führer came to power and imposed *real* discipline."

"I will study the notes on Brundage before we leave for Stockholm. One can never be too prepared."

On first meeting, Hans von Tschammer had liked the young man. Rolf had blond hair and blue eyes, the embodiment of Nazi youth; he stood over six feet, mostly muscle. Except for the scars on his back, which raised a few eyebrows, he exhibited flawless Aryan skin. At the suggestion of von Tschammer, Rolf had had his back tattooed with an Iron Cross, which effectively disguised his welts.

Hans replied, "It is the wise man who prepares in advance. Now I want you to meet Karl Ritter von Halt, who will be in charge of the meetings with Brundage. Like you, he speaks perfect English."

Avery Brundage set sail for Europe on July 29, 1934. Given his wealth and his stature, he traveled first class. Even the few famous people sailing on the same ship paid due deference to this man who felt himself charged with the responsibility of seeing that the Berlin Olympics took place, and that its detractors, whom Avery regarded as principally Communists and Jews, would not prevail. He ate at the captain's table, danced with socialites in the ballroom, took the air on deck with his wife, Elizabeth Dunlop Brundage, and swam two miles every morning in the ship's pool. A former decathlon athlete, he prided himself on being trim, forceful, and honest. His critics would have agreed with the first two qualities, and would have snickered at the third.

A skirt chaser, he eyed all the pretty women on board, accompanied one to her stateroom, poured her champagne, and then turned out the lights. He felt that most of the passengers were not his equals. Having risen from poverty to wealth, he had little patience for the out-of-work and those on the Roosevelt dole, as he called it. He often said that with self-discipline and hard work virtually anyone could succeed. His was a Calvinist work ethic joined to a roué's morality. In his late forties, he regarded himself as a self-made man, having overcome a broken home and poor eyesight to earn a college degree in civil engineering and start his own construction business. He regretted only two things: the day that he learned his myopia would require him always to wear glasses (he was ten), and the day, in the 1912 Olympics, that he quit the decathlon before the last event, the fifteen-hundred-meter race. He was exhausted, having already competed in the pentathlon, but others, he later told himself, were equally tired and had finished the race. To excise the memory of having given up, he dedicated himself to remaining steadfast when opposed, lest he regard himself once again as a quitter. Now he and Elizabeth, a plain, retiring woman with impeccable manners, were sailing for Europe, where he would argue that sports and politics must live in separate realms.

Dario Lorca, whose Castilian family dated back to the twelfth century, invited the Brundages to dine at his table. The ballroom was all chandeliers and waiters in stiff uniforms and a five-piece ensemble playing Viennese music and two professional dancers gliding across the glistening floor. Avery appeared in a white linen suit, sporting a boater banded in red, and Elizabeth in a light pink, long formal dress. Dario's table, the most elegant, included Baroness Annuska Polanyi from Hungary, Count Stefan Galati from Rumania, and Francesca Bronzina, an Italian singer, all of whom had left the United States with a sense of foreboding, but for different reasons. Having seen the ravages of the Depression in America, they wondered out loud how Roosevelt could persuade his southern and conservative colleagues to take the steps necessary to end the chronic joblessness. The only person in the group who did not believe in collective action was Avery Brundage, who equated the New Deal with hated socialism, and said so, to the chagrin of his wife.

Mrs. Brundage touched her husband's arm and excused herself, complaining of seasickness. Avery wondered whether she was truly ill or just escaping from a discussion of politics.

The baroness, dressed in a frilly gown, an outdated boa, and with feathers in her hair, felt certain that it would be better for her to move her mother and two brothers to France than to wait until the feckless Hungarian government settled the disputes between Russophiles and Ukrainophiles and became autonomous from Czechoslovakia. "The country is paralyzed and ripe for a dictator. Then what'll happen?"

Brundage replied, "Look at all the good that has come from Hitler in Germany. Maybe a strongman is the answer. America could do worse than electing a Hitler."

The baroness raised her plucked eyebrows, lifted her chin, and protested, "The man is a barbarian, a monster. He hates the upper classes and the intelligentsia, probably because he is a guttersnipe."

"Look at all the improvements that Mussolini has brought to Italy," said Signorina Bronzina, who seemed to prefer a liquid diet of champagne to the main course. "I know people scoff at the idea that Il Duce has made the trains run on time, but the fact is that he has. And some of the train stations are architectural monuments."

Exuding nobility in his English-styled tuxedo, Dario mumbled, "The man's a buffoon."

"*Non sono d'accordo,*" said Francesca rather proudly, arching her back and extending her ample bosom, which was at war with the stays of her corset and her elegant dark blue gown. She had won more than a few arguments by thrusting her chest into the fray.

Dario Lorca, who spoke six languages fluently, including Italian, responded, "*Il uomo é un pavone.*"

Brundage, like most men of his midwestern class, spoke only English, equating multilingualism with spies. "He seems to have put the Communists where they belong: in jail."

"He was one himself before he became a nationalist," Dario said.

Avery's expertise was business and sports, not history, and he felt out of his element. In his correspondence with the German Olympic Committee, he had made it clear that he would, at all times, need a German translator, one who understood colloquial American diction. He hazarded, "At least Mussolini saw the light. A great many people in America have yet to do so."

Count Stefan Galati, silent during the discussion, smoked one gold-tipped Turkish cigarette after another. Dario turned to him: "Count, you have recently been to both Italy and Germany. What is your impression?"

Galati's English was of the British variety, formal and terse. He blew a cloud of smoke through his nose and said, "Yes, like you I have been to both countries. I don't suppose our opinions differ much on the matter of fascism. Italy is authoritarian and Germany totalitarian. Distinctions *with* a difference."

"Ah, then you agree with me," said Francesca, running a hand through her long, blonde hair, "that Benito is not so bad."

"If he ever runs afoul of Hitler," replied the count, "Italy will be doomed."

"Why do you say that?" asked the baroness, massaging her neck as if to dispel the wrinkles.

"The Italians are laughter and food," answered the count, "the Germans, mirthless and maniacal."

Reciting her words as if trilling up and down a scale, Francesca recounted singing in Vienna, Berlin, and the Rome opera house with both Mussolini and La Sarfatti present.

"Who is Sarfatti?" asked Brundage.

"Benito's favorite mistress," said Francesca.

Brundage seemed uncomfortable. "I don't approve."

Dario looked nonplussed. "Of what?"

Like most men who preach morality but practice its opposite, Brundage answered self-righteously. "I believe in the sanctity of marriage."

Dario laughed. "As Shaw remarked: 'Confusing monogamy with morality has done more to destroy the conscience of the human race than any other error.'"

The guests tittered; all but Brundage, who asked, "Is that George Bernard Shaw?" Dario nodded. "Wasn't he a socialist?"

"My dear Mr. Brundage," said Dario, "I think that you have an idée fixe about socialism. Hitler's party is the National Socialists, and yet you seem to have no qualms about Germany."

Discomfited by this remark, Brundage suggested that now was not the time nor the place to continue the discussion. He would gladly meet Dario for a walk on the ship's deck to continue it later, perhaps tomorrow. The next day, as good as his word, Brundage invited Dario to join him for a stroll. A hot day, the calm sea offering no cooling breezes. Avery fanned himself with his straw hat, sweating from his white blazer jacket and striped linen trousers. Dario wore a cotton tan suit. Both men were tieless.

"Damn hot," Brundage said.

Dario, carrying a Derby walking cane with an ebony shaft and a pewter collar, pointed it toward the ocean. "Calm one minute, feverish the next, like the human condition." He paused to study the pewter. "Needs polish." Again he paused. "In 1930, you opposed Berlin and supported Barcelona. What changed your mind?"

Brundage studied Dario's face for a minute and then exclaimed, "I thought I had seen you before. You were an observer at the 1930 meeting that chose Berlin."

"Quite right, and I am now a supporter of the People's Olympics in Barcelona."

A dyspeptic Brundage replied, "You'll never be able to compete."

Dario shook his head. "Perhaps not, but we will at least have made a statement about our disapproval of the Nazi Olympics."

"Why do you object to Berlin? Is it Spanish nationalism?"

"No, racism."

Brundage breathed deeply. His next words would take some courage. "My dear Señor Lorca, I have been told that the main reason for the Aryan movement in Germany is that the Jews, who hold a prominent position in the affairs of German life, have misused their position, as Jews often do."

Dario tapped his cane on the deck, as if asking an audience for quiet. He then wordlessly turned and walked away from Brundage.

"Have I offended you?" asked the American, calling after him.

Dario stood motionless. "Avery, if you will allow me to call you by your first name . . ."

"Please do."

"I have visited Germany, you have not. Let me tell you that Adolf Hitler is not what you think. You may admire him, but he would not admire you: your poor eyesight, your thinning hair, your education, and, most of all, your money. He despises the wealthy, though he does not hesitate to use them, just as he will use you."

Never having been spoken to in this manner, Brundage expressed his resentment, as he always did, by stiffening his already ramrod straight back and insisting that the principal opponents of the Berlin Olympics were Communists and Jews.

"You are sadly out of step with history," said Dario. "Those arguments were tried—and failed—in the last century. I will tell you what you are lending yourself to." By this time, a number of passengers had gravitated toward the two men, who still stood apart, arguing. In addition, the baroness Polanyi, who had been relaxing in a deck chair and reading a book, put down her lorgnette, and stared incredulously.

"Perhaps it would be better," said Dario, "if we separated."

As a gesture of reconciliation, Brundage took the Spaniard's arm, and they strolled down the deck. "Dario, believe me: Barcelona is a dead issue. Why continue?"

"I will tell you. The Berlin Olympics are not about sport but about Nazi propaganda. Every building, every anti-Semitic poster being removed, every newspaper report . . . all of it is designed to impress the foreign visitor, people like you. Then you will return to the United States and praise German wealth, order, security, hospitality, and organization. Your German hosts will not have shown you the concentration camps and the countless number of democrats and poets and intellectuals who are languishing behind barbed wire. So I beg you. When you arrive in Germany, ask to see the prisons and camps, ask to speak to gypsies and Jews, ask to see the training facilities for non-Aryans. Leave the Olympic site. Go off alone and walk down the side streets and avenues. Do you know what you'll see? Frenzied brown-shirted thugs roaming the avenues, arresting and assaulting, even murdering, any person who they think violates the purity of Aryan blood: Jews, gypsies, cripples, the blind, socialists, Communists, dissenting Christians. And the police will not lift a nightstick to help. Nor will judges convict or sentence any of these barbarians. They fear for their own lives. You will see broken windows and stores painted with anti-Semitic slogans. You will see Nazi flags fluttering from every building and lamppost. You will see children dressed as soldiers, and their parents wearing Nazi pins and heiling their neighbors. And then there's the noise. Trucks regularly pass through the streets blaring Nazi slogans and propaganda. And it seems as if every building in Berlin has a loudspeaker playing martial music. You cannot but conclude that you have reached a level of hell that even Dante would find unimaginable."

Brundage, never having read Dante, could say only, "They are compensating for all the bad years . . . lifting their spirits."

"With murder and mayhem?"

Feeling at a disadvantage owing to his lack of languages and familiarity with Germany, Brundage decided to break off the discussion. But as was typical of the man, he wanted to have the last word. "I will say just this," Avery declared adamantly, "Hitler and his party have halted Communist gains in Western Europe, and to my mind, Communism is an evil before which all other evils pale.

For that reason alone, Berlin deserves to host the Olympics." Now red in the face, he stopped to catch his breath and adjust his glasses. He then added, "I fervently believe that amateur sport and fair play can rise above sectarianism and put an end to national hatreds."

This last comment, a non sequitur, led Dario to say what he did. Making no attempt to hide his contempt for this provincial, bigoted American, he calmly remarked, "You mention politics and sport in the context of the Berlin Olympics, but you fail to indicate that the real issue is not Communism nor amateur athletics but humanity, for which you seem to have little regard."

The men parted. They never spoke again and dined at different hours. The count and baroness joined Dario; Elizabeth and Francesca joined Avery. As if in response to the roiling opinions of the passengers, the sea grew stormy, so that by the time Brundage arrived at the International Amateur Athletic Federation (IAAF) meeting in Stockholm, he complained of a queasy stomach. In need of moral support, he found it in Karl Ritter von Halt, a bronze-faced diplomat and steadfast Nazi, whose tipped nose bore a passing resemblance to Bob Hope's. The round-faced Brundage and the sunken-cheeked von Halt had competed against each other in the 1912 Olympics. Five years later, the German government honored him with a nobleman's title for acquitting himself bravely during World War I. A member of the International Olympic Committee, he was told to shepherd Brundage through the Stockholm meeting and serve as his interpreter and guide in Germany. Their common values—the virtue of amateur athletics and the superiority of the Aryan race—led to an enduring friendship.

In Stockholm, the IAAF meeting took place at a villa outside the city. Rolf Hahne drove. Autumn's bright arrival had turned the woods red, yellow, and orange. Von Halt asked Brundage to tell the other delegates the position he'd taken before leaving the United States. "The German committee is making every effort to provide the finest facilities. We should see in the youth at Berlin the forebears of a race of free, independent thinkers, accustomed to the democracy of sport, a race disdainful of sharp practice, tolerant of the rights of others, and practicing the Golden Rule because it believes in it."

After the meeting, Avery and Elizabeth joined four German officials for lunch in Stockholm. One of the guests was Jewish, Justus W. Meyerhof, a member of the Berlin Sports Club and the IAAF. When the talk turned to politics, Elizabeth excused herself to walk on the terrace. Brundage was shown documents to prove that German-Jewish athletes were welcome to participate freely in sports and to train for the Olympic team. Avery asked Justus if the documents were accurate.

Meyerhof answered obliquely. "As a non-Aryan, I offered to resign from the Berlin Sports Club, but my offer was not accepted. I was seldom as proud of my club as at that moment."

Brundage, visibly impressed, repeated, "Just as I thought, just as I thought."

That night the Brundages had dinner in Stockholm's Gyldene Freden restaurant, a warren of small cozy dining rooms. Accompanied by von Halt and three other men, one of whom had brought his wife, the Brundages and the others ordered sauerbraten, schnitzel, *rouladen*, and *rippchen*. After the meal, the men asked for permission to smoke. The two women excused themselves. Von Halt asked Rolf, posted outside the dining room, to look after them. Brundage called for champagne, and toasted his German colleagues and "pure sport, which rewarded the natural aristocracy of ability and pointed to the right principles for the proper conduct of life."

Ritter von Halt asked about the state of the proposed boycott in America. "As you heard from Meyerhof, we do not discriminate against Jewish athletes."

Brundage scoffed. "Who are the Jews to complain? I don't hear them saying anything about the condition of the Negroes in the South." A poor public speaker, Brundage often strained reasoning and misdirected his words, as he did now. "Besides, America is a free country. My own country club won't admit Jews."

The other men were too polite to question Brundage's logic, but one of them asked, "In your opinion, will the Negro athletes compete?"

Now much in his cups, Brundage said, "Their own newspapers object to a boycott. They want their Sambos to show just how good they are, though I suspect that the Aryan athletes will eclipse them."

On September 12, the Brundages arrived in Germany at Konigsberg in East Prussia. Karl Ritter von Halt and Rolf Hahne had preceded them to prepare for Avery's visit. Taking a train to Berlin, the Brundages checked into the Kaiserhof Hotel, as the guests of the German government. The next day, Avery was introduced to Hans von Tschammer und Osten. So well did they get on together that Avery regarded him as a soul mate. For the next five days, Brundage interviewed German officials and Jewish sports officials, but always in the company of Ritter von Halt, who did all the translating, and of other Nazis, including Rolf Hahne. When interviewing Jewish figures, Brundage's questions never varied.

"Are conditions as bad as the foreign newspapers suggest? Are there any obstacles to Jews making the German Olympic team? Can Jews and Aryans train together?"

To the last question, von Halt explained that Jewish athletes preferred to train with their own kind. When Avery asked the Jewish officials if von Halt's explanation was accurate, Hahne conspicuously put a hand to his holster. The Jews looked at each other, at the Nazi officials in the room, and then at Brundage. "Yes, von Halt has told the truth." Rolf visibly relaxed and shifted his hand.

Avery smiled broadly and commented that as a matter of fact he personally believed in "separate but equal treatment," an approach that worked in American schooling and public facilities and athletics. What was good for America was good for the Olympics.

The night before Mr. and Mrs. Brundage were to leave Berlin for the United States, they had dined well at the hotel restaurant, Elizabeth having ordered ginger glazed salmon filet with wasabi cream. An especially pretty waitress, Heidi, had been assigned to their table, and had been particularly attentive to Avery. After dinner and toasts and appreciative speeches, von Tschammer and von Halt announced that the German government, fearing for the safety of the Brundages, had arranged for Rolf Hahne to accompany them on their boat trip to the United States. More appreciative words followed. Rolf merely bowed, silently.

As Elizabeth Brundage prepared for bed, Avery stood expectantly looking out the hotel window. Before he had left the dining room, von Halt had slipped him a note. Now he waited. Soon there was a light tapping at the door. Elizabeth had already climbed into bed and reached for a book. Avery, still dressed, opened the door just a crack, enough to see standing before him the pretty blonde Heidi, who had served him liver dumpling soup, duck with *spätzle* and red cabbage, and a bottle of Chardonnay. She smiled and bent her index finger in a gesture of "Follow me." Avery nodded and told Elizabeth that von Halt wished to see him.

"Don't tire yourself," said Elizabeth, "and if you return late, please don't turn on any lights."

Avery closed the door behind him and followed Heidi to an upstairs room, which shed an amber light from a small chandelier. Without so much as a word, she suggestively undressed. Brundage watched as she sat on the edge of the bed and removed her stockings, revealing a small patch of black between her legs. She slid under the comforter and smiled. He asked would she mind if he dimmed the lights. She shook her head no. Darkness.

At the dock, Rolf looked after the luggage. The Brundages had a stateroom and he a cramped single. No matter, he had space enough to review his instructions and plot a course of action. A feeling akin to pride suffused his body. The SS authorities had entrusted him to find a means to silence the loudest voices of boycott and to dig into the relationship between Axel Kuppler and Arietta Ewerhardt, whom they suspected of being in the employ of a "moral pervert," whose pro-boycott links reached from New Jersey to California. He had come well equipped for his mission. One of his two bags held the three dental picks, a pistol, a vial of cyanide, and a small photograph of Fräulein Ewerhardt. Arrangements had been made in Germany for Axel to meet him at the dock in New York. He would soon find out whether Axel had transmitted secrets to Fräulein Ewerhardt and whether she had transmitted her information to others. To occupy his time during the ocean crossing, he lifted weights in the men's gym and rode a stationary bicycle. Passing the women's gym, he saw an attractive blonde woman, Francesca Bronzina. He nodded, she smiled, but he refused to follow up, focusing on the Brundages and their welfare. The German SS Intelligence Service had assigned Rolf to guard the Brundages not only to insinuate Rolf into the country for their own murderous purposes but also to see that Avery Brundage landed safely in New York. The SS had received unconfirmed reports that two Jewish commandos, dispatched from Haifa with false passports, might be boarding the boat at Bremen to assassinate Avery Brundage. Although the ship's manifest had been carefully screened, the police found no suspicious passengers.

The first day at sea, Rolf haunted the ship trying to identify any would-be killers. Two men were sitting in deck chairs, with an empty chaise lounge between them. After several minutes, one of the men stood, dropped his newspaper on the empty chair, and departed. The other man casually reached for the paper and studied it. Were these the two? Perhaps the first had merely been doing a crossword puzzle that he failed to complete; and the second took up the challenge. Rolf watched. If the second failed to write in the paper . . . but what if he were equally stumped?

Rolf needed more proof than a discarded newspaper retrieved by another.

As the second day passed into the third, Rolf decided to use Brundage as a lure. Until now, Avery had stayed well away from the deck rails, where an unseen assailant could shove him overboard. Rolf suggested that Avery, without Elizabeth, stroll to the outside railing, pause a minute, and then return to the glass-enclosed deck. If anyone made a move to follow, Rolf would of course be at Avery's side to protect him—and might have a better idea of the persons assigned to harm Brundage. But nobody followed, and Avery returned to his wife. Standing by himself in the stern of the ship, admiring the great propellers leaving a wake behind the liner, Rolf heard a dog barking in the distance. Around a corner came a German shepherd running toward him. Its owner was nowhere to be seen. The dog playfully sniffed Rolf's leg and turned its head, as if looking for its master. At that moment, Rolf leaned over, scooped up the dog, and threw it overboard. A few seconds later, the owner came scurrying around the corner looking for "Schatzi." He was an elderly gentleman, well attired, and sporting a monocle. Had Rolf seen a dog? Yes, but it took off down the other side of the ship. The man had spoken in German. He thanked Rolf, bowed slightly, and disappeared.

After dinner, Rolf accompanied the Brundages to their stateroom. As always, he entered first, looked around, and then, seeing there was no danger, stepped aside to admit the couple. Outside the door, Rolf saw a young cabin boy coming his way carrying a tray of food. He stopped the young man to ask if any of the passengers had been inquiring about the location of the Brundage stateroom. The boy hesitated. Rolf flashed his SS badge and handed him a ten spot.

"As a matter of fact, since we left Bremen several passengers have asked me that question."

"Old or young?"

"Mostly old, except for one person, who never leaves the cabin. But I don't think . . ."

Rolf interrupted. "What about meals?"

"Good question. I have no idea."

"Perhaps a friend . . ."

"I've never seen one."

"Room number?"

"It's . . . it's 218."

"Not a word about this matter," said Rolf. "I am here as a representative of the German government. Secret business."

The cabin boy's eyes grew as wide as portholes, and he shook his head vigorously. "Not a word, sir, I promise." And then, still balancing the tray of food, he hastily left.

That same evening and the next day, Rolf shadowed Room 218, but no one entered or exited. So he descended below deck to the kitchen, where he found his way blocked by a small, cadaverous man who belied the belief that all cooks are fat.

"No passengers allowed," he said in German.

Dozens of people were dashing about: cooks preparing food, scullions scouring pots, pans, and dishes, and waiters and waitresses carrying plates in and out of the kitchen. Once again Rolf flashed his SS badge. The skeletal cook forced a smile, revealing a mouth of bad teeth.

"A word, please," said Rolf.

The cook wiped his hands on his apron and walked to one side. "Be quick, the diners are waiting."

"Are you in charge?"

"I am the head cook, Benedict Strassen."

"Herr Strassen, do any of the passengers require a special diet, for example, a kosher one?"

"Why do you ask?" said Benedict suspiciously.

"I am looking for a man . . ."

"For this you interrupt me. No, we don't serve kosher."

Rolf thought twice before he spoke again, wondering whether Herr Strassen could be trusted. "A Jewish killer. Perhaps two of them."

Without replying, the cook waved his hand to a meat cook preparing pork chops. As the man approached, Benedict greeted him as Friedl and repeated Rolf's question.

Friedl looked at Benedict. The head cook wiped his perspiring face with his apron. "Tell him," said Benedict. "He's with the SS."

"Some rooms, not many," said Friedl, "have dumbwaiters. We can put the food on a tray and hoist it directly to the passengers."

Benedict added, "The shaft for the dumbwaiters was built to guarantee a person's privacy, like royalty and diplomats and high government officials."

"And a Jew who doesn't want to be seen."

"I wouldn't know about that," said Benedict.

Rolf was convinced that one assassin occupied Room 218, but where was the other? Unless the cable from Palestine was in error, and only one killer, directed to kill Avery in New York, was on ship. He would have to be sure, lest he put himself and both Brundages in danger.

"Do you serve anyone else using a dumbwaiter?"

"No, only the one—who paid handsomely for the service."

Rolf was silent.

"Ask the purser," said Benedict. "*Ach*, look at the time. I have wasted precious minutes talking to you. If the passenger is a criminal, arrest the person. Don't bother us."

The cooks returned to their work. Rolf decided that the steamy kitchen, with its chopping block and pots and pans suspended overhead, was an uncongenial place to glean any more information. He would confront the purser about the man in Room 218, and try to learn his name, his country of origin, his special arrangements. But he knew that the man was unlikely to be traveling on an English passport, even though Palestine was a British mandate. If the man knew German, then he probably came from an Eastern or Central European country. He would know in a minute, once he heard the man's accent.

Bernd Fuchs shook Rolf's firm hand when Rolf introduced himself. Having worked as a purser for German cruise liners since he turned twenty, he thought that he knew the characteristics of passengers and their schemes. But he had never before met anyone like Rolf Hahne, who had materialized in a black shirt and black suit, and had assumed a stiff, resolute, and menacing posture. Fuchs always dressed in white for Atlantic crossings, even in winter: white gloves and a white hat with a black beak. He spoke several languages and particularly prided himself on his fluent English. Trained to be discreet, Fuchs was disinclined to reveal the identity of the passenger in Room 218, even when he saw Rolf's SS badge and diplomat's passport. Besides, he had no special love for the Nazis and, in fact, despised their arrogance and presumption of superiority.

"A person is entitled to his privacy," said Bernd.

"Not when he intends to assassinate Mr. Avery Brundage."

"Where is your proof?"

Rolf could hardly produce a cable that indicated some commandos *might* be aboard ship. "You'll just have to trust me."

"Power is a trust, and I don't intend to abuse mine."

Rolf glanced around the purser's office. He took note of the filing cabinets, the combination safe in the corner, the desk strewn with papers, and the lock on the door. As part of his SS training, he had been schooled in breaking and entering. The lock on the purser's door was a Schlage, difficult to work the tumblers but not impossible. Perhaps his dental picks could serve more than one purpose. His only fear was that the papers he wanted were in the safe and not in the filing cabinets. But . . . German officials were famous for putting the combinations of locks in files labeled "Snuff." Why they had selected that name, he never could fathom.

Fuchs felt uneasy in the presence of this SS man. To break the impasse, he suggested that he would call the ship's main office in Bremen for instructions bearing on this matter. His superiors would know what to do.

"The matter is secret," said Rolf.

"Then I can't help you."

At that moment Rolf was tempted to choke the man to death. It would have taken no more than a minute or two. The two were alone. No witnesses. But he chose to pursue another course of action. That evening, when he could try the door and the safe, he would know how to proceed.

After midnight, Rolf made his way to the purser's office and found to his raging impatience that he could not pick the lock. Had the purser shown up at that instant, Rolf would have killed him. The door to the purser's office had a small window, fitted with thick smoky glass. Rolf went to his room and returned with a blanket, which he wrapped around a fire extinguisher that he used to break the window. Reaching inside the door, he disengaged the lock and entered. He would have to work fast, before someone reported the break-in. Every time he heard footsteps in the corridor, he gripped the pick and feared what discovery would mean. Unequipped with a flashlight, he had to risk turning on the lights. He moved quickly, rifling through the cabinets. No file marked "Snuff." What did his SS trainers know? They were all working from manuals printed during World War I. The safe was locked. He had often heard it said in jest that all the safe combinations in Germany were set to Hitler's birthday: 20 April 1889. He tried 20-4-89; it didn't work. He tried 20-4-889. No luck. Then: 20-4-1889. His last attempt was equally unsuccessful: 4-20-1889.

He entertained the idea, but only for a second, of taking a fire axe to the safe. But the noise would awaken the ship's crew. After rustling through the papers on the purser's desk and in his drawers, he knew that the information he wanted was in the safe. But if he had no way to access it, he would just have to assume that the man in Room 218 was an assassin—and kill him.

In the morning, the ship's captain alerted the passengers to an attempted robbery of the purser's office. Everyone should take special care to guard his valuables. A malefactor was afoot.

The dumbwaiter shaft ran from the kitchen to a cabin on the top deck, four levels above. Room 218 was on the second deck. If he could gain access to the shaft at level three or four, he could effect his purpose. He would have to discover who occupied Rooms 318 and 418. But first he had to gain entrance to the dressing room of the cabin crew responsible for changing linen, making beds, and cleaning berths. He confidently opened the door and confronted two young men. Before either man could speak, he flashed his leather identification case with its SS badge. Asking where the uniforms were kept, he removed a jacket and pants from the supply cabinet. Later that morning, he knocked on the door of Room 418. No answer. In Room 318, he could hear people stirring. An elderly couple were just preparing to go on deck to read. Rolf introduced himself as the new attendant in charge of preparing their room. When they asked what happened to their regular cabin boy, Rolf dangerously said that he'd taken ill. If the couple, having left the cabin, ran into the lad, Rolf knew he'd have some explaining to do. He therefore had to work quickly. With his Swiss penknife, he removed the small screws from the dumbwaiter panels. He could smell the food being prepared down below. But what if the man in 218 didn't eat lunch or had decided to forgo it today? Rolf was unlikely to have another chance like this one. He heard the sound of wheels. A trolley in the hall. Seconds later, a polite knocking on the door. The cabin boy with his supplies had arrived to make up the room. Muffling his voice, Rolf requested that the boy return after lunch. He waited. The trolley moved on.

Several minutes passed, while Rolf opened and closed each blade in his knife. Then he fingered the vial in his pocket. He peered into the shaft and contemplated whether he had the space to lift himself, hand over hand, up the ropes. Strength was not a problem. He had excelled at rope climbing during SS training exercises. Suddenly, he heard the ropes moving. As soon as the platform passed the opening he had made in the shaft, he seized one of the ropes and stopped the dumbwaiter. Reaching for the vial, he could hear the cook's complaint coming from the kitchen. But Rolf took less than a few seconds to empty half the vial into the cup of steaming coffee. He then released the rope to exclamations of relief from the cook.

Once he had replaced the panels, he removed his uniform, opened the room's porthole, and threw the clothes into the sea. He then went in search of the Brundages. Avery was in the gym using a treadmill. Rolf stripped to his shorts and entered the weight room. As he cradled the dumbbells, he imagined the following scenario. The elderly couple would see the cabin boy and ask about his health. The boy would say that he was feeling fine. "But another fellow showed up to clean our room with the excuse that you were ill." The boy would say, "But you asked me to return after lunch." The couple would say that no such conversation ever took place. "Perhaps it has to do with the attempted robbery," the cabin boy would say in an effort to clear up the confusion. The captain would be summoned. He would ask the couple if they could identify the man if they saw him again. "Yes, of course." The captain would then ask the couple to attend both sittings for every meal and scrutinize every person they passed. Rolf could not afford to hide himself lest he leave Avery Brundage unguarded. A second assassin might still be on the loose.

When Room 218 stopped taking meals—first dinner and then breakfast—and had neglected to return the dishes from lunch the day before, the purser entered Room 218 and found the little-known, blonde Swedish actress Ingrid Paiken dead in a parlor chair, wearing only a dressing gown and a string of expensive pearls. A tray of rancid food stood on the tea table, and a coffee cup lay on the rug.

The news electrified the ship. A promising movie star had been on board, had been traveling incognito, and had been found dead. No one knew the reason for the secrecy or the cause of death. But gossip, which is like a choir, gives rise to all manner of voices. The explanation most often repeated was that Ingrid had been traveling to America to meet a lover, and in fond expectation of falling into his arms, had suffered a heart attack.

But the shipboard tragedies didn't end with the young woman's death. Less than a day before docking, the elderly couple in Room 318 had been reported missing. The only clue was traces of blood found on the frame of the porthole. Nothing of value was stolen. The man's wallet and the woman's purse were still in the room. Their passports were untouched. The few valuable pieces of jewelry the woman owned had been safely stored in the ship's safe. When the question of motive arose, the cabin boy told his story of someone having replaced him to clean the room, and the cook related the trouble he'd had with the dumbwaiter. On close inspection of the shaft, a ship's mechanic declared that the screws to the panel had been tampered with and suggested that possibly the same person responsible for the disappearance of the elderly couple was responsible for the death of the Swedish actress. The captain, aghast, wired ahead to New York requesting that a squad of detectives meet the boat.

Sitting down for dinner with the Brundages the night before docking, Rolf was introduced to a pretty, dark-haired woman whom Elizabeth had become friendly with on the crossing. Her name was Elspeth Botinsky, an émigré from Ruthenia. As Rolf listened to the conversation between the women, he heard in Elspeth's speech a few pronunciations that led him to speak to her in German. When she responded, he could hear in her Deutsche a Yiddish inflection. It was then that he realized his error. The commandos sent from Palestine were not men, but women. One was now dead and the other sitting across from him. Before the ship docked, would he be able to get Elspeth alone? If not, she would disembark in New York, lose herself in the crowd, and stalk Avery Brundage. For the moment, she was sitting just a few feet from him. He couldn't squander his chance. Excusing himself, he returned to his room and took the vial of cyanide and a dental pick. Back in the dining room, the passengers were eating their desserts. He would have to wait.

Later that evening, before the passengers retired to their rooms, the captain distributed champagne to toast the ship's safe arrival, albeit under trying circumstances. The orchestra played some mood music, and several people took to the dance floor. As Elizabeth and Elspeth sipped their champagne—Rolf and Avery were teetotalers—Rolf asked Elspeth to dance. The Brundages followed. Rolf deliberately spun Elspeth around several times, until she pleaded dizziness, and he helped her back to the table, where she pushed away her champagne glass. Rolf eyed it hoping that she would take a last sip. When she lowered her head to the table, he spilled the remaining contents of his vial into the glass and urged her to finish it off—for good luck.

"No, no," she said, "I couldn't. My head is spinning."

Lest anyone accidentally drink the poisoned champagne, Rolf leaped to his feet and tossed the glass over his shoulder.

"An old German custom," he said, apologizing to the waiter who came running to mop up the broken glass and champagne.

After this public episode, Rolf decided that he would have to act below deck. With Elspeth feeling ill, he accompanied her back to her cabin. The next day, as the liner entered New York Harbor with all the expectant passengers crowding the railing and most of the steamer trunks and baggage neatly arranged for the handlers to move them by hand and by dolly to the dock, a coast guard cutter brought the ship to a halt short of its berth. Several policemen boarded and summoned all the passengers to the ballroom. Here each person was questioned as to the unhappy events that had occurred during the crossing. One person was missing, Elspeth Botinsky. Although her luggage had been brought to the deck, she was nowhere to be seen. The police made careful notes and then allowed the boat to dock and the passengers to proceed to passport control.

Rolf showed his black-covered diplomatic passport, which allowed him to carry his luggage through customs free of an inspection that might have discovered his pistol and knife and dental picks. He then waited for the Brundages. When they arrived, they asked him if he had seen Elspeth.

"One minute she was there," said Elizabeth, "the next, gone."

"Strange, very strange," said Avery, and turned to Rolf. "You saw her to her cabin. Did she say anything? Did you have any inkling of something amiss?"

Rolf put his palms up gesturing innocence and said, "I saw nothing."

A redcap carried their luggage to the curb. The cabstand was crowded. As Rolf and the Brundages waited, Francesca Bronzina also waited, out of sight. When the next vacant cab pulled up, Rolf embraced Elizabeth and then Avery, promising to ring them at their hotel. If he was needed, or if they heard from Elspeth, he could always be reached through the German consul in New York. The Brundages bundled into the backseat of the taxi, which immediately turned into the flow of traffic. Rolf waved. The Brundages never saw him again.

On leaving the pier and reaching the street, Rolf waited. Moments later, Axel Kuppler drove up, identified himself, introduced Rolf to the beautiful woman in the passenger seat, Arietta Ewerhardt, and opened the back door of the sedan for Rolf, who was delighted to learn that Axel had saved him the trouble of locating Fräulein Ewerhardt.

Once Rolf had left, Signorina Bronzina stepped out of the shadows, waited her turn for a cab, and handed the driver a piece of paper with an address in West Orange, New Jersey: the home of Abner Longie Zwillman.

After all the passengers had disembarked, an unclaimed steamer trunk remained on the dock. When the customs officials forced the lock, Elspeth Botinsky tumbled out. Her killer had left behind the dental pick used to pierce her jugular vein.

3

A line of cabs waited to pull up at the curb to disgorge women in furs and men in camel-hair coats, fedoras, and mufflers. When Arietta and Jay stepped out of the Checker hack, a hatless, yellow-haired young man, wearing black jodhpurs, polished knee-high boots, and a swastika armband, shoved a flyer into his hands. "A Call to Aryans! The nigger 'art' of the Kinney Club is so barbarous and depraved that many a Negro would justifiably refuse to see his own race on stage or acknowledge any part in the performance of such filth. Do not enter!!!" Jay crumpled the flyer and tossed it, inciting the young Nazi to call them "Jew-Communists" as they brushed past and greeted the doorman.

According to Puddy, Newark's answer to the Cotton Club attracted underworld figures ranging from swaggering gunmen, gorillas, and gangsters to syndicate bosses and high-class pimps, prostitutes, gamblers, and hustlers. One look around and Jay knew that the joint also drew gawkers who came to see the demimonde. They paid no admission charge, climbed up a long flight of stairs, turned right, and walked back toward Arlington Street into a large dimly lit hall crowded with tables sporting red-and-white-checkered cloths. Jay slipped the headwaiter a buck, and he seated them near the door. Maybe for a fiver, thought Jay, he could have been seated at a table next to the stage. The club served no food, only booze, with beer going for fifteen cents a glass. Jay gathered, from the number of bouncers, this was a rough place, even though sprawled at a table were four uniformed cops, no doubt on the take. A dozen waiters and waitresses, who also sang, darted among the tables as deftly as ballet dancers. An emcee introduced skits and a small band accompanied the vocalists.

They had come to see Clara Smith, the Queen of the Moaners, second only to Bessie Smith. Clara and Bessie had been close friends until, one night, Bessie got drunk and assaulted Clara. That event, eight years before, and a brief romance with Josephine Baker gave Clara a reputation for living on the wild side. Round faced with a large tipped nose that flared at the nostrils, she had sparkling eyes and glowing hair that she wore parted down the middle and looped over her forehead and ears. She made her wide mouth function as an incomparable musical instrument, mournfully singing "Shipwrecked Blues," "Look What You Done Done," "Cheatin' Daddy," and "Tell Me When." She followed her blues routine with several gospel numbers and then teased the band with her sassy and sardonic wit.

"Leon," she said to the trumpeter, "you is so black that I reckon lightning bugs follow you around in the daytime."

Leon ran up and down the scale on his horn.

"Sketch," she said to the saxophone player, "I hear you're colored blind."

Sketch played an off-key note and replied, "Heavens, Clara, I hope you is wrong, because I just got married last week."

"Clara," asked the drummer, "do you keep all your old love letters?"

"You bet I do, Henry, 'cause some day I expect them to keep me."

She continued this repartee, to the boisterous delight of the audience. If laughter is an outward sign of an inward state, then these partygoers were enjoying the night.

As she left the stage, Jay heard a man at the next table say, "Clara's on her way down. At thirty-nine, she don't have the power to moan the blues the way she used to."

"But her stories are still sharp as a tack," said his companion.

Arietta had struck a contemplative pose.

"What's on your mind?" Jay inquired.

"I was just thinking of my father and the grand piano we used to own. We even had an eighteenth-century violin from Cremona, until we had to sell it."

"Times are bad for everyone."

"Except the rich. Clara's gospel numbers reminded me of Papa's singing. He wanted a career in opera."

A waiter hovered over them expecting an order for another round of drinks. Jay would have ignored him had not one of the bouncers begun staring. Requesting two more beers, Jay heard the waiter grumble, "The last of the big spenders."

"The opera," Jay said, trying to pick up the thread of Arietta's conversation. "Where?"

"In Rome . . . after he left the priesthood."

Jay blinked and tried to tell himself that he had misheard. Arietta, seeing his expression, continued. "He was a Jebby. My mother and her two sisters bumped into him on the steps of St. Peter's . . . they came from Germany . . . on a pilgrimage with a group from Stuttgart."

"Your father was a Jesuit *priest?*"

"Once. But he loved women more than God, or so he says."

To step back a moment: The evening had begun with Jay being grilled by Mr. Magliocco. After having called Arietta no fewer than six times—where women were concerned, he believed in the adage that success is nine-tenths persistence—he dropped by to see her at Castle House, where she worked as a part-time dance instructor when the school needed an extra coach. As he sat on the sideline watching the klutzes shuffling across the polished wooden floor, she told one, a rotund fellow no taller than she, "Don't shake the hips or twist the body . . . don't flounce the elbows or pump the arms." At the end of the lesson, she took a break.

"What are you doing here?"

"You wouldn't say yes on the phone, so I thought if I made a personal appearance, I might persuade you."

She looked around furtively. "It's that nasty business at Dreamland. My father wants me to cut all ties to it and anyone associated with the place. But I did ask him to make an exception for you."

"Maybe I should speak to your parents and show them I'm okay."

"Mother's dead."

"Sorry." Pause. "Well, what do you think?"

Removing her black patent leather shoes and rubbing her feet, she gave him a gnomish smile and said, "All right, but if he doesn't approve, you'll just have to understand."

He shook her hand. "I accept your terms. How about Saturday night . . . about eight?"

"Where?"

"The Kinney Club."

"Not *the* Kinney . . ."

"Why not?"

He took a taxi to her house on Littleton Avenue, a two-story brown-brick dwelling dwarfed by big trees that left the interior dark. Arietta opened the door and stopped him in the foyer, which had framed photographs of famous opera stars, mostly Italians, like Enrico Caruso and Amelita Galli-Curci.

"Don't mention the club to my father. Say we're off to a movie."

"Which one?"

She thought a moment. "*Bombshell,* with Jean Harlow."

"You won't believe this, but I met Harlow once and we became friends."

She smiled skeptically and said, "Be sure to admire his plants."

In the living room stood a stunted piano covered with faded photographs in silver frames. The mission-style furniture, with its dark wood and Dick Van Erp hammered copper lamps, casting warm yellow shadows through the vellum-like shades, bespoke a time when arts and crafts design was all the rage. Now it all looked dated and dreary. Only a profusion of houseplants mitigated the sense of decay: spider and rubber plants, a Boston fern, a large philodendron, and a plant that Jay had never seen before. Mr. Magliocco sat in a parlor chair with rimless spectacles perched on the end of his nose. Jay's arrival had interrupted his reading. Arietta introduced them. Mr. Magliocco placed his book face down on his chest, invited Jay to take a seat, and asked Arietta to pour them each a glass of Strega. Extending his hand, her father said, "Piero Magliocco."

"That plant?" asked Jay curiously, failing to introduce himself.

"An ornamental monkey-puzzle tree. It's native to Chile and Argentina. The name comes from an Englishman who thought that the tree would be a puzzle to climbing monkeys. Ironically, monkeys are not native to the areas where this unique specimen comes from."

"It looks prehistoric. By the way, my name," he said belatedly, "is Jay Klug."

"Klug . . . what kind of name is that?" Before Jay could answer, Mr. Magliocco left his chair and insisted on showing him the framed photographs on the piano. Mostly prewar, the pictures of his wife and her blond wealthy family had been taken on terraces, in formal gardens, on picnics, on pleasure boats. Mr. Magliocco pointed to his wife posed in her First Communion dress and coming-out dress, the latter inscribed on the bottom: "Silvesterabend 1911."

Turning to Jay, the older man observed, "You could pass for a German . . . the blond hair," pointed to two chairs, and said, "Let's sit."

"I'm Jewish, sir. My father comes from the Ukraine." To curry favor, Jay added, "He speaks Italian."

"And do you?"

"I wish I could. It's a beautiful language. My father sings Puccini and Verdi arias."

"Does he?" Mr. Magliocco exclaimed. "I studied opera in Rome and even appeared in *Tosca* at the Teatro della Pergola in Firenze."

"Do you still sing?"

"For my own pleasure. Arietta accompanies me on the piano. These days most opera companies have folded. No one has the money to stage a production. How do you support yourself?"

"Journalism. The *Evening News*. I do movie and theater reviews."

"Under your own name?"

"I just started."

"You're lucky to have a job. Until recently, I worked all the time . . . as a truck driver . . . hauling liquor." Piero chuckled, remembering. "Kristina never approved."

Jay took Kristina to be Arietta's mother. "My dad says Prohibition was a full-employment act."

Arietta brought the drinks. They clinked glasses and toasted each other's health. Mr. Magliocco sipped his drink and expounded:

"He's right. It took thousands of law-enforcement officers to police it and even more people to break the law: shippers, sailors, smugglers, truckers, bodyguards, warehouse watchmen, nightclub owners, bankrollers, bribers. The guys who brewed their own had to buy barrels, malt, brewing machinery, cooperage coating, air compressors, cleaning compounds, kettles and pipes, hops and yeast. If they repaired their beer barrels, they needed heads, shooks, and rivets. Those who did their own delivering had to buy a fleet of trucks, gasoline, oil, tires. Yeah, Prohibition created a lot of jobs and brought good times. Even Kristina had to admit it."

Jay gathered that his wife's upper-class background made it difficult for her to countenance his illicit work. Suddenly, Mr. Magliocco changed the subject.

"Arietta is all I have," Piero said, leaning over and taking her hand. "She's my support. Without her . . ."

How could she have supported him on a part-time job as a dancer? Surely, instructors didn't earn that much.

"Your plants are magnificent. I particularly like the monkey-puzzle tree. You must have a green thumb."

"Gardening and opera: my two passions."

Jay walked to a flowering geranium resting on a window sill and made a point of cradling the orange bloom in his hand.

"That one comes from a trash can. I found it on a walk in the neighborhood. A little pruning and plant food and *ecco*!"

"Lovely."

"You'd better hurry or you'll be late for the movie."

Whew, what a relief! The father had approved of Jay's dating his daughter. "I hope in the future to see a lot more of Arietta," he replied gaily. Oops, would Mr. Magliocco hear the double entendre? Jay decided that he would take Arietta and her father to dinner just as soon as he could afford it.

Between acts, two familiar-looking toughs, wearing black homburgs and white silk scarves, entered with a couple of whores. It took Jay a minute to realize that these were the men he had watched from his Prince Street window. They worked for Dutch Schultz. The headwaiter seated them next to the stage. Jay would have ignored them except that one of the women in their company removed her hat and he recognized Margie Smith. Before Jay could say hello—he had been woefully delinquent in not sending her flowers and inquiring about her health—Johnny Fussell, back from Europe for a short tour, tapped out onto the floor for his specialty number, dancing while seated on a chair. His bow tie and white shirt quickly lost their starch as his face and neck ran with sweat from the furious beat: tap-a-tap-tap. Swinging his arms and skipping, Johnny swept from one end of the stage to the other with a fluency and rapidity that left the audience breathless.

At the conclusion of his number, people spilled change and bills on the tables, which Fussell swept into his black derby as he made his way through the room. Arietta enthused knowledgeably, "He's the best, the very best. Leave him five dollars." Five dollars! Who did she think he was, a Vanderbilt? His reluctance led Arietta to sing:

> When me and mine am blue and broke,
> Wishing to 'scape the common folk,
> We throw money at our cares,
> Though we ain't no millionaires.

Maybe Barbara Hutton and her friends used conspicuous wealth to thumb their noses at the Depression, and maybe the determined gaiety at the Kinney Club was designed to ignore the world outside, but he knew that some families could live two weeks or more on a fiver. So he put down two greenbacks. Looking contemptuously at his offering, Arietta shoved it back at him, opened her purse, and balanced a fiver atop her beer glass. He figured her father wasn't wrong in saying that she supported him. Perhaps her mother had left her a trust.

Shamed, he excused himself to greet Margie. Her deep-cut dress accentuated her breasts. One of the hoods showed his appreciation by lasciviously staring at her exposed anatomy. She leaped up and embraced him, to the annoyance of her escort.

"Boys, I want ya to meet an old friend of mine, Jay Klug. We used to go marathon dancing together. The night I got sick, Jay was my partner." Jay shook hands with the men, whom Margie introduced as Mandy Weiss and Charlie Guzick. "This is Charlotte. She's one of the girls." The young woman, balancing a cigarette holder in one hand and wearing a sheer pink dress that brought to mind Jean Harlow, smiled and cracked a piece of gum. He nodded—and wondered how one could chew gum while smoking. "Sit down," said Margie. "Take a load off your feet." She turned and looked over her shoulder. "Who's the lady?"

"Sheesh," said Charlotte, "she looks like a movie star. Maybe I ought to ask for her autograph."

"After they drove you to the hospital, I teamed up with her. She teaches at Castle House."

"Pretty soon you'll get so good you'll be high hatting me."

"Not you, Margie. You're an old pal."

Weiss kept staring at Arietta. "How does a punk like you rate a doll like her?"

Margie shook her head censoriously. "Behave yourself, Mandy. We're here to have a good time."

But Mandy persisted, "Well, kid, how come? You got a bulgin' bankroll or somethin' else in your pants?"

"We both like to dance."

Mandy laughed uproariously. "With a babe like that, why spend your time waltzin'?"

Jay didn't like the company Margie kept. Standing up to leave, he foolishly taunted, "The pleasure's been all mine. The conversation's been illuminating. Maybe we can meet again, on Prince Street."

Mandy and Charlie exchanged knowing looks. Forcing Jay back into his seat, Charlie put his hand inside his jacket. "Mandy, I think pretty boy here's tryin' to tell us somethin'."

"Yeah, he's soundin' real smart."

Margie foolishly blurted, "Sure he's smart. He went to college."

"See, I told you, Mandy, pretty boy's got a head on his shoulders—unless he loses it."

Nightclub shootings were not unheard of, and the gunsels usually escaped in the confusion. This party was certainly unlike Longie's. Gang leaders were one thing, gorillas another.

"My friend Charlie has an itchy finger. Maybe if you tell him what's on your mind, he'll stop scratchin'."

Trusting that Margie would restrain her friends, and that Abe's magical name would protect him, he replied, "I'm merely an errand boy for Longie Zwillman. My boss likes to keep tabs on his friends."

A contrite Charlie Guzick offered to buy Jay a drink, and Mandy amended his remarks. Immediately, Jay began to trade further on Zwillman's name, suggesting that he had long been in the employ of "Abe."

"Some of us," said Charlie, "ain't real happy about Longie puttin' out the no-go sign for drugs in the Third Ward. He oughta know that a guy's got a right to make a livin'."

"I hate when friends fall out," said Mandy. "You end up scraggin' your own."

Charlotte said impatiently, "Hey, we're here to dance, not chew the rag. They're playin' some good swing music." She stood and grabbed Charlie's hand. "Come on, Romeo." Charlie seemed uninterested. "Forget how to dance?" Charlie got to his feet and hit her forehead sharply with the palm of his hand, dazing her. She plopped back in her chair and sat there looking off into space.

Arietta had to be troubled. Jay mumbled something about his date waiting for him. Margie grabbed his arm and pulled him toward her.

"Drop by Polly's. I'm there every day but Mondays."

When Jay returned to his table, Arietta asked, "What was that all about?"

"The woman in the blue dress . . . she's the one who took sick the night I met you. The others I don't know."

"They seemed awfully friendly for strangers."

Her suspicions made him uneasy. She'd never see him again if she thought he ran with the mob. "Honest, I never met them before."

"All that back slapping and laughing made me wonder."

"We were just swapping stories."

"On what, mad hatters?"

"I don't follow."

"Headwear. Chapeaus. Caps. Lids. Skimmers. Homburgs."

"Arietta, you'd better translate."

She studied her glass and said, "The ticket taker at Dreamland said that the two men in the getaway car wore black homburgs."

A second later, he remembered that Mandy and Charlie entered the Kinney wearing homburgs. "Hey, thousands of men wear them."

"You *do* seem to show up at the wrong places at the wrong time—or perhaps the right places."

Now, what the hell did *that* mean? "You're speaking in riddles, and frankly I'm lousy at solving them. Could you be more precise?"

"If those are the same men who drove the getaway car . . . your being palsy-walsy with them doesn't look so good."

"What about you?" he said snappishly, feeling abused. "You asked the victim to dance. Maybe yours was the kiss of the spider woman."

"Yes, I went to Dreamland, but while I rested in the tent, you hung around. Why?"

"The triggerman looked fishy."

Could she really believe that he had anything to do with the murder? If she did, why would she spend the evening with him? Something else had to be up. "Look, Arietta, I'm no gangster. Just a journalist who . . ."

She interrupted, ". . . is on Longie Zwillman's payroll."

How did she know that? He hadn't told her.

"I can hear what you're thinking, Jay. Where did I get my information?"

Losing patience with her, he blurted, "Yeah, you read my mind perfectly."

The same waiter began to eye them, so he ordered another beer; but Arietta held up her hand indicating that she had had enough. Disgruntled, the waiter went off for one beer. Jay told himself that when the guy returned, he would slip him a buck and ask him to leave them alone.

"During Prohibition my father trucked in beer from the shore to Newark. He has friends among the Zwillman gang."

But that didn't explain how she knew Longie had hired him to write reviews for the *Newark Evening News*. The only two people present at that meeting were Jean Harlow and Abe. And the only person he'd told was Puddy. Crap! Puddy probably told Moretti. "Does your father know a Willie Moretti?"

"It's the Italian connection," she said. "They both began small. Moretti advanced, my father didn't."

"If your father trucked booze, then why are you grilling me about knowing a few gangsters?"

"You admit, then, that you know those men."

He could see that he wasn't helping his case. She seemed intent on twisting his words.

"Until a few minutes ago, I never laid eyes on them."

"They were certainly chummy with your friend in the blue dress."

Ah, maybe her real beef was not the hoods but Margie? That argued she might have a yen for him. He smiled.

"Margie," he said casually, trying to assuage her jealousy, "has a husband and two kids." But once again he misjudged her cleverness.

"Then why the hell is she hanging out with other men? The morals of your friends leave much to be desired."

He lied. "Her old man is out of work. She has to support him— any way she can."

"What's her husband's name? I'll ask my father if he can find him work. Hungry kids are no joke."

"That won't be necessary . . . because, you see, uh, um, the guys Margie's sitting with have agreed to give him a job. That's what the powwow was all about."

Arietta said simply and without anger, "I don't believe you."

A disconcerting pause ensued; he then laughed and admitted that his embarrassment had led him to lie. She made him promise that he would always level with her. Encouraged by that word "always," he convinced himself that if she cared about his future behavior, then maybe she'd agree to return with him to the Riviera

Hotel. So when the band took a break, he used the occasion to ask. She lowered the lids over her fascinating eyes and peered at him as if she couldn't make out the person in front of her.

"Please, Jay, we hardly know each other."

He wanted to say "What better way to get acquainted," but sensed that beneath her skin was a mystery that sex was unlikely to solve. For a moment, he entertained the idea of telling her how much she entranced him, but guessed that, if she knew, he would be her toy, always at her beck and call. Maybe he was already. . . . The wiser course, he decided, was to act nonchalantly, pretending that all gentlemen, as a matter of form, propositioned their dates. In response to her comment, he replied, "Since we have so much ground to make up, let's go out next Saturday."

"Any place special?" she said rising from the table and pocketing the book of matches that had been lying in the ashtray.

"The Park movie house to see *Bombshell*."

He dressed in a tan suit and draped around his neck a brown silk muffler. As the cab passed the B'nai Abraham Synagogue, the spectral worshippers sparkled in the illumination of the incandescent moon. His thoughts became reflective. Terrible events were unfolding in Italy and Germany, but the Lord gave no sign of His displeasure. What would it take, he wondered, to disabuse people of their belief that the Almighty would protect them? At the door, not Arietta but Mr. Magliocco greeted him, scowling as if somehow the old guy knew about Jay's propositioning Arietta. Instead of retiring to the living room, Mr. Magliocco led him to the back of the house and into the damp and moldy air of the garage, where autumn flies buzzed in the light of an old standing lamp that illuminated a motorcycle and a "Toga Maroon" Waterhouse 1929 DuPont Model G five-passenger sedan, in mint condition.

"DuPont Motors made only about 625 of them," Mr. Magliocco said, "from '29 to '32. It'll go 125."

With its six "Borgia Wine" wire wheels, two of them spares resting in the fender wells, a rearview mirror strapped atop each, silvery aluminum bumpers, and the glowing maroon exterior finish, one could see that the car had been lovingly cared for.

"A reminder of adventures past," Mr. Magliocco said. "If this car could talk, the tales it could tell. . . . Shall we take a spin? We could circle the park . . . and talk privately."

Jay's confidence fled. What could he say if Arietta had told her father about his forwardness? Perhaps her father merely objected to a Jewish suitor with shady connections. Or maybe Piero just wanted to learn whether the lad's intentions were honorable. This much Jay knew: He wanted to take her to the hotel, not to the altar. At least not yet. Marriage happened when one had the means, and never before the age of twenty-five.

Driving smoothly and deliberately through the city, the old guy chatted about joyful felonies, bootlegging in particular, and the death of his wife from cancer—"she made me promise I'd raise Arietta a good Catholic." Like a kid who digresses but eventually returns to the subject, Piero kept coming back to the DuPont Model G Waterhouse. It fascinated him, particularly its pedigree.

"I understand you know Longie Zwillman."

"He got me my job at the paper." Hoping to look like an innocent, Jay added, "Though I'm not sure why."

"Longie has a big heart. He gives lots of money to the Catholic soup kitchens, and believe me they need it in these times." Slowing the auto to a crawl as they entered Weequahic Park, Mr. Magliocco said, "He gave me this car."

"Really?"

"Zwillman bought it from a guy in Pennsylvania, a fellow by the name of Robertson. Family owned thousands of acres. Abe figured that since most of the leggers hauled liquor in 'Henry's Lady,' a classier car like this one wouldn't be stopped—or caught, because it could outrun the feds. Zwillman originally got it to move liquor from Canada to Kansas City, but when the Pendergast people started buying from the local shiners, he used it to carry booze from Quebec to Atlantic City. I worked as a hauler. It suited me fine because I'd sneak off to visit a friend from Italy, Luigi Baldini, who had a farm near a small town not too far from Vineland, called Norma. Once his wife died, he hired a Negro housekeeper to keep up the place. He eventually gave the farm to her. That was Luigi: generous. Would you believe . . . 'Hump' McManus once hid out in Luigi's bunkhouse after he shot Rothstein in the stomach. Ever hear how the Big Bankroll refused to tell the cops who plugged him?"

"Some of the story but not all of it."

"One of these days we'll go to the diner and talk."

Half a dozen kids, taking advantage of the shining night, were biking down the "Sugar Bowl," a favorite hill in winter for the Flexible-Flyer crowd. He had done the same himself and, as a very young child, had often spent many a summer day rolling down the grass and arriving at the bottom in a vertiginous state.

Mr. Magliocco stopped the car. "Kristina came from money and would've liked another child," Piero said offhandedly. "But her health wouldn't take it. So she put all her mothering into Arietta: a tutor, music lessons, dancing classes, etiquette, religion . . ."

"She must have been lovely. You can tell from the photograph that Arietta's very much like her."

"Yes, though Kristina was blonde." Piero lapsed into memory. "She wore her yellow hair in a long braid down her back, not looped on top. Me, I resemble a Turk. Her skin was white as porcelain. Perfect teeth, thin face, dark eyes, high cheek bones, like royalty." Pause. "When she disapproved of my behavior, she called me 'Mr. M.'"

A boy came flying down the hill. Approaching the gully at the bottom of the Sugar Bowl, the kid bailed out, letting his bike nose-dive into the trench.

"Once they discovered the cancer, she went fast. Toward the end, she spoke only German." Tears welled in his eyes. "Do you know what it's like to have your dying wife whisper to you, and you can't understand?"

"You don't speak German?"

"Never learned. Arietta did . . . she always wanted to be just like her mom."

In the ensuing silence, Jay thought about how a woman's eyes purloin a man's love. Intuitively, he knew that eventually Arietta would steal all of him, even his faith in free love.

"You're probably wondering why I asked you to take a drive with me. If I was in your place I'd wanna know."

"Well, to tell you the truth it did cross my mind."

Jay turned to face him squarely, and in doing so, his knee hit—and opened—the small cabinet at the end of the instrument board provided for gloves or parcels. Mr. Magliocco leaned over and closed it, but not before Jay saw a pair of black gauntlet gloves.

Mr. M. lit a Wings cigarette, rolled down the window a couple of inches, and flipped the match outside. Jay noticed the matchbook: Kinney Club. Piero took a long draw as if he needed to fill his lungs to come out smoking. On the exhale began the lesson.

"Arietta's mother, like I said, made me promise to see that she grew up right. I don't want her falling into bad company. My own background is raw enough, first the priesthood business and then the bootlegging."

Knowing very well what had prompted his comment, Jay tried to evade it by waxing sentimental. "My parents have few equals for kindness and goodness. They never judge people by their purses. They respect all churches. My mother would cut off her right hand before she would ever say an unkind word to anyone, and my father would rather die than steal. That's the kind of family I come from, Mr. Magliocco."

To Jay's amazement, Mr. M. produced a business card for the Jea-nette Powder Puff Company. "I checked into your father's factory. He's everything you say. Honest Ike, right?"

Like a landed fish gulping the unfamiliar element of air, Jay opened and closed his mouth soundlessly. He felt overwhelmed by Piero's genuine concern for his daughter.

"Nothing's too good for Arietta. I check out all her friends—and their friends. The rackets taught me never to sleep." Mr. M. took another monster pull on his cigarette and exhaled. "You never went to the Park movie house. You spent the evening at the Kinney Club—and ran into some people I don't want my daughter around. It's bad enough I know those people."

No question: Mr. M. had Jay dead to rights, but who had spilled the beans, Arietta or someone else? It mattered. If she'd yakked, he might as well forget about their ever playing the dirty blues. But if the snitch came from the crowd at the club, which one? He decided then that the first commandment of the underworld should read: "Be extra careful when dealing with people who survive by knowing more than you."

"If you want to see Arietta again, take a page from your father's book. Don't lie. Understand?"

"I apologize, Mr. Magliocco. It will never happen again."

Piero smoked in silence, trying to decide whether to give Jay a second chance. "How come you live at the Riviera Hotel?"

Jay interpreted the question to mean: Where does your money come from? To lead him off the scent, he replied, "Are you asking why I don't live at home?"

"A lot of big shots live in that hotel."

Jay had guessed right. Mr. M. wanted to know how he could afford it. Having just promised to be straight with him, he now found himself in a position where he had to lie. If he told him that Longie paid his rent, Mr. M. would surely conclude that he was one of Longie's boys, one of the toughs, and ask for an explanation. ("You see, Mr. Magliocco, Longie's putting me up so that I can write glowing reviews about Miss Harlow." And Mr. M. would reply, "You gotta be kidding. All that dough for a movie review?") Street life had taught him, when in doubt, dissemble.

"I moonlight as assistant super of the hotel," he said, figuring that Longie could arrange with the owner to back up his story. "In return they give me a place to stay."

Mr. M. looked skeptical, said nothing, and lit another cigarette from the previous one. "A place to stay," Piero ruminated, "yes, I know the importance of that. I joined the priesthood as a young man to escape poverty. The Jesuits gave me shelter. But on a trip to Rome, a thunderbolt struck me, as the Sicilians say. In front of St. Peter's, a young woman stopped to ask me the way to the Sistine Chapel. I gave her directions but wound up following her. One thing led to another.

"Once I could no longer pass as a celebrant of chastity, I was defrocked—and brought her to the United States. Her family dis-owned her. Though she had a tiny inheritance from a sympathetic aunt, the money went on hospital bills." Here Piero broke off and began to speculate whether his wife's death came as a result of his sin or for some other reason. Jay tried to assure him that the Lord does not despise lovers. But what proof did he have, what right to speak for the Almighty? When he asked Mr. Magliocco how one reconciles faith and fact, the former priest gave him a peculiar reply.

"A beautiful aria proves that something greater than ourselves made it possible for the composer to create the music."

Jay left the subject. On the way back to the Magliocco house, they passed St. Lucy's Church, where a line of poorly clothed people stood waiting for bread and soup.

"Longie's money," said Mr. M.

"I suppose that gives a new meaning to laundering money. A good cause cleans it."

Mr. Magliocco looked surprised. "Yes, that's it, the source of the money doesn't matter, only what it's used for." Jay could see that some moral quandary had just been cleared up in Piero's mind.

At the house, they sat down to a cup of coffee with Arietta, resigned to missing the first movie, *Little Caesar*, but catching the second, *Bombshell.* As they chatted about films, Arietta said suddenly, "Did you know, but of course you don't, that my mother knew Mary Astor's parents, Otto and Helen Langhanke? She met them in Manhattan. Mother had a cousin in Quincy, Illinois, where the Langhankes once lived. She always tried to keep up her German connections."

Mr. M. insisted on driving them to the theater. Jay told him they would take a cab home, but Piero wouldn't hear of it. The wily ex-priest had checked on the movie, knew when it ended, and would pick them up. Enticing Arietta to the Riviera Hotel seemed a fading hope.

In the Park movie house, he saw standing at the popcorn concession the short, tattooed, dark-haired man with whom Arietta had been dancing before he quit and she took Jay as her partner. He gave Arietta a nudge and a come-hither smile. The tendons in her pedestal neck tightened, and her face turned ashen. Squeezing Jay's arm, she led him into the darkened theater, where she whispered that she wanted nothing to do with him.

"Just because he ran out of steam on the dance floor?"

"No, because he's called several times since and won't take no for an answer."

Jay, now jealous, led her to a seat at the back, some distance from the closest person, hoping to snuggle her when the movie got hot. The credits began with a background shot of a burning fuse on a bomb and ended when the bomb went off.

"I asked him to drop out of the marathon."

"Who?"

"Charlie Fernicola, the man you just saw."

The name sounded vaguely familiar, but before Jay could question her, the bomb dust cleared, and the film opened with splashes in newspapers and magazines of Lola Burns (Jean Harlow). Cut to a wealthy California home. A colored maid wakes Lola, who has an interview with a woman reporter representing a movie magazine. Absorbed in the action, Arietta and Jay began to mimic Harlow's slang.

"Why dump him?" he whispered.

"He's a twit."

"If he'd hung on you might've made a load of clams."

"Don't make me feel like a skunk."

Lola's publicity man, Space Hanlon, keeps her in the news by scandalizing her life. At the Coconut Grove, she is dancing with a European gent who is arrested. Publicity ensues.

"Where did you meet the rummage-sale Romeo?"

"At our church."

"He doesn't look the type."

"If I'm lying you can cut out my appendix without ether."

Space Hanlon talks about the speed of news reporting. A few minutes after an event occurs, it appears in the papers.

"What did he say when you dumped him?"

"That he felt like a worm."

"I'd be sore as hell."

"I guess I did play him for a chump."

"You really are a corker."

"And yet he keeps calling. He refuses to see daylight."

"Just give it to him right from the shoulder."

"He doesn't believe me. Says it's all feminine guff."

"Does he come to the house?"

"No, but if he did I'd bust him one in the bugle."

Lola's designing father and family enrich themselves by exploiting her, until everything collapses like a punctured balloon.

Before they left the theater, Arietta ducked into the ladies' room. By the time she reappeared, the place had emptied out, and Jay could see her father parked at the curb. Pausing in the foyer, he asked:

"Was he really a twit?"

She turned her pixy peepers on him and smiled. "He moved like a patent-leather peanut vendor. Besides, I wanted to dance with you."

"What a lotta banana oil."

"It's true. I saw your partner faint, and I'd noticed that you danced a lot better than Charlie."

As they moved toward the car, he felt strangely affected by the movie, almost as if he had just been a part of it, and, like Harlow, thought he'd been used. Her explanation about the guy she'd been dancing with sounded phonus-balonus. She had sworn him to truth, but what about her?

"Arietta!"

She stopped.

"What's the grift? I think you're just giving me a line about your partner at Dreamland."

Looking hurt, she said, "In that case, fade."

And fade he did—for several weeks. During that time, he wrote a glowing review of *Bombshell*, remarking how the movie mirrored Jean's offscreen life and how the language captured the wise-cracking spirit of people trying to make the best of a beastly Depression. It must have been a good piece, because the editor of the *Evening News* dropped by his desk to congratulate him on the way he had used the review to comment on conditions in the country. The editor then asked whether Jay knew Jean Harlow well enough to grill her about Zwillman and the Jewish gangsters trying to squash the upcoming Olympics. According to him, Abe and others were putting money in the mouths of politicians to persuade them to call for a boycott of Berlin. Jay admitted to being aware of Zwillman's concern, but was dark to any details. His editor then went on to say that it was a story Jay might want to cover. Apparently, Zwillman and some other Jewish gangsters had created a network of like-minded people across the country to persuade their representatives, local and national, to introduce legislation that would keep the U.S. team at home. Avery Brundage, having got wind of this tactic, was, not surprisingly, inveighing against the Jewish influence in government and newspapers—and threatening to call for an investigation.

"It's not just the Jews," Jay said, "plenty of Irish and Italians agree with Abe."

"Brundage says they're all members of the same gangster class."

"I suppose I could ask around."

"According to the little information we have, Zwillman has some heavy hitters working for him who are respectable citizens."

"I would hope so."

"One rumor has it that he's even put some women on the payroll. That's why I thought of Harlow."

"Beats me."

The editor left and Jay made a beeline for High Street, to Polly's brothel, the Parrot. With Arietta gone, he needed to keep up his spirits and a part of his anatomy; he also wanted to ask Margie if she had heard anything, since she was often in the know.

Polly ran her business like an old boys' club that often seemed not to be about women at all. Decked out in a sumptuous mixture of décors, the house looked like a museum, with plush Turkish carpets, expensive furniture in the style of Louis Quinze and Seize, valuable antiques, first editions of Robert Benchley and Dorothy Parker, and paintings by artists who had traded canvases for sex.

When he entered, the place sounded like Kaplan's, with different accents and conversations reinforcing the pungent aromas. A local businessman and one of the girls were playfully teasing.

"You did."

"You did not."

"You did so promise . . . a chain bracelet with piglets."

George S. Kaufman and Moss Hart, buried in adipose parlor chairs, were kibitzing with two local gangsters.

"Da only one of yous guys that ever got it right was Damon Runyon," said the hood. "He knows how the guys and gals talk."

"Joey's right. The rest of you ain't got a glimmer. The only reason I buy the papers is to read Runyon."

From the mah-jongg room came a clicking of tiles and voices.
"My move."

"No, Trish's. You oughta remember."

"Geez, she takes so long, I forget."

At the bar, he could overhear one of Joe Adonis's boys and a lo-cal politician playing backgammon and drinking.

"Who the hell did he think he was talking to, some greenhorn just off the boat?"

"I don't need no map, Councilor, I'll take care of it. You got no worries."

Polly greeted him and immediately sent for Margie, whom he had met the year before, when his Uncle Al introduced him to the enchantments of the Parrot. Although he never asked her age, he guessed twenty. Born in Denver, she said her father had brought the family east so that he could work in the bootlegging trade; but the Depression had wiped him out and led her to Polly's to help support the family. This particular evening, trade limped. Four girls, two of them high yellows, were occupied polishing their fingers and toenails. He gathered that only one of the girls had some real action. The other bedroom doors stood open. Margie, reeking of perfume and dressed in a kimono with large yellow and orange orchids printed against a black background, greeted him on high heels decorated with sequins. As usual, a wad of chewing gum kept her mouth in motion.

"Sure was good seeing you at the Kinney Club. What happened to Miss Beautiful?"

"She doesn't give me what you do."

"You never want to marry someone lousy with looks. Her puss is like neon, a come-on for every lug on the make."

Sensitive about Arietta and his feelings toward her, he changed the subject. "Guess what? I met Jean Harlow."

"You gotta be kiddin'! What was she wearin'?"

"Next to nothing."

"The movie mags say she ices her tits to make them stick out straight."

"They got a point."

A second later, the door opened and Polly greeted the man whom Arietta had identified as Charlie Fernicola. The guy wore an overcoat and a steel gray fedora. Jay couldn't hear the exchange between him and the madam, but she handed him a key and pointed upstairs. Without looking around, Mr. Fernicola headed in the direction of the closed door.

"Rico Bandello," Margie murmured.

"What?"

"The bruno who went upstairs. A real greaser."

"His name's Charlie Fernicola."

"Bunk. That guy burns powder for Zwillman. He's a torpedo."

"You're sure?"

"Absolutely."

With Margie as a decoy, Jay led her upstairs, as if they intended to flop in the feathers. Stopping outside the room that Rico had quietly opened with a key in his gloved hand, Jay peered over his shoulder. Rico was pointing a revolver at a man holding his *putz*, in full penile flight ready to enter a woman from behind.

"Blix!" Rico barked.

The preoccupied mark had failed to hear Rico enter. At the sight of the gunman, the guy raised his hands and fell back on the bed, his dick turning into a wet corn husk. A second later, the woman, realizing the situation, screamed, grabbed a robe from a chair, and rushed into the hall.

Rico commanded, "You got one minute to get a stander or I shoot off your nuts."

Seemingly oblivious to their presence, the hit man looked at his watch and counted off the last ten seconds. The pigeon, unable to coax his pecker to rise, begged for mercy.

"I'll get outta town. Anything Longie wants, but don't shoot."

Rico grabbed the fellow's clothes, which hung on a wall hook, and, removing a roscoe from the guy's jacket, said, "If you ever push drugs again in the Third Ward, you're dead. That's Longie's message to Dutch. Now get the hell out of here."

Leaping out of bed and using his hands as a fig leaf to cover his genitals, the man said meekly, "Can I have my clothes back?"

"No, you can just go home in your skin. Take a powder."

The man fled from the room naked as a newborn, down the steps, and out of the brothel into the street. Rico turned and sneered:

"Who the hell are you and what's your game?"

Margie immediately extricated herself from Jay's arms and ducked into one of the rooms.

Shoving his shaking hands in his pockets, he said casually, "Longie pays my salary too. I happened to be on the premises. When I saw you go upstairs alone, I figured you were on a job and might need some backing up."

"And the dame?"

"Window dressing. She's like Polly: Mum's the word."

Skeptically, they guy asked, "Ain't I seen you before?"

For safety's sake, Jay continued to trade on Zwillman's name, saying, "Maybe we met at his party for Harlow and Jolson."

Rico seemed to relax as he grunted, "I missed that one."

Downstairs, Bandello insisted on buying drinks. "I'm having a Scotch, and you?" Jay requested a beer.

"Not one for the hard stuff?"

"It ruins a boner, and I've got someone upstairs waiting for me." Rico snickered and eyed Jay suspiciously as they sipped their drinks. "You sure we ain't met?"

"I can't imagine where."

Although bursting to ask him about Arietta, he felt he needed to ask her first why she had lied about Rico's name. If Jay got too curious with this guy about that fateful day at the dance hall, he might be putting her in danger. But without healing the rift with Arietta, how could he approach her?

"I'm Jay Klug," he said. "We haven't introduced ourselves."

"Rico Bandello." They shook hands.

Margie was right, unless this guy, like a number of hoods, used different names. Jay decided to test him.

"You wouldn't happen to know a Charlie Fernicola?"

Rico, sipping his Scotch, put his glass down.

"You kiddin'?"

"No, I'm on the up and up."

"Funny that you should ask because . . ."

"Yes?"

"Never mind." He took a swig of his drink. "If you mean the Fernicola who pitched for the Newark Bears, yeah, I seen him throw once. He didn't last long in the league."

Jay knew now why the name sounded familiar. But why had Arietta invoked it? "Any idea where he works?"

"Charlie? He took over his father's barrel business. At least that's what I heard. How come you want to know?"

Jay gulped. "Um, you remind me of him. Same, uh, walk."

"Never noticed. So you seen him pitch?"

"Yeah, against Montreal, I think."

For a while, they sipped their drinks in silence. Rico seemed lost in thought, but Jay sank into despondency. He could see no reason for Arietta's lying.

"Whatta you do for Longie?"

"I write, uh . . ." If he said reviews of Jean Harlow, he knew Rico would never believe it, so he replied, "Letters for Abe. I'm his . . . amanuensis."

"What's that?"

"His private secretary."

"I didn't know he had one."

"Hired me recently."

Rico finished his drink and joked that Jay could write his future love letters. They shook hands, and Rico left.

Upstairs, Margie, fully dressed, sat on the bed. She said, "I told Polly, no hit men. Anyone else, okay. I hate gunplay and try to stay clear of the droppers."

She clung to him for a long while, until her body slowly relaxed. Jay asked if she knew anything about Abe and the Olympic boycott. She looked as if he were speaking Greek. Eventually, they fell back on the bed and undressed one another, screwing slowly and caringly, without passion. The whole time, he tried to imagine himself entering Arietta, but the absence of abandon did not fit his dream of how he and Arietta would make love.

As Jay lay spent on the bed, Margie asked, "How come you never picked up the blower to ask how I was?"

"Didn't you hear about the killing at Dreamland? It happened right after you went to the hospital."

"I never read the papers. All they got is bad news. I wanna laugh, not cry." She rolled onto her side and walked her fingers from his chest to his scrotum. "Whatta you say we become steady? I'll be your regular."

Damn, what does a guy say to a swell gal when she makes an offer like that but he knows it will never work? Not to hurt Margie, he told her he was planning to go back to college.

"What for? You already went."

"Maybe law school."

"Will that make getting a real job any easier?"

Margie thought of college as a trade school. If the degree didn't result in a good paying job, the whole experience was worthless.

"Look at it this way, Marge, it's college or my old man's factory."

"If it ain't you, it'll be someone else."

"Maybe a rich fancy man who'll keep you out of sight of his old lady."

She sighed resignedly. "More likely I'll hook up with a pimp or a pigeon."

They hugged. He kissed her. She had tears in her eyes. On the street, outside of Polly's, he heard a newsboy crying the late evening headlines: "Dutch Schultz Investigated for Racketeering!"

Longie's name never surfaced, which was surprising, because when Dutch had failed to support the boycott, Longie had coldly said, "He'll earn his fate."

A week later, Jay received an invitation from Mr. Magliocco to have dinner with him and Arietta at the Tavern. Perhaps she had told her father about Jay's behavior at the movie. They all met in front of the restaurant. After the usual wait, Sam seated them. Although Arietta said virtually nothing, an unusually garrulous Mr. Magliocco regaled him with the details of a recent lively reunion at the Robert Treat Hotel with some of the old rumrunners.

"Even a few of the young fellows joined us. In fact, one of them knows you. Rico Bandello."

"What a coincidence, you and Fernicola," Jay said, looking at Arietta.

Mr. M. laughed raucously. "Don't blame Ari. Rico knew I'd never let her go dancing with him, so he called himself Charlie Fernicola. She didn't know they were the same guy until Rico drove me home from the reunion and stopped at the house for a nightcap."

Jay looked perplexed. If Mr. M. was being straight with him, then how come Rico hadn't leapt out of his skin when Jay asked him if he knew a Charlie Fernicola? What other small deceits and sinful games were this pair up to?

"You said, Mr. Magliocco, that Rico mentioned me?"

"Yes, he spoke of you in a friendly way. Something about you trying to help him if things got out of hand."

Apparently, thank god, Rico had left out the location.

Jay shrugged. "It's hardly worth repeating."

"An interesting guy, Rico. Like you and Arietta he loves dancing. Did he tell you that?"

"No. We spoke for only a couple of minutes."

Sam took their orders, leaving a plate of *forshpiesers* that included slices of gefilte fish. Skewering one with a toothpick, Jay let it slowly dissolve in his mouth, waiting for Mr. M. to continue his indirection, clearly intended to worm something out of Jay, but what in particular, he couldn't tell.

"Surely he must have mentioned Longie?" Mr. M. said with a rising inflection.

"Yes."

"He works for him."

"So he said."

Mr. Magliocco sampled a piece of herring. Arietta sat mum as marble, staring out the window.

"Of course, when you saw him dancing with Arietta, he was out on the town, on his own time, between jobs."

"Really? He didn't say. In fact he never mentioned the dance marathon . . . or what happened."

Mr. M. sighed. "Terrible thing, that murder. You know, when the police interviewed Arietta, they asked her a lot of questions about you. Why would that be?"

Jay looked at Arietta, but the stone maiden seemed utterly content to let her father speak for her. At that instant, he would have given a C-note to be with Arietta alone in a solitary place where he could try to get to the bottom of his suspicions. Mr. M. migrated into an anecdotal discussion about his adventures during Prohibition. Arietta occasionally smiled at some of his confessions but wouldn't look at Jay. At meal's end, Mr. M. excused himself and left the table to light up outside. His daughter never so much as gave Jay a glance.

"Why did you come to dinner if you weren't going to talk?"

"You still owe me an apology."

"For what?"

"For saying I had grifting motives."

She was clearly hurt. He decided then, sitting there, admiring that faultless face, that growing up in the house of a bootlegger had given her speech a larcenous veneer, as she herself had suggested the first time they met, but that underneath she was really quite as innocent as she appeared.

"I apologize."

It took a moment, but slowly a smile softened her face and she said, "Apology accepted."

A few tables away, the diners were speaking German. That he had not noticed it before was probably owing to his absorption in

Arietta. Four people rose to leave. The women went first, followed by the men. Apparently the German dislike of the Jews didn't keep the local Deutsche population—even Newark Nazis—from frequenting the Tavern.

As the group passed their table, the last of them, a tall, thin, romantically handsome man, no older than thirty, with a dueling scar across his left cheek, stopped and bowed slightly. In acknowledgment, Arietta smiled politely and nodded.

"So nice to see you again, Fräulein."

"Scarface" then followed the others to the front of the restaurant to collect his overcoat and dissolved out the door. Jay tried to get a better look at him, but could see only his straw-colored hair as the fellow removed his hat to enter a cab.

"Quite handsome. What's his line of work?"

"My mother would have said hard times make good men bad."

"But she would have approved of the German connection."

"Yes, she was proud of her roots, which is why she had me home-schooled by a German tutor, Fräulein Bauer, a real stickler."

"I would like to have met your mom."

Arietta's eyes misted, and she looked away, wandering to another place, another time. "She died on my tenth birthday. I have never celebrated my birthday since. When I was a child, she used to play hide-and-seek with me in the house. In those days, we had Persian rugs and Waterford glass and Wedgwood ceramics. After she died, I went from room to room looking for her. In my dreams, I often find myself opening doors, but the person I'm looking for is never there."

"Is that why you maintain your German ties?"

She seemed inclined to answer, but Mr. Magliocco returned, full of Italian good cheer, talking with both mouth and hands, filling Jay in, as promised, on the details of Arnold Rothstein's death, which had become the stuff of myth. Rothstein had received a call at Lindy's and had left. The Big Bankroll was then found in a hotel, shot and dying.

"All the famous ones—gone. A.R., Legs, Joey Noe, Bo Weinberg, Vincent Coll." He shook his head. "Now the tax men are closing in on the Dutchman. I wonder where he's stashed his money. Dutch was always stingy. He must have a fortune." Mr. M. picked at a nicotine-stained finger. "Probably somewhere in the Third Ward."

Jay said nothing, fearing that Mr. M. sensed a connection between him and Schultz's Third Ward drug operation.

He waited a few days before calling Arietta again. The evening with her father had left him feeling peculiar. Why had Mr. M. asked him to dinner? No reason was ever given. Was it to heal the rupture between Jay and his daughter? Perhaps that explained his cigarette break. Or did the invitation have something to do with the Fernicola-Bandello falsehood? But that confusion had been dispelled with a plausible explanation. Something lay below the surface, or was Jay being his usual suspicious self? Surely Mr. M. couldn't imagine that he knew where Schultz's loot was?

After a fortnight, his unease abated and he invited Arietta to a revival of Kaufman and Ryskind's musical play *Of Thee I Sing*, a 1931 winner of the Pulitzer. The *News* had given him two comp tickets. When she inquired what to wear, he told her she would look good in a *shmattah*, which he had to explain meant a rag, and requested she tell her father that they would be late and not to stay up. He planned to take Arietta to dinner afterward and then try to steer her to the hotel.

Their fourth-row seats positioned them just behind Kaufman and his companion, the movie actress Mary Astor. He knew that George had a wife and Mary a husband and therefore figured they were just old friends. Whew, was he wrong! It all began innocently enough. Before the curtain went up, George kept Mary in stitches with his corny one-liners. Once the theater darkened, they played "kneesies," and George slid his arm over her shoulder, cupping her breast with his hand. She responded by putting a hand between his legs. By the time the play ended with the audience humming, "He's the man the people choose—loves the Irish and the Jews,"

Jay's temperature had risen several degrees. He would have gladly skipped dinner and grabbed a train back to Newark, but Arietta wanted to ask Kaufman and Astor for their autographs. In the press of people, they temporarily lost them. A few minutes later, Arietta saw them walking down the street, hand in hand. They discreetly followed. When George and Mary entered an eatery just off the boulevard, Jay looked at Arietta. She said, "Why not?" They entered, got them to sign their programs, and decided to stay for dinner.

Kaufman and Astor sat at the back of the restaurant. Jay could see them but Arietta could not. They seemed perfectly at ease, and periodically George leaned across the table to kiss her. Jay saw him rest his hand on her knee, and she, dropping a shoe, put her stockinged foot in his crotch. Arietta asked him why he kept staring—"Are they still making whoopee?"—to which he replied, "You ain't kidding."

As Jay related the scene unfolding behind her, she cut him off, as if to send him a signal: don't get any ideas. He would find out soon enough. With their meals unfinished, George and Mary left; they seemed to be in a hurry. Jay could guess why. Mentally, he was writing Walter Winchell's next day's column: "Flash. Deskman at a midtown hotel says Kaufman and Astor arrived around midnight. Took the elevator to her sixth-floor room. Did not emerge until morning." In his own review, he merely observed that the author graced the audience in the company of Mary Astor.

By the time they reached Newark, Arietta requested that they take a cab from Penn Station right to her house, no detours. Crestfallen, he complied, and then returned to the hotel to jack off.

Finding her presence addictive, he had to give it one more try; and the next date, wherever he took her, he'd leave plenty of time to return to the Riviera. After giving it some thought, he decided on the Chanticler club in Millburn. Erwin Kent and his band would be playing. They could make the early show. When he rang, Mr. Magliocco answered the phone and to Jay's surprise said, "I thought she was ice skating with you at Irvington Park?" He hastily assured him that they had been skating and that she was now on her way home. Would she please call when she returned?

A little more than an hour later, she telephoned, full of apologies and thanks for his backing up her story. But she didn't say why she had used his name or where she had been. In an appreciative mood, she agreed to join him the following Sunday for an afternoon of dancing and an evening of dining at the Chanticler.

Three days later, he had an unexpected visit from two cops, Detective Barbarash and Sergeant Muger, still investigating the murder of Heinz Diebel. They found him in his Prince Street room, writing and vainly watching for hoodlums.

"Who pays the rent?" asked Detective Barbarash, as he and his pal pulled up a couple of chairs.

"I do."

"On this place *and* the Riviera?"

Fortunately, Longie had, at his request, directed the hotel manager to tell anyone who asked that Jay worked there as an assistant super. When he explained that he received a room at the hotel in return for services rendered, the detective mumbled:

"Yeah, that's what the manager said. I just wanted to hear you say it. And this room? Your landlord said someone else rented it for you, Puddy Hinkes. A friend of yours?"

"He found the place for me. His office is just down the street."

"We know that."

Sergeant Muger began shuffling through a stack of Jay's papers and examined the sheet in the typewriter.

"Hey, do you have a search warrant?"

"We don't need one," said Muger.

"Why would I have anything to do with the death of Diebel?"

"You're Jewish," said Detective Barbarash.

"And so is 20 percent of Newark. Try them."

"They weren't at Dreamland. You were."

"I know nothing about the murder."

"You know Arietta Magliocco."

"What's she have to do with it?"

Sergeant Muger, absorbed in Jay's manuscript, read out loud, "May bananas grow in their throat; my god, I am passing . . . out!" Then a moment later, "Bleeding from two large holes in his chest, the stricken man gasped for air and uttered some unintelligible German words. His partner sank to his side and took his hand. While trying to whisper in her ear, the victim expired." Muger looked up from the page and said, "This sounds like a description of Diebel's death. How come?"

"I'm a journalist."

"Yeah," said Barbarash. "The News gave us copies of your reviews. You really laid it on with a ladle about Harlow. Could the reason have anything to do with Longie Zwillman?"

"Who?"

Detective Barbarash reversed his chair so that he was now leaning over the backrest. "Knock it off, Jay. We had police stationed outside Abe's house the night of his big party. We've got you on film. You and Puddy."

"All right, I went to a bash. There's no crime in that."

Detective Barbarash looked at his associate. "Armen!"

Sergeant Muger, still reading from the manuscript, said without looking up, "What do you know about Arietta Magliocco?"

The police, of course, knew that he had been dancing with her just before the murder. They had questioned him on that point at the time of Diebel's death. But did the cops know that they had been dating? He saw no reason to lie and readily admitted that he had taken her out a few times. Where had they gone? He told them.

Muger continued. "Ever been to a meeting of the Friends of the New Germany, in Irvington?"

"What the hell would I be doing there?" he said indignantly. "You said it yourself: I'm Jewish."

Detective Barbarash held up a hand, as if to signal Muger to wait. "Zwillman has been known to plant some of his boys in these meetings to gather information and sometimes even to foment a fight."

"I write reviews, not reports about Nazis." Turning to Sergeant Muger, he urged, "Read through every page on the table. You won't find a one that concerns the Friends of the New Germany."

Muger smiled. "Not yet. I already checked."

"Why do you suppose," Detective Barbarash said languidly, "that Arietta Magliocco attends these meetings—at least some of them?"

"I don't believe it."

The detective removed an envelope from his breast pocket and spilled on the table several small photographs. "Take a look for yourself. Isn't that her?"

Indeed, the shots depicted Arietta heading into and coming out of the Nazi meeting hall. Not knowing what to say, he shrugged and held up his palms. Barbarash collected the photos and said:

"So you're unfamiliar with these activities of hers?"

"Absolutely."

"Disloyalty kills." The detective handed Jay a business card with his telephone number. "If you hear anything, please let us know. Your own safety may be involved."

For a long time after they left, Jay sat in a distracted state, trying to make sense of what he had just heard. Should he call off their date at the Chanticler? A number of times, in the next few days, he went to the phone, but then in his imagination he would see her delicately sculpted face and radiant eyes. Try though he might, he could not dispel her image. She haunted him. He saw her in beautiful women on the street, in paintings, in carvings, in ads, in movie actresses. Finally, he persuaded himself that he owed her the chance to explain her behavior. On the Sunday, he borrowed Puddy's car, collected Arietta at her house, admired her yellow sweater, and motored to the Chanticler in Millburn.

Driving up the circular drive, he stopped in front and handed the car keys to an attendant. The chandeliers' silver radiance reflected off the black-and-white marble floors, lighting the entry hall and the winding staircase leading up to the bridal suites. They left their coats with the hatcheck girl. At the bar, to the right, he could see a large late-afternoon crowd. He pushed aside the serge curtains leading to the lavish red-carpeted dining room and gave his name to the maitre d'. The tables—arrayed on two tiers, one at the level of the dance floor and the other two steps up—glowed in their starched linen brightness and silver settings. They sat close to the oval dance floor, facing the central bandstand, where shortly Erwin Kent would play the piano and direct his small band.

To the chagrin of the waiter, he and Arietta ordered two ginger ales. Without any soft soaping, he broached the subject of immediate concern: her relationship to the Friends of the New Germany.

"The police came to see me."

"Me, too, for the second time."

"They asked me why you would be attending a Nazi meeting."

"My mother's older sister, Aunt Hilde, begged me to go. I hated every minute of it."

"Then why did you return?"

"For the same reason I went the first time, as a favor to an old woman. Would I do it again? No."

"The police seem to want to tie us into the murder, somehow."

As Maestro Kent and his fellow musicians seated themselves at the bandstand and launched into "I Get a Kick out of You," the bar crowd began to migrate to their reserved tables. In no time, the place filled up with swells.

"Where does your aunt live?"

"What?"

"Your Aunt Hilde. She must have an address."

Arietta said matter-of-factly, "You don't believe me."

In fact, he didn't, but he also didn't think that she sympathized with Nazis. So why had she attended those meetings? The cops said Longie had spies in the meetings, but women? Perhaps she worked for the cops. No, they wouldn't have pushed so hard for information about her if she'd been one of theirs. Maybe FBI? That would explain the source of her money. But if the FBI had employed her, wouldn't they have tipped off the police? Maybe yes, maybe no. Perhaps the bureau wanted the cops to keep a protective eye on her, given the circles she was traveling in. But why then would the cops have questioned Jay about her loyalty? No, they had to have been nosing around independent of the feds. He reasoned that since the cops were in charge of the Diebel investigation, they undoubtedly had put the Friends under surveillance, and when Arietta showed up, they saw a connection. Present at both the murder and the meeting hall, she was a likely suspect.

Arietta leaned across the table and rested a hand on his. "You must trust me, Jay. I can't talk about it."

"But what does your presence at those gatherings mean?"

"I am not a Nazi or a Friend, if that's what you're thinking."

"The word on the street has it," he said, trying to draw her out, "that the group plans to launch a violent anti-Semitic campaign."

But she ignored the bait. He felt helpless, like a child subject to its parents' whims. She held all the cards. A particularly gorgeous smile animated her face.

"You saved me from getting into hot water with my father. I am in your debt."

Indeed! And what about *that* little lie? Was she meeting her contact or maybe someone worse?

The band struck up "I Only Have Eyes for You." For some reason, his mind wandered to the misplaced "only." Did the lover have *only* eyes and nothing else? Not a head, a torso, a dick? What he hoped to hear one day from Arietta was "I have eyes only for you."

When Sylvia Kent came on to sing "Blue Moon" in her torchy voice, he and Arietta danced, to the appreciation of the other diners. All his fears and reservations about Arietta disappeared as he twirled her around, held her at fingertip length, and then brought her close. She rested her head on his shoulder and kissed his neck. At that instant, he knew that the IOU he held would be paid on this lustrous lunar night.

Without comment, she snuggled him in the car as he drove her to the Riviera Hotel. He listened to their shoes clack across the tiles in the foyer and up the marble steps, as they made their way to the second floor, where he had a small back room that looked out on an alley. They sank into the settee. His head began to throb, and his hands shook. Weeks later, he had no memory of their small talk, but he did remember her saying playfully, "I should warn you, I keep a diary," and his replying recklessly, "I'd like to star in it!" Extending a hand to him, she silently rose and let him lead her into the bedroom. She crossed her arms and grasped the bottom of her sweater, slowly raising it, revealing no slip, only a bra. She stared at him until the sweater came over her face, her arms stretched overhead, entangled in the yellow sweater, her body extended. He stared at her white bra and could see the outline of her nipples. Dropping the sweater at her feet, she smiled at him. He lost himself in her eyes. Her smile seemed to be asking him if he knew what her undressing meant to her, and to him, and reached behind her back with both arms. Having forgotten to pull the shade in the bedroom, he watched the moon washing over her right side, from shoulder to knee, as she unhooked her bra, bringing her arms forward and crossing them on her chest. Holding the straps of the bra in her hands, she dropped it on the floor. Her breasts were bountiful, the areolas a deep red, the nipples erect.

She continued to look at him. As she pulled her skirt down over her hips, his eyes devoured her body. In the moonlight, her dancer's legs induced him to think of the pleasures to come when she locked them around his waist. Wearing only panties, silvered by the luminous sky, she fixed him with her wild eyes, exuding anticipation and desire. His body ached from lust.

"I hope you won't be disappointed," she said provocatively, removing the last item of clothing, and giving him the frightening impression that she was completely aware of her sensuality. As she slipped into the shower, he was beside himself with urgency and prayed that she would offer him immediate relief. In her absence he undressed. A few minutes later, she exited the shower, dripping, and kissed him chastely, but her nearness violently affected his blood heat, which coursed madly in his temples, his cheeks, his fingertips, and his member, causing him no little embarrassment.

Driving her home that night, oblivious to traffic lights and streets, he still felt aroused. Where had she learned so much? Possessed by concupiscence, he kept thinking, "Let it always be, the passion, the voluptuous breasts, the wet womb." Aphrodite had risen!

4

As he reached over to spear another piece of *broost*, his Pop said:

"I've tried reaching you several times at the New Jersey Vending Machine Company. Maybe I have the wrong number: Waverly 3-3165."

When he had moved from their house on Goldsmith Avenue to the Riviera Hotel, he had told his family that to pay the rent he was working two jobs, publicity and journalism. Of course he had never set foot in the offices of the vending machine company, although he had alerted the secretary to the possibility that his mother or father might call there. He therefore checked in with her regularly and requested that she leave messages for him at the newspaper. Having always returned his parents' calls, he figured they'd never pursue the matter any further.

He noticed on the table a butter dish, which constituted a small victory for his father. His mother had come to the marriage from an orthodox family, and his father had insisted on maintaining a secular home. In dietary matters, though, his mom often clung to the old ways, refusing to mix dairy and meat. His father, however, liked buttered bread with his meals and had often told the story of his first dinner at the house of his future in-laws. Jay's grandmother had served a boiled chicken, which his father likened to a beggar in tattered clothes, what with the meat hanging off the bone. Seeing no butter to *schmear* on his bread, he requested some. Jay's mother kicked him under the table, forcing him into an ignoble retreat. This Friday night, his father had prevailed.

Upon moving out, he had promised that he would not lose touch and made it a point to have dinner at Goldsmith Avenue every Friday night. His mother would light Sabbath candles—his father dared not interfere with that custom because she associated it with burning a *yahrzeit* candle in honor of her dead parents—and would say a prayer in Hebrew before the meal. Actually, his father knew Hebrew far better than she, but always deferred to her in matters of worship. Even Jay knew, from his synagogue training, that her pronunciation often went awry, but neither of them ever corrected her.

"So tell me," his father continued, "what do you do for the vending company? I see your articles in the arts section of the *News*, but you never show us any examples of the publicity you write."

"It's just internal stuff, like reminders to the salesmen of what points to make with prospective customers."

"You seem so sedulous," his mother said.

He knew without even seeing her how-to-improve-your-vocabulary book that "sedulous" was one of the words.

To be playful he answered, "Actually I'm quite pococurante."

She asked him how to spell it, ran to her dictionary and returned to the table.

"Indifferent. I would never think of you as insouciant," she said with a satisfied smile.

Her charming dedication to self-improvement didn't provide the shortcut to learning that she longed for (she woefully lacked a grasp of history and logic), but it did make for some splendid word games and had put Jay leagues ahead of most English speakers.

"You seeing anyone?" she asked tentatively.

He knew what her tone meant: Was he dating Jewish girls? "Yes, I've been seeing an Italian girl who lives on Littleton Avenue."

His father chuckled as his mother repeated, "Italian?"

"Yes, I know. If you marry your own kind, you have fewer prob-lems, more in common. A better chance at happiness. Right?"

"Since you know that, why then . . ."

But she couldn't finish the sentence. Her generosity forbade cen-sure. He could, however, sense her disappointment.

"Once you meet her, I'm sure you'll feel different. She's almost as beautiful as you, Mom."

"And her parents?"

"Her mother died a long time ago and her father's currently out of work."

From his mother's expression and quick glance at his dad, he knew what to say next. "She supports him, as a dancer and . . . a government worker."

His father, who regarded FDR as too conservative, but very much believed in federal projects to keep the poor employed, asked what she did.

"To be perfectly honest, I don't know. I think she works in an office that keeps tabs on German immigrants."

"Germans!" his mother exclaimed.

Again he knew what she thought. As far back as he could re-member, he could discern her meanings. In her book of errors, "Catholic" held a prominent position, but "German" stood right at the top of the list because it meant anti-Semite. The first problem could be fudged, but not the second. Nevertheless he jumped into frigid waters, convinced that a quick immersion would cause less pain than a protracted one. "Her mother was German, and she speaks the language."

After an interminable pause, during which his mother studied the white linen tablecloth and drew lines in it with her fork, she began her set speech. "So many nice Jewish girls I see at the syna-gogue. Single ones. Why not them? They come from good families. Take the Bernstein girl, for example."

At this point, as often happened, his father came to the res-cue. "Are we not all human beings . . . the same under the skin?

Religion! Just a cloak for a lot of *mishugunah* beliefs that lead to hatred and wars."

His mother, unable to defend her religious feelings on empirical grounds, always retreated to cultural ones. "Our Bible is not theirs; our sacred values, not theirs; our habits, not theirs; our . . ."

His father interrupted. "All decent human beings think alike, whatever their church or skin color. Look at socialist theory if you want to see what the world could be. All races, all religions . . ." His father typically broke off in the middle of a political statement, knowing that his wife shared neither his love for nor his knowledge of left-wing politics.

"When do we get to meet her?"

He knew that bringing her to the house for dinner would not be a problem. His mother, a model of courtesy, would treat any guest of his graciously. In private, she might *noodge* him or drop hints as subtle as cannon balls, but in public, she behaved like royalty. So too would his father, though he might be inclined to probe the guest's political beliefs.

"Perhaps you'd like to meet her father at the same time? I'm sure Mr. Magliocco would like to meet you."

Ever formal, his mother demurred. "I think that including her father would suggest a degree of seriousness that your friendship has not yet arrived at."

Little did she know, and he did not intend to enlighten her.

His father, having no patience for parochial views, changed the subject. An earnest socialist, he couldn't understand why Jay hadn't joined the American labor movement or volunteered his services to the Soviet Union, which was advertising in the *New York Times* for field hands and industrial laborers. For the first time, he brought up the idea of Jay's going to Spain.

"According to the *Daily Worker*, German and Italian fascists are sneaking into Spain to help overthrow the democratic government."

His father's dependence on the *Daily Worker* for his news had more than once led him astray. He tried gently to downplay the veracity of that organ.

"Nonsense, they have reporters in the field. And you can't deny that the church and the army would like nothing more than to repeal the reforms of the 1931 constitution."

Well aware that to plead ignorance about the constitution would have subjected him to a lecture, he said, "Dad, be reasonable. I don't even speak the language."

"You could learn it."

"And what would I do?"

"Whatever was needed."

"Their needs and my skills are unlikely to match up."

His dad looked dismayed. "Why can't you do something socially useful?"

He nearly asked him if making powder puffs qualified, but refrained from hurting the feelings of this tall, gangly man, whose political passion he admired but did not share.

"At least I'm not on the dole."

"Don't ever disparage welfare. Those who seek it, do so reluctantly. The measure of a great country is not how well it treats the rich but how well it treats the poor. Just think of the Nolans in the attic space."

Jay and his parents lived at 172 Goldsmith Avenue on the first floor of a two-story house with a small room at the top, home to the Nolans, dependent on government handouts for survival. The owner, Mrs. Denholtz, who occupied the second floor and fashioned herself a capitalist, tormented his mother with small indignities, like taking their window screens, which his father had himself repaired, and substituting her own broken ones, and refusing to give their dealer's coal truck access to the basement chute as she did for her own deliveries, requiring the truckman to carry the coal on his back in canvas bags and to double the cost. Unlike the Nolans, they owned a few furnishings worth mentioning: a piano and a china closet that held his mother's *Shabbas* dishes. The piano was her prized possession, perhaps because it had come down to her from a beloved uncle. Convinced that no piano should remain unused, his mother arranged for him to take lessons. He started at seven and quit at fourteen, the lure of shouting kids at their street sports proving a greater attraction than the keyboard. And yes, he had since come to regret his decision. After seven years, he was actually pretty good. His mother, in particular, rued his refusal to practice; his father, preoccupied with work, seemed less concerned.

His mother, who kept the books for the Jeanette Powder Puff Company, had herself at fifteen been forced to leave school—and discontinue piano lessons—to help support her family when her father died from mercury poisoning, the result of working in a hat factory. That death, which his dad often cited as an example of the evils of American capitalism, had cheated his mother of an education. A kind and generous woman as well as a strikingly beautiful one, she was ill equipped to face the world of ideas, even though she had been raised in New York City and had a great deal of street savvy. Limited by her truncated schooling, she coped by reading vocabulary-building books and by subscribing to optimistic platitudes and clichés.

His Russian-born dad presented another story, one that he thought of as an impermeable membrane separating memory from meaning. Although his dad could recall numerous childhood events, how they had affected his life he never said, leading Jay to conclude that motives were inscrutable, born of the protean moment. A learned man, his father had undoubtedly married his mother for her loveliness and gentleness. Intellectually, they had nothing in common, except the dream of building a successful business. His fluency in six languages, including English, set him apart from so many immigrants who spoke with heavy accents. On arriving in this country as a teenager, his father studied opera to perfect his speech. Result: impeccable enunciation; and after two bars, his father could identify the composer and relate the libretto. His mother never shared her husband's taste for classical music; popular dance tunes captured her fancy. He supposed his love of dancing came from them both. Having taken ballroom dancing lessons for many years, they could cut a rug with the best professional hoofers.

He learned from them. They also tried to teach him the rudiments of business, but he had no head for commerce, only books and writing. Since grade school, he had kept notebooks with sketches of people, places, and plots. His mother knew that he stored these scribbles in his closet and encouraged his writing, though she agreed with his dad that education and making a living came first.

"Jay, what kind of life is it . . . this dancing?" his dad had lamented upon hearing the story of the shooting at Dreamland.

"Everything will turn out for the best," said his mother, trying to defend him. "You'll see."

His father scowled.

"Who knows," he quipped, "maybe I'll end up dancing in Hollywood."

"Jay," his father reproved, "there is a dignity to honest labor, no matter how slight. Don't demean it."

"Come," his mother said, taking his arm and extricating him from his domestic discomfort. "I need you to quiz me on the L's: languor, lassitude, lethargy."

As he and his mother disappeared into the next room, his father called out, "Factories are the heartbeat of the country. The sight of honest people at work is the realization of the Golden Medina, marred at the moment by the absence of good jobs."

How well Jay knew the sights and smells: the sewing machines, the circular dies, the mixing machine, the long cutting tables for the bolts of velour, the Negro cutter, and the aromas of perfumed powder and eye rouge blending with the chemical odors of the mascara vat.

At one time his father had employed thirty-five women as sewing machine operators and a dozen men, a workforce that had shrunk to two gals and four guys. The business had prospered until the Depression. Unable to obtain a loan, he sold it to a Russian émigré, Helena Rubinstein. But that event occurred after Jay had enrolled in law school on a scholarship made possible by a person the FBI regarded as one of the most dangerous men in America.

When he had worked for his dad as a shipping clerk, his Uncle Al, his Mom's younger brother, whom his father kept on as a favor to her, provided an unusual education for which he would always be grateful. Having apprenticed as a locksmith, his uncle had taught him how to pick locks and break into cars, a skill that he exercised more than once. Also a ladies man, his uncle arranged for a condom dealer to show up regularly on the street below. They would then lower a basket with money and haul up the goods for their use with the young office girls in the building. It was his uncle who explained how to satisfy a woman. Contemptuous of screw-and-bolt men, Al lectured him in how to delay ejaculation and prolong the pleasure. His uncle also taught him positions other than the missionary and different ways to effect a climax in a woman. Had Jay's mother known the lessons her brother was transmitting to her son, he guessed that for all her sisterly love she would have disowned him. But except for the sexual initiation he owed to his uncle, he resented both factory work and marketing. To sell their products to F. W. Woolworth, their principal buyer, required meretricious rhetoric on a grand scale. So the evening he had run into Puddy at the Tavern, he was ripe for the picking.

Arietta and Jay now saw each other regularly on weekends. When work permitted, he even dropped into the dance parlor, though she usually had only a few minutes to spare between lessons. Having heard her occasionally play on the academy piano, he decided to buy an upright for his apartment. On Prince Street, at the Bodian Pawn Shop, for only twenty bucks, he found what he wanted: a Sears-Roebuck Beckwith. Although bearing the imprint "Concert Grand Chicago," it belonged in a dive. While she played, he sang in his best countertenor. At home, his father had often observed that his son's voice was sadly wanting. Wonderful at harmonizing, Arietta would let him get a good start and then come in under his line. They had a thousand laughs, and he thought the piano—almost as much as dancing—bridged their cultural differences.

And yet in the midst of his bliss, he entertained doubts; he felt that Arietta had a secret life. Twice when he called on her at home, he could hear her on the Ma Bell speaking in German; and once at the Riviera, she excused herself to use his phone, closing the door behind her. Even so, he caught the occasional *ja* or *nein*. When he asked her to whom she had spoken, she replied, "Oh, just a friend." But she never took him into her confidence, and her lack of openness gnawed at him. He presumed that the calls had to do with the work she couldn't disclose, but he refrained from asking her directly. He did, however, hear her distinctly say on the phone "Friends of the New Germany," as he waited in her living room to take her to a movie.

To put his suspicions to rest, he decided to visit one of these German meetings, normally held in Irvington. On a Wednesday evening, he dressed in a black suit and dark tie, took a bus that dropped him off two blocks from Montgomery Hall in Irvington, and walked the rest of the way. When he tried to enter the building, a young man with a red armband held up his hand and asked to see a membership card.

"I've never been here before. I want to join."

The man directed him to a table just inside the front door, where a husky, blond guy, with a crew cut and a fascist uniform including a Sam Browne belt and swastika armband, asked for some identification. Since he had deliberately left his driver's license at home, he could open his wallet and plead insufficiency. The Teutonic avatar seemed none too pleased.

"Why do you want to join?"

"To promote the ideals of the homeland."

"And what are those?"

Good question. From all reports they involved race hatred, anti-intellectualism, a celebration of militarism, and a gagging sentimentality in things having to do with the *volk*.

"Blood purity, honesty, strength, honor . . ."

Prepared to continue, he stopped when asked his name. Klug might mark him as a Jew, so he gave him the name of the composer his father liked least, Richard Wagner.

"The Führer's favorite! A glorious name."

Jay added, "His music makes my father cry," not mentioning why.

Told he'd have to swear an oath, he took the paper, raised his right hand, and recited:

I hereby declare my entry into the association of the Friends of the New Germany. The purpose and aims of the association are known to me, and I pledge myself to support them unequivocally. I recognize the principle of leadership according to which the association is conducted. I am not a member of any secret organization of any kind, Freemasons and so forth. I am of Aryan extraction, free from Jewish or colored racial admixture.

Scribbling his "name" on the bottom of the page, he asked what else was required.

"Ten cents, please."

He gave him a dime and received a membership card; then both men saluted. The meeting began with a song in English that included the line "Our greatest joy will come when Jewish blood flows through the streets." What he'd failed to anticipate was that the speakers would address the audience mostly in German, a language he could partially comprehend owing to his knowledge of Yiddish. When they lapsed into English, he faithfully made notes, as if drinking at the fount of Germanic wisdom.

One man said that the anti-German propaganda of World War I and its aftermath had led to the loss of German-American identity. Children growing up after 1914 had come to doubt and suspect the Fatherland. They had grown to distrust their parents and accept as fact the vile propaganda that Germans had crucified Canadian soldiers and cut off the hands of Belgian babies, and that Germans had introduced poison gas into the war.

The audience, for the most part silent and sullen, would rise in tumultuous salute when the speakers periodically shouted, "Heil, Hitler." Toward the end of the meeting, a familiar face took the stage: the man from the restaurant, the one with the dueling scar, who warned, in English,

> Without proper instruction in the ways of the Fatherland, German-American children will drift into pool halls, learn bad language, read obscene literature, see evil movies, smoke cigarettes, and drink alcoholic beverages. They will, like so many American adolescents, become swarms of human parasites. Just look at American society now. It is overrun with depraved Orientals, Blacks, and Jewish scum from southern and eastern Europe. In their place we need Aryans, German-Americans to shape the course of U.S. history.
>
> Why do you think Heinz Diebel was murdered? Because every day he exposed the vomit this sick government feeds on, a government composed mostly of Jewish politicians who protect and coddle Bolsheviks and their own spawn: swindlers, gangsters, white slavers, dope peddlers, pickpockets, gunmen, and brothel keepers.
>
> Heinz Diebel knew that America was becoming a nation ruled by Jews and Communists.

Raising his eyes and extending his arms to heaven, the speaker implored, "Dear God, bring forth a man in this nation who will lead us out of our misery, who will do for America what Adolf Hitler has done for Germany through the National Socialist philosophy, who will bring about salvation at the last hour."

The crowd loved him, applauding his screed wildly. At the end of the meeting, the group sang the "Horst Wessel" song.

What Jay had heard scared him; but what he had not understood might have been worse. As he left the meeting, he told himself that languages constitute a code and that not to know them is to render yourself vulnerable. On his way home, he stopped at the Saba bookstore and asked the venerable owner if he had any German grammar and phrase books. The store owner complied, handed him his change, and smiled mischievously. "Italian is the more beautiful tongue."

The next day, using the *News* archives to check up on the hate-spewing Nazi sympathizers, he came across a brief description of Horst Wessel, who wrote the song he had heard. To the dismay of his father, a well-respected Protestant minister, Horst had given up his law studies to lead brawls and street fights as a Nazi storm trooper. Enamored of a prostitute, Horst was murdered—shot in the mouth—by her pimp, a German Communist, and thus became an instant political martyr. The more Jay learned about the votaries of National Socialism, the more he realized that these people all began as haters: of parents, of learning and teachers, of outsiders, and, not least, of themselves. They brought to mind Ahab, who "piled upon the whale's white hump the sum of all the general rage and hate (read: Jews and Communists) felt by his whole race from Adam down; and then, as if his chest had been a mortar, he burst his hot heart's shell upon it."

Anxious to speak to Arietta about scarface, he suggested they take the train to Coney Island. An unseasonably warm autumn had inspired a spate of newspaper ads trumpeting the park and its rides. Arietta wore a pink dress and he, white ducks with a boater. The subway overflowed with Sunday outers smelling from the foods of their different cultures and sweating from the closeness of the car. Wicker baskets provisioned the revelers from virtually the first moment the train pulled out of the station. Papas with big bellies gave orders to mammas thin as needles from bearing and raising the flocks of kids huddled around them. Fortunately, he and Arietta had seats. Amid the press of bodies and the clickety-clack of the rails, he decided not to say anything until they had a chance to walk, hand in hand, in a setting more conducive to intimacy and confession.

As they pulled into Coney Island, the station teemed with food vendors hawking sausages, peanuts, and salted pretzels among the sound of steaming trains arriving and departing. On the street, cars honked for apparently no reason, and pawn-brokers manned folding tables where the cash-starved traded brooches and other baubles for enough money to enjoy the rides and concessions. They bought tickets and entered the park to the sound of bands playing oompa, oompa, the Cyclone roller coaster eliciting screams of delicious fear, merchants crying their wares and services, parents in myriad languages disciplining their recalcitrant children, guns crackling at the shooting gallery, the surf pounding the beach, and everywhere the cricket voices of children expressing their delight. A barker outside the vaudeville hall engaged in a patter of one-liners as a come-on. "I knew a fellow who kissed a girl on the cheek and died of painter's colic. She was the kind of girl that five minutes with her and you were a man with a past. Just step inside for the laughs of a lifetime— and seven other acts, including dancers and a melodrama, 'Tilly's Punctured Romance.'"

As they traversed the grounds, he wondered what attracted people to bumper cars, saucer dishes, slides, roller coasters, moving sidewalks, barrel rolls. What was the fun of being spun, upended, hurtled, tossed, thrown, toppled, and tripped? Why should disorientation be pleasing? To his mind, staying upright was hard enough.

He asked Arietta what tickled her fancy.

"Let's begin with the merry-go-round."

As they rose up and down on their painted horses, he had a glimpse of the fierce imagination of the children, who lovingly spoke to their mounts and happily squealed. Real equestrians lacked the pleasure of imagining their horses.

The Ferris wheel gave them an overview of the park and a perspective that brought to his mind the distance of the rich from the poor, and the politicians from the populace. He would have broached the subject of the man in the restaurant had not Arietta been so absorbed in the sights, leaning this way and that to point out another landmark.

Leaving the Ferris wheel, they stopped for a Nathan's hot dog and some caramel corn. On the boardwalk, a small band played while a waif-sized busker danced and sang the lyrics, "I can be happy, I can be sad; I can be good, or I can be bad. It all depends on you." Arietta suggested they stop at the penny arcade, where they peered through the viewers at the vaud tricks and watched the flashing cards tell "Sadie Simpson's Secret."

Near the arcade they stopped to watch the weight guesser, always watchful for the trickster trying to swindle a prize. A short, skinny guy stepped on the scales, registering 190 pounds. The concessionaire patted the man's pockets and told him to empty them. Handfuls of ball bearings spilled out, making Jay wonder about the importance of the unseen. At his suggestion, they headed for the fortune-teller's tent. On the way, they passed a juggler, who seemed to keep four or five balls suspended above his outstretched dexterous hands in defiance of gravity. Taking Jay's arm and pausing to watch, Arietta made a strange comment:

"Every gigolo's dream."

The crystal gazer, dressed in a yellow robe with black moons and crescents, introduced herself as Madame Blotofsky. Although they asked for separate fortunes, she insisted that theirs were intertwined. Mumbling a lot of mumbo jumbo, which included a few Yiddish words that caused Jay to shake his head skeptically, she quoted the biblical line, "Who can find a virtuous woman? For her price is far above rubies."

Refusing payment, she said the "reading" was a gift from the other world and they should tell their friends about Madame Blotofsky and her profound pronouncements. He noticed that she did not say predictive powers.

Before he could steer Arietta to the beach, she insisted they had to stop at the shooting arcade and the fun house. Plopping down two dimes, he waited for the attendant to prime his pistol, but Arietta took a clip and expertly loaded her own. They faced two kinds of targets, one composed of animals, like bears and bison, and the other of World War I German objects, a submarine, a soldier, a tank, a plane. Jay fired at the second targets, forgetting that Arietta's mother came from Stuttgart. Before he had finished his allotted shots, he stopped, put down the gun, acknowledged his bad manners, and murmured "Sorry." Without responding, Arietta proceeded to knock down all the wildlife without a single miss, earning a stuffed giraffe.

In conspicuous silence they walked to the fun house. The first room, with its floor-length mirrors, gave them a distorted glimpse of themselves. Wishing to redirect her attention from his faux pas, he said that depending on the lenses people saw through or the cast of their minds, Jay and Arietta might actually appear to some observers in these grotesque shapes. She fired back, "Anti-German feelings, for example, lead people to behave abominably, and those targeted do equally terrible things."

To recover lost ground, he observed, "We all suffer from our heads getting in the way of what we see. Just think of all the craziness afoot in the world."

She looked deep in thought. Taking his arm, she walked toward the "Tunnel of Love." As they waited in line to board one of the cars, he asked, "Where did you learn to shoot? I couldn't hit the side of a barn."

She laughed and said, "Of course you could, especially if you'd practiced enough. My mother belonged to a gun club in Germany and won several awards. She introduced me to the sport."

"I learn something new about you each day." Before she could reply, an empty car arrived, the attendant seated them, and they entered the darkened tunnel. When the couple in the car in front of them started necking, he said, "Let's," and they kissed deeply, whispering endearments. Ten minutes later, they exited, hand in hand, and made their way to the boardwalk.

"Yoo hoo!"

Arietta and Jay turned to see Margie Smith waving her parasol. Damn! What an unfortunate coincidence. Why here? Now? Embarrassed by memories of the Kinney Club, he feared what Arietta would think. Dressed in a tight-fitting black skirt and silver blouse that accentuated her breasts, Margie had a red boa wrapped around her neck and wore an outrageous picture hat with ostrich feathers. The man holding her arm was none other than scarface, the very one about whom he wanted to know more. His high style and Margie's low tastes made Jay wonder if this guy was her fancy man.

Pickled in perfume, as always, Margie had a wad of gum in her mouth, which she repeatedly cracked. Although she had the bust to compete with Mae West, she lacked the wit; nevertheless she tried hard, introducing her date as Axel Kuppler, a "butler" who worked for a ginger ale "buttling" company. Then she laughed too loudly at her own joke.

Dressed in a black Eton jacket and gray slacks, Mr. Kuppler bent at the waist in greeting and said in a slight German accent, "I have had the pleasure of meeting Fräulein Ewerhardt, but not you, sir."

"Miss Ew . . ." he started to say, trying to clarify the mistaken identity, but Arietta elbowed him in the side.

Turning his back to the women and bowing slightly, Jay took Mr. Kuppler's hand and murmured "Richard Wagner," since he had registered with the Friends under that name. He would tell Arietta later.

"Anyone who exhibits the good taste to spend a day out with Fräulein Ewerhardt has my admiration."

The sweet talk this guy exuded brought to mind Huck Finn trying to save his life on the raft. After the compliments ended, they all walked to the boardwalk railing and watched the sea and the bathers. Several men, no doubt of the poorer class, wore union suits instead of bathing costumes. Eventually, a policeman directed them from the beach. Margie, standing next to Jay, oohed and aahed at the thrill of the breaking waves, and then leaned over and whispered, "It's like sex . . . rising and falling." She knowingly

nudged him with her elbow. "I'm leaving the Parrot," she continued confidentially, "to be on my own. Axel's volunteered to drive
the car and balance the books."

A foot or two away from Margie, Mr. Kuppler and Arietta were
quietly chewing the rag, so he took the moment to tell Margie
about his phony name and promised he would try to see her. He
then eased himself into the other conversation.

"Did I hear you mention Germany?"

Mr. Kuppler, looking ill at ease, replied, "I was just recommending to Fräulein Ewerhardt a Beethoven concert. Beethoven, one of
the German greats."

Skeptical, Jay deliberately tried to discomfort him. "And where
is it being held?"

Mr. Kuppler glanced at Arietta and then back to Jay. "Frankly,
it's a private concert, just for members."

"Do you mean for the Friends of the New Germany?"

His eyes widened and fixed Jay in their stare. For a moment, he
felt like a butterfly skewered on the end of a pin. But unlike those
monarchs of the air, Jay took the initiative. "Yes, I am a member."

With that admission, he thought Arietta would faint. Her legs
went wobbly and she reached out a hand toward him, which he
took as she righted her balance.

"I heard you speak a couple of weeks ago. You're quite an orator.
Impressive."

"Ach, then you approve of our movement and our ideals?"

"Absolutely."

Mr. Kuppler visibly relaxed, no doubt relieved that Jay was one
of them. Arietta, though, clenched his arm, and not, he thought,
for support. Margie cracked her gum and suggested they go to the
vaudeville or the dance hall. As he hoped, Arietta demurred.

"Well, then," said Margie, annoyed, "Axel and me, we'll just go
see the show and have dinner later . . . by ourselves."

After another deep bow, Axel led Margie down the boardwalk,
and he steered Arietta toward the beach and the numerous folding

chairs spread near the water. While the parents sat and ate, their kids tossed balls, flew kites, played tag with the tide, and leap-frogged over each other, laughing when the "bridge came falling down."

"Arietta, I must confess. I sometimes wonder if I really know you."

She tried to dismiss his concern by playfully alluding to one of the biblical meanings of the word "know."

"Oh, you know me!"

"This Mr. Kuppler, what's his story?"

She paused to kick some sand. "I like Coney, but the beach at Sea Girt is far nicer." She paused. "He's a man I met . . . at a meeting. He came to the house once or twice."

"Is he sweet on you?"

One of the kites, trailing a tail of shredded rags, lost height and began to drop toward the sea.

"I suppose so . . . but I have no special feelings for him."

"He talks like a Nazi sympathizer."

"Maybe you can tell me what *you* were doing at a meeting of the Friends of the New Germany!"

The kite fell into the ocean, and the kid, yanking on the string, tried to bring it back to land.

"Looking for you."

She stood watching the efforts of the young boy trying to reel in his kite.

"I didn't lie to you at the Chanticler. I'm not one of those types . . . but I can't explain now."

"The day you told your father that you had an ice-skating date with me, you met Axel. Right?"

At last, the shaver landed his kite, which looked battered owing to its buffeting by the waves.

"Yes."

"Why?"

"He's my excuse for attending meetings of the Friends."

What was one to conclude from this admission, assuming it was true?

"The next thing I know, you'll be telling me you're also a member of the movement."

"No, I'm more Magliocco than Ewerhardt."

"Then why attend meetings of the Friends as Fräulein Ewerhardt?"

"For my own safety."

He halted and, ignoring those people spread out on blankets, begged her, "Please stop speaking in riddles."

"Sometimes, Jay, you ask too much of me." She turned and started back toward the boardwalk steps.

Now more at sea than before, he might as well have been trying to ride a wave to the beach and, for all his efforts, been overturned, landing on his head. As he followed after her, he looked back and saw Axel Kuppler peering in their direction through binoculars.

Catching up to her, he said, "Your friend seems to be training his binocs on us."

"How can you be sure?"

"I can't. But how can one be sure of anything?"

"Faith, I guess."

"Faith is not a proof. It's a hope, and hope blinds us to reality."

She turned her generous smile on him, the look that said, you're the only person in the world I care about, and remarked, "I have faith in you."

"To do what?"

She paused and then replied softly, "To tell me the truth." He waited for her to continue, guessing from her expression that she had something in mind. And she did.

"What was Margie saying to you?"

"Margie used to work in a brothel and . . ."

She interrupted. "Is that where you met her?"

"Yes."

"Well, I do admire your honesty. Did she mention Axel?"

"Margie said she'd left the brothel, and he was her pimp."

Angrily, she shot back, "I don't believe you!"

The energy of her protest unsettled him. She had asked for the truth, and he had honored that request. Feeling ill used, he rubbed it in. "Yeah, that's what she told me: 'I'm on my own now, and Axel's my one and only very special pimp.'"

She mumbled, "That bastard."

Suddenly he wasn't so sure of the landscape. Was this guy a government agent or a pimp? Or both? He could see his analysis going up in smoke. Back to square one.

"Why do you care?"

"It's degrading."

Here was his opening. Perhaps he could finally learn more about him. "For whom?"

"Me!"

But what did she mean? If his behavior degraded her, she must be either working with this guy or seeing him on a personal basis. For all their closeness, he still found himself groping for answers. Persuaded that the ends justified the means and that nothing less than betrayal, of person or perhaps country, was at stake, he decided that when the time was right, he would trail her.

As if nothing had changed, he brought Arietta to Goldsmith Avenue for dinner the following Friday night to meet his parents. She gave them a lovely serving plate packaged in wood shavings and boxed with a ribbon. His mother was speechless, his father troubled, since Jay had told them the Magliocco family had once been well off, but no longer. Where did the money come from? Arietta wore a blue velvet dress with a pink sash and black soft-leather shoes. When she had first arrived and handed his father her coat to hang up in the front closet, he noticed him nuzzle the mink collar. Frankly, he wished that Arietta had dressed less tastefully and guessed, not incorrectly, that his father's dinner conversation would lead to the subject of money. His mother, as expected, behaved sweetly, completely charmed from the first moment Arietta crossed the threshold, a sure sign that the religious issue would not be a part of the postmortem.

When Arietta asked about his father's business, a throw-away question since Jay had already described the Jeanette Powder Puff Company, his father repeated what she already knew and observed that people had stopped buying cosmetics because of the Depression.

"And you, what do you do?"

With a quick glance at Jay, she replied, "I'm a dance instructor at Castle House on Bergen Street."

"In these hard times does anyone take lessons?"

"A few."

"If you're on commission that has to hurt."

"We're hoping it will pick up."

"And your father?"

"He's disabled with a bad back. Too much heavy lifting over the years, I guess."

"A lot of people have to hold down two and three jobs to make ends meet. Of course they're the lucky ones. Thousands can't find any kind of work."

That comment had written all over it "fishing expedition." Clearly his dad had not bought her dancing instructor explanation, and asked, "I suppose that's true of you, as well?"

Reluctantly, she murmured, "Yes."

Since he had never heard Arietta admit to anything more than working at Castle House and at another job she couldn't tell him about, he paid close attention. She was obviously ill at ease, fingering her napkin and staring at her unfinished first course, chopped liver. For what seemed a painfully long time, she said nothing.

"I work as a German translator."

Not knowing whether to laugh at this fabrication or to applaud her chutzpah, he said lamely, "I thought I told you about that, Dad."

"I think I would have remembered."

Again the table grew silent, as everyone waited for Arietta to fill in the details. When she paused, his father persevered, "Who's your employer?"

Without precisely answering him, she explained, "Nowadays the authorities like to keep tabs on the German-language newspapers. I read them and translate those articles that seem seditious."

A good answer. But was it true? Arietta went on to talk about her adored mother, and the good woman's lessons in Deutsche.

"When I was a child, she always spoke to me in German and paid for lessons. If I answered in English, she pretended not to understand. Before long, I could speak the language. Now if only my father had done the same in Italian . . ." She trailed off.

His mom, for the first time, said something that didn't bear on the dinner. "How did your parents communicate?"

"Mostly in English and, believe it or not, sometimes in Latin, which both had been taught and took pleasure in speaking. I think that must have been one of the attractions when they first met in Rome. They charmed one another, as it were, in a classical way."

Arietta's mention of German newspapers and sedition led his father into a discussion of the Weimar Republic and the observation that ardent Nazi university professors counted among its harshest critics. "I've never been able to understand how an intellectual could be drawn to National Socialism. Democratic socialism, yes, but fascism, no."

Arietta appeared genuinely interested. "From the papers I read, I can tell you what the issues are: the unfairness of the Versailles Treaty, excessive war reparations, unemployment, inflation, the belief that Communists and Jews are threatening the Fatherland, and of course, Hitler's promise to restore Germany to its former medieval glory. At the moment, nationalism and patriotism are rampant."

Jay's father, a well-read man, huffed and quoted Dr. Johnson, "Patriotism . . . the last refuge of a scoundrel." Arietta looked nonplussed, leading him to add, "When reason and argument fail, wave the flag."

Arietta's claim to reading the German newspapers certainly appeared to be true, but for whom did she work? When she observed that the German government had its doubts about the steadfastness and intentions of American Nazis, Jay decided the time was right to start observing her activities.

The evening ended literally on pleasant notes with Arietta playing their baby grand while his father sang Italian and Russian arias. She had the good manners not to compare his voice to her father's. Jay knew the evening had been a success because Mr. Klug sang for others only when he was enjoying the company, and concluded the concert with the "Volga Boat Song," even though the last few hours had been smooth sailing.

Arietta and Jay spent Saturday together, seeing a movie and returning to the hotel where she played the piano and he croaked out a countertenor of "My Grandfather's Clock." Then they danced to a record of "Stardust." On this particular evening, after they made love, she whispered, "I love you."

"Does your love earn me the right to enter the adyta of your heart?"

"Whatever that means."

"I want to share your private thoughts."

"Then they wouldn't be private."

"In other words . . ."

She silenced him with a kiss.

Intentionally, he stayed away from her house on Sundays, figuring that she might want to attend church or some Catholic social event. He knew that she was in the dance studio every day but Thursday. So on that morning, he sat in Puddy's car, parked down the street from Arietta's house. Watching for her out of the rearview mirror, he decided that detection was not his line of work. You spend most of your time waiting, and if you want to interrupt the boredom by looking at a paper or magazine, you run the risk of missing your mark. By the end of the day, he called it quits. Both his bladder, on the point of bursting, and his head, dizzy from a day of sitting, told him that he had to find relief. He looked at the dashboard clock: two minutes after five. Bold as brass, he turned the car around and pulled up in front of Arietta's house. She answered the bell and looked genuinely pleased. But before they could get cozy, he asked to use the bathroom. When he returned, she asked what had brought him. The few minutes in the bathroom had given him enough time to concoct an explanation: he wanted to write an arts piece on Mr. Magliocco and his former operatic glory in Italy.

"We have so many immigrants who were performers in the old country," he explained. "Wouldn't it be nice to recognize them? Who knows, it might lead to something for your father."

Jay hung around talking to Mr. M. for almost an hour but could see that Arietta wanted him to leave. Glancing at her watch, she mumbled that she had an engagement at seven. He deliberately stalled for several minutes, thanked the old gentleman, gave Arietta a chaste hug, and left. As he got behind the wheel, a black LaSalle pulled up a short distance behind him and discharged a very dapper looking Axel Kuppler. Jay slowly pulled away, but not before he saw Arietta meet Axel on the front steps, take his arm, and lead him to the car.

Here was Jay's chance. He went to the end of the block and parked. When they came down the street, he ducked until they had passed and then followed. Axel drove to Springfield Avenue, pulled into a dark alley, and parked the LaSalle behind a building a few doors away from the Schwaben Halle, a favorite meeting place for German-Americans. Jay parked nearby. The second-floor lights in the building barely showed behind drawn blinds, but the back door stood slightly ajar. Deciding to risk more than he had originally intended, he started up the wooden stairs. Creak! He removed his shoes and took pains to place his weight on the sides of the steps. At the first landing, a door read: "Frank Beer and Sons: Accountants." As he crept up toward the second level, he heard voices and halted. Though he couldn't make out the words, he could tell that the parties were in heated disagreement. When the tempers subsided, he left his perch, descended to the bottom of the stairs, put on his shoes, and, hugging the wall, returned to the car.

The next day, he and Arietta dined at a small posh restaurant in a bucolic setting. Reaching across the table, he took her hand, gave her an affectionate smile, and told her how much she meant to him. She responded that she hoped to have a place in his future.

Fearful of mentioning Kuppler directly, he approached the subject obliquely.

"Do you still have your giraffe?" Arietta looked uncomprehending. "You know, the stuffed animal you won at Coney Island."

"Yes, I keep it on the bookcase next to my bed."

"You have no idea how surprised I was running into Margie Smith on the boardwalk."

"The whore?"

She said the word so derisively, he wanted to reply that her friend Mr. Kuppler apparently didn't mind making a living off a streetwalker's earnings. But he held his fire, electing to dissimulate.

"She called the other day . . . wants to know if I'll enter a marathon dance with her in Brooklyn."

"I thought you were through with marathons."

"That's what I told her. Maybe she'll ask her . . . her friend Mr. Kuppler."

She replied contemptuously, "Unlikely!"

"Unlikely that she'll ask him or that he'll accept?"

"The latter."

"You must know him pretty well to predict his response."

She poked at the food on her plate. "There's something I ought to tell you, Jay. I used to date Axel. For a while, we saw a lot of each other."

"How much?" he asked sarcastically.

"What do you mean? It's all over now."

"How much of you did he see: some of you, all of you, dressed, undressed?"

She put down her fork. "I don't care for your attitude."

"Well, I don't care for my best girl carrying on with a Nazi—or is he a double agent?"

He had never seen Arietta look so hurt. She bit her lip and tears came to her eyes.

"Why do you think I am telling you about him? It's because of my feelings for you. But apparently you don't feel the same toward me."

His guilt lodged palpably in his throat, paralyzing his speech. Yet what she said couldn't be true; she'd seen him just yesterday. Forcing himself to speak, he said, "You've been honest with me. I'll be equally candid with you. I saw you leave with Axel last night."

"Yes, we went to his office. He asked me to resume our . . ."

"Affair!" he said nastily.

"Former romance. I told him that I had found someone else. He made some disparaging comments about you and said he would settle the matter in his own way. I replied with some unladylike things, and then Axel took me home. You can ask my father what time I returned. I was gone for less than an hour."

Feeling that he had rewarded her sincerity with abuse, he tried to excuse himself with the observation that "a person in love imagines slights and sees obstacles where none exist."

"Didn't your mother ever tell you not to wear your heart on your sleeve?"

"I suppose I could keep it out of sight, but the delicious pain reminds me of your infinite variety."

She snorted, "Plagiarist."

A few nights later, he returned to the building where she and Axel had fought. Casing the joint from the outside, he eventually found a way in: a cellar door, rotted from years of exposure to the elements, gave way with a good kick. In the dark of the cellar, he upbraided himself for not bringing a flashlight and other tools of the housebreaking trade. He would know better next time. That occasion presented itself two nights later, when he brought a flashlight, locksmith's pick, gloves, and, just in case, a crowbar. Pushing aside cobwebs and old wooden boxes, he found the staircase and made his way to the second floor. The door, which on his first reconnaissance mission he had missed because he had stopped at a bend in the stairs, had a window that said: "Bavarian Imports." He used the pick to unlock the door and enter the office. On the wall hung a picture of Adolf Hitler, and in the corner stood a pedestal holding a flag with a swastika. Some German slogans adorned the walls, but the only one he could make out was "Death to the Jews."

A battered desk, several spindle chairs, and two wooden filing cabinets constituted all the furniture. But before he could start nosing around, he heard a car pull up in the alley. Fear gripped him, and suddenly he needed a toilet. Some second-story man! He couldn't even keep his bowel under control. Looking through the Venetian blinds, he caught sight of a man entering the adjacent building. He eased himself out the front door, found a lavatory, and waited, trying to decide whether to bolt. Recalling some of the mystery movies he'd reviewed, he wondered what causes the greater terror: when the victim and the audience are both surprised by the intruder's sudden appearance or when the audience, but not the victim, knows in advance that someone is approaching? He decided the latter and, but for the sound of a car door slamming and a car driving off, would have skedaddled. His ruminations, however, inspired him to move quickly.

The locked desk gave way to his pick. Rifling through it, he found nothing of real interest. In one of the filing cabinets that he picked, he came across a letter informing the Friends of the New Germany that a major Nazi dignitary (unnamed) would be addressing the faithful in New York City at the Jaeger restaurant in Yorktown and in Newark at the Schwaben Halle. The date for the latter meeting was two weeks hence.

A manila envelope with receipts showed that Kuppler, among others, had taken a number of bus and rail trips, many of them out of state and as far west as California. Kuppler had also frequented the Robert Treat Hotel, occasionally staying overnight and running up a few bills in the restaurant.

In a folder labeled "Publicity," he stumbled across several memos listing public figures that might be assassinated for the good of the cause. One of the names leapt off the page: "The actress Jean Harlow has a worldwide reputation. The death in 1932 of her husband, Paul Bern, remains unsolved. If it could be made to look like murder at the hands of the Jewish gangster Abner Zwillman, it would prove helpful to our anti-Jewish campaign. (Motive: Zwillman and Harlow were once lovers. We could say that Zwillman was jealous.)" He stuffed the memo in his pocket and the next day sent it to Zwillman with a letter of explanation.

A second item, a cablegram, tersely said, "We've convinced Brundage. The Olympics are on. Silence the Reds and Jews and all talk of boycott. You have the list." Signed: von Halt.

The other filing cabinet, which he also picked, had only one folder of interest: an alphabetical membership list. Under the letter E appeared the name Ewerhardt, Arietta.

Several nights later, he introduced Arietta to the heart of the Jewish quarter. As they strolled along Prince Street, a few pushcarts, lit by kerosene lanterns, still remained open for business. She stopped to finger some *shmattahs*, and bought nothing more than a pair of shoelaces. They stopped at Kaplan's for a Danish and cup of coffee. She observed that several old men cooled their coffee by spooning it into their saucers, and asked why they balanced a cube of sugar between their teeth as they drank their coffee or tea. What he took for granted, she found exotic.

"They like their drinks saturated in sugar. If you look closely, you'll see that most of them have V-shaped front teeth, from the sugar having eaten away the enamel."

Comparing Jewish and Italian culture, they concluded that the two groups had more in common than one might suppose. Still intent on getting more information about her and Kuppler, he segued awkwardly, "Italians are one thing, but the differences between Germans and Jews could fill volumes, except of course for German Jews."

"Why single them out?"

"They have always disdained other Jews as beneath them intellectually and culturally."

"From what I read in the German papers, many of them think they will escape the Nazis' wrath, but I don't think so."

"From your sources," he said, hoping that she wouldn't just cite newspapers but would give him something more substantial, "what do you think the Nazis have in mind for this country?"

"For the Nazis to mobilize the people, whether in Germany or here, they have to persuade them that they are threatened by a common enemy. In both cases, they say it's the Communists and Jews. Some people, as you might expect, regard them as one and the same. Newspapers all over Germany are full of this rubbish."

Noting that she failed to mention Kuppler and his Nazi colleagues, he confided that to learn more about the doctrines of the Friends, he planned to attend one of their upcoming meetings.

"When?" she asked, alarmed.

"A week from this Saturday at Schwaben Halle."

"Don't!" she said urgently.

"Why not?"

"What if you're discovered and the meeting turns violent?"

"The worst they can do is throw me out."

"Or worse. Some of the men might be armed."

"Have you told the police?"

"No."

"Why not?"

"Jay, just trust me."

Further questions elicited equally vague responses. When they parted, he paid a cabby to take her to Littleton Avenue. She rolled down the window and said, "Please, be careful."

With that, she left him standing on the curb in front of Kaplan's. To clear his head, he walked back to the hotel. That night, he thrashed about in bed, sleeping little and wondering about her warning: What precisely could it mean and what was its source?

He didn't see Arietta again until after the riot. On the Saturday night in question, he arrived early and stood across the street, out of sight. A car pulled up and two men, one of them Nat Arno, carried a tarpaulin into the dark alley next to Schwaben Halle. Not until other cars arrived later, disgorging rough-looking guys, did he learn the contents of the tarp: iron pipes, baseball bats, and clubs. The "Minutemen," dressed in shirt-sleeves and polo shirts, positioned themselves in the courtyards of apartments opposite the hall. When the Friends, many of them dressed in Nazi uniforms, entered the hall, the Minutemen challenged and taunted them. He gravitated to the back of the building, where he saw the ex-boxer Abie Bain and some of his pals slashing tires and breaking windshields, presumably of cars belonging to Friends. A long ladder, leaning against the rear wall, reached to the second-story windows that faced the auditorium. He wondered whether the attack would follow the same plan as the one the Minutemen had launched in the fall of 1933.

Returning to the street, he gathered from the chattering Friends that Fritz Julius Kuhn, the "American Führer," would be addressing the faithful. Having joined the Friends in 1933, Kuhn had risen rapidly from head of the Detroit local to leader of the midwestern units, and was now *the* major figure in the American Nazi movement.

At the front door of the Schwaben Halle, two young men, holding batons in their gloved hands and wearing swastikas, black jackets, brown shirts, and jackboots, checked membership cards. He weighed Arietta's warning and decided to enter, but only long enough to see if he could spot Axel Kuppler. One of the myrmidons checked his card and stepped aside. Planning to slip out early, he stood in the back, a plausible choice since most of the seats were taken. As many women as men were in attendance, also a large number of teenagers. The stage held three empty chairs and a dais with a Nazi flag. Suddenly a drum roll, played by a uniformed young man, ushered in the notables, among them Axel Kuppler. The first man to speak introduced himself as the head of the Newark Friends. Quickly moving from English to German, the man elicited a great deal of hand clapping, though Jay couldn't follow well enough to figure out why. Axel followed and said in his polished English that it was his great pleasure to introduce Fritz Julius Kuhn, "who is known to you all as one of our greatest German-American patriots." Other than decrying "the efforts of Jews and their hirelings to boycott the Olympics," Kuppler said nothing inflammatory, concluding by clicking his heels and saluting Kuhn, a gesture that brought the audience to its feet heiling.

Kuhn began his speech in German. The English part consisted of anti-Semitic attacks against prominent Jews, like New York Governor Herbert Lehman, and a diatribe against the Roosevelt administration for "its concentration of Jews in government." Jay headed for the exit, Kuhn's voice still fulminating. "I can assure you that 95 percent of Americans agree that we must attack the filthy Jews in every realm—politics, economics, and culture—and that the battle to destroy this detestable race will be very agreeable."

The uniformed guards, standing at the doors in the back of the hall with their arms across their chests and their legs anchored, seemed in no mood to let him leave.

"Diarrhea," he whispered, indicating his stomach, though he could just as well have pointed to the speaker.

The guards probably would have continued to block his way had a stench bomb and a rain of rocks not broken the rear windows, dispersing the crowd with glass shards and putrid smells. By the time he reached the street, dozens of Minutemen, armed with baseball bats, brass knuckles, chains, and clubs, had formed a phalanx in front of the hall. One of them would have brained him had not a familiar baritone yelled out:

"He works for us. Let him go."

It was Puddy Hinkes, and next to him stood Nat Arno.

Jay started toward the two men, but Nat waved him off, saying, "Get outta here, kid, this ain't any of your business."

He lingered just long enough to see the ferocious beatings inflicted on the Friends: the hail of bricks, the screaming women, the blood, the downed men trying to crawl away or retreat into the hall for shelter. The enforcers picked out for particular pummeling those displaying armbands or other kinds of Nazi dress. Even from a distance, he could see heads laid open, men felled by blows to their knees and legs, jaws and faces struck violently; the men lay on the ground trying to fend off kicks to their backs. But nowhere in the crowd could he see Fritz Kuhn, who had presumably stayed behind to greet well-wishers and had escaped the carnage. The avengers, unfortunately, had no idea what Kuhn looked like. Animated by that idea, Jay darted into the alley just in time to see Kuhn and Kuppler enter the very building that he had broken into. Racing back to the street, he yelled that the Nazi leaders had gotten away and pointed out where they had taken refuge. But before Puddy and his friends could reach them, police sirens sounded and patrol cars came into view. He knew damn well why they had taken so long, and wondered how much it had cost Abe. Breaking up Nazi meetings had become a specialty of his, and the absence of police was his trademark.

Less than twenty-four hours later, Arietta called, said that she had to see him immediately, and recommended an ice cream parlor on Bergen Street. Facing each other in a booth, they leaned across the table talking and sipping black-and-white sodas.

"After I told you not to," she said, "you went to the Friends meeting."

"I even got a story out of it, though not a byline. The editor called it a scoop."

"Why did you go?" she asked anxiously.

"To be perfectly honest, Arietta, I wanted to see what role Mr. Kuppler would play."

"He recognized you."

"I thought he might. I was standing in the back."

"Do you have any idea how close you came to jeopardizing . . . that is, getting yourself killed?"

"Is that what Axel said?"

"He certainly wanted to know if your presence had anything to do with the . . . aftermath."

"And what did you tell him?"

"No."

Jay sipped on his straw, thinking of what to say next. "Arietta, what do you know that I don't?"

"Have you any idea how ruthless these people are, how demonic? Even if I didn't care for you as I do, I would try to keep you away from these people and their deceits. See no evil . . ."

"I appreciate your concern, but frankly, I'd rather be in the know."

She turned her magnificent eyes away from him, and her face took on an expression of great sadness. "That man, Axel . . . I met him in Parsippany at a picnic for young German-Americans. The Friends were trying to bring together eligible young people. I enrolled. It was my way, foolish as it turned out, to honor my mother's memory. I even assumed her maiden name, Ewerhardt, when I attended. Axel and I dated—his aristocratic manners and expensive clothes impressed me—but it didn't work out. He still calls me Fräulein Ewerhardt."

"And now he thinks I'm a member of the mob that attacked the Friends. Is that it?"

"I told him he was wrong."

The few facts that Jay had at his disposal didn't seem to lend themselves to a credible interpretation. Why did she continue her friendship with a man she no longer saw romantically and knew to be a Nazi sympathizer—or was he? And whom did she really work for? She had used the word "jeopardizing" and then corrected herself. If Jay had nearly ruined some operation, what was it? He tried to trap her.

"From interviews I conducted after the riot, I know that some Friends have doubts about Axel's loyalty."

She looked amazed. "You're lying!"

"Not so," Jay prevaricated.

"If you're right, his life is in danger."

"I can't get too excited about a dead Nazi sympathizer."

She paused. "I may no longer have any romantic feelings for Axel, but that doesn't mean I want to see him dead."

Jay's churlish response had not won him any points; worse, it had not shed any further light on her relationship to Axel and his—or hers—to the Friends.

They finished their sodas in silence. Arietta's brown study told him that she was mulling over his lie.

"What exactly did you learn about Axel? Did anyone say why they thought he was a plant?"

Stumbling through a flaccid explanation that he feared would expose him as a self-serving liar, he ended up repeating himself, "That's what some of the Friends are saying."

"But in what context? How did it come up?"

"They said that for some time now, they have felt as if all their private meetings and correspondence have been known to the authorities in advance."

"That's hardly surprising," she whispered, "given their beliefs . . . but why Axel?"

Grasping for a reasonable explanation, he said, "Maybe it's because he's been seen with you and you were present at the time of Heinz Diebel's murder."

In a panic, Arietta exclaimed, "What in the world would I have to do with it? Why would my company or my presence at Dreamland jeopardize him?"

There was that word again. He began to feel as if he had entered some other dreamland where appearance and reality had merged so completely that he had no way of determining one from the other. But then, he had contributed to the Alice-in-Wonderland effect with his own fabrications. He decided that the only way out of the labyrinth was to get Arietta to come clean.

"You must tell me, Arietta, who you work for, besides Castle House. Why have you been attending Friends meetings? To what end? Surely you know how I feel about you. Isn't it time you told me the whole story?"

Her silence felt like a thousand years. When she finally began to speak, he sat terrified that her words would prove fateful.

"You may not want to hear what I'm going to say, but since you insist . . . Frankly, I'm ashamed. As I told you, Axel and I once dated. After we broke up—I objected to the sordid side of his life—I heard that he had a new girlfriend. Although I had started dating you, my jealousy got the better of me, and I wanted to see who this person was. I knew from my own breakup with him that he hoped someday to meet a woman who shared his political convictions. That's why I went to the meetings . . . to spy. Isn't that awful of me? I hated myself for it."

Was she still carrying a torch for scarface? The secrets people store in their ghostly hearts endure for a lifetime. Her frequent absences from the city—she would be gone for days on end—made him wonder whether she and Axel were rendezvousing elsewhere.

Arietta started to cry. Moving to her side of the booth, he put his arm around her. "There's no shame in caring for another person."

"Yes, but while seeing you, I was watching him. I feel as if I've betrayed our . . . closeness."

"Nonsense. Since meeting you I've seen Margie."

"You have?" she said clearly alarmed.

"At first, but not since we've become . . ." He paused, searching for the particular nuance he wanted, "paramours."

Her body relaxed, and she rested her head on his shoulder. "I wouldn't want to lose you, Jay." As an afterthought, she muttered, "At least not to a whore."

"Margie's a good friend. I could never think of her as anything but a pal."

"Well," she said playfully, wiping away her tears, "I'd prefer it if you thought more of me and less of her."

5

In the ride from the pier to Newark, Axel and Arietta had found Rolf Hahne good company. He spoke flawless English and, when he said that he loved opera, sang a few bars from several Italian operas in response to Axel's request. When Arietta mentioned her father and their plan to attend an opera at Carnegie Hall, Rolf enviously sighed that he wished he could too.

"You're welcome to join us," said Arietta.

"Really? How would I get a ticket?"

"Leave that to me."

At the opera, Rolf charmed both Arietta and her father, insisting on taking them afterward to the Plaza Hotel for tea. As a result of the good conversation and Rolf's generosity, he and Arietta became friendly, meeting from time to time to discuss music and, on occasion, current affairs. But their get-togethers left her feeling odd. Rolf always found some way to avoid talking about himself and turn the conversation to Axel or to her "friend" Jay. She had the sense that she was being used. In fact, during one of their dinners, she told Rolf that she was not an informer, a word that he scoffed at and dismissed as entirely out of place given their friendship. But why then was he always trying to find out which information she and Axel shared and for whom she worked? Of course, Rolf asked in the name of security and the greater good of the country. But which country, the United States or Germany? And he never failed to introduce the subject of the Olympic boycott, wishing to know who was *really* behind it. After all, the committee would be making a decision shortly, and Germany had already, at great expense, embarked on preparing for the games.

Although Arietta tried, she could never learn where Rolf lived in Newark. Was it a residential hotel, a rooming house, a bed in a friend's home? In fact, she wondered about his friends. Did he have any, and where did he work? He never wanted for money, but what was its source? They were sitting on a bench in Weequahic Park, where the fall leaves gave the woods a fiery look. In response to her questions, he insisted that he served as a liaison between the German Olympic Committee and the American members of the IOC, and to prove it, he produced his diplomatic passport. He also claimed that he and Avery Brundage were good friends. December 6–8, at the Commodore Hotel in New York City, would decide the fate of the boycott. It was then, just two months away, that the Amateur Athletic Union of the United States would be voting on whether or not to participate in the Berlin Olympics. It was therefore imperative, Rolf insisted, that he know the names of the silent financial contributors to the boycott.

He seemed convinced, owing to German wiretaps, that Arietta had gained that information from a gangster called Longie Zwillman. But when Arietta swore that she and Axel knew nothing, Rolf grew livid. "I will not be lied to!" he raved. Arietta looked around. No other people were in hearing distance. She wondered whether to run or to stay. A new person had suddenly materialized out of Rolf's skin. The previously courteous gentleman with whom Arietta had attended the opera had transmogrified into a minatory maniac. "You and that Casanova of yours are playing a double game." When she tried, calmly and reasonably, to explain that he was mistaken and that she and Axel were no longer close, he grew all the more menacing. "I don't intend to pay for the information I want. Give me the names or it will cost you your lives." Arietta began to cry. "That won't help. My own life is at stake if I don't get the names." He laughed insanely. "In fact, whether I fail or succeed I'm a marked man. But I'd rather die winning than losing. My advice is don't cause yourself pain."

And so matters stood until Margie found the body.

Arietta and Jay celebrated the New Year, 1936, in a muted mood. Despite Jeremiah Mahoney's best efforts, the Amateur Athletic Union had voted 58.25 to 55.75 to support the Olympics, a two-and-a-half-point margin. (In July 1936, Ernest Lee Jahncke was expelled from the International Olympic Committee for his opposition.) After the vote, Avery Brundage issued a statement implying that a boycott would encourage anti-Semitism in America. "There are maybe five percent of the population which is Jewish. A study of the records of the Olympic Games shows about one-half to one percent of the athletes are Jewish. And responsibility for actions of this kind [a boycott], right or wrong, would be charged to the Jews, I think."

What Berlin and Rolf Hahne quickly realized was that in spite of the vote, the pro-boycotters would continue their campaign until the day the boat set sail for Germany carrying American athletes. Rolf Hahne's mission, therefore, continued, made all the more difficult by Arietta's refusal to cooperate or even meet him.

Until early spring, she and Jay continued to see each other, though newspaper work taxed his time. During that period he wrote numerous reviews and articles, without a byline, a situation that actually suited him because his editor had asked him to cover the Nazi movement in Newark, and he had no desire to be mugged or even worse. In addition, at the paper's behest, he was following the murder investigation of three men, allied to the cause of the boycott, gunned down at a Chinese restaurant by a lone assailant, who had escaped. The men, all Catholics, had helped Jeremiah Mahoney rally their fellow congregants to continue opposing the Nazi Olympics.

Given his deficient German, Jay persuaded Arietta to accompany him, in his role as Richard Wagner, to meetings of the Friends. The paper even agreed to pay her. Aware of the risk he was running by putting Arietta and Axel in the same locale, he convinced himself that Arietta no longer cared for Axel. But he did become suspicious when she predicted the increasing radicalization and fragmentation of the Friends, who in fact eventually became the nucleus of the Bund. And his suspicions grew when Axel stopped attending meetings and she began to break dates. For reasons unknown, Jay and Arietta's affair seemed to be cooling.

Wishing to turn up the heat, he suggested they dine at the restaurant in the Robert Treat Hotel. Arietta had suggested a less swank place on Elizabeth Avenue, but he wanted to put on the dog. She wore a red velvet dress and he a three-piece black suit. In the cab he took her hand, and she smiled. At their table, she looked around a great deal; but he could see nothing amiss. During dinner, they disagreed about some silly things and migrated to the topic of a movie that he had once reviewed, *Our Daily Bread*, which celebrates a commune that makes its own bread.

"If the Depression continues," he said, "I think we're going to see more films like it."

"You sound like your father."

"He never goes to the movies."

"I'll bet FDR asked the producers to make that film," she said. "It's terribly biased."

"I thought you liked it. If I recall, you even praised my review, saying that I captured the 'spirit of the dispirited.'"

The piece of lamb on her fork never made it to her mouth. Putting it down, she remarked, "I really do think we need a film industry that is more even-handed and hires fewer foreigners."

This was an Arietta he had never seen before. "What about the Jews?" he asked sarcastically. "Most of the big movie companies and producers have names like Goldwyn and Warner and Selznick."

She bit her lip and apologized. "I really didn't mean what I said. Just ignore it."

He knew then that Arietta had undergone a sea change. Thinking about the implications, he concluded that what mattered was not the source but her impressionability. Or were the two causally related?

For the remainder of the dinner, they ate in virtual silence, neither one of them venturing to say anything that could be misconstrued or that could lend itself to a political interpretation.

At the Riviera Hotel, in no mood to be jovial, he plunked down in the parlor chair. Arietta sat on the piano bench, the lower part of her body turned toward him but the upper facing the piano, which she lightly teased with her right hand. He took the News from the coffee table, which separated them, and crouched over to read it. Clearly, neither of them had any interest in making love. To anyone looking in, his indifference and her aloofness would have conveyed a picture of profound sadness. The wistful loneliness of the scene stood in dour contrast to the first night they had become lovers. Although neither of them spoke, Jay was sure that she wished as earnestly as he to be somewhere else, apart.

That evening, they neither sang nor danced. After a short while, he sent her home alone in a cab. A few days later came the murder. Axel Kuppler was found dead in Margie's apartment. During Margie's absence, someone had shot him. Spitefully, Jay persuaded the paper to run a headline that read: "Pimp Killed!"

The day of the killing, he had called the Magliocco house to ask Arietta if she knew anything about it. But no one had answered the phone. For the next two days, he failed to get a reply. Borrowing a car, he drove to her house. The place stood completely dark and the doors locked. He looked in the garage. Mr. M.'s Waterhouse was gone. His instincts told him that if he ever saw Arietta again, it would not be in Newark. In his bones, he knew she and her father had fled.

Quite naturally, the police questioned him. He was becoming a regular on their list of suspects, to the despair of his parents, who had hoped that journalism would change his life. The police knew that Arietta had bolted and asked if he knew why and where. He refused to talk about her "friendship" with Axel, even when the police said they had evidence that the two of them in the past had spent nights together in the Robert Treat Hotel. As to the whereabouts of father and daughter, he swore in complete honesty that he had no idea where they had gone.

The same day, to his great surprise, Gerry Catena telephoned; the "big man" wanted to see Jay that very evening, if possible, and Gerry would collect him at the hotel. "Sure," he gulped. He shaved, slapped on some aftershave lotion, and changed into his best suit, the black one that he'd worn the last time he saw Arietta. Catena arrived twenty minutes later and drove them to an opulent apartment in West Orange. All the furniture, in different pastels, had a Parisian look. The end tables and lamps reminded him of ads in fashion mags; the mahogany coffee table held a hand-carved chess set, and the mantelpiece African carvings, some in ebony, some in ivory, others in stone. Longie, dressed in a tie and jacket and exuding cologne, was sitting on the couch talking to a beautiful blonde, leggy woman who spoke with an Italian accent. On the coffee table was a silver tea set and a book, *The Heart of Darkness*. When he and Gerry entered, Longie introduced him to his guest, Signorina Francesca Bronzina, asked him what he wanted to drink, and sent Gerry to the kitchen to fetch it.

"Miss Bronzina sings opera," said Longie. "Her father was arrested in Rome for opposing Mussolini."

"I work for the underground," said the singer.

Gerry returned with Jay's ginger ale.

Thinking of the Italian connection, he asked, "Are you and Arietta Magliocco friends?"

"No. I'm here to watch someone and discover his contacts."

As Jay rocked the ice cubes in his glass, he wondered what her specific assignment could be. But before he could ask, Longie nodded to Gerry, who left the room in the company of Francesca.

At first, Longie said nothing. Jay began to feel like an insect under glass, as Longie eyed him. Finally, the big man said, "Until recently, you spent a lot of time with Arietta, around town and at the Riviera."

Everyone who worked for Longie said that he made it his business to know who sneezed, where and when. Jay had just become a believer.

"For a while I was really sweet on her."

"No more?"

He used an English expression he had heard. "It seems to have gone off the boil."

Longie chuckled. "The police who came to see you . . ."

"Which time? There were several."

"When they told you about Arietta's being seen at the Friends' meeting hall."

"I'm listening."

"They questioned you because I sent them." Jay's jaw went slack. "They reported everything you said."

"But why?"

"To make sure you didn't know enough to upset the apple cart."

"I don't understand."

Longie stood and, leaning against the mantelpiece, picked up one of the ivories. Fingering its polished surface as delicately as he might a flower petal, he remarked aimlessly, "A fertility goddess," returned it to the mantel and said, "She worked for me, and now, as you probably know, she's disappeared. Why?"

"Worked for you?"

"She kept an eye on the Friends. And she served as a courier."

If she had been a courier for Longie that would explain her frequent absences. "What kind of courier?"

"She carried cash to people around the country who are running ads and sending out letters to promote the boycott. We could hardly have sent checks that the feds and tax men could trace."

He could see where Longie was heading.

"We owe her, and we always look after our own. I'm worried about her safety. She was threatened by a Nazi hit man that I wanted to take out immediately, but she asked us to wait, hoping to pump him for information about other German agents in the country. I begged her to watch her step, and also her language; you know, sound sympathetic to the swine."

That would explain her recent changes in attitude, Jay thought. Protective coloration. Longie was behind it. Then he remembered the words in the cablegram: "You have the list." What list? Did Arietta know about it?

"Kuppler's death really complicated matters. The Nazis put a price on her head. They're convinced that she killed him or arranged it."

A conscience-stricken Jay exclaimed, "How many more reasons do you need for her taking a powder?" A moment later, he nervously asked, "Did she in fact kill him?"

"I don't know. All I can tell you is we didn't and she's disappeared . . . and I'm worried." Longie opened a pocketknife and began to clean his fingernails. "The question running through my mind is will she shun her old contacts, approach them for help, or continue her efforts on behalf of our cause? I do admit: She's tough. Once she agrees to do a job, nothing stops her."

At that moment, Jay experienced both a rush of guilt and exhilaration. While she had been risking her life, he was thinking only of romance; but he also felt in a strange way that if he could find her, he could find himself. "I want to help," he volunteered. "If there's anything I can do, just ask."

"Her and her father," Abe added.

"At the moment, Longie, I haven't a clue. I wish I did."

"When she started seeing you, Kuppler threatened her. He said she belonged to him. 'Belonged' was his word."

The story had started to take on a new dimension that left Jay not only confused but frightened. "I'm not following you."

"I originally employed her because I knew that Kuppler had broken off their romance, and that a spurned woman would be a perfect source of information. And she was."

Jay tried to sort out these revelations. How in the world had Longie learned about Arietta's personal life? "I'm listening."

"She told us what she'd known about Kuppler during the time of their affair and, more important, what she found out later, when she kept on attending Friends meetings and reporting on him and his associates."

"If Kuppler tried to woo her a second time . . ."

Longie interrupted. "He did. We were bugging his home and his whore's place, as well as Mr. Magliocco's house. Arietta was furious with his pimping and demanded he give it up."

It occurred to Jay that if Margie's place had been bugged, Longie might have the murder scene on his recorder.

"All we have are a few words: 'Believe me . . . I can explain.' Then a shot and a muffled cry. It sounds like he double-crossed someone, maybe his whore."

Knowing Margie as a true soldier, he felt called upon to defend her. "Margie hates violence. She'd be the last person in the world to kill him. Maybe the Friends did. It was whispered that he questioned Hitler's sanity."

"If so, he was damn discreet about it. But I'm glad you're willing to help us find her. It's what I hoped."

"Any living relatives?"

"None in Piero's family. Two aunts of hers, an Amalie in Wildwood, New Jersey, and an Agna in Milwaukee."

"Their addresses could be useful. Anything else?"

"Here's what we know. The Bundists think she killed Kuppler and want to get their hands on her. The Nazi who threatened her presumably entered the country to suppress the Olympic boycotters. We're looking for him now. It's my guess he's behind the three recent murders at the Chink restaurant. We have good reason also to believe that Arietta is a prime target. She has to be protected from both: the Bundists and this guy."

"You sound as if you know who he is."

"I don't, but Francesca does. She's part of the Haganah, fighting for an independent Palestine." Longie cracked his knuckles. "She thinks his name, which may not be his real one, is Rolf Hahne. Francesca can describe the man for you. Women are always better at that sort of thing than men. If I had a picture of the guy, I'd give it to you. She'll fill you in."

"Do you have any married names for the aunts?"

Longie shook his head no and handed Jay an envelope. "Here's a record of the telephone calls Arietta and her father made in the last several months. Two are to Wildwood, one to Kansas City, and three to Milwaukee. If we can get this information, so can others. You'll also find the names and addresses of people supporting the boycott—those we funded. They too could be in danger, especially our man in K.C., J. L. Wilkinson, the owner of the Kansas City Monarchs. Arietta may well seek him out." Longie reached into his pocket. "And here's a key to the Magliocco house. Maybe you can find something we missed."

"Just for the record, I'm prepared to do whatever I can, even though it means quitting the paper, but what makes you think I can find her when you can't?"

"Two reasons. One, you're a member of the Friends. If I were in your shoes, I'd plead ignorance about her and Kuppler and try to learn something from them. Second, you know her habits better than anyone else. As to the job, I promise it will be there when you get back."

Mentally calculating what it would take to find the Maglioccos, Jay said that he would need money, a car, and an assistant. When Longie asked if he had anyone in mind, he suggested Francesca.

"She works alone, always has and always will. I promise: She'll keep an eye on you. Can you think of anyone else?"

"T-Bone Searle, a friend of mine, a Negro. We play pool checkers together."

"A *schvarze?*"

"He speaks Yiddish better than you, and oozes muscle. He's also got an eye for spotting trouble."

Longie thought a moment and grinned. "Maybe he's from one of the lost tribes."

"Believe me, a lion of Judah. Do you want to meet him?"

"No, I trust you."

He and Longie shook hands, and the very next day, Wednesday, May 22, Jay began what was to become an odyssey of self-discovery through an America that he had never seen before, swept along by events not of his own making. Free will? Impossible. Most people are nothing more than picaros propelled by jobs and romance down winding roads, hoping that each new encounter will be more promising than the last.

Jay's first step was to attend a Friends meeting. The hall in Irvington, seething with conspiracy theories about Kuppler's death, grew silent when he entered. He quickly learned that these creeps thought that Arietta had killed Axel because he had tried to end her affair with Jay, a.k.a. Richard Wagner. To Jay's disclosure that Axel and Arietta had once been lovers, they puritanically held that Axel Kuppler would never have polluted his body with such filth. When Jay reminded them that Axel had of late been working as a pimp, they accused him of spreading "Jewish propaganda."

A particularly evil-looking fellow with a vicious habit of slapping his wife and kids across the face to command discipline poked his index finger into Jay's chest and informed him that sexual crimes were the province of Jews, and that a friend of his at the *News* had told him that the story about Axel's pimping had been concocted by some unnamed Jewish reporter. By any chance, did he, Mr. Wagner, know him?

"This is the first I've heard of it."

A crowd slowly encircled Jay.

"You and the Ewerhardt woman," said a guy shaped like a water hydrant with a bullet head, "often attended our meetings. The two of you spied on us to undermine the German-American cause— and to kill Axel." By trying to implicate Jay, the fireplug had immeasurably increased the danger.

Jay argued that at the time of the killing, he was at a bowling alley and that ten witnesses would bear him out.

"Probably all Jews!" a thin-lipped fellow sneered.

"As a German faithful to the Fatherland, I make it a point to surround myself only with Aryans."

When his antagonists shifted their focus back to Arietta, again accusing her of being complicit in Kuppler's death, Jay insisted that even after the breakup, she regarded him fondly.

But they scoffed at the very idea of the two having been romantically involved.

How could one argue with their Nazi logic? At least they hadn't accused him of having played a part in the riot. Axel had done him a good turn, probably to ingratiate himself with Arietta, by not voicing his suspicions.

The man who claimed to have a friend at the *News* knew that Jay was employed at the paper.

"In what capacity?" he asked.

"I write movie and theater reviews."

"Filth!" a man missing his upper front teeth whistled.

How often had he heard the Friends urging their members to see German movies and to boycott American ones? Probably every meeting. He really felt in no position to start extolling Jean Harlow or Mary Astor, whom they regarded as whores. Ransacking his memory, he mentioned a German play he had reviewed, Georg Kaiser's *From Morn to Midnight*. But the moment he mentioned Kaiser's name, he remembered that he had been critical of Germany during World War I. Sure enough, they greeted his statement with expletives. It was time to get the hell out of there. But what could he use as an exit line?

"Gentlemen, let me remind you," he said in his best tutorial manner, "Kaiser's play satirizes the cheapness and futility of modern society. Isn't that a position we all share? Aren't we trying to bring about a better one?"

A particularly intractable Friend, Friedl Kretch, objected that true patriots of the Fatherland found Kaiser's work contemptible and unworthy of production in the new Germany.

He decided it was now or never. "Had I known about this feeling coming out of the Fatherland, I would never have agreed to review the play." Before they could react, he requested a list of works that they would like to see treated in the *News*. As their suggestions tumbled forth, he assured them that he would be as good as his word. Taking the omnipresent pad from his pocket, he scribbled down the titles. "Don't forget," he prompted, "Leni Riefenstahl's brilliant new movie *The Triumph of the Will*." That seemed to turn the tide in his favor, as they oohed and aahed with orgasmic pleasure. Judging the moment ripe for an escape, he pushed through the circle and left the hall.

As he rode the bus back to the office, he ruminated about the uses of art and Leni's mesmerizing film: its stark beauty, its terror, its power to make evil look good, and the zero demands it made on one's intelligence. How could one combat such effective appeals to pure emotion? The bus passed a billboard with a catchy phrase, advertising Fisk tires: "I know when it's time to retire." Puns were clever, but the best propaganda hit people in the gut. *Deutschland über alles* told the Germans that they and their country mattered most. Add a midnight torchlight parade, martial music, uniforms, choreography, and an exaltation of the spirit (not the mind), and you could understand why the population took to the streets. Yes, he had to admit, Leni's film was art. Not great art—that engaged the head as well as the heart. But since the public preferred not to think, great art was in short supply. He began to see the frightening nexus between sentimentality and totalitarianism. What was he doing spending his life reviewing saccharine films that aimed no higher than the groin? At that moment, he wondered whether he wouldn't be better served attending law school. But what was he thinking? He wouldn't be sitting in any classrooms or writing reviews again until the Maglioccos were found.

Longie had given him a key to Arietta's house that his locksmith had made. With T-Bone at his side, they entered the premises and began looking for clues. Jay had offered T more money than he could make working on the federal building projects, and had filled him in on the nature of the search, including a candid account of Mr. Magliocco's relationship to Longie's gangster activities. T readily agreed to exchange his overalls for street clothes and to join him, even though they might be on the road for months without any guarantee of success.

"Hey, man, it's a chance to see America. I ain't been out of Newark in several years."

T-Bone scoured the upstairs and Jay the down. It didn't take a detective to conclude that Arietta and her father had left the place in a hurry. Strewn about were personal items: old letters, mostly in German, a picture postcard of the Admiral Hotel in Cape May, clothes, costume jewelry, bedding. He concluded that the Maglioccos must have been pretty scared to have left so hastily. A photo of Muehlebach Field lay on the floor. The only thing he had to go on, and no small thing, as he subsequently discovered, was the absence of the "Toga Maroon" 1929 DuPont Model G Waterhouse five-passenger sedan. Not many people in the world drove such a car.

As they prepared to leave, T-Bone removed from the piano a small framed picture. "Looks like the place I grew up in," he said.

Jay glanced at it: a pen-and-ink drawing of a ramshackle bungalow and bunkhouse.

"Somethin' wrong? You sure is lookin' at it hard."

"No," Jay exclaimed, "something is right. I'd bet ten bucks to a nickel that what we're looking at are farm buildings in some small town near Atlantic City. I can't remember the name of the burg, but if I see an atlas, I'll know."

"I ain't followin' you."

"If I'm not wrong, Mr. Magliocco used to visit a friend there. Also, some guy, reputed to have scragged Arnold Rothstein, holed up in those houses."

T whistled. "I see how you're figurin'."

Jay held up two thumbs, and T-Bone, smiling, said: "Maybe our little adventure ain't gonna take as long as you figured. I hope you don't mind if I bring along my checkerboard."

"Not at all, let's hit the road."

In the Newark Public Library, he opened an atlas and located Norma. Longie, as good as his word, generously supplied them with two grand and a car, a 1931 Ford Roadster that Abe had bought off an ex-legger in Paterson whose growing family needed a larger vehicle. Although the car had racked up a few thousand miles, except for the discolored wide seat upholstered in Bedouin grain leather with narrow piping and the rumble seat, it looked none the worse for wear. Behind the seat, Longie had lodged a loaded shotgun with two shells. "Just in case," he had said.

When Jay asked him how to find George "Hump" McManus, the man tried and acquitted for murdering Arnold Rothstein, Longie replied:

"He lammed it until he felt he could clear his name."

"Mr. Magliocco knew him."

"I had no idea. But frankly, I think you're barking up the wrong tree. Hump keeps to himself and has no phone. A while back, some of my friends and I wanted to see him about a private matter and had to drive to the shore."

With nothing to lose, Jay decided to talk to McManus. For safety's sake and fairness, he gave T five C-notes. As he wheeled down the coast road, he could have sworn that in the rearview mirror he saw a car trailing them.

Arriving in Sea Girt at dinnertime, they ran into difficulty with lodging. After numerous inquiries, they found a Negro boarding-house. The owner, a skinny woman with a parchment face and varicose-trellised limbs, agreed to rent a room to T-Bone but not Jay. She said his presence would raise eyebrows. So he went to a small oceanfront hotel.

Instead of trying any of the restaurants, where T would likely be turned away, they bought some food at a small neighborhood grocery and ate in the car. A few people eyed them warily, but no one objected. The address that Longie had provided took them to a small house on a wooded lot two blocks from the sea. The shingled cottage had a front porch and manicured lawns. Around eight, Jay knocked on the front door. It had begun to rain. The April showers drained the air of light but released the sweet smell of the earth. He could see through the shaded front windows two lamps in what he guessed was the living room. He breathed deeply to control his nervousness. Fully expecting to be greeted by a floozy-blonde gangster's moll, he momentarily lost his tongue as a well-groomed elderly woman answered the door. She courteously asked him his business, but before he could respond, she glanced over his shoulder at the sidewalk, where T, huddled under a tree, began to back away from the door. "George," she summoned. A husky, gruff fellow said "Yeah," and would probably have closed the door in Jay's face had he not said, as politely as he could, "Abe Zwillman asked me to see you. I work for him. My name is Jay Klug." Before McManus could object, he added, pointing to T, "He works for Mr. Zwillman also." He then showed him Longie's business card, which McManus reluctantly took, studied, and, turning it over, saw Longie's private number.

"Inside," Hump said grudgingly.

Jay motioned to T, who came shuffling up the walk, doffed his cap to McManus, and acted deferentially, a routine that he witnessed many times in the coming months and one that always made him feel ashamed of being white. They followed McManus into the house, where the old lady stood at a distance, watching cautiously.

"Mother," McManus said, "how's about some coffee?"

Hump led them into the living room, a gloomy space with brown walls and ugly green and maroon furniture made of some kind of bristly tufted material. A card table stood off to one side. Jay gathered from the arrangement of the cards that someone had been playing solitaire. McManus rested his arms on his knees and waited.

"Longie would have called to tell you about us, but you have no telephone."

"Yeah," the old gambler grunted, "whatta you want?"

Again Jay breathed deeply. "I understand you once met Piero Magliocco . . . at the Norma place."

McManus squinted and tore a cuticle with his teeth. Jay could see the wheels in his head turning. "Yeah, I met him once. So what?"

From his tone of voice, Jay decided the sooner he moved the discussion from Mr. Magliocco to Arietta, the better chance he had of eliciting any information. "His daughter worked for Longie. Some pretty nasty people would like to kill her. Longie wants to protect her but can't unless he knows where she is."

McManus lit a cigarette and inhaled deeply. "Mother," he called, "where's that coffee?"

She told him to hold his horses.

Hump was stalling, deciding whether to talk. Otherwise this weather-beaten relic would have immediately denied seeing Piero Magliocco since Norma and denied knowing anything now about him or his whereabouts. But Jay knew Hump was unlikely to blab without first looking into his story, and unlikely, even if the story checked out, to be completely forthcoming. There was nothing to be gained.

"Longie always takes good care of the people who help him," Jay said, hoping to encourage McManus.

What Jay didn't know, nor did Longie, was what had transpired between the two men when they had met in Norma. Perhaps the encounter was innocent. On the other hand, since McManus was lamming it at the time, Piero could have proven valuable to him, feeding him information, making calls, and generally acting as a go-between in the weeks after their meeting and preceding McManus's trial. Or was Jay reading too much into one fact?

The old lady brought them all coffee and some rather bland cookies. When she put the tray down on an end table and poured everyone a cup, she gave T an awfully long look. Taking his cue, he hastily said:

"This smells like the most wonderful java I ever had the pleasure of enjoyin'."

"How do you know till you taste it?" she said tartly.

"Smart thinkin'," T mumbled and took a sip. "It's even better than it smells."

Her chilliness did not disappear, but she did stop staring.

Taking refuge in his role as a journalist, Jay tried to give McManus a chance to open up by asking about his most famous moment: his trial and acquittal for the death of Arnold Rothstein. Before leaving Newark and the paper, he had looked through the archives and fortified himself with a great deal of detail. "Would you mind if I asked you a few questions about the Rothstein affair?"

Exhaling smoke through his nose, Hump said with a skewed smile, "A guy can't be tried twice for the same crime, so ask away."

"The papers said Rothstein got a call while eating at Lindy's. Did you make the call?"

"That soft blob of shit," McManus blurted. "He has me line up a card game with two California gamblers, loses a bundle to all of us, and walks out without peelin' the green from his wad. A week goes by, maybe longer, and we don't see the kale. When I call him, he says the game was fixed and he ain't gonna pay." His face reddened and his narrative grew impassioned. "My reputation's on the line. I run card games and make book. If someone I brought into the game don't pay, *I* have to. Understand? Me! Even Mr. Big's pals couldn't forgive him for welshin'."

At the time of the shooting, two people had agreed to testify that McManus had gunned down A.R.: a chambermaid and one of the players, Alvin C. Titanic Thompson. Before the trial, the chambermaid changed her story, and on the witness stand Thompson suffered an inexplicable memory loss.

"That trial," continued Mcmanus, "was the worst thing that ever happened to me. A guy in my line of work has to stay out of sight. The newspapers made me famous. From that day on I was finished. The police began watchin' me and my business petered out. No one wants to make bets with a bookie who's been in the news. So I retired down here with the old lady."

"Quite a coincidence," Jay said cautiously, "that both witnesses went blank."

McManus lit another butt. "Ask Longie, he'll tell you."

"Why not save me the trouble of asking?"

Hump immediately extinguished the cigarette in the dregs of his coffee cup. "All I'll say is this, look at who took over the Brain's empire . . . which guys . . . it will tell you somethin'."

They left the subject of Rothstein and chatted about the people McManus had known during his heyday and the nightspots of New York. The guy liked reminiscing about the high rollers and the city, but would say nothing about Norma and the Maglioccos, even when Jay hinted broadly. As he started with T for the door, feeling low about having come up empty-handed, McManus said, "Come back tomorrow." When Jay reached the car, Hump shouted, "Nice chariot."

"Yeah," Jay said, "courtesy of Longie," emphasizing the name.

Jay drove around the corner, returned to McManus's street, and parked in the next block, to see him, no more than fifteen minutes later, leave the house and walk to a gas station to use the telephone.

"That guy and the old woman," said T-Bone, "give me the heebie-jeebies."

Jay wondered if all American Negroes spent their lives in a state of anxiety.

The next day, making it a point not to arrive early and earn the displeasure of an ex-gangster accustomed to waking at noon, Jay and T-Bone bought a bouquet of flowers that they gave to the old lady. Although unsmiling, she seemed resigned to their presence. They arrived about one and found McManus sitting on the couch, still in his bathrobe and slippers, sipping coffee and smoking. The ashtray next to him looked as if the chain smoker had gotten an early start on his habit. Hump waited until his mother had left the room and then said sotto voce:

"Longie says you're legit."

"What did you tell him?"

"Nothin'. It's you I'm doin' business with, right?"

Hump McManus clearly played his cards close to the vest. It took almost an hour and a C-note to wheedle this out of him:

"Piero stayed here one night with his daughter. He parked his car out front. When my neighbors got a gander at that buggy, they thought I had hit the jackpot."

"Did he say where he was going?"

"To tell you the truth, I can't be sure." McManus shook a cigarette loose, lipped it right from the pack, ignored the handsome silver table lighter, lit his weed from a matchbook, and, in a cloud of smoke, said, "They mentioned several places." Hump walked to the window. "Still mistin' out there?"

The aimlessness of his question suggested to Jay that he was finding it difficult to talk about the Maglioccos. Jay hazarded a guess. "He did you some favors, right?"

"Yeah. I met him in a dump called Norma. We got along good and stayed in touch."

Although willing to confirm his friendship with Piero, McManus said nothing about the nature of the favors. But neither of those facts really mattered; what counted was where they had gone.

"Do you remember which places they mentioned, besides Norma?"

"I didn't say he was headed there. Frankly, Piero's fear of American Nazis sounds pretty farfetched."

"Abe ought to know. He's had people on the inside of those organizations for a long time."

McManus walked to the kitchen door, peered in, and returned to the couch. "Mother don't like it when I talk to strangers."

"Longie's no stranger."

"No, but you are. How come he didn't drive down himself? I always like seein' what kind of car he's got."

The rain had begun in earnest and splatted loudly against the windows. McManus opened the front door, explaining that the smell of wet earth was good for his lungs. Jay sensed that McManus regarded his talking about Piero as the betrayal of a friend. T-Bone must have had the same idea, because he said:

"It ain't as if you're tellin' us where they went. Like you said, they coulda' gone anywhere. It's just that a few names makes anywhere somewhere. Now I can assure you, Jay here doesn't want to waste his youth lookin' for a needle in a haystack. But if you'd rather Mr. Longie come down to Sea Girt and talk to you, well . . ."

McManus, clearly feeling put upon, replied dyspeptically. "God, I hate bein' caught in the middle. Piero said nothin' about Nazis. He whispered to me, here on this very couch, that his daughter was wanted for a murder she didn't commit. So do I believe him or Abe?"

"That's up to you," Jay said.

"Abe I know from business. Piero risked his neck for me."

"What if he had refused?"

"Huh?"

"Just because someone does us a favor, does that make him a friend?"

"Of course."

"Sometimes people do us a favor by not doing us a favor."

"I'm not followin' you."

"Supposing you want me to join you in a bank heist, but I refuse on the grounds my gut tells me the job will go bad. You're furious with me, but change your plan. As matters turn out the bank that day had an audit requiring the presence of extra cops. By not doing what you wanted, I probably saved you." Jay waited a second to let the idea sink in. "How do you know that you wouldn't have been better served if Piero had refused to do what you asked?"

The blankness of McManus's face suggested incomprehension, but a lengthy silence seemed to readjust his sight. "Yeah, but in this case it was a favor, though I admit it could have gone wrong and cost me."

"Think of it this way, Mr. McManus. Maybe by telling us where Piero and Arietta might have gone, you may actually be doing them a favor."

McManus came back to Mr. Magliocco's story. "Have you heard about any murder concernin' the girl?"

Jay shaped his reply to emphasize why her life might be threatened, spelling out the connections between people and parties. McManus visibly relaxed, sighed, and at last gave them some leads.

"Norma. A small town southwest of here. He said they needed to get to Cape May. You know the name Satchel Paige?" T's eyes lit up. "Piero's daughter been trying to get him to support some cause of hers. And in Milwaukee a Gehrig, like the ballplayer. That's how I remember. But it's a Mrs. Gehrig."

Thanking Mr. McManus and handing him a pack of fine Turkish cigarettes bought that morning in a tobacco shop, Jay remarked, "I'm not sure you need these coffin nails."

Hump took his guerdon and said enigmatically, "You know, don't you, that A.R. hated cigarettes?"

The rest of that day, Jay and T-Bone drove south to Vineland, delayed by a puncture owing to the rutted roads. As soon as they pulled into Vineland, he stopped at a gas station and bought a new spare tire. A talkative young man on duty gave them directions to Norma and Luigi Baldini's old place, and added that the current owner, a Negress, Leonora Wells, had inherited the property from Mr. Baldini.

"A gospel lady. She sure does have some strange ideas. Me and the wife sometimes run into her at the outdoor market and right off she starts talking about good and bad, evil and such."

Jay paid for the tire and left him with the flat one. "It's yours." The young man thanked him. "Tell me, you haven't by any chance seen a 'Toga Maroon' 1929 DuPont Model G Waterhouse five-passenger sedan around here? I'm something of a car buff."

The garage attendant's eyes lit up with recognition. "I seen that boat sail through here a few days ago. It sure didn't come from these parts. Too rich for our blood. Myself, I drive a flivver."

"Do you remember which direction he was headed?"

"Yeah, the same way that gets you to Leonora's shack."

Jay and T-Bone drove down Landis Avenue and turned onto a dirt road with a sign that pointed to Norma. A short way along they came to a drive that led into the woods. A number of stalks and wild flowers had been crushed under the weight of a car, whose tire tracks could still be seen faintly. The woods, dark with pines and poison ivy and poison oak, opened up around a bend to reveal a clearing and a building that resembled a one-room schoolhouse with an outdoor pump. Peeking out behind the building stood a bunkhouse and woodshed. Every structure came equipped with a rain barrel. Before they could exit the car, a tall, stately high yellow appeared at the door. She wore a house dress that accentuated her thinness and had fashioned her hair in a bun, held in place with a wooden barrette. When T-Bone greeted her with a biblical line— "In the Lord put I my trust"—her surprised expression gave way to one of pleasure.

"Psalm eleven," replied the African queen, who said, "I'm Leonora Wells, owner of this Eden."

Some Eden! The grounds had gone to seed. Dead corn stalks and blighted strawberries littered a misconceived garden. A few chickens, haphazardly fenced, pecked at the sandy soil, and a sow rooted in a mucky pen. Invited inside the house, the two men discovered that the place had in fact once been a country school. A big room on the right, at one time a classroom, had a long dinner table, leading Jay to suspect that in the past this place had fed a number of guys on the run. The kitchen, on the left, had a woodstove, a dry sink, and an ice-box, stocked with regular deliveries. In the one bedroom, behind the kitchen, stood a large bed and a cot. Although the house had no running water—hence the pump and the rain barrels—Leonora did have electricity and a wall phone, which explained how her number had shown up on the list of calls made by the Maglioccos. The bathroom was a two-holer with a camphor cake hanging on the wall to dispel odors. On the roof of the woodshed, an oil drum served as a cistern for showers. A hose ran from above to a roughly rigged wooden enclosure that provided a modicum of privacy.

Under the kitchen, Leonora stored her provisions in a dirt root cellar with shelves for the jars of canned fruits and vegetables, behind which bull snakes dined on mice. Both the school and the bunkhouse used kerosene lamps and of course attracted a plague of moths. Outside the bunkhouse, Leonora had hung a tractor-tire swing from a maple tree for her grandchildren. (They learned later that Mr. Wells, a mechanic, had been crushed to death under a tractor.) Grasshoppers leaped in the scraggly undergrowth and millions of mosquitoes hovered in the pine trees. Jay couldn't understand why anyone would stay here, especially in the winter, and how Leonora could cook in this inconvenient and uncomfortable place. But she lived here year round and, while they stayed with her, managed to materialize marvelous meals.

Jay explained that they were trying to find Piero and Arietta Magliocco, friends of Luigi Baldini and, no doubt, familiar to her. Leonora never acknowledged whether she recognized the names, but did invite them to stay with her as long as they liked. After dumping their valises in the bunkhouse, which Leonora had stocked with towels and soap, they joined her for a glass of lemonade.

Returning to the topic of the Maglioccos, Jay asked whether she had ever made their acquaintance. Instead of answering him, she took a large leather-bound family Bible that lay at her elbow on an egg crate that she used as an end table and read them the story of the Good Samaritan. Whether she intended the story as a cautionary tale (be a friend and don't look for them) or an encomium (I approve of what you're doing), he couldn't tell. But then most of Leonora's religious utterances left him confused. Even T-Bone, who had a good grounding in the gospel, couldn't stay with her philosophy, which she called Gnosticism, a name Jay had never before heard. She said that what attracted her to this belief was its various approaches to God.

"If you think, for example, the virgin birth is unbelievable, the Gnostics say you don't have to regard everything else as hooey."

She also liked the fact that Gnostics often told the story of the Garden of Eden from the viewpoint of the serpent. "He's not evil but an aspect of divine wisdom. It was the later Christians who changed the nature of the devil—in order to beat up on the Jews."

Over dinner that first night, T and Leonora talked more Bible than Jay had heard in his whole life. Whereas T wanted to assign a certain meaning to a statement—"I hold this as gospel"—Leonora would argue for many meanings. Jay supposed that you could say the same for a good book.

The one subject that Leonora steered clear of was the Maglioccos. Rising from the table to her queenly six feet, she strode the boards of the room and lectured, "Is murder wrong because the Bible says 'Thou shalt not kill?' Shucks, the Bible is full of slaughter and mayhem. So how do we know right from wrong, and good from bad?"

Jay remembered what the gas station man had said and figured that Leonora would be at this subject for quite a while. Hanging around just long enough to hear T-Bone argue that a law-abiding country depends on consensus about what constitutes wrongdoing, and to hear Leonora counter with the view that laws are often in the eyes of the beholder, Jay went to the bunkhouse to unpack. Three cots, each separated by its own egg crate and kerosene lamp, constituted the amenities. A rope with clothes hangers had been stretched across one corner of the room to serve as a closet. Feeling dusty from the road trip, he took one of the towels Leonora had provided, entered the shower in the woodshed, and turned on the hose. What greeted him was a rush of cold water. He had forgotten that the cistern worked off the oil drum, which in turn depended on sunlight. Staying no longer than a few seconds, he grabbed the towel and while drying himself made a dash for the bunkhouse. He then crawled into bed with G. B. Shaw's *Major Barbara*, as the insects incinerated themselves in his kerosene lamp.

A frustrated T-Bone returned from his colloquy fulminating about her heresies. "That woman," said T, "is really temptin' the infernal fires of Hades with those sinful ideas of hers."

With Bernard Shaw on his mind, Jay said, "What constitutes a sin? Is it the act, the motive, the laws that protect the privileged, or maybe the conditions that drive people to break those unjust laws?"

T sniffed the air. "Jay, I think those kerosene fumes have got to your head, because I sure hope it ain't what that crazy woman in there's been sayin'."

"I've been reading a play that says poverty's a sin."

"Now you listen to me, Jay, it ain't no sin to be poor. I oughta know. Just remember what the good book says about a camel passing through the eye of a needle. That's how hard it's gonna be for a rich man to reach heaven."

"Then why would anyone want riches?"

"Good question. Now blow out the light."

6

They rose about ten, ate a hearty breakfast of eggs, waffles, and bacon, then, finding some horseshoes, pitched a few games. Jay took T to the cleaners. After the game, which had kicked up clouds of dust, he decided to shower. This time the water came out warm. As he stood there soaping himself and washing off the residue, he noticed stuck in the coarse boards of the wooden enclosure several long strands of hair, the color of Arietta's. Turning off the water, he dried himself, dressed, and then gently removed the strands, carefully placing them in a fold of his towel. When T-Bone showed up, he showed him the evidence. T seemed convinced.

"But you gotta persuade that queen of hair-splittin', 'cause you can bet she'll come up with some excuse or what she calls 'interpretation' that will explain them away. That woman could make you believe you ain't who you are."

Instead of immediately confronting Leonora, Jay decided to wait until supper. In the meantime, he and T-Bone drove into Vineland to see the garage man who had first directed them to the farm. The young man, cheerfully wiping his hands on his overalls, asked if they needed help.

"Got a real dirty job in there," the man said, referring to a car on a lift. "The oil case broke."

They asked him the location of the other garages in and around town, because they had to find the driver of the Waterhouse sedan. The attendant led them into a cubbyhole of an office and, shoving aside some papers, discovered a pencil stub and drew a rough map of the area with X's indicating the other gasoline stations. As they started to leave the fellow pointed at T and said to Jay:

"He goin' with you?" His question caught Jay by surprise. Before he could reply, the fellow added, "Not all the garage mechanics round here's as open-minded as me."

Jay didn't know whether to laugh, cry, or thank him. In his most noncommittal manner, he mumbled, "Yeah," and left with T at his side.

Their labors took longer than they expected. First, in this piney wilderness they had to find the gas pumps; second, they had to overcome the skepticism of the mechanics, who seemed in no mood to answer their questions. Although he hated to admit it, Jay was greeted more warmly when he parked the car out of sight and T stayed behind.

Still no luck. The Waterhouse sedan had not gassed up in the area. Their failure made Jay's impending confrontation with Leonora all the more important. After a chicken dinner with mashed potatoes and a local beer to wash it all down, he brought in a few pails of water that they heated on the woodstove and then poured into the stoppered sink where they washed the dishes. Relaxing around the dining room table, they moved aimlessly from one subject to another until Jay said:

"You do know, Leonora, why T and I made this trip down here?"

"Sure, you're looking for some people."

"It's to save a friend's life. I'll pay you well for information."

"You know, son, a long time ago, I learned that silence keeps a body out of trouble."

Detecting an opening, Jay said, "That's where you're wrong, Leonora. For a woman who assigns such importance to interpretation,

I'm surprised that you don't realize that silence leaves itself open to all kinds of meanings. Do you want to leave interpretation to others or do you want to have some say in the matter?"

Leonora looked perplexed and then hazarded, "There's laws that say just because I keep my peace doesn't make me guilty of a robbery I didn't commit."

"You must know the old saying: Silence is consent."

"Maybe yes and maybe no. Like you just said, a person's silence can signify a lot of different things."

Without her realizing it, Leonora had moved toward his position.

"Yes, and that's the trouble. You want your silence to signify innocence. But someone else might read it as guilt."

Leonora shrugged as if to suggest she wasn't changing her mind.

Removing the hairs from his handkerchief, where he had moved them, he gingerly slid them across the table.

"What's that?"

He chose not to bluff but to show her his hand. "Some strands of hair from Arietta Magliocco. I found them caught in the shower boards." Before she could deny his flimsy proof, he added a personal note, figuring that a blow to the heart beat one to the head. "I was once a suitor, and I kissed her hair enough times to know its heavy texture and color." He paused to let that statement sink in. "My guess is that the two of you stayed in your bedroom and Mr. Magliocco slept in the bunkhouse. If I'm right, I'm sure that you and Arietta got pretty thick. I'd be willing to bet that if I carefully examined your room, I'd find some evidence of face powder or rouge or mascara or maybe even a strand of hair that matches these."

Leonora was the sort of woman you wanted on your side in a revolution. She did not flee at the first whiff of gunpowder. Without conceding a single point, she tried to move the discussion into the realm of the theoretical. "It's hard enough to understand ourselves, much less other folks. To know what moves a person requires the wisdom of Solomon. That's why I look at what people do—not what they say—and ask myself how that doin' affects me.

I return kindness with kindness, for example, and I'll bet you feel the same way."

Jay had his answer. The Maglioccos, and especially Arietta, had, as he suspected, treated her well.

Leonora ran a hand over her mouth and adjusted her hair bun. Then she studied the handkerchief in Jay's hand. "In all my born days, I've known preciously few men wanting to find someone so as to save him. Just the reverse. Do you get my meaning?"

For all she had said about the impenetrability of people's motives, he concluded that she thought she knew theirs.

"You've got us all wrong on this one."

"But, son, if I'm right, what then?"

Perhaps recklessly, though certainly not insincerely, he said, "If you feel that way about us, I suppose we'd better move along."

Leonora paused as if weighing in the balance some intangibles; then she went to a cabinet in which she stored pots and pans. Lifting the lid of a saucepan, she removed a linen napkin, which she unfolded. Inside was a handwritten note to Leonora, giving her the Maglioccos' address in Cape May. "They're living there at a rooming house," she said with downcast eyes, "under the name of Clark."

As they motored south, he guessed from the car in his rearview mirror that his pursuit of Arietta was being tracked by another.

Rolf's contacts had traced a telephone call from Piero Magliocco to Leonora Wells, who lived in Norma, New Jersey, where Rolf pulled into a nearby garage driving a 1934 Packard 120 sedan with white-wall tires, a spare in the right well of the fender, and bullet-shaped headlights. As Rolf had requested, the car resembled one suited to a family, nothing ritzy or conspicuous, even though the car was costly. The garage was the same one at which Jay and T had stopped; and Rolf asked the same question. Had the attendant seen a "Toga Maroon" 1929 DuPont Model G Waterhouse five-passenger sedan? The attendant shook his head in disbelief.

"Is someone offering big money for that car? You're the second person in a few days to ask about it."

"Who else is interested?"

"A couple of guys, one white, one Negro, who drove off to see Leonora Wells."

Rolf handed the garage man a fiver and asked him about this woman. A few minutes later, Rolf reached her house. As was her custom, she came to the door to greet the visitor.

"Good to meet you, Miss Wells," said Rolf, extending his hand.

She had a dish towel in her hand, which she twisted nervously, wondering how this stranger knew her name. "I don't think I've had the pleasure."

"Rolf Hahne," he said, and pushed past her into the house.

She followed. To her astonishment, when he turned to face her, he was holding a pistol.

Surprised, though not frightened, Leonora said, "Now, son, you don't wanna be behavin' like a misfit. We got enough of them runnin' around as is. If there's somethin' I got that you want, just ask. Hope, faith, and charity . . . I live in those words. And as you know the greatest of those . . ."

"Shut up!" Rolf commanded. "If I need Bible lessons they won't come from a monkey." He waved the pistol indicating that he wanted her to sit, which she did with folded hands at the kitchen table. He pulled up a chair next to her. "Where did the others go?"

"What others?"

Rolf pointed the pistol at her. "The two from last night, and before them you housed a girl and her father."

Leonora shook her head. "I don't know no girl and her daddy."

Rolf slapped Leonora's face. Blood trickled from a split lip.

"Don't lie to me, you black monkey. You belong in a jungle."

Touching her puffy lip, Leonora said, "The way you behavin', son, I'm there now."

"All blacks are savages."

"It ain't me doin' the savagin', but you, s'far as I can tell."

Rolf eyed the kitchen, side to side, top to bottom.

"Can I get you somethin' to eat? I got some nice apple pie."

Her question completely disoriented Rolf. He began to stutter. "Eat? Now . . . here? Me?" Having expected Leonora to beg for her life, he was unnerved by her charity. He thought of his mother, but refused to allow that a black person could be imbued with her sensibilities. Trained to treat non-Aryans, particularly Jews and blacks, as an alien species, he tried to regain his balance. "You're like a parrot; you've learned to mimic others. You don't mean a word that you say."

"Maybe you want somethin' bigger. I got a pot roast. But maybe you'd like me to cook up some chili."

Rolf slithered out of his chair and rose to his full height. "Stop talking!" His breath came in pants, and his pounding heart felt as if it were trying to burst through his rib cage.

"What you want, son?"

"I'll spare you if you just tell me where they went."

With the note no longer in the saucepan, Leonora said, "Look around. See for yourself. Ain't nobody here now or before."

Rolf pulled down books from her cedar bookcase mounted on the wall near her rocking chair: cookbooks, dime novels, an atlas, a pocket dictionary. Fingering her Bible, he paused and then threw it against the wall.

"What you lookin' for, son? If it's truth, you just tossed it on the floor."

"Where are they?" he wailed like a wounded animal. "Tell me and I won't kill you."

The sound of a car bouncing along the rutted road could be heard coming their way.

"Is there only one road in and out?"

"You can follow the Indian trail at the side of the house. It bends back to the Vineland road. But it ain't easy goin'."

Peering out the window, Rolf asked, "Where else does it go?"

"Son, you saw when you come up here that you got two choices. One way is Norma, the other Carmel. Of course, beyond those towns are others. And beyond them still others. Your best choice is the holiness road."

Misunderstanding her meaning, he said, "Which one is that?" He pointed out the window. "The car's stopped. An old Ford." He paused. "Carmel!" he exclaimed.

She added wistfully, "The mountain in the Bible, where Elijah and Elisha walked among the vineyards."

"That's what you mean," he cried. "That's where they've gone."

Leonora stood and touched Rolf's cheek. He couldn't have been more startled if a snake had struck him. As he recoiled, he pulled the trigger, and Leonora Wells slumped to the floor. But before she passed into unconsciousness, she looked up at Rolf and said:

"At heart, I know you're a good man."

A short ways out of town, T-Bone had said he didn't feel right. Jay, thinking his friend might be car sick, offered to stop the car.

"I got me a real bad case of the heebie-jeebies. I don't want you pullin' off the road, I want you to return to Leonora's place."

"What's bothering you?"

"When I get to feelin' this way, I know someone's sendin' me a message."

Like Leonora, once T made up his mind, there was no changing it. Jay reluctantly turned the car around and headed back to Norma. When they left the main road for the dirt one, they could see fresh tire tracks in the dirt. Maybe, Jay mused, T had second sight of some kind, and asked his friend to reach behind the seat and remove the shotgun.

"If it's the Lord you're hearing," said Jay, "better armed than not."

They bumped along the rutted road for a minute until they heard a gunshot. Then Jay hit the gas, eliciting from T the comment, "Who do you think you are, Barney Oldfield?"

They pulled up a short distance from Leonora's house just as a man bolted out the front door and made for the Packard. He shielded his face with one hand and brandished a pistol with the other. Jay yelled out the window for the man to stop. A bullet pierced the windshield between Jay and T. They rolled from the car into the cover of the tall grass. Another shot hit the grille. Obviously the man was trying to disable the Ford.

It was then that T-Bone, still holding the shotgun, let loose a blast, which brought myriad birds out of the trees, squawking and screeching as they flapped their wings taking flight. Jay could see a spot of red on the man's cheek. Clambering into the Packard, the man caromed down the Indian path, kicking up a cloud of dust, as T-Bone unleashed a second shot at the vanishing car.

Finding Leonora dead, the two men, according to their separate beliefs, said a prayer over her body, telephoned the police, and debated whether to bury her. T-Bone spoke for them both. "With a killer out there, I think the sooner we hit the road and find the folks we're lookin' for, the better."

On the two-lane road to Cape May, Jay and T-Bone thanked their good luck and the car's sturdiness for surviving the assault. They stopped at a gas station, had the windshield replaced, picked up a few noshes, and asked the garage man if he sold shotgun shells. He did not. They asked for permission to use the privy out back.

"It's a two-seater," said the garage man, eyeing T suspiciously.

"Our sitting here side by side, bare-assed, could get us killed," said Jay. "You know that, don't you?"

T thought a moment. "When I die, I pray that you're as close as we are now." He then guffawed.

As they continued their drive, T-Bone remarked casually, "Two grand total. Isn't that what you said Longie gave you for expenses? And you gave me five hundred of it. When we return with the

Maglioccos, maybe he'll let us keep what's left. And then, if you ain't got no objection to splittin' it up . . . I'll have a lot of money."

Jay began to consider what a thousand dollars would mean to T: a chance to start his own checker parlor, or travel, or even buy a small house. The one time Jay had come to his apartment, T had said he'd give his left arm to have his own place.

"Sure thing," Jay replied.

A famous gingerbread town of once brightly painted Victorian houses, Cape May had, like every other resort in America, suffered from the ravages of the Depression. As a child, Jay had seen it when colorful tents lined the beach and all the honky-tonk concessions exuded a raucous energy. But with revelers long since gone, the few people on the streets walked listlessly, and the once bright life of the waterfront attracted only a downcast population. The city seemed sunk in hebetude. Those stores not boarded up offered sales of 50 percent off, and those hotels not left to die in the salt air and the rain were renting rooms for three dollars a week. You would have thought that with business so poor, Jay and T could have had their choice of places to stay. Not so. They faced the usual racial prejudice.

In the rental section of a local newspaper, Jay saw an ad that offered a bed and three meals a day. No mention was made of Negroes, Jews, or Catholics. Located on Franklin Street, a low-lying area called Frog Hollow because it frequently flooded during heavy rains, the boardinghouse was owned and administered by a Miss Sue Patulous, a comely woman with black hair and a shapely figure whose skin looked as if it had been bleached bone white, except for an occasional brown splotch. She reminded Jay of an albino woman his father had once employed. Miss Patulous's house had two floors: downstairs, a comfortable parlor with a card table holding an unfinished jigsaw puzzle, a dining area off the kitchen, and a small solarium for plants; upstairs, four small guest bedrooms and a larger one in which she slept. At the end of the hall stood a bathroom. To the delight of Miss Patulous, T and Jay took separate digs; instead of making seventy-five cents for a room with twin beds, she earned fifty cents apiece.

"You gentlemen in Cape May for some special reason?"

"Actually we've come to visit a friend."

Asking Miss Patulous how to find the address that Leonora had provided, they made straight for the rooming house and asked for the Clarks, only to learn they had left the day before. Their departure convinced Jay they had decamped for Wildwood and Aunt Amalie's house, which Longie had traced through her telephone number. So the two men backtracked to Wildwood, where they easily found Dune Drive, near the ocean, and Aunt Amalie's Queen Anne house with a wraparound porch and a mailbox with the name "Holz." When they came up the steps to the front door, their hearts sank. The place was closed for the season. Apparently, Aunt Amalie spent the fall and winter in another location. But where?

Desolate, they drove back to the Patulous boardinghouse, where they retired to the parlor. Jay sat down at the table on which Miss Patulous had spread her jigsaw puzzle, about half of which she had completed, no mean feat given that the box indicated the number of pieces at 5,012. Studying the cover picture, a Dutch landscape of a field in Holland, he quickly realized that the predominance of yellow from the sun and hay made it almost impossible to discern patterns and to identify the subtle shifts in shades.

"I belong to a club." Miss Patulous had come up behind him. "We exchange puzzles. It takes me about two weeks to complete one."

"It would take me forever. I could figure out the edges but nothing else."

"Color's the main thing. You isolate them and then see how one tint shades into the next. Of course, the shape matters too. If you have an eye for geometry—I was always better at algebra—you can see at a glance what the next piece has to look like. Here, for example, you can tell that you need a yellow piece with five prongs, two of them thin, three of them fat."

T rose from a parlor chair and came over to look. Miss Patulous reached for a piece and started to put it into the yellow field, when T said, "I think you'd be better off with this one," leaned over, and put another in its place. The next thing Jay knew, T and Miss Patulous were seated side by side whipping through that puzzle like nobody's business. Her genuine kindliness toward T impressed Jay for its uniqueness and courage: a white woman in a southern-like society befriending a Negro. You really had to admire her.

After Miss Patulous served a dinner of roast chicken with mashed potatoes and peas, and refused to let them wash the dishes, she changed her clothes and led them down to the massive U-shaped Admiral Hotel, said to be the largest in America. She thought they'd like the architecture. Remembering Arietta's postcard, Jay was keen to see it. Perhaps she and her father were staying there. As they neared the Beaux-Arts style building, they found themselves in a crowd and were swept up the steps to a front plaza, which they crossed to reach the elegant archway and the grand lobby featuring large columns, marble floors, a glass-domed Tiffany ceiling, and a staircase bending in two directions to the upper levels and the hundreds of rooms. The crowd flowed into a dining room rearranged to serve as a lecture hall, with hundreds of folding chairs. They followed. Besides T, Jay saw about a dozen other Negroes, all of whom looked like liveried servants attending patrons, a scene that must have made T feel like a freak. Sue whispered that this hotel attracted a wealthy clientele who came here by train from Philadelphia and New York City and seemed untouched by the stock-market crash. Jay looked around but did not see Arietta and her dad.

A stand at the front of the room held a conspicuous white placard with black lettering: "Bishop Alma White, God's Emissary on Earth."

A plain-looking woman in a baggy white blouse and a drab, brown, ankle-length skirt, Bishop Alma White had a flat, broad, unflinching face. Her stern eyes made Jay think of a generation of weather-hardened midwestern settlers. From her chair, she looked over the faithful as she waited for a local preacher to celebrate her "struggle with Satan and the Scarlet Mother," the Catholic Church. Although no Gerald L. K. Smith, or Huey Long, or Father Coughlin, she could still rattle the rafters. Grabbing the sides of the dais as if preparing to climb a ladder to heaven, she spoke without notes and was repeatedly interrupted with applause.

"Our religious and political foes are within our gates," she began,

coming by the hundreds of thousands from the chaos and ruin of old European and Asiatic countries to un-Americanize and destroy our nation, and to make it serve the purposes of the Pope in his aspirations for world supremacy. The "Scarlet Mother" wants to destroy all the God-given rights of a free and liberty-loving people. For reasons heretofore mysterious, the Jews have made common cause with the "Scarlet Mother," enabling her with Jewish wealth to menace our civil liberties and institutions.

This unlikely marriage between Jew and Catholic has much to do with the former's adamantine behavior. I call your attention to the story of Jonah and the whale and ask you to think of the whale as Protestantism. After three days there was not a bone in Jonah's body broken, for he had successfully resisted the powerful digestive machinery in the stomach of the monster. What an illustration we have here of the Jew! For the past two thousand years, the Gentile powers have been unable to digest or assimilate him or break his solidarity or make him disavow the old doctrines as they were when he rejected the Messiah.

She took a sip of water and continued. "Now the Jews are telling us to boycott the Olympics." The crowd hissed at the very suggestion. "In the Olympics we will see German Protestantism at its best. Only a Jew could object."

She concluded with the ominous suggestion that "a great force was now gathering in Europe that would purify the race and protect the faith."

T whispered, "I don't suppose she's gonna lead us to the promised land."

"The only place she's leading me to is the door," Jay replied and started for the boardinghouse in high dudgeon. Miss Patulous and T followed. Outside the hotel, she touched Jay's arm and effusively apologized for having led them to the Admiral Hotel and to that "hateful woman."

"You didn't know," he said, "it's not your fault. But just for the record, I'm Jewish. And personally, I don't think her kind of religion leads to the salvation road."

She looked ashen and led them back to Franklin Street. At the house, he felt obliged to say to Miss Patulous, "If you'd like us to leave, I'll pay for our rooms even though we haven't slept in them."

"No, please stay."

Jay could see that she was wrestling with some troubling idea, so he asked rhetorically, "Surely, you don't countenance anti-Semitism? Your newspaper ad is free of discrimination."

"It's easy enough for me to ignore what the bishop said. But then I wonder: Is my religion really of that kind?"

"Not if you live up to your name."

She looked puzzled. "I don't follow."

"Open, flowering."

"I never knew my name had a meaning."

"All names do, literally or figuratively."

Before they retired for the night, Miss Patulous served them some cheesecake and freshly brewed coffee. Jay had the feeling she wanted to show them that, unlike her friends, she had an open, spreading nature. In the morning, they awoke late and puttered around the house, helped her fix her lawn mower, and changed a washer in a leaky faucet. T volunteered to cut the grass, but Miss

Patulous told him the weed patch was not worth it because she planned, just as soon as she could afford it, to plant some trees and shrubs that would survive in the salt air.

That afternoon, they started cruising the streets of Cape May and local townships looking for a 1929 Waterhouse parked outside a rooming house. When that search proved fruitless, they started grasping at straws. Talk about setbacks, false leads, reversals, and all the other stage machinery of mystery stories . . . they encountered them all. They sought aid from the police, firemen, hotels, boardinghouses, restaurants, fraternal clubs, churches, community houses, soup kitchens, charities, rental agencies, garages, green grocers, drug stores, hospitals, banks, and newspapers. From time to time, Jay had the feeling they were being followed, but he could never confirm his suspicions. One late afternoon, after deciding that their search was a lost cause, he suggested they go to the local shooting range, which was tucked away in the pine trees. He had remembered that Arietta liked pistol shooting, but the place was deserted. In the distance, he saw several wicker chairs and a dozen large berms. The sole building on the property, a locked shed, probably held the targets. A closer look at the berms bore out his guess that they either held the targets or served as a backup to arrest the bullets. T and Jay started to leave just as a decrepit truck pulled up, discharging a fellow in overalls and a long white beard, who removed from the flatbed a scythe. Old Man Time, Jay thought, and chuckled.

"Range closes at four," he mumbled, as he gummed a plug of chewing tobacco. "Most do their shootin' in the late mornin' to avoid the 'skitas and 'fore the afternoon heat sets into the pines real good. But in the fall, any time's good. Name's Clarence, Clarence Herbert. Groundskeeper here. Keep the grass cut and the place clean. Used to be a gardener when people had money and fancy lawns and would spend summers in Wildwood."

They chatted with Clarence in general about the town and which rooming houses were the most likely to be able to garage a fancy car. Clarence eyed them suspiciously, as if trying to make up his mind about something.

"Say, you boys ever shoot a Thompson submachine gun?"

Their negative responses led Clarence to open the shed and remove a shiny, fully loaded, newly oiled 1921 tommy gun. The old guy removed one of the targets, positioned it at a distance of about fifty feet, and, handing the gun to Jay, explained how to gently engage the trigger and cradle it against his shoulder. So quickly did the instrument spew bullets that it seemed to take only a second to fire off a round. The smell of oil and sulfur hung in a blue haze, befogging Jay's senses before he realized that he had hardly grazed the target. Happily, he passed the gun to Clarence, who reloaded it and handed it to T, who reluctantly agreed to have a go. Feet astride, shoulder steadying the gun, eye peering down the barrel, T let off a burst of spitfire that ripped the target to shreds. Clarence exclaimed through pursed lips, "Whew," but T's accuracy left Jay mute. Suddenly, he saw him in a new light, as a warrior taking the fight to the Hun and leaping from one foxhole to the next and slaying the enemy. T must have been thinking in similar terms because he said reverentially:

"In my whole life, I've never been drunk like this, never with power. Now I know the thrill Legs Diamond and Vince Coll musta' felt squeezing off a round. With a Thompson nobody would get in your way. My god, Jay, do you know what it means to have so much power at your fingertip? No one to push you around, order you off the sidewalk; no one to send you to the back of the bus. A tommy gun makes you an equal with one pull of the trigger. Jesus, just think what it would be like if the colored baseball leagues with one squeeze could join the white leagues. *This*," he said, holding the weapon over his head, "is a miracle worker."

Clarence added, "For some folks a gun's a god."

"My Lord," T said proudly, "if the Negro races had some of *these*, the world would be a different place."

Jay didn't have the heart to tell him that armed Negroes would incite every fear and prejudice in the white community, and that all the bigots in America would love nothing more than to take up arms in a race war. Tommy guns would not provide the answer; with any luck, the legal system and education might.

A minute after the three men sat down in front of the shack to chew the cud, a shot rang out, splintering the wooden boards above Jay's head. He and Clarence instinctively hit the ground, but T-Bone grabbed the Tommy gun and would have raced into the woods to pursue the shooter had Jay not told him to stay put, fearing T might kill the wrong person.

Several minutes later, all one could hear was the murmur of the wind in the trees.

"Some folks around here are plumb crazy, usually moonshiners. They're thick as 'skitas in these woods." Taking the gun from T-Bone, Clarence said he guessed the danger was past and insisted on showing them his pride and joy, a small stand of apple trees, neatly pruned and fenced. "I love when ripe apples drop about my head. This here patch gives me happiness, and a green shade."

Jay suddenly had a green thought. "How would you like to land-scape a lady's house on Franklin Street?"

Clarence smacked his lips and spat some evil-looking black juice. "Right up my alley but . . ."

"Yes?"

"Will she pay?"

"No, I will."

Opening his wallet, Jay removed a sawbuck. "You decide what plants she needs and keep something over for your labor."

Clarence took the money and asked for the address of the lady who needed his expert gardening skills. Later, Jay wondered if he should have asked for a receipt, but T assured him the old man would show up and do a good job in the hope of getting more work.

That evening Jay told Miss Patulous about Clarence, bringing to her face a blush that spread from the roots of her hair to her neck. She protested that she had done nothing to deserve such generosity, but broke off when T said simply, "You let me stay here."

In the morning papers, they read that another prominent member of the anti-Olympics crusade—the fourth in two months—had been shot to death. The victim was opening his garage door when someone hiding in the bushes pumped two slugs into him. His wife, hearing the shots, ran to the front of the house and found him lying in a pool of blood from wounds to the head and chest. Jay's concern for Arietta now bordered on the desperate.

His attention was also drawn to a newspaper article about the opening of a gun show, to be held under a large tent in Cape May Township. Knowing Arietta's pistol skills, he thought, why not give it a try before heading back to Newark? He wondered if they would run into Clarence, who, in fact, was one of the first to arrive. Jay parked in the large lot next to the tent. A few yards away, a Packard sedan pulled up, and a fellow in a sporty tweed suit, white collar, and striped shirt stepped out, carrying a black briefcase. He had a mangled left ear that resembled a cauliflower.

If intuition is a mixture of savvy and luck, Jay had both, because when they entered the tent, he saw Arietta admiring a long-barreled pistol, with her father some distance away studying the floral display that ringed the tent. Arietta was dressed in a natty suit with a jaunty black hat and looked fetching. She revealed more leg than other women were inclined to show, giving her the appearance of a John Held model on the cover of *Vanity Fair*. Mr. Magliocco, seeing Jay approach, reacted with astonishment and then pleasure. "Do you know that fellow?" Mr. M. asked in a troubled tone of voice, pointing to the cauliflower ear who was bearing down on Arietta.

"No, but I'll check."

Unnoticed, he approached Arietta and Cauliflower. When he spoke, they swiveled as one.

"Miss Ewerhardt," said Jay, deliberately using her undercover name, "you have no idea how glad I am to see you."

On seeing him, Arietta cast her eyes so low, he thought they'd suffered an eclipse. Cauliflower, on the other hand, stiffened his back and set his jaw. Before she could respond, Jay added:

"This is my good friend T-Bone Searle."

Arietta introduced her "friend" as Rolf Hahne, with whom Jay shook hands and feigned cordiality, remembering all too well what Francesca Bronzina had said about a man of that name. Arietta's expression bespoke relief, which suggested that Cauliflower was menacing her.

"At last I've found you," Jay said. "We've been sick with worry, but we can't talk here. Would you mind accompanying Mr. Searle and me to the parking lot? Your father can join us."

An uninvited Rolf Hahne followed a few steps behind.

Stopping under the leafy gold canopy of an oak, Jay said loud enough for all to hear that he would be only too glad to drive her back to Newark. T-Bone and Mr. M. could follow in the Waterhouse sedan. Before he could say more, Cauliflower opened his briefcase, removed a Luger, and stepped forward.

"She'll be traveling with me," Hahne said, placing a hand on her shoulder and pointing the gun toward his car. "The fourth one on the left . . . the Packard."

T suddenly bolted behind the line of parked cars. For a moment Jay thought he'd done so from fright. But T had found Hahne's Packard and, kneeling on the far side of the back wheel, was letting the air out of the tire. Rolf, after shoving Arietta into the passenger seat, came to the driver's side, saw T, and pistol-whipped him.

Jay and Mr. M. had stood transfixed, worried about Arietta's safety.

"Get rid of your car keys," Jay muttered to Mr. M. "I just tossed mine into the bushes."

Cauliflower immediately returned with Arietta in front of him.

"Your car keys!" Hahne demanded.

Jay turned out all his pockets to show that he had none.

"Give me yours," Hahne said to Mr. M. "And don't tell me you have no car."

Mr. M. also turned out his pockets. Nothing. By this time, all the commotion had attracted the attention of a policeman patrolling the grounds. Jay could see panic in Cauliflower's face. Without a car, what could he do? Take Arietta hostage, but where? Spying a man in the distance entering his car, Cauliflower forgot about Arietta and raced toward it. When the car started to ease out of the parking spot, Cauliflower ordered the driver from it, slid in behind the wheel, and drove off. The owner of the hijacked car came running toward the policeman, yelling:

"Stop him, stop him. He stole my car!"

"Who is he?" asked the cop.

A badly frightened Arietta replied, "A man from Berlin."

At that moment, T-Bone, temporarily blinded by the blood running down his forehead and into his eyes, staggered toward them.

"I'll get out an alert at once," said the cop. "And let's get this man to the hospital for stitches."

But T refused to leave, using his handkerchief and Jay's to stanch the bleeding. When the Maglioccos suggested coming to their rented cabin where they could attend him, Jay insisted that they all return to the Patulous house.

But Arietta seemed to think that she and her father were safe in their current digs. Mr. M. agreed, fetching his car keys and, with Arietta in tow, making for his auto.

"Where are you staying?" Jay shouted, but they made no reply.

"Those folks huntin' you," mumbled T, "are bad 'uns. You'd best hear what Jay has to say."

The Maglioccos listened, but Jay could sense that more than the fear of Nazis had driven them to flee. They did, however, collect their belongings and stay with Jay and T at the Patulous house. They all ate together that night in Frog Hollow, with Jay and T taking turns keeping watch outside the Maglioccos' bedrooms. By morning, they looked and felt pretty ragged. From afar, Sunday church bells sounded. When the Maglioccos appeared, Jay said they should leave directly for Newark; but Arietta insisted that they first had to drive to Chatsworth, in the Pine Barrens, to see her Aunt Amalie's son, her cousin. He knew that in matters concerning her mother's family, there was no point in arguing. She described the area, which sounded prelapsarian, and suggested a picnic and swim to put them both in a better mood. He grudgingly told himself that another day wouldn't matter. Arietta packed a straw basket and took some towels from the linen closet.

"A swim in one of the cedar lakes would be absolutely divine," she said. But Jay found her enthusiasm insincere; moreover, the water in May could be pretty damned cold.

Mr. M. volunteered to take T fishing, on an excursion boat, so that Arietta and Jay "could have some time alone." They all agreed on that plan, with T and Mr. M. leaving first. As Jay said goodbye to Miss Patulous, she whispered:

"Your friend is quite a beauty. Good luck."

Jay gassed up at a station on the other side of the causeway and continued north. At first, he and Arietta said nothing, but slowly they reestablished a communion of words, seeking safe ground by identifying the wild flowers as they inched along the road in the Sunday traffic. Once they had exhausted the innocuous subjects, they gravitated toward the real one.

"You are wondering how I knew about Axel's death. An anonymous caller rang me and said that unless I cooperated—his word, cooperated—I would be the next one to go. Frantic with fear, I told my father about the call. It was he who insisted we leave at once."

"I thought there might be more to it."

She nodded. "There is." She studied a fingernail and looked out the side window. "I feared that my work for Mr. Zwillman would be exposed."

"You supplied him with information, until Longie asked you for a favor that was a bridge too far. Right?"

Putting one hand on the dashboard and the other behind his seat, she turned to face Jay and, in this S-shape, marveled at his disclosure. "How did you know?"

"Longie told me."

"Frankly, I liked working for him—he paid me well—until he asked me to steer someone to a particular Portuguese restaurant near the station."

"Axel, you mean?"

"I'd rather not say."

"A man marked for murder?"

"For roughing up, I was told. When I refused, he threw a paper-weight against the wall, swore, and walked out."

In light of Longie's extravagant praise, her story rang only partially true. Jay couldn't believe that one refusal would have angered him; she must have not only refused the assignment but also cautioned Axel to lie low. That would explain his absences from the Friends meetings. If Arietta had indeed saved his skin, albeit temporarily, it made sense that Axel would shower her with affection. But apparently she rebuffed him. Jay didn't like the direction of his logic. If Longie hadn't hit him, then who had? Jay wondered if that enigma might explain her running away.

"Who do you think killed Axel?"

She bit her lip and resumed her former posture, looking straight ahead at the road. They bumped along, past shacks and gritty farms and thousands of blueberry bushes, through stands of pitch pine and different kinds of oak—white, scrub, black, and chestnut—smelling the wild laurel and the heavy air, until finally she spoke. "If I give you a name, you'll be equally at risk." Resuming her former S-shape, she pleaded passionately, "Don't you see? That's why my father and I can't return. Mr. Zwillman knows that I know."

"Knows what? I'm confused."

"There were two murders: Heinz Diebel and Axel Kuppler. As far as the police are concerned, they both remain unsolved."

Jay could hardly keep his eye on the road. "Do you know who shot them? Was it one of Longie's boys?"

"Please don't ask me that question, Jay. As far as Mr. Zwillman's concerned, I'm the unknown, the X factor, the person who could be caught and made to talk. Of course, I would never say anything, but could I convince Longie of *that?* He wants to pack me off to Canada, for safekeeping."

If true, Jay's involvement in her return would make him complicit in her . . . what? Disappearance? If untrue, his assistance in her escape would earn Longie's displeasure. It suddenly occurred to him that Longie had never said what to do if Jay found Arietta. Was Jay to bring her back to Newark? Find a safe place in another state? Leave the country? He needed time to think, time to clear his head and find in this state of unknowing some safe harbor. Unfortunately, Arietta would not give him time.

"Just do this one thing for me," she importuned, "let my father and me slip away. I promise that I'll never breathe a word of it. Then, in a few years, when the matter's long since forgotten, I'll write to you, God willing, and we can be as we once were."

He probably would have been tempted, but for that staged, insincere "God willing."

"Let's enjoy the day," he said lamely, "and I'll give you my answer later."

Her crestfallen expression spoke volumes, but she did not plead her case any further. Just as if a veil had been cast over the past, they stopped trying to pierce it and spoke only of the present and her work as a courier.

"Are you still part of the pro-boycott movement?"

"I am, but it's fruitless. Most Americans are too preoccupied with making a living or finding a job. Why should they care about the Olympics when they have little or nothing to eat? I've seen parts of the hinterland they call rural America. It's a wasteland. I hate to say so, but Negroes don't see much difference in the treatment of Jews in Germany and colored people in America. A boycott won't stop the spread of fascism. Jobs will."

Jay had no desire to test that hypothesis. For now, he just wanted to get Arietta safely back to Newark, but first they had to taste the enjoyment of Chatsworth, which they soon reached. The dirt road leading into the town ran past a barracks maintained by the New Jersey mounted State Police, who patrolled the pines for criminals on the lam and for big-syndicate stills, which, according to the pasty-faced, porcine owner of the local general store, the locals usually exposed. Apparently the police turned a blind eye to small bootleg operations but intervened in the larger ones because they attracted thugs from the city. At the general store, Jay inquired about boat rentals. Down the road, they were told. As they descended the wooden steps, he asked Arietta where her cousin lived. Dropping her head on her chest, she murmured:

"I lied to you. I have no cousin in Chatsworth."

They returned to the car and for several minutes sat silently. He then told her about his going to Wildwood and finding her Aunt Amalie's house shut. "Where does she spend the fall and winter?"

"Los Angeles. When she finds a place she normally writes to me. But now that I'm on the run, I don't know how we'll connect."

Arietta brightly smiled, as if she hadn't just led him on a wild goose chase, and suggested they not waste the day.

"Let's rent the canoe you wanted and go to the river."

The day had warmed up pleasantly. He reluctantly agreed, though once again he felt emotionally used. They stopped at the rental shop. She selected a canoe, and he strapped it to the top of the car. The road took them north, and he parked in a stand of trees. They intended to paddle a short distance to Chatsworth Lake and swim there, but given the pristine, Edenic beauty of the river they paddled only a short distance before they banked the canoe and undressed. Although both of them had brought along bathing suits, Arietta insisted that their past intimacy entitled them to swim au naturel. Before he could dive in, she had disappeared in the breath-stopping cold water. He stood and watched, waiting for her to surface. At last, she exploded from the deep like a geyser, rising up to her waist with her hands extended overhead, and then sank again. She performed this rising-and-falling act several times, dripping water from her hair and glistening breasts as she rose and then disappeared completely from sight in the slow black current. Every time she submerged herself, he feared she'd disappeared. She called him to join her. He knew that her swimming skills eclipsed his; nevertheless, he stroked toward her in the middle of the river, but as he approached, she turned and swam to the far bank, where she disappeared into the woods. As naked as Adam, he followed, plunging through the scratchy underbrush.

He discovered her lying in a small open area covered with moss. She had brambles in her hair from running in the forest, and her body, like his, still exhibited the slime of the mossy slope. Holding out her arms in a come-hither manner, she eagerly embraced him, a reminder of that first night when her nipples stood rigid with anticipation. But he could not control his pent-up anger, which led him to take her not gently but roughly. Lying down next to her, he put one hand behind her head and brought her lips to his, holding them against his own till she gasped. He wanted to ravenously devour her mouth and tongue, but she murmured, "Don't!" Pressing her breasts together, all the better to suckle her nipples, he would have bitten her had she not said, "Be gentle!"

Breathlessly, he slid his penis down the length of her body and rested his head between her legs while she ran a hand through his hair. Tonguing her labial lips, he quickly induced lubrication and then slammed into her body wanting to knife his penis right through her. Furiously, over and over again, piston-like, he drove into her soft flesh. Wrapping her legs around his waist, she forced him into a sitting position; a moment later she sat astride him with her hands pressing his head to her breasts. Suddenly her body stiffened. She turned his head and pointed. A small water snake slithered across the moss and disappeared in the ferns. Her body relaxed, and she, now in postural control, took his face in her hands and kissed his mouth, whispering, "Just tell Mr. Zwillman you couldn't find us."

Without answering, he slipped his arms around her waist and they gently reclined. Her smile and eyes said yes, yes, so they recklessly loved until she drove her fingernails into his back, which so excited him that instead of spilling his seed on the ground, as he had intended, he poured it into her. They lay on the moss for a long time, until she wordlessly rose and ran further back into the woods. Reaching a small tributary, she slipped into the water and, as before, disappeared from sight into the blackness. He swam to the spot where he had last seen her, but she miraculously appeared yards downstream, beckoning him to follow. Again he lost her. When she materialized, she climbed the bank and, heedlessly jumping over tree roots, made her way deeper into the woods. He trailed her into a part of the forest that must have resembled the original darkness and oozy wetness that fecundated the earth. The only sound came from birds cawing against the intrusion into their world. Ducking under branches and dashing through the sumac, she finally came to a halt. Her expression, one of radiant contentment, seemed to suggest that she had at last arrived in that primeval place from which came the first simple light. Spellbound, he took her again, but this time tenderly as if the woods shone and they, Adam and maiden, were the progenitors of creation.

Lying in a postcoital reverie, they said nothing. At last, she murmured one word, "Yes." He knew what she meant.

Later, she spread a small tablecloth on the ground and from her basket took fruit and cheese and bottled sodas that she opened with an opener she had thoughtfully packed. As they ate, he observed that the ground seemed to move, not violently but ever so slightly.

Arietta laughed. "We are floating on a sea of water. Underneath this sandy ground lies the Cohansey Aquifer, a reservoir estimated to contain twenty trillion gallons of some of the purest water in America." He had read once that you could fill a jug with aquifer water and it would still be potable twenty years later. Moonshiners simply dig a hole in the ground four or five feet deep and set up a still in a swamp, using apples, blueberries, peaches, or corn.

Darkness began to erode the light when they decided that they had better start back to Cape May. He knew that he had left

Arietta's plea unanswered. She folded the tablecloth carefully and then rose slowly from the ground. He interpreted her deliberate motions to mean she wanted a reply before they departed. When none was forthcoming, she asked him if he would give her a driving lesson in the Ford. Odd, for some reason he had the impression that she already knew how to drive. After they packed the car and fastened the canoe to the roof, he showed her the basics and, sitting beside her, let her meander jerkily down the road toward Chatsworth. She parked in front of the rental shop, and he removed the canoe. To his amazement, before he even reached the front door, she suddenly turned the car around and expertly sped in the opposite direction.

He waited inside the shop, hoping she'd return, and then started down the road toward Chatsworth, assailed by insects. He put out his thumb to hitchhike. Fortunately, a car stopped almost immediately, but blinded by his anger, he failed to study the driver. As he slid into the front seat, he was met by a pistol aimed directly at him. Behind the wheel sat Rolf Hahne.

"I'll drop you off at the next side road," Hahne said sarcastically, only to realize a moment later that it would be impossible for him to steer, change gears, and train a pistol on Jay.

"You drive!" Hahne commanded.

As Jay exited the car, he looked for a chance to run. No such luck. Hahne ordered him to stand in front of the car with his hands on the hood, and then slid into the passenger seat while Jay took the wheel.

"I'll tell you where to turn. I saw a deserted spot a mile from here. Since you left Cape May, I've been following you and your turtledove. When she flew the coop, I could see no way of running her off the road. Too much Sunday traffic. So I came back for you."

As Jay drove, he decided he had nothing to lose and perhaps something to gain by turning the car into the oncoming lane.

"Are you trying to get us killed?" Hahne growled.

"That's the idea."

Jay could see beads of sweat on Hahne's forehead.

"The side road is up there. Get back in the right lane and turn into it."

But Jay didn't stop. They passed the turnoff as oncoming cars honked and swerved to miss him. To his right, drivers looked terrified. Straight ahead and coming their way was a hay wagon, too wide to avoid. Darting back into the right lane, amid the din of outraged horns, Jay veered off the road through a field and across an expanse of lawn toward a church. Stopping a few feet from a group of children playing croquet, he leaped from the car and threw his arms around an indignant pastor, as Rolf roared off.

"Are you mad?" cried the pastor.

"Just anxious to pray and give thanks," Jay said contritely.

An hour later, a parishioner drove him back to Cape May.

He arrived at the Patulous house after dinner and gave no excuse for his lateness. He supposed that when Arietta showed up alone to collect her father, she had given T and Miss Patulous a good explanation for his absence. Unless asked what happened, he saw no need to alarm them. T-Bone had occupied himself waiting for his companion, bent over a new jigsaw puzzle that fittingly depicted the major transcontinental roads and rail routes. Jay knew that before too long they would be heading down some of those roads—pursuing Arietta and her father.

After a few hours of sleep, Jay took some breakfast with T. With the early morning light falling across the oilcloth on the table, T asked:

"What now?"

"On your fishing trip, did Mr. M. mention Kansas City or J. L. Wilkinson? That's where Hump thought they were headed."

"Jay, I know the city and the man. Leave it to me."

"I was hoping that Mr. Magliocco might have confirmed Longie's suspicions."

T, who refused to shave until they had found their quarry and returned to Newark, scratched his beard. "All that man wanted to talk about was opera and fishin'. Him and the boat pilot had a whale of things to say about bluefish, but no one on that five-seater knew anything about two women he kept mentionin', Aida and Lucia. You woulda' thought they were old girlfriends he'd been wooin' for years."

"He'll be courting them his whole life, I suspect."

Procrastinating about calling Longie, Jay watched as T and Miss Patulous sat down together, hip to hip, to work on the jigsaw puzzle. When Jay finally reached Longie, he told him, without going into detail, that the Magliocccos had slipped through their fingers, and that they had good reason to believe the two were heading for Kansas City. Longie's response set off alarm bells.

"It's time to put some professionals in charge. Pay your bills and get back here. Irv and Rico will take over. They can handle K.C."

Perhaps Arietta was right: Longie wanted her found because he feared for his safety, not hers. With the gunsels Sugarman and Bandello looking for the Magliocccos, the urgency of finding them both was immediate.

"You and the *schvarze* can brief us when you get back."

Not wishing to compound Arietta's danger and to fail in the eyes of Mr. Zwillman, Jay said, "We're not giving up yet, Abe, we're prepared to keep looking."

"Not on my nickel. Bring back the car and the dough."

Jay pleaded that he give them more time.

With uncharacteristic truculence, at least toward Jay, Longie replied, "I put my money on airy hopes once, not twice," and hung up.

Jay weighed the consequences of continuing the journey and perhaps making himself a marked man, but he felt that Arietta's life was at stake, and he still deeply cared. They had enough money to live on—and a car. Although he felt like a thief, he decided there was no other choice. One day, he would explain his motives to Longie.

T and Sue, relaxing in the parlor over a cup of coffee, had finished the puzzle. They sat jawing, to Jay's amazement, about race, as in skin color. Miss Patulous was speaking with some vehemence.

"That's why they killed him. For no other reason. They beat my daddy to death in a police station."

Had Jay heard her correctly? Her daddy?

T gave her a modest hug, stepped back, and then hugged her again, this time with real feeling. Jay couldn't hear what T whispered to her, but when they disengaged tears were streaming down her face.

As they climbed into the car, she followed them to the street, and as they pulled away, she stood there waving.

"It's none of my business, T, but what went on between you two?"

T looked back and after a moment answered quite matter of factly, "While you were gone, I asked Sue if she had any pictures of her family and her eyes wetted up. That's when she showed me a picture of her parents. You know the one-drop rule? One drop of Negro blood makes you black, even though you may be white as alabaster." T breathed in deeply as if summoning the strength to continue. "Her parents were light-skinned Negroes passin' as white. Somehow, it was found out. Her daddy paid the price."

7

Driving to Kansas City presented them, once again, with the problem of housing. Their choices were few. The hotels in the cities were closed to them because of T's color. They would have to find housing on the roads, which had tent cities, public campgrounds, municipal parks, and picnic-sleeping spots in a field or schoolyard. The road, a windy boulevard for indigent transients and migrant workers in search of employment, also attracted auto gypsies in old rattletrap cars piled high with tents, and tin-can tourists in model T Fords, loaded down with six children and a birdcage, wandering the country in search of the quintessential rural America and finding, not an Edenic land, but failing farms, auto garages, telephone poles and wires, billboards, ramshackle food stands, and litter.

Occasionally they took heart from a dairy and wheat farm that seemed to have escaped foreclosure or a vast blooming field that could be seen in the distance as the road opened. With auto pumps few and far between (they could make only twenty miles to the gallon) and restaurants outside major cities scarce, they stopped an itinerant kitchenware salesman and purchased utensils, two pots, and a pan. From farmers along the route, they bought milk, butter, eggs, and vegetables and cooked over rough fires in deserted places so as not to invite hostile looks from other campers who might resent T's presence.

They averaged only thirty miles an hour owing to the numerous flat tires that halted traffic (a new inner tube cost ninety-five cents) and to road conditions where the pavement would suddenly end and miles of dirt stretch would follow. Occasionally, disabled cars that had misjudged the depth of a mud hole would block the road, and they and other motorists would attach ropes to extricate them. On some stretches of road, billboards warned motorists to fill up at the approaching station because the distance to the next one would tax the limits of their tank—and recommended buying a can for "emergencies" (metal can, one dollar; gasoline, nineteen cents a gallon).

The words "See America" may have had a special meaning for Jay's parents and their friends, who took their first automobiles on the road to learn about life outside the cities and willingly stayed in tent camps or put up their own canvas coverings, but for T-Bone and Jay auto camping held no attraction. They sought out tourist cabins (one dollar a night) or cottages (two dollars a night), aiming for those advertising community kitchens and toilets, showers with hot and cold water, and the occasional extra service, like a haircut (thirty-five cents). The community kitchen enabled T, a brilliant cook, to establish himself as an equal among those who mostly prepared the meals, women. Once the guests sampled his freely offered fare, they stopped noticing his color. The picnic tables brought together people from every walk of life, poor and rich, ordinary and gifted, even the eccentric, like circus people, quack medical peddlers, Russian noblemen, cowboys, and wandering poets.

But above all, the car served as a common denominator; irrespective of the type of automobile—from Fords to Pierce Arrows—people rubbed shoulders and exchanged stories about their home states or the best route to Joplin or recipes or weather conditions or the world situation or mosquitoes or the best resting place for the night. Protocol dictated that you could say whatever you wanted about yourself, except your name; Jay suspected that the practice originated with unmarried couples.

Their third night on the road, they rented a cottage, but not before two people who had arrived before them tried to chisel the price down.

"You just ought to see what we had last night. The loveliest cottage with a toilet, bath, and hot and cold water—and all for one dollar. Why we've been getting them all along the line for that amount."

The manageress, deeply tanned and wrinkled, listened patiently and finally agreed to their price, knowing that her "vacant" sign could remain out all night. A buck was better than nothing. It would pay for her groceries. Hoover's filthy depression had brought out the worst in many Americans and made the rest vulnerable to the chiselers and cheats.

The cottage that Jay and T rented had two beds and a few pieces of furniture, so Jay willingly offered the woman three dollars, which she reluctantly took when he said that his three and the one she received from the couple in front of them made it an even four. Hell, the night before, the two of them had shared a bed in a cabin that had once been a chicken coop, and the smells still lingered. This time they had a place with cotton-stuffed mattresses, a store-bought table and chairs, a bureau with a framed mirror, coat hooks behind the door, a throw rug, and a gas plate. After a communal dinner, which the manageress laid on for an extra quarter per person, the guests sat around comparing notes. All agreed that this place, called "Kozy Kottages," was a special treat.

"Christ," said one of the guests, sopping up the gravy with a bread crust, "the last place I stayed in would've moved you to tears. It was a miserable little shack that would've blown over in a high wind. It was plastered with tin signs advertising every vile potion, from tobacco to so-called medicines. The manageress was a slattern in a soiled bungalow apron and a breakfast cap. Her husband, the general handyman, whined endlessly about the customers."

At this point, a fellow, to the amusement of the others, imitated a guest at his last stop. "Why, some feller had th' nerve to ast, 'Is they a bathroom in connection with the room?' Bathroom! Huh, what does he think this is, the Waldorf-Astory? An' I says to him, 'No, they ain't no bathroom, but they's a pitcher of good cold water in th' room, an' a cake of soap,' and he looked at me like I was a pizen snake, and got in his shiny sedan and drove off. I dunno what folks are comin' to these days."

With everyone in a cheerful mood, they moved out of doors, where the manageress's son had laid a fire in a stone enclosure. One of the guests, a drummer with pomaded black hair and a gold tooth in the center of his mouth, talked about a snake oil salesman.

"He done said he had medicines that can raise the dead and change your skin color. He calls himself 'Doc Wonder,' and has a medicine show just down the road apiece."

T asked him how long it would take to reach the show.

"It opens for one week in East St. Louis. Even if you drive slow, you'll make it in plenty of time. Look for the signs and the large white tent on the outskirts of town. You'll hear plenty from the doc' about the Energy Elixir. Get there early if you want a seat. After hearin' Doc's speechifying, you may just want to buy a case."

"Have you ever been to a medicine show?" T asked.

"Don't need to," Jay said. "I've read all about them."

"Jay, it seems to me you put far too much trust in readin'."

"How else can I learn about what I'll never experience for myself, like ancient Rome?"

That response stumped T, who finally conceded, "I guess there's some things from long ago worth learnin' about."

The medicine show, booked into East St. Louis, attracted quacks and characters the equal of Mark Twain's Duke and King. The billowing tent on the banks of the Mississippi held about two hundred folding chairs, a platform, and a lectern. Dozens of small tents dotted the landscape with camp followers and accommodations for all the peddlers. Cars of every type and age covered at least an acre of ground. Whether the suckers came for the medicines or the show, Jay had no way of telling, but the strutting and the posturing and the proclaiming and the testifying were certainly worth watching. Where else could you enjoy such free entertainment? No wonder the locals poured into the tent, their white shirts exhibiting great ovals of sweat under the arms, their pants supported by suspenders, and their straw hats used as fans to move the unstirring heated air and chase away the bugs. A sallow lady in a neck to ankle *shmattah* banged a rinky-dink piano, alternating march tunes with martial and sentimental ones. Next to her, a young boy, no more than thirteen, scratched a violin. He resembled the woman, and Jay guessed that his mamma had dragged him into this meeting with the promise that he could earn a nickel or dime.

Although they arrived early, the only seats were toward the back because of the size of the crowd. When T sat down, an indignant lady stood up and changed her seat. Jay assured T that they would not spend the night in this town.

Different charlatans took turns haranguing the audience about the diseases of modern life brought on by the economic collapse of the country and how their nostrums could dispel every conceivable ill. Time and again these drummers of dreams likened their products to miracles and stressed the need for "the patient" to believe. (Herbert Hoover had purveyed virtually the same message: be patient and believe.) As the quacks hawked their products, shills in the audience came forward to buy a bottle of the promised cure with a statement to the effect that they had tried everything and that if this stuff worked, then it was indeed miraculous. Upon purchase, the shills drank the beverage and a minute or two later leaped into the air and declared themselves cured. One fellow, who made his way to the front of the tent, carried a tapping cane and looked off into space as if blind. Upon gulping the liquid, he immediately discarded the cane and declared himself free of darkness. Other shills behaved in a similar manner, including a white man who claimed to have once been black. When the hallelujahs subsided and people rushed forward to buy the "miracle medicine," the drummer always pleaded a shortage, which created a frenzy to purchase. Sending a young man to bring his entire stock from the car, the huckster would then urge the audience to purchase two and three of his bottles because he would not be back this way "for some time."

Jay suspected that most of these quacks would never pass through these parts again owing to the bogus nature of their goods; he also suspected that since medicine and religion so often go hand in hand, a relationship that probably goes back to the beginnings of both, the religious diction that the drummers used was intentional. He silently wished someone would discover a potion for finding persons on the lam; wouldn't that be a wonder drug?

The show ran for two hours twice an evening, from six to eight, and eight to ten. They left after the first, but not until T had bought two bottles of the elixir. On exiting the big tent, they encountered a group of forlorn men, standing around a Negro seated at a card table with a checker board. Across from the man sat a "Weary Willie," a hobo, wagering pennies. The onlookers were also betting among themselves, for or against the players. The amounts ranged from a penny to a dime. To listen to these men, you knew at once that they had turned to gambling in desperation after having roamed the country for work, begging on the streets, besieging back doors, standing in endless soup lines.

In age, they ranged from fifteen to sixty-five, in education from zero to a Ph.D., in background from the cabbage patch to Back Bay. Mostly they came from the lower depths: generously tattooed, eating food out of a can with a knife, and using the double negative. Many of the men seemed to know each other and addressed their pals by monikers fashioned from some physical characteristic adjoined to a city, for instance, Chicago Slim and Denver Dopey. Generally, though, they used confected first names like Red, Whitey, Blackie, Shorty, Heavy, Crip. Jay gathered that they eschewed last names because they didn't want friends and kinsmen to know their condition or their whereabouts. As one man said, "Tellin' the truth can only get you into trouble."

For over an hour, T-Bone and Jay watched the colored man beat the pants off all comers. Unable to resist the temptation, T finally jumped in and challenged the fellow to a game.

"I'll pay you in hard cash if I lose," said T, "but if I win, you give me your board. It looks special."

"That's jake with me," said the fellow, who introduced himself as "Memphis Mike." "This board is special, so let's begin with a deuce."

T threw down two dollars, to the oohs and aahs of the crowd. While their hands flashed, Memphis Mike broke into song.

Hand me down my walking cane,
Oh, hand me down my walking cane.
I drank and whored and used cocaine.
I'm gonna catch that Jesus train,
'Cause all my sins have caused me pain.

As the action heated up, Memphis repeated this refrain ever faster until Jay could hear the train and feared the chant would have a mesmerizing effect on T. To his credit, though, T got on top of the game and Memphis by intoning his own verses.

I'm gonna win Mike's checker board,
I'm gonna win Mike's checker board.
Carry it home as my reward
For all the sins I done abhorred.

With a flashing display of jumps and captures, T at last prevailed, but not easily. In a gracious gesture, T told Memphis to keep the deuce and walked off with the board under his arm and the box of checkers in hand.

T-Bone was to repeat his winning ways wherever they stopped for the night, collecting a few bucks for an evening's play. The gamblers included the full range of the human bestiary, from professor to priest, all wearing the rags of poverty. Their floating checker game attracted two college boys, as broke as everyone else, who whined about FDR infringing on their personal liberties but took umbrage when T reminded them that the bribe of big business—whose bread I eat, his man I am—had done more to undermine a person's rights than any FDR program.

Once they had extricated their car from the mass of tin cans that passed for automobiles, they drove through town, past boarded buildings and innumerable for-rent and for-sale signs. East St. Louis looked as if the entire place could be let or bought for a song. Jay could understand why its residents flocked to the medicine show. In hard times, liquor sales go up, also gambling and quackery, not just medical but political and spiritual as well.

They'd intended to bunk in St. Louis to catch Joe Frisco's show at the Commodore Club and hear Louis Armstrong play the horn. But in light of the *St. Louis Post-Dispatch* cover story about the polio epidemic in the city and across the state, they decided to drive through the night to Kansas City. A pelting rainstorm made the roads difficult, particularly since some drivers slowed to fifteen miles an hour in the downpour. As they poked along, T began to reminisce about his playing days with the Kansas City Monarchs.

"Baseball meant I didn't have to work in the stone quarry, or the meat-packin' plant, or the steel mill. I'd sweated in all those places, even on a celery farm. The other black boys felt the same way. They knew baseball would give 'em more dignity than washin' dishes or workin' in a dinin' car or bein' a Pullman porter. Yessirree, I told myself, baseball will put money in my pocket and let me see America. But the America I saw was from a bus, which I slept and ate in 'cause white-owned hotels and restaurants in small towns refused to serve Negroes. But at least I didn't have to earn a livin' shovelin' snow, or haulin' coal, or scrubbin' saloon floors.

"'Course since '31, the Monarchs ain't played in a league, only barnstormin' and the players workin' for a percentage of the gate."

In the current hard times, white major leaguers had expressed an interest in playing against some black teams—for the drawing power and money. But Judge Kenesaw Landis, the baseball commissioner, had a policy barring "regular" teams from playing black ones. Landis, fearing that if the latter won, the white major leagues would be undermined, sanctioned only barnstorming teams, composed of so-called all-stars; then if the barnstormers lost, he could always say that they were nothing more than a motley collection of players, not a unified, well-organized team.

T's memory waxed warmer the closer they got to K.C. "Know what Satchel Paige said about James 'Cool Papa' Bell? He was so fast he would flip the switch and get into bed before the room went dark. And as for Satch, you can't hit what you can't see."

Jay remarked that Arietta was hoping to win over Longie by getting Satch to endorse the boycott. Then other black athletes might follow suit.

"He ain't political," said T, and then fell into a reverie. On the outskirts of the city, T remarked, "I once tried to hit against Satch. No luck. He struck me out on four pitches. Him and Hilton Smith . . . the best pitchers who ever lived. Satch could make the ball invisible with speed or come in on a change-up so slow you could fall asleep waitin'. He threw bloopers, loopers, and droopers. He had a jump ball, bee ball, screwball, wobbly ball, whipsy-dipsy-do, a hurry-up ball, a nothin' ball, and a bat dodger. But his best pitch was his fastball. Why, Satch could smoke the ball across the plate so fast, the friction with the bats almost caused them to catch fire."

T directed Jay to Eighteenth and Vine: Street's Hotel. Jay could see that the Depression had really taken its toll in the Negro areas. "The Monarchs and the other black teams," he said, "must be hurting badly."

"Hard times ain't gonna matter that much to the teams 'cause they've had a depression most of their lives."

They checked into the airless and silent hotel. One man sat reading a paper in a parlor chair next to a potted fern and a floor fan. The deskman took a while to appear, even though T banged the bell a few times.

"What you been doin'," T asked, "stealin' the brass spittoons?"

The humorless deskman shoved a ledger in front of them and told them to sign. Perspiration dripped from his head, staining the book and causing the ink to run. The man seemed dumbstruck when T requested one room with twin beds, and tentatively inquired, "You isn't a couple of nances, are you?"

"You don't see us wearin' red ties, do you?" T snapped.

"Just askin'. Where's your valises?"

"We're parked out front," T replied. "We can bring 'em in ourselves." The dejected deskman looked ready to cry. "But you can carry 'em up to the room," T said, handing the guy a quarter, which elicited a reluctant smile.

After a number of calls, Jay learned the address of Satchel Paige's house. But before they left the hotel, he gave the deskman a five spot, in exchange for five dollars in nickels, and called his parents in Newark. His mother answered the phone with a spiritless voice.

"Mom, it's Jay. I'm in Kansas City . . . on business. What's wrong? You sound different . . . upset. Is something wrong?"

"The business is failing," she said.

"I'll send you some money."

"There's no need."

"I'll send it anyway." She didn't object, but she did ask when he'd return. "As soon as I finish the . . . assignment I'm on."

"We tried to reach you at the tobacco company."

"What did they say?" he inquired, suddenly overcome with self-loathing.

"They said you were traveling . . . and as soon as you called in they would tell you to phone us."

He apologized. "I've been delinquent in not keeping you posted about my whereabouts. From now on, Mom, I'll stay in regular touch."

"Hurry up and finish what you're doing. I miss you."

"I promise to be home soon."

They motored to Paige's house without calling first. A teenage boy answered the door and said that Satch had gone out with Mr. Wilkinson and two others. Where? Likely Muehlebach Field. Jay's optimism became was palpable, and T said some homemade pie would be jsust the thing.

"Let's go to Luther's," said T. "He's got the best diner in K.C., and lots of important black folks eat there."

They pulled up at an old railroad car that had been converted into an eatery. On top of the place, a sign badly in need of paint said, "The Heavenly Diner." Jay parked in back, and they walked along a gravel path to the front of the joint. The exquisite smells inside made up for the shabby exterior. With most of the booths along the side occupied, they took seats at the counter. A hefty colored lady with gray hair pulled back in a bun and wearing a rakish red beret wiped an imaginary spot from the table and asked:

"What kin I get you?"

T folded his arms over his chest and smiled broadly at the woman. "Don't remember me, do you, Mae?"

Mae put her gnarled hands into an apron pocket and removed a pair of specs. Holding them up to her face, she peered through the glasses. "Luther," she shouted, "come here!"

Poking his head through the hatch connecting the serving area to the little kitchen in the back, a short rotund fellow with a patina of silver beard framing his jaw and wisps of white hair perched above his ears inquired, "Yeah, what is it?"

"Look who's back in K.C.!"

Luther stared and blinked and stared some more. At last, recognition dawned on him. "Well, I'll be blown full of joy if it ain't T-Bone Searle, the prodigal son, returned home to see his own people." Coming from the back room, Luther wiped his hands on his soiled cooking apron and extended a paw to T. "How long it's been, son?"

"Too long," said T.

"Where you been?"

"Out east."

"Playin' ball?"

"No, I never got over that torn Achilles tendon. It still bothers me to this day."

"And your mamma, how's she?"

"Laid to rest."

"I'm heartsore to hear that. She was a good woman."

Mae shoved a menu in front of them and said, "The dinner's on the house." Luther momentarily raised an eyebrow, but Mae glared it away.

"Just a piece of pie," said T. "What's your special today?"

"Banana cream or apple. But I also got cherry, blueberry, and lemon meringue."

"I'll take the apple."

"And you?" she said.

"His name's Jay Klug and he's a friend of mine. Jay, this is Mae and Luther Johnson. Luther and me used to play ball together."

Luther immediately declared that he had never had the talent of T. "His arm was so strong, he could scoop up a grounder behind third and throw out the fastest player in the world, Cool Papa Bell . . . and could hit the best pitchers, 'ceptin' Satchel Paige. Young kids followed him round the ballpark and town just like the man was royalty. Fact, the kids gave him the title T-Bone, right, T?"

"That's right."

"Bullet Joe Rogan bet that T couldn't hit five pitches out of ten. T said, 'not if you throw them in the stands.' Rogan said, 'I'll put them all over the plate'—and darned if he didn't. And darned if T didn't hit all but two of 'em."

"Submarine balls," T mumbled.

Luther continued, "Bullet Joe bet T-Bone a steak dinner. Ever after, the fans called him T-Bone Searle."

Jay turned to T. "How come you don't use your real first name?"

"Randall? Sounds sissy-like, don't it?"

"Well, I wouldn't say that, but I much prefer the moniker."

"What's that?" said Mae.

"A nickname."

"Well, why the hell didn't you say so in the first place? What's wrong with you, boy, you ain't even told me what kind of pie you want." She turned to T and visibly winked. "I think this feller is short of some goods."

"No, he's all right," said T, "he just got his brain a little muddled in college."

Luther whistled. "I never before met a college boy."

"Well," sighed Mae, impatiently strumming the counter, "what's it gonna be?"

"Cherry pie, please."

While she dished out the two pies, and T and Luther traded stories about the old days on the diamond, a Negro in a Panama hat with a colorful band entered the diner carrying a young boy. Luther looked up and said:

"How's he doin', Ernie?"

Ernie stood the boy down on the floor and held his hand. Tentatively, the lad took a few steps to the applause of Luther. Jay noticed that one of the boy's legs was as thin as a toothpick.

"As soon as we can pay for it," said Ernie, "we're gettin' him a brace. Once it's fitted, Leroy will walk real good."

Mae cut a slice of banana cream pie and slid it across the counter to Leroy, who thanked her in a whisper, made shy, Jay suspected, by his atrophied leg. With every bite, Leroy looked up at her and smiled.

Jay gathered the kid had been stricken with polio, a fact that he confirmed when Ernie and his son left the diner. "How much do braces cost?" Jay asked.

"What did he say the time before last, Mae? Thirty-five dollars for a child's size?"

"Yeah, I think so."

Jay opened his wallet and took out two sawbucks. "Here, give them to Ernie. Tell him the money's from Longie Zwillman."

"Who's that?"

"A crook with a big heart."

Luther and Mae exchanged puzzled glances.

"Goin' to the game tonight?" asked Luther. "The Dean All-Stars and Monarchs are playin'. The team's got a portable lightin' system attached to the back of a truck. But the light ain't real good, so the players lose sight of the ball. With Dizzy pitchin', our boys better be wearin' their specs."

T said they would see the game, and slapped a bill on the counter. "Thanks for the pie."

"I don't want your money," Mae protested.

"Tell you what," said T, "put it to the cost of the kid's braces."

Jay and T-Bone drove through a Negro neighborhood to Muehlebach Field, at Twenty-Second and Brooklyn, where they bought two seats for the game. After changing their clothes at the hotel, they returned to the stadium, arriving just before game time. An attendant holding a pennant and wearing a rumpled light green seersucker suit led them to their box seats. A vendor sold them a bag of peanuts and some salted pretzels. When they reached their box, Jay saw his ardent hope realized. Dressed in their Sunday best and seated in the next box were Satchel Paige, Arietta and Piero Magliocco, and an older man. T nearly flew out of his skin.

"Wilkie," exclaimed T, leaning over the railing to shake the gent's hand. "This here man," said T, "is the owner of the Kansas City Monarchs, J. Leslie Wilkinson."

Jay was exultant. Mr. Wilkinson was on Longie's list of good guys, a pro-boycott supporter and a local legend. Having earned the respect of the Monarchs and the other teams for his fair and generous treatment of the players and his professional conduct in league affairs, Wilkinson was the only white owner of a black baseball team. His appearance was unremarkable, pale and balding, looking more like a banker than a sports figure.

After shaking his hand, Jay casually introduced himself to the Maglioccos, as if father and daughter were strangers, and asked what brought them to Kansas City.

Piero replied, "I used to deliver liquor from Windsor, Canada, to K.C. Prohibition had no effect on this stadium. They sold beer under the stands." Mr. M. chuckled. "You could buy it as easily as you could a bag of peanuts."

Jay remembered very little about the game, just that Ed Mayweather, the Monarchs' first baseman, hit one out of the park against Dizzy Dean and that Leroy Taylor, the Monarchs' right fielder, hit a game-winning double in the bottom of the ninth. Mr. Wilkinson excused himself to join the players in the clubhouse. Everyone shook hands, and Satchel Paige left. On the way to their respective cars, Jay whispered to Arietta:

"With Rolf Hahne trailing you, every contact you make for Longie puts that person in danger. You must let me help you."

"After Kansas City, I'm through with Longie."

She started to walk away. Out of exasperation, Jay grabbed her arm and muttered, "You must trust me."

She evinced a pained look and replied mysteriously, "I can't. You'll just have to understand. I tried to warn you."

At that moment, he knew his intuition was right. "It was you who fired that warning shot at the range. Right?"

"You were getting too close. We had rented a cabin in the woods nearby."

Then she fell silent and the moment was gone. Joining her father, she walked to their car. Jay and T-Bone followed them to a garish steak restaurant near the stockyards, where they sat a few tables away at a large glass window overlooking animal pens. The room admitted a slightly acidic odor from cattle manure.

The menu made it clear that Kansas City was a meat-and-starch town and that K.C. had the best beef in America. A wheezing fan overhead made it hard to hear. Jay strained just to catch what T was saying. They sat in this tawdry restaurant, with its pink and red striped wallpaper, eating ribeyes and sirloins smothered in onions with a side dish of baked potatoes. No greens, no salad. As Jay expected, T talked about baseball, but Jay hardly listened, keeping an eye on the Maglioccos. Although he needed desperately to see Arietta alone to tell her about Rico and Irv, he worried she wouldn't believe him. Based on what Hump McManus had said, he figured she wanted to reach Milwaukee. The German population in that city would provide safe haven, especially if she had friends or family there.

At the end of the meal, he asked Arietta to join him for a drive along the river. To his surprise, she consented. T volunteered to grab a taxi back to the hotel. Piero told his daughter not to be late. Jay's mind was already racing ahead. How would he persuade her . . . to do what? Protect herself? Others? She was obviously on the run looking for a good place to hide.

On a bluff overlooking the Missouri River, they sat in the car and watched a barge with lanterns at bow and stern. As it floated south, he drifted into a plea.

"In the woods, I thought you actually cared."

"I do, Jay."

Her invoking his name sounded contrived, like the bonhomie of a used-car salesman.

"Is that why you left me? Your idea of caring and mine have little in common." He then told her about his escape from Rolf Hahne.

"Now you see why no one must know where we're headed, not even Longie. For my father and me, it's a life-and-death matter."

"May I ask: Why Kansas City?"

"I came to talk to Satchel . . . my father to ask for money," she said simply. "Mr. Wilkinson told my father to contact him if money was short. Wilkie always insisted that my dad did him a favor by delivering beer to the stadium during Prohibition. We had no time to sell the house before leaving Newark. So we took him up on his offer."

The lack of invention gave her explanation the ring of truth. They talked, heedless of the time. It was now late, and Arietta asked him to drive her to the hotel. She described the Muehlebach as an Italian Renaissance palace with, on the main floor, a warren of shops and, at the top, celebrity penthouses. (Tom Pendergast was reputed to maintain one.) He accompanied Arietta to the front desk and told her that in the morning they had to talk. Intending to call her early, he asked the desk clerk for her room number. His raised eyebrows hinted at sin.

"Her room is a single, sir!"

"I have no plans to join her."

Arietta smiled sweetly. "Room 422," she replied and entered the elevator. Sure enough the Otis stopped at the fourth floor. Jay retreated to the lobby for several minutes pondering Longie's motives. Why not let Jay bring them back; why the need to send two of his boys? If protecting them was uppermost in Longie's mind, that concern might explain his haste to send out his mugs. But why would Arietta resist such protection? Something was missing. In the far reaches of his memory stirred a quotation from some long-forgotten statesman: "There's your side, my side, and the right side." If Jay substituted the word "truth" for "side," he would be implying that truth depended on the teller, that perception, and not some universal all-seeing sage or substance, was the source of one's truth. Small wonder people believe what they want to believe, and woe to the Teiresias who divines differently.

By the time Jay bedded down, the clock showed nearly three. But though dog-tired, he couldn't sleep. He kept mulling over motives and what Arietta and he would say to each other in the light of a new day. About eleven the next morning, T went off to see some friends, and Jay met the Maglioccos at the Muehlebach. He treated them to breakfast in a corner cafe that Mr. M. declared had "something like real coffee." As they settled into a booth, several sorry- and lonesome-looking men sat at the counter morosely eating.

"You know what I liked about the priesthood," said Mr. M., clearly not expecting an answer, "the camaraderie. I felt as if I belonged to a world of like-minded people, to a group devoted to the same ends, the improvement of the community's spiritual life."

"The socialists say the same thing, don't they, except they're concerned not with heaven but with food and jobs?" The moment

Jay made that comment he realized that Mr. M. might find it offensive.

He needn't have worried; Mr. M.'s next comment flirted with the same point. "The only groups like it are the trade unions and gangsters."

At first, Jay found the inclusion of gangsters strange, but when he mulled it over, taking into account mutual interests, companionship, self-protection, and, not least of all, money, the idea made sense.

"Do you miss it—the priesthood?"

"To worship an abstraction, the Mother of God, or a real woman, Arietta's mom?" He breathed deeply, paused, and, on the exhale, murmured, "I made the right choice."

As in Jay's past encounters with these two, Arietta said little in the presence of her father, whether from deference or fear or for some other reason. When Jay tried to include her in the conversation, she seemed out of sorts, replying tersely and even imperiously to whatever he asked, as if his questions were unworthy of a response. When Mr. M. said that he had an appointment at twelve-thirty with Mr. Wilkinson, Jay accompanied her back to the hotel, where they settled into a couple of deep leather lounge chairs and sat staring at each other for so long that he thought maybe it was a contest to see who would blink first. Unable to stand being pinioned by her great green eyes, he weakened and sighed:

"I give up!"

She smiled wanly and crossed her legs, causing her pleated skirt to hitch up above her knees. His loins pulsated as he imagined her wrapping those gorgeous gams around his back while he sank into her delicious body. Of all the unbidden thoughts that came to him in unexpected moments, uppermost was the image of her legs, long, shapely, elegant, suggestive . . . sleek for the flight into sex. He wanted to take her upstairs in the hotel and make delirious love. Forcing himself to rearrange his mind, he tried to focus on her motives, not her legs, and tried to elicit more information.

"How much does your dad know about you and Axel, or for that matter, about you and Longie?"

"Enough."

"Is that why he came away with you?"

"He's my father."

For a moment, Jay weighed that comment, realizing how little respect he had shown his own father, who had always appeared as "old world," even his socialist beliefs. His manners and habits, his style of dress, his formal speech patterns all struck Jay as old-fashioned. But was that any reason to value him less? He felt certain that Arietta would have said that the very characteristics he found disagreeable were well worth honoring.

"You must care for your father a great deal."

"He's my father," she repeated.

"Yes, but some fathers beat their wives and kids; they drink, womanize, goldbrick. I don't think they're worth caring about."

"The kind of man you describe is not my father."

He took that statement as a rebuke. "Well," he said in a conciliatory tone, "tell me who your father is. I hardly know him."

She puckered her lips, as if savoring her tongue, and replied laughingly, "Like all priests, he has a devious streak. You have to if you want to get ahead in the church. Hierarchies are just that way. To rise or be assigned a good parish, you have to know when to ingratiate yourself with the monsignor and bishop and when to stand up for a principle. My father fiercely fought against hunger and want, always asking his superiors for more money to buy food and clothing to aid the poor. He did the same for my mother and me."

Her last sentence left Jay speculating whether Mr. Magliocco had approached the church for personal assistance, to help him and his daughter during these hard times. If yes, Piero must have felt deeply uneasy, given his desertion of the Jesuits for a life of the flesh.

"My father would go to any lengths for his family."

"Even . . ." Jay broke off unwilling to give his thought words.

"You were saying?"

"Arietta, let's quit the shadow boxing. You're in terrible danger, and I am as well."

She shivered and hugged herself. "How do I know I can trust you? What you're saying could all be for Longie."

"I swear to God!"

"So does every heretic."

"Please, Arietta, listen to what I'm saying—and tell me what you know about the two murders."

But she wasn't forthcoming. He could see that the only way to make her believe him was to win back the old confidence between them.

"Would you like a cup of tea?" she asked. "I would."

Catching the attention of a waiter, she requested a pot of green tea. While waiting, they again lapsed into an uneasy silence.

"What are you thinking?" he asked, not wishing to be stared into making some frivolous statement.

Looking at her folded hands in her lap, she said softly, "I was remembering the woods outside of Cape May."

"Idyllic . . . perfect."

"If you're really free of Longie . . ."

"I am."

"Then it all depends on you."

"What?"

The waiter brought a tray with a pot, saucers, and cups. As Arietta sipped her drink, she brazenly seduced Jay with her bewitching eyes as she had so often done. He knew that look all too well: You can have me if you're up to it.

"Arietta, I would like nothing more than for us to . . ."

She interrupted. "Would you marry me?"

Speechless and bewildered, he could see in her eyes that, for Arietta, his muteness belied his disavowal of Longie.

"I thought so," she said sadly.

"But I haven't answered."

"Yes, you have, Jay."

"What would it mean?" he asked incoherently, trying to gain time.

"Marriage?" She downed her tea in three gulps. "That you would stand by me—and mine. That you would be loyal, even if not sexually faithful, though that would be nice, but always loyal."

His head was spinning. He had neither the intention nor the means to marry; and in all honesty, having no precise idea what she meant by loyalty, he had misgivings. It sounded ominous and strangely illegal.

"While you think over my proposition—I trust, you realize, that *I'm* the one asking you to marry *me*—I'll just use the ladies' room."

Fifteen minutes later, he asked a woman hotel clerk to look in on Arietta, to make sure she hadn't taken ill. When she returned, she said that the lavatory was vacant.

On a hunch, he called Mr. Wilkinson's office. Yes, Piero had been there and left. How long ago? In the last twenty minutes. Doubtless Mr. M. had arranged to pick up Arietta somewhere outside the hotel at an approximate time.

Proceeding on his supposition that the Maglioccos were heading for Milwaukee, Jay and T wearily packed their belongings and once again hit the road, lodging at the usual cabins and cottages. They drove through Des Moines, Iowa City, and Davenport. On discovering that the opera house was featuring Gilbert and Sullivan's *Pirates of Penzance*, they stayed the night, though the only accommodations they could find were in a fetid tent camp; then they continued to Moline, Sterling, and Rochelle. Before Jay turned north to Rockford, T asked him if he'd mind dropping him off in Chicago.

"That's where my niece Janice and her daughter, Melanie, live. I'll give you their number. You can pick me up on the way back."

Jay drove through Chicago to a brown one-story brick house with a large stoop. A young black girl skipping rope in front stopped when T called her name. As T emerged from the car, she hugged him and then shot up the steps, yelling for her mother, who a moment later flew out the door. Jay could see that T had come among loved ones; so after being introduced to the family, he left.

The roads out of Chicago teemed with the dispossessed and the homeless, living in and out of their rattletrap autos and trucks. In the gullies and next to culverts, families sat holding up signs that read: "No money for gas or oil or food. Please help!" Ragged-looking children sat on their parents' laps, presumably to induce travelers to take note of their condition and stop. In fact, he did pull over for one family because the mother and two children, lying on a threadbare blanket, appeared dead. The mother, crippled by polio, could only crawl; her husband held out a bony hand and begged for relief. Jay slipped them a deuce and thought the man would die from ecstasy. The poor man embraced Jay's legs and started kissing his shoes, to Jay's painful embarrassment. He remembered what T had said when they passed through some desperately poor areas in Iowa, "America ain't all that it's cracked up to be." Jay had replied, "Not for the poor." To which T had added, "And the fat cats don't seem to notice."

Crossing into Wisconsin, Jay made for Milwaukee. West of Racine, he saw some men striking a local cheese factory and soliciting money. He gave them a few bucks, noting the paradoxical contrast between the rich chernozem fields and the wretched workers. The prosperous farmlands would have led one to think that the Great Depression had never touched this part of the world. But the towns themselves told a different story: the usual boarded-up stores, decay, half-empty streets, and ragged people out of work.

He had never been to Milwaukee, the beer city on Lake Michigan. Approaching it from the south, he stopped at a small grocery in a Polish neighborhood to grab a bottle of soda and look at a telephone book. He left the car engine running. The effluvium of sausage pervaded the store. In a corner stood a religious icon with a votary light. The counterman saw him staring at it and said, "The black Madonna"; "of Czestochowa," the man added. "She's sacred to all Poles." Not Jewish ones, Jay thought. Thumbing through the directory, he found a Reinhard Gehrig Jr. at 334 Sixteenth Street. The telephone number matched the one on Longie's list. In Sea Girt, George McManus had mentioned a "Mrs.," but women usually took their husbands' names. The grocer eagerly asked if Jay wanted anything else, recommending the cheese, which he bought. A surly motorcycle policeman greeted him at the car.

"This your automobile, sonny?"

"Yes."

The cop gratuitously sneered, "Well, I knew it didn't belong to no darkie, 'cause those guys have to steal 'em to afford 'em."

The logic of that statement caused Jay to blink. Why would stolen cars be less expensive to maintain than ones purchased legitimately? Undoubtedly the bull meant to say that the only way a black person could obtain a car would be through theft. But when Jay thought of some of the Monarch baseball players and the chariots T told him they had once driven, even that statement did not stand up to scrutiny.

"Got the papers to prove it? And while you're at it, let me see your license."

As Jay pulled out his wallet, he intended to show surprise at the absence of the ownership slip, but when he saw the cop eyeing his cash, he peeled off a fiver, folded it in half, and put the license inside. The cop never uttered a word as he pocketed the money.

"What's the best way to get to 334 Sixteenth Street?"

The cop said, "Follow me, I'm goin' off duty and headin' to that end of town." Jay slid in behind the wheel. Ten minutes later, they found themselves passing shops with German names—Helmick's Bakery, Stoskopf's Shoe Repair, Meyerhof's Hardware—and at the intersection of Fond du Lac, Center, and Twenty-Seventh Street, the cop pointed Jay in the right direction. When Jay asked about small hotels in the area, the cop suggested the Decatur, told Jay how to find it, and drove off with a friendly wave.

The hotel, a small place two doors away from the Wittenberg Tavern, greeted Jay in the person of Francis Glenn Irwin, a bald, bespectacled doctor, who subsequently explained that keeping an inn could make him more money than working as a physician. Jay had to admit that it gave him some comfort to think that if he took ill here, he would have someone on the premises who could attend to him immediately. Doc, as Jay and the other five guests called him, had extremely large hands, a cherubic ashy face, and a shuffling gait. The sawbones never seemed in a hurry, even when a neighbor would come to the hotel and ask him to assist with a birth or emergency in the neighborhood. His wife, a dark-haired, frail retiring woman, had a slight squint. Generous and gracious people, they apologized for lodging Jay on the second floor in the back room, the only vacancy, overlooking a tenement building that, Dr. Irwin said discreetly, "occasionally provides views that are not for genteel eyes."

Before dinner, Jay walked around the neighborhood, composed mostly of white bungalows on small, well-maintained lots, probably no deeper than forty or fifty feet. Stopping at the Wittenberg for a shot of Scotch with a free glass of beer as a chaser, he stayed long enough to have a meal. The liquor culture and German influence were much in evidence. A young woman in Tyrolean dress plucked a zither using the fingers of one hand and a plectrum with the other, while a waiter in a long white apron served sauerbraten with the suds, and a few lively people danced the polka. He heard more German spoken than English and saw several men reading the *Deutsche Zeitung*. From an adjoining booth, he overheard two guys expressing opinions of the kind that had inspired Longie to send his boys to break up Bund meetings with baseball bats.

"If we had a Hitler, instead of a Roosevelt, this Depression would have been over a long time ago. Just look at all the Jews in FDR's cabinet."

"They belong in concentration camps. If we could round them up, and all the pansies and Communists, we'd have this country on the road to recovery."

"Amen."

Jay paid for his meal and slipped out the restaurant without voicing his anger. Back at the hotel, he went directly to his room and sat down on his coffin-sized bed with its hammock mattress to ponder strategy. With only the name Reinhard Gehrig to go on, he decided to cruise by the house to see if the Waterhouse was parked nearby. Doc Irwin gave him a key to the front door, and he clambered into his car. Creeping slowly down Sixteenth Street past number 334, he saw nothing untoward—no car, no bodies, no clues. Step number two: call the house. His watch indicated a few minutes past eight. Although his mother told him never to call anyone after eight o'clock, he figured he could bend her rule. Driving to a gas station, he told the attendant to fill her up, eased himself into the outside telephone booth, and called the Gehrig house. A woman with a German accent answered.

"Mrs. Gehrig?"

"Yes?"

"I hope you're the person I want. I'm a friend of Arietta Magliocco's. She gave me your number. I'm passing through town and thought I would call. I hoped you could tell me her whereabouts."

"It's late! You have the wrong number," she said abruptly and hung up.

(Mom, you were right.)

He returned to the hotel. Before turning off the light, he began to reread Bernard Shaw's *Major Barbara*, a fitting play for difficult times. But his mind kept wandering. The woman on the phone had acknowledged her name, but had she told him the truth? The Maglioccos were most likely hiding at her house. For a moment, he wished that he could just barge into number 334, look around, and make his escape with Arietta and Piero. He kicked himself for not acting as if he knew Arietta was there and just asking Mrs. Gehrig to call her to the phone. Too late now.

The next morning, arriving before seven, he waited outside 334 Sixteenth Street. When a man left, he followed him to a hunting goods store around the corner from the Schwabenhof

Restaurant, on Twelfth and Teutonia. The shop had the usual kinds of mounted wall displays: antlered deer and elk, stuffed fish, photographs of hunters standing next to a fallen bear, and anglers standing on a boat surrounded by their catch. Two things caught his eye. The first was a framed photograph of an older woman who resembled the picture he had seen in the Magliocco house of Arietta's mother. Surely this was the third sister, Agna. The second was a document taped to the cash register certifying that Mr. Reinhard Gehrig Jr. was a member of the Friends of the New Germany. The dwarfish round-faced fellow in attendance wore an ill-fitting faded brown seersucker suit that had seen too many washings.

"Yes?" the little man asked dourly, tugging at his lapels.

"I'd like to speak to Mr. Gehrig."

"He's currently on the phone."

A minute later, a door at the end of the shop opened and a balding martinet, with a paunch and bespectacled colorless eyes, entered, presumably Mrs. Gehrig's son.

"Frumpf," ordered the martial voice, flecked with a German accent, "the toilet is blocked again. See to it."

Mr. Frumpf said deferentially, "Sir, this gentleman wants a word with you."

Mr. Gehrig, peremptory and probably no more than twenty-five, was already losing the muscle tone in his face, which had begun to sag. His bulbous lips reminded Jay of some Negro horn players. From his pasty face, the incipient Nazi removed his thick-lensed glasses and said brusquely, "Yes?"

"I'm interested in a pistol, but I don't know how to go about selecting one. I figured it's always best to talk to an expert . . . about guns and politics."

Mr. Gehrig scrutinized Jay as if taking his measure and replied, "How right you are," and then asked, "You German?"

"Wagner. My parents come from Hamburg."

"Mine from Stuttgart. If you like, you can call me Reinhard."

With this information, Jay decided to take a chance. "My parents live in Newark. They knew a woman from Stuttgart, a Kristina Magliocco. If I recall correctly, they said she died young, leaving a daughter."

Mr. Gehrig again removed his glasses, wiped them, adjusted them to his nose, and said indifferently, "I don't know the name."

From his wallet, Jay removed his New Jersey membership card for the Friends and placed it on the counter. Mr. Gehrig reached for it tentatively as if it might bite, and then visibly relaxed. A smile played around his lips.

"You didn't say . . . Mr. Wagner."

"One can't be too safe."

"Exactly! But why do you ask about her?"

"We used to attend Friends meetings in Irvington."

"That explains why you chose to be so indirect."

"In our business . . ." Jay deliberately broke off.

"Yes, secrecy never betrays."

Fearing that they were wandering from the subject, Jay continued. "Now about Arietta . . ."

Mr. Gehrig reflected briefly and then said, "My cousin. *Ach*, such a beautiful girl. She's visiting."

"Is there any chance of my seeing her?"

"Impossible, she's preparing to go to California."

"I trust Mr. Magliocco will be accompanying her."

"Of course. Such a close family."

"You wouldn't happen to know her Friends contact in California?" Jay said casually, pretending to be knowledgeable about such matters.

"You'd have to ask my mother. But she and I are at odds."

Desperate, Jay took a shot in the dark. "With Mr. M.'s interests, I'd guess Southern California."

Mr. Gehrig laughed heartily, the first time he had done so. "You are so right! Movies and gangsters. It all fits, doesn't it?"

"Like a tailored suit."

Hoping to encounter Arietta, Jay expressed an interest in meeting with the Friends the next day. "If so, where?"

Reinhard opened a small black book and studied it. "Why don't we plan to have dinner around the corner, at the Schwabenhof. Say around eight. I'll bring along some friends, for the *gemütlichkeit.*"

"Bring Arietta. It will be wonderful to see her again. Tell her Mr. Wagner sends his regards . . . Richard Wagner."

How dumb could he be? At that moment it struck him that she might well remember that name as the one he'd used to join the Friends.

"I'll ask."

"On second thought, don't. It's best to keep our contacts to a minimum . . . until the new order . . . but you understand."

"Not a word," Reinhard said and grinned as if they had just entered into a vast conspiracy.

"What do you need a pistol for, Mr. Wagner?"

"Protection. Prowlers and that sort of thing."

"Then I recommend the model P-35 Browning. It's a military pistol, made in Belgium. First-rate."

Jay purchased the gun, exchanged pleasantries with Mr. Gehrig, and started for the front door. Had Jay left a minute or two earlier, he wouldn't have seen the man approaching the shop. Through the window he recognized Cauliflower. Placing his package on the floor, he bent down and tied his shoelaces as Rolf Hahne entered and walked past him. Jay quickly left. His hands were shaking and his head spinning, so he went around the corner for a beer at the Schwabenhof. As he sipped the bitter ale, he tried to sort out his disparate thoughts. Young Reinhard seemed to be in charge; his father, Jay guessed, had died and left his son the store. He wondered if the mother shared her boy's political views. If she did not, perhaps he could use that as a lever to induce her to put Jay in contact with Arietta. But how?

He went down the street to a public telephone booth and called the Gehrig residence. She answered the phone.

"Mrs. Gehrig, this is Police Detective Gerhardt Mueller. I'm calling about your son and his participation in an organization that we have some concerns about, the Friends of the New Germany. I wonder if I could come to the house to speak to you . . ."

She cut him off. "I have nothing to do with those Nazi swine!" and slammed down the receiver.

Conclusion: Mother and son did not see eye to eye on politics. Anything else? Reinhard lived at home and probably supported her. The Maglioccos were temporarily hiding at 334, and Mr. M. was parking his car elsewhere. But if Jay waited outside the Gehrig house and Arietta and her father failed to appear, what then? But having no other choice, he parked a few doors away and sat peering over a paper. Around noon, a police car materialized, slowly moving in his direction. Jay guessed that a neighbor had probably complained about a fellow loitering in his car out front. Pulling away from the curb, he drove around town and took in some of the sights: the city hall, a brewery, a small art museum. That evening, he caught a showing of Mary Astor in *Red Hot Tires*.

The next morning, he awoke around five, found a small restaurant, ordered some waffles with maple syrup, drove to Sixteenth Street, and parked, but this time in front of a different house. Around nine, he saw the Waterhouse coming down the street. The driver parked in front of number 334. Jay could not see anyone else in the car. Perhaps that was best. He would be able to confront Mr. M. and explain his concerns. One of his legs began to shake uncontrollably. A man with cotton knickers and matching lid exited the auto and briskly strode to the front door. At first, Jay thought his eyes had deceived him. Not until he had a close look at the man in plus fours was he convinced that this fellow was not Piero Magliocco. Perhaps this guy garaged the car and was now bringing it to Mr. M. for his use. Jay approached him. With his heart thumping wildly, he said, "Pardon me, sir, I'm looking for a friend who used to drive this same car."

The fellow jerked back his head and squinted as if he could see objects or people only at a distance. "Oh, you mean Mr. Magliocco?"

"Yes."

"A fine old gentleman."

Jay wondered about the stilted reply and the adjective. The man looked at least ten years older than Piero, but Jay just nodded in agreement and said, "Will he and his daughter be here this morning?"

The fellow replied with what Jay could now identify as a slight English accent. "I should hardly think so."

"Why's that?"

"He sold the motor to me, I gathered, to pay for train tickets, and to cover his expenses in California. Agna Gehrig and I are old friends."

Jay's head whirled, and the earth beneath his feet shook. Certain that he had misheard, he asked, "Would you kindly repeat what you said?"

"Mr. Gehrig introduced me. Reinhard knew that I was in the market for a Waterhouse. It was all rather sudden."

"Cal . . . uh . . . fornia?" Jay stuttered.

"Piero, he had located a job there and needed to leave at once."

"But he loved that car," Jay mumbled to no one in particular.

"Understandably. A wonderful motor car."

"He sold it," Jay repeated reflexively.

"Good price, too," the gent said. "Must go, Agna expects me."

"You wouldn't happen to know when Piero intended to leave?"

"As a matter of fact, I think today."

Jay thanked him, darted for his car, and raced to the train station. Leaping from the Ford, he dashed for the platforms. A ticket taker at one of the gates, seeing his anxiety, volunteered to help.

"I'm looking for the train to California."

"Which one? We have two, a morning train that has already left for Los Angeles via Chicago and another leaving this afternoon for San Francisco with a stop in Minneapolis."

Having no choice, Jay hung around the station to wait for the afternoon train. When the San Francisco boarding was announced, he stood out of sight watching the gate. Arietta and her father most likely had left on the morning train for Los Angeles. A moment before the gate closed, a man came rushing up, waving a ticket: Cauliflower.

Using a station phone, Jay called Janice, who said T had taken her daughter to the movies. He left a message: He would be picking him up to take him to sunny California, the land of citrus groves and walnuts and cotton. If T wanted to know why, she should tell him that the two people they wanted had gone to Los Angeles. The woman on the other end of the line let out a low whistle and said, "I wish you'd take me."

Of course, Jay had no idea whether the Maglioccos would be staying right in L.A. They could have taken a train there but migrated elsewhere, like Pasadena or Santa Monica or the San Fernando Valley. And yet in light of Mr. M.'s comment that the only job he'd prefer to rum-running would be the movie industry, and Reinhard Gehrig's reference to Los Angeles, Jay had a hunch that father and daughter would gravitate to the Hollywood area.

Returning to the hotel, he gathered his belongings. As he drove south to Chicago, he briefly wondered what Reinhard would think when he failed to show. Shortly after crossing the border into Illinois, he picked up a hitchhiker, an elderly man with rheumy eyes, wispy hair and beard, and a large pouch of loose skin under his jaw that brought to mind a turkey gobbler. The man said he needed to cover ten miles and felt much obliged that Jay had stopped for him. The two of them exchanged introductions, Jay Klug and Stine Becker. On his way home from following itinerant jobs in Wisconsin, Mr. Becker explained that his wife and three boys used to travel with him until that proved too costly.

"Now she and the kids stay with her mother while I travel around looking for work."

"What kind?"

"I'm not particular, if it pays."

Traveling through small towns that had little to show for their devotion to the Protestant ethic, Jay deduced from the number of American flags mounted on front porches that army recruiters found most of their fodder in these hamlets, where the out-of-work young men eagerly signed on for regular meals, clothes, shoes, and a small allowance. Although Mr. Becker's age would have kept him from service, Jay could imagine his sons joining up in response to the local patriotism and the promise of a new life.

"Do you normally hitchhike to get around?"

"Depends. If I can, I ride the rattlers . . . freight trains."

"I'm headed to Los Angeles after a stop in Chicago."

"Route 66. Just take it all the way, from Chicago to Springfield to St. Louis, Tulsa, Oklahoma City, Amarillo, Albuquerque, Flagstaff, L.A. Before I lost my job to a fellow a lot younger than me and willing to take a lot less money, I used to be a truck driver. I know 66 like the palm of my hand." Mr. Becker opened the road map that Jay had wedged on the top of the dashboard and studied it. Running his index finger along the black-lined highways made him appear like a man feeling the pulse of a nation. "Hardly a one I haven't traveled." Mr. Becker folded the map and leaned his head back against the seat, murmuring, "Old 66. Some folks call it the mother road. I call it the river of rue."

The old guy then launched into an amazing aside. "Sixty-six is the path of people in flight, refugees from dust and shrinking land, from the thunder of tractors and shrinking ownership, from the desert's slow northward invasion, from the twisting winds that howl up out of Texas, from the floods that bring no richness to the land and steal what little richness is there. From all of these, the people are in flight, and they come into 66 from the tributary side roads, from the wagon tracks and the rutted country roads. Sixty-six is the mother road, the road to flight."

Jay sat speechless. What can you say in the presence of such talk? But as he drove, he kept stealing glances at Mr. Becker, hoping that he would lean back and again become reflective. No such luck. At Heywood Junction, Jay dropped him off and continued on into Chicago, retracing the route he'd taken when he had left T behind.

Janice met him at the door. Jay stayed for both dinner and the night. Over pork chops and sauerkraut, she related how her husband had been in the meat-packing industry and had died of blood poisoning contracted from some contaminated beef. Her daughter, Melanie, sat listening.

"He stood in a line with a lot of other hog butchers cutting the meat carcasses as they came through. I always worried about the sharp knives they used and the speed of the line. But those things didn't kill him, some disease did. Even though he wore rubber gloves, his arms were bare. He had a cut on his arm, and it must have rubbed up against the infected slab. The doctors gave him sulfur drugs, but his temperature just kept rising till his body burned up. I asked the Cudahy people for money to help me and the girl. They said no. Without T and some others, I don't know how I would've got by. Lucky for me that Melvin bought this house when he could. Otherwise we'd be living with kin."

After washing the dishes, Jay discussed the impending trip. He felt that the leads he had come up with left them looking for a mote in a sunset.

T observed that "without somethin' like the names we got from Mr. George McManus, I think we're startin' out on a fool's errand."

"Ignis fatuus," Jay mumbled.

"What in the hell's that?"

Jay told T the story of a professor he had once studied with, Ralph Cohen, whose vocabulary kept classes breathless. One day he uttered the phrase "ignis fatuus," and when they all looked blank, Professor Cohen explained its meaning and told them that someday they would have an occasion to use it.

"So what does it mean, you still ain't said?"

"I'll give you the short answer: a deceptive hope, a delusion."

"That's exactly what Los Angeles is, a dreamland. I played ball there once. The place ain't hardly real. So why go chasing after the Maglioccos in a place that's just all smoke and mirrors?"

They argued until Jay reminded him of Longie's generosity. The money he'd shower on them for finding Arietta would beat fixing potholes in Newark.

"Yeah," T said, "government work ain't gonna make a man rich, and worse of all, it ain't even steady."

Hitting the road early with only about four hours of sleep, they left before Janice and her daughter awoke. T slipped a tenner into Janice's purse. Driving south through Springfield, they crossed the Mississippi River, flowing lazy and muddy, entered St. Louis, and continued southwest through a corner of Kansas and into Oklahoma. Neither of them was prepared for what they saw in the Sooner state, where single-crop farming had impoverished the soil, leaving it to utter ruination from the pitiless droughts and the wind. Some people called it the Dust Bowl, but Jay figured a better name would have been the Valley of Ashes.

As usual some cottages and cabins turned them away because of T's skin color, so they pulled into a tent camp. Without sleeping or cooking gear of their own, they rented some from the manager. But having no food, they were reduced to asking other campers if they might sell them a can of beans and some bread with a few bacon strips. No luck. Jay told T that they could stand to go without a meal; they were still better off than some of the other campers. A rain of locusts suddenly blew in from the south, causing them to beat a hasty retreat to their tent. As they stomped on the bugs, a middle-aged woman with pale blue eyes, leathery skin, gray hair, and discolored teeth pushed her head through the door flap and asked if they would like to share a meal with her family. Hungrily accepting her offer, they followed her to her campsite. Three tents housed thirteen people: the woman, called Ma, her husband, her parents, her brother, six children, a son-in-law, and a preacher man by the name of Casy. Even though her group clearly had more members than any other, she insisted it would be no trouble to feed two extra mouths.

Using a small kerosene stove and pan, she brought a wad of bacon grease to a sizzle, added dough and taters and then some greens and onions. They ate with bent silverware on chipped plates. Jay suspected that his parents would have gagged at the greasy-smelling concoction, but he thought it tasted like manna from heaven.

After the meal, Ma said, "Since no one said grace before the eatin', Preacher, how's about you shoutin' up a thanks to the Lord for sendin' us a full stomach."

What Ma called a full stomach, Jay regarded as a scant mouthful. Other members of the family must have felt the same, as they took crusts of bread and sopped up the last bits of grease in the pan.

Casy explained for the sake of the two guests that he had given up preaching but in appreciation for the meal would say a few words. "We thank those responsible for the growin' of the fruits of the earth and the pasturin' of animals for what we've just et. Their hard labors, and that of others, keep us goin', even though the rich foxes try to spoil the vineyards. Someday, though, when we harvest the grapes, the people, I pray, will rise up in wrath against the spoilers. Amen."

The family chimed in and fell to telling stories. Jay gathered from some of them that the oldest child, Tom, had done time in Oklahoma for killing a man in self-defense. Ma's son-in-law, married to Rose, babbled stupidly about the money to be made once they arrived in California. His lack of sense made him think that enrolling in a night-school class and learning how to repair radios would enable him to afford a home with electrical appliances in Hollywood. Similarly, Ma's second son, Al, resolved to find a job in a garage fixing cars and to spend his money on lovely long-legged aspiring actresses. From his talk, Jay concluded that Al knew a great deal about engines and was the person responsible for keeping the family truck running, an old Hudson that looked as if any moment it might quit.

Ma, who provided the moral strength of the family, urged T, who had briefly played baseball in Los Angeles, to tell what they could expect to find there.

"The city fathers call it the City of Angels, but I think of it as the city of dreams. Even then, back in the twenties, all the failed and frustrated folks from around the country had started to move to the coast, 'specially hopeful actors. What I remember was the weather, the sameness of it, and the orchards and the movie studios abuildin' out toward the beach. Them hills overlookin' the city on one side and the valley on the other sure were pretty. The best town of all, though, was up the coast a bit, Santa Barbara. Now that place, if you had enough money, would be my idea of landin' in paradise. From the city, you can see up on the hillside a mission datin' back to the Spaniards. Hikin' up to that church, I got to speak to the padre. One of my sweetest memories is of that man in his brown robes and rope belt."

Back in their tent, Jay asked what the padre had said. "That God was color blind."

In the morning, as they loaded the car, Jay could see Ma and her family packing up their Hudson truck. She waved. Jay folded a fiver in his palm and asked T to join him in saying goodbye to these kind folks. When they shook hands with the old lady, Jay transferred the money and closed his hand around hers, whispering, "Promise you won't look until we've left the camp." She reluctantly agreed. They thanked the family for their hospitality, shook hands all around, and once again took to the road. The Texas panhandle lay ahead.

They stopped at a campground outside of Amarillo, and T set up his checker board, as he had done many times before, to earn a handful of change. As usual, Jay hustled players, going from one tent and cooking pit to another announcing the start of the game. On this particular evening, they attracted about twenty players, each good, Jay figured, for at least a dime. What he didn't count on were the cops showing up with lights flashing and night sticks waving. Hauled off to jail for breaking Texas gambling laws, T and Jay were questioned about their age, place of birth, residence, last job, education, name of father, maiden name of mother, length of stay in Amarillo, destination. Jay wondered what all these questions had to do with gambling. Eventually, they were turned over to the turnkey, who told them to follow him. They found themselves in a cell measuring about ten-by-fifteen feet. Five men were already in the cage when they entered, and by midnight the number had increased to ten. Everyone lay on the cement floor in all sorts of positions. Jay was doubled like a jackknife; T was trying to sleep sitting up; and a hobo felt no reluctance to use Jay's stomach as a footrest. The last two men who entered the cell arrived drunk and, for want of space, were forced to sleep with their heads against the toilet bowl.

Well past midnight, Jay felt someone trying to take his watch, one of the two drunks. When he shoved him aside, the man grew truculent and struck Jay with his boot. A second later, T had him in a neck lock. His companion tried to help him, but T kicked the man in the groin, ending the night's adventure and attracting the turnkey, who proved susceptible to a bribe. The bull led them out the back door of the jailhouse into a darkened street but not before hitting T with a nightstick on the back of his head, a lacerating blow that exacerbated the ones administered by Rolf Hahne and caused T no little blood and pain.

As they approached their car, they saw a drummer and his tart, whose giggle sounded strange in the perfect deadness of the hour, and a family sleeping in a doorway, their two young children hunched over with their faces hidden in the mother's skirts. What dreams obsessed the parents? Probably dreams that swallowed up the night. Reaching the car, they drove west toward New Mexico with its beautiful mesas and dry desert stretches. Slowed by the sea of souls in every conceivable conveyance making their way down 66, they gave up any idea of making good time. Vehicles lined the road for miles. It looked as if all of America was resettling from east to west. Reaching Albuquerque two days later in the late afternoon, they slept on the outskirts of town. A blistering sun greeted them in the morning. Before setting out, T bought some curios and an Indian blanket for Janice and Melanie. The desperately tedious drive through New Mexico and Arizona ended with their arrival at the Colorado River and an agricultural station checking for plants. By the time they rolled into Needles, California, where they luck-ily found lodging in a tent camp, T had just about consumed his second and last bottle of Energy Elixir. Perhaps the stuff partially worked: T hadn't become a white man, but Jay's faithful friend had manhandled two thieving drunks and kept him from harm. Unloading their gear from the car, they heard familiar accents: Ma and her family. Although they had left Oklahoma before Ma, the endless queue of cars and their arrest had put the two men only a short ways behind.

Sitting on the ground in front of their tents, they wheezed from the aridity in Needles. Ma miraculously produced a bunch of ba-nanas and offered them some. As they reached for the fruit, out of the darkness came cacophonous sirens, the wailing sound of police cars. A minute later, four state troopers appeared, angrily question-ing their intentions in California. The family explained how they had left Oklahoma in the hope of gaining employment as harvest-ers in the fruit orchards and cotton fields.

"There ain't no work," said one trooper.

"You Okies are just shiftless bums," said a second.

A third brandished a flashlight that he seemed to enjoy shining in their eyes; and a fourth stood to one side watching amusedly while sucking on a toothpick.

When Tom, Ma's oldest son, defended their right to enter the state, the third man repeatedly shoved his flashlight into Tom's chest and snarled, "You tellin' me what I can and can't tell worth-less drifters like you?" The trooper shone the light right in Tom's eyes and waited for an answer.

The reply came swiftly, but not as the bully expected. Tom grabbed the light and with one swift blow crowned the guy, who dropped like a limp john. In the darkness, his three companions reached for their pistols. Immediately, Tom wrestled one of them to the ground as T and Casy jumped the other two. Curses, blows, and grunts sounded. With all four troopers on the ground, Ma's other kids weighed in, as did Jay. Somehow, the four police pistols ended up in Jay's possession. Racing to the river, he hid in the reeds and buried the guns in the mud, keeping his own. In the confusion, Tom and Casy and T also took refuge in the thick tangle of reeds. For several minutes, an eerie silence prevailed, and then they heard gunfire. The troopers had returned to their patrol cars for shotguns, which they trained on the river. When the fusillade ended and the cop cars drove off, Tom and Casy moved further downstream. T, who had hidden next to Jay, still lay face down. Jay tried to rouse him. But T did not respond to his touch. Turning him over, Jay saw blood oozing at the site of the injuries he'd suffered in Cape May and Amarillo. Had a shotgun pellet found its mark and worsened the wounds? Peeking out of T's hip pocket was the unfinished bottle of Energy Elixir. Jay trickled some into T's mouth and prayed that it would awaken him; then he pressed his ear to T's chest, but he failed to detect a heartbeat. Choking with sadness and guilt, he cradled T's body in his arms and cried unabashedly. Had he not asked T to accompany him to California, his friend would still be alive. Innumerable memories crowded his mind: the deli and the checkers and the Bible debates with Leonora and the drive across country and the places that turned them away and those that invited them in and the Kansas City Monarchs and of course Janice, whom he would have to call to tell about the death of her uncle and to whom Jay would forward T's belongings. Later that night, by which time Tom and Casy had returned, they buried him in a marshy spot at a bend in the river, and the preacher said a few words over the makeshift grave.

"Death ought to be reserved for the legions of selfish and mean people in charge of this world. Kindly men, like T, deserve to live on, not just in memory but in life, so as we can enjoy their many gifts. Why good people die young remains a mystery. Black or white, the just will stand before the Lord, one color, in His radiant light. And if'n I make it to heaven, the first question I intend askin' the Lord is 'How come you don't rid the world of the bad uns and keep alive the beautiful?'"

On a late afternoon in July, after enduring the dreary expanse of southeastern California, Jay reached a valley of endless fruit and nut groves: apricot, orange, lemon, avocado, and walnut. Los Angeles, indeed, seemed like the City of Angels.

8

The Franklin Arms, a small residential hotel just off Wilshire Boulevard, provided Jay with a splendid view of manicured grass lawns and swaying palm trees. But for the depressing sight of homeless people, he would have thought that he had arrived in Eden. The lush smell of gardenias competed with orange blossoms, suggesting southern corruption and the possibility of all manner of romance. From the mountaintops to the sandy beaches stretched Los Angeles and environs, a fecund land waiting to be ravished. It was said that in this city the impossible could happen.

And indeed, serendipity struck when outside a hardware store, Jay ran into John "Jinx" Cooper, an Englishman who used to buy from Honest Ike and now owned Sierra Powder Puffs on Adams Boulevard. Out of friendship for Jay's father, Mr. Cooper willingly hired him as a pattern cutter, enabling him to support himself.

The hotel staff, most of them would-be thespians, kept Jay current on the Hollywood gossip and, when word got around that he tipped generously, delivered his groceries. They also arranged for him to have a private telephone so that he could regularly call his mother to ask about the family business, which was entering bankruptcy. At least once a week, he received a call, not from his mother but from someone else. He would be called to the hall tele-phone, and the feminine voice on the other end would ask, "Jay?" He would reply "Yes," and the person would hang up. From the accent, he inferred the calls were placed by Francesca Bronzina; and from time to time, he would see in the hotel parking lot a yel-low Studebaker, which Longie, during their last conversation, said she'd recently bought to fit in.

Evenings he walked along Wilshire to enjoy the cool night air and the scents of the city. His perambulations led him past the glamorous Ambassador Hotel housing the Coconut Grove, cur-rently hosting Tommy Dorsey's band and featuring Glenn Miller. They also gave him a chance to reflect on how one goes about find-ing two people among half a million. His first few weeks in Los An-geles he tried several ploys. He ran an advertisement in three of the local papers asking for help locating two lost friends. He stopped by several government hiring agencies to learn if the Maglioccos had signed on with them. He called the movie studios and asked the same question. He read the newspapers to see if they had run an ad, like so many others, seeking work. He even interviewed a private eye on how to proceed with his search, a fruitless endeavor that cost him a fiver.

Seven weeks passed, and he was still working as a cutter. Then, an opportunity to get back into journalism presented itself at the end of July, when all the local papers were headlining what promised to be a juicy story, the actress Mary Astor's custody case. Astor's complaint stated that at the time of her divorce from Dr. Franklyn Thorpe (April 12, 1935), Thorpe had threatened to ruin her screen career unless she agreed to a judgment awarding him their four-year-old daughter, Marylyn. Now, fifteen months later, she was suing for custody and seeking to change the divorce decree to an annulment, claiming that at the time of her marriage to Dr. Thorpe, he had a common-law wife, Lillian Lawton Miles, a comely blonde widow with a saccharine southern accent, named as a codefendant. All the hotel staff buzzed about the case. Within a few days, people were lining up, lunch satchels and knitting bags in hand, to witness the court proceedings. Jay tried to attend one of the sessions to see the lissome Titian-haired beauty in person. He recalled Arietta saying that her mother, Kristina, had once met Miss Astor's parents in New York and hoped that the link would lure Arietta to the courtroom. Alas, thrill seekers queued the night before to see the trial, and Jay had no hope of gaining entrance unless he wanted to sleep on the sidewalk and wait for the bailiff to open the doors in the morning.

A few days later, however, when the Los Angeles newspapers hinted that Dr. Thorpe's attorneys might introduce into the trial, as evidence of Astor's immoral conduct and maternal unfitness, her two-volume diary—reputed to be an illuminating record of her love life before, during, and after her marriage to Dr. Thorpe—it occurred to Jay to call the *Newark Evening News* to ask if they would secure him a press pass and pay him a salary. His editor said the newspaper could get full coverage from the Associated Press, United Press, or International News Service, all of which the *Evening News* had used before. Although Jay knew that star reporters, people like Roger Dakin of the *New York Daily News* and Sheila Graham for the North American Newspaper Association, would be covering the proceedings, he pleaded that he could fashion the story to fit the *Evening News* readership.

The conversation would have ended with a "No" had Jay not mentioned his old friendship with Jean Harlow and his plan to reconnect and induce her to comment on her friend Mary Astor and on what one paper called "the worst case of dynamite ever to reach Hollywood." The editor agreed and told Jay to include not only Jean's comments and all the salacious details but also descriptions of Mary's dresses "for the ladies back home." For safety's sake, Jay requested that his name not be used.

Forty-eight hours later, Western Union delivered a money order and credentials. Now he could leave Sierra Powder Puffs and join the other members of the fourth estate behind the heavy oaken courtroom doors and, unlike the milling mob attempting to find seats, take his in the jury box, reserved for the press, ready to streak for a telephone should mention of a name or a situation mean a news flash.

To celebrate Jay's good fortune, Jinx Cooper took him to the Brown Derby Restaurant for lunch. How Jinx managed to obtain a reservation was a mystery, because a table at the Brown Derby was the hottest seat in town. Jay wore his one summer suit and straw hat. They had a good view of the other diners but not the front door. As they started eating, Jay felt a hand brush his back. Before he could turn, the person swept past him. It was a woman. Her companion followed a few steps behind. When they arrived at their table, she pointed him to a seat that made it impossible for Jay to see his face. But Jay saw hers. It was Francesca Bronzina. During the course of the meal, the man entered the lavatory. On his exit, Jay recognized Rolf Hahne.

So Francesca had finally decided to beard the Nazi. Jay wondered how she had found him. A number of pro-Nazi groups in Los Angeles advertised their meetings. Perhaps they had run into each other at one, where she had passed herself off as a believer in the cause and capitalized on her good looks and acting ability. All Jay could think of was the cobra and the mongoose. Would she be able to stay out of his reach? Or would Jay shortly be reading about a woman's body found with her throat slit?

On leaving the restaurant, Jay made it a point not to be seen by Cauliflower, dissolving into the crowd waiting at the front to be seated.

Jay's first day in court, he looked around and saw James Cagney, George Raft, Paulette Goddard, Franchot Tone, Edward G. Robinson, and the bandleader Horace Heidt. Everyone stood when Superior Judge Goodwin "Goody" J. Knight entered. A youthful thin-lipped man with a splayed nose that looked as if he had taken one on the nozzle, he was presiding without benefit of jury, a request agreed to by both parties. Whether or not the judge knew it, all of Hollywood was counting on him to preserve filmland's reputation.

On Monday, August 3, for the first time, Miss Astor entered the courtroom. Although Jay had seen her in New York City, he couldn't get over her stunning good looks. A soulful, dark-eyed, ethereal wisp of a woman weighing barely one hundred pounds, she was even more beautiful than he had remembered. Film cameras failed to capture her essence: her gorgeously chiseled, slightly uneven but lovely, cameo-like features, her throaty sensuous voice, her full lips and Titian hair. Whether flanked at a table by her two lawyers (only one of whom spoke), or on the stand, she became the fixed star of the courtroom.

Behind Jay sat the peanut gallery, a vast sea of staring eyes and listening ears, composed mostly of middle-aged and elderly women, who perched in their chairs, wearing their proper hats and holding their paper bags. Their mood decidedly favored Miss Astor, despite Dr. Thorpe's good looks. Jay gathered they were willing to forgive her indiscretions because of her readiness to risk her career for the custody of her daughter.

The strategy on both sides was the same: to prove the other party morally unfit to care for the child. Marylyn's nurse, a plain looking bespectacled woman in an ugly frock, approvingly pointed out that Mary kept the child in virtual isolation every summer to protect her from polio. Her view of Dr. Thorpe was less kind. She testified that beautiful women often came to the house to spend the night, and even took breakfast in bed with him the next morning. Miss Astor's attorney, a roly-poly, round-faced fellow with an unruly shock of curly hair, went so far as to suggest—to the gasps of the courtroom—that Dr. Thorpe entertained more than one woman in bed at the same time.

Dr. Thorpe defended himself against these charges by using his patrician bearing to good effect. A handsome, curly headed, debonair, well-spoken gynecologist and surgeon to the movie stars and other rich women, Thorpe responded through set teeth:

"Untrue . . . all of it untrue. I feel very sorry for Miss Astor that she would allow her hired help and attorney to resort to such slanders. But by doing so, she leaves me no alternative . . ."

The doctor broke off without finishing the sentence, an interruption that left everyone wondering: Did he mean to publish her diary? Not until Miss Astor took the witness stand did the courtroom learn that the two large ledgers, bound in black cloth with bright red edges, resembling a grocer's account books, had indeed been entered into the trial as Exhibit A. The public and press, though, did not get to see all the pages, covered with Miss Astor's distinctly feminine handwriting in deep purple ink, but only those that Dr. Thorpe's attorney, a bald ex–narcotic agent, chose to release. Although she acknowledged that she'd mentioned many men in her diary, she claimed that much of what Dr. Thorpe's lawyer released was a forgery. Listening to her tearful testimony, Jay was inclined to believe what she entered into the record as her "real diary":

"Nothing could have been more sincere than my love for Franklyn a short while ago and yet—we are now simply worlds apart. I am not myself with him. Sometimes it's pretty bad—we don't think alike; and we're not interested in any of the same things. All we have to talk about is the doings of the day: some patient of his who won't pay a bill, the servants, the gardener, the baby, her discipline and cute ways, money matters, the trouble with my family—and that's all. Franklyn has no sense of humor whatsoever. I like laughter and people and he sits around with them like a bump on a log. He doesn't know what to discuss, except politics and medicine."

After meeting the playwright George S. Kaufman, whom she adored immediately, she tried in her diary to make sense of her feelings.

"Does this happen over and over again? Am I going to keep on forever thinking this is it? What the hell is it? And what do I want? First of all I've come to the conclusion that the reason for my constant restlessness and dissatisfaction with life in general is because I don't like to be alone. I'm scared to death of independence, and the result is I'm always tying myself up imagining myself deeply in love with someone I've no right to be tied up with."

All of the people following the trial had the same question in mind: Did she author the racy parts? Perhaps Jean Harlow would know. Jay had promised his editor that he would include Miss Harlow in his reports. Now was the time to call her.

"Do you remember me?"

"Of course Jean remembers you. We played poker together and Jean predicted that one day you'd visit her in Hollywood—and she was right. Come on over. Here's how you can find her house."

Directions followed. Jay drove to the leafy Bel Air and Beverly Hills area and eventually located her estate. Jean answered the door wearing a sheer silver shift that offered no more than a nod to the convention of dress. She might just as well have come to the door naked, which he understood she sometimes did. Leading him through the house to the pool, she excused herself. He sat in a padded deck chair and admired the view of the city. Returning a few minutes later with a tray of drinks and noshes, she put it on a white-enameled table, shaded by a green awning, and stretched her gorgeous body on a chaise longue. They drank and reminisced until suddenly she stood up, wriggled out of her shift, and dove into the blue water.

"I don't have a bathing suit," Jay said stupidly.

"Neither does Jean."

Feeling terribly self-conscious, he stripped and cannonballed into the pool trying to cover his nakedness. They swam and splashed each other playfully, until she pulled him up against her body and kissed him with tongue and lips. What he feared most happened: he sprouted an erection. Jean laughed and said:

"There seems to be an eel in the pool."

Torn between wanting to ravish her and fearing that some mobster would kill him, he exited the pool, took an enormous bath towel from a trolley piled high with them, and wrapped himself up like a mummy.

She returned to the chaise longue and lay undressed, letting the water evaporate off her body in the warm light that had not yet shaded toward evening. He had an urge to lick the drops off her, running his tongue across her perfect alabaster skin and into hidden places. Thank goodness for the bath towel. Once again he was rampant. Forcing himself to focus on her face and not her body, he said that he had been attending the Astor-Thorpe trial and wanted to know what she thought about the discrepancy between the ruminative and the rutting Mary.

She surprised him by responding, "You can ask her yourself. Jean will call her now," and went into the house, standing naked just inside the open French doors talking on the telephone. He could hear her say, "Fine, we'll drive over about nine, after we've gone out to dinner."

"Jean will just throw something on and be back in a jiff." At the door she turned and smiled. "Jean told you that someday we'd dine together. Jean knows these things."

They ate at a small restaurant on Sunset Boulevard—salmon and a salad. When Jean mentioned Longie, Jay asked her not to tell him they had dined together. His request seemed to flatter her. She wanted to pay for the meal, but he wouldn't hear of it. They drove in Jean's red Cadillac to Miss Astor's Toluca Lake mansion, where she retreated each night after court. A tired, wan Mary greeted them in the living room, with the lake glistening beyond huge windows. There they sat among the great thick rugs and luxuriant pillows, soft lights, and profusion of indoor plants, including an ornamental monkey-puzzle tree that reached to her cathedral ceiling, comforted by the knowledge that the great iron gate and the solemn night watchman would combine to restrain the reporters camped outside her house.

"I love this place," she said. "It's everything that the Quincy and Chicago apartments were not, the holes where I grew up. Did you know," she said aimlessly, "I once placed second in a beauty contest to Clara Bow. The 'It' girl had more to show physically, and I more mentally."

At first Jay thought her comment strangely self-serving, but soon realized that she had a first-rate mind, even if she was emotionally immature. Jean and Mary, like two teenagers, giggled and joked, sometimes at Mary's expense. When the subject migrated to the diary, she rued Dr. Thorpe's confiscating it and the descriptions of men easily identified. Otherwise, she felt perfectly satisfied that her diary had served her well as a faithful confidante.

Jay specifically asked her about George S. Kaufman, who held center stage in the "thrill omnibus." With admirable candor or foolish indiscretion, Mary told them a part of the story surrounding their affair, beginning with the breakdown of her marriage.

"The fact that I was in love with George had nothing to do with my wanting a divorce, but of course Franklyn thought it did. The real reason was I didn't love Franklyn anymore. I was unhappy and bored with him, and I didn't think one should live with a person feeling that way."

Jay could feel the pain of this troubled woman; her loneliness and need for love palpably filled the room. To break the tension, he pointed to the monkey-puzzle tree. "That's some tree. I've seen only one other like it. Did you grow it yourself?"

"No, my current gardener installed it. He's very good."

She returned to her memories of George. "We had rapturous moments, delicious, sublime. We'd sing at the piano and talk about books and shows. The great bane of modern life, boredom, never assailed me when I was with him."

Jean, who had been unusually quiet, said rather too crassly, "Love 'em and leave 'em. That's Jean's motto." She shifted the gum in her mouth and added, "Well, it's all over now."

Mary replied heatedly, "Not until I have Marylyn *and* the diary!"

Jay could understand her desire to have her daughter legally assigned to her, but it seemed a little late to worry about the diary. "Just words," said Jean, with a wave of her hand.

"Franklyn has his own reasons for taking the diary," Mary said cryptically.

On the way back to Jean's house, Jay started to wonder. The doctor had a wide practice among Hollywood stars, not as a psychiatrist or therapist, but as a surgeon and gynecologist. According to rumor,

Jean's numerous affairs, as well as those of other actresses, had led to several abortions. Had Mary used a code to identify these people? If Thorpe had performed illegal operations, Jay could understand why the doctor would want the diary.

Certainly he couldn't ask Jean. When they returned to her place, she reminded him that at Longie's party he had agreed to play poker with her in Los Angeles and insisted that he honor his word. In an upstairs sitting room she had a table laid out with cards and chips, as if, like Miss Havisham, she was waiting for the suitor's return. They played well into the night, and Jay had the feeling that he might have been able to share more than her card table if he had stayed on; but he wanted to return to the courtroom before other reporters grabbed the best seats in the jury box and he was forced to sit at a distance.

He kissed Jean goodnight and promised to return in a few days to take her to dinner and then to the Trocadero. She said wistfully:

"Longie and Jean used to go there."

Outside Jean's house, the silver moonlight had miraculously turned the lawns blue, and the sky, vibrant with stars, seemed just one dream away from descending and, like the arms of Arietta, embracing him with astral brilliance.

On two hours of sleep, he attended the next day's court session. Miss Astor gave him a radiant smile and sat down next to her attorney. Garbed attractively in a dazzling white ensemble of sharkskin silk, she also wore a sheer brown blouse, a tan felt hat adorned with an orange-tinted feather, white sandals, tan stockings, and brown gloves. A jeweled brooch shone at her throat.

Some of the quotations from Mary's diary that had appeared in the physician's affidavit charging her with "continuous gross, immoral conduct," the ones she deemed forgeries, now surfaced.

"Once George lays down his glasses, he is *quite* a different man. His powers of recuperation are amazing, and we made love all night long. . . . It all worked perfectly, and we shared our fourth climax at dawn. . . .

"We saw every show in town, had grand fun together and went frequently to Seventy-Third Street where he fucked the living daylights out of me. . . .

"Was any woman ever happier? It seems that George is just hard all the time. . . . I don't see how he does it, he is perfect."

When Kaufman came to Los Angeles, she saw him at his hotel.

"Monday I went to the Beverly Wilshire . . . he tore out of his pajamas and I never was undressed by anyone so fast in all my life. Later we went to Vendome for lunch, to a stationer's shop . . . then back to the hotel. It was raining and lovely. It was wonderful to fuck the entire sweet afternoon away . . . I left about six o'clock."

Shortly thereafter, Kaufman and Moss Hart went to Palm Springs. Miss Astor followed.

"Ah, desert nights—with George's body plunging into mine, naked under the stars . . ."

Judge Knight issued a subpoena for George S. Kaufman.

At the conclusion of that day's testimony, Jay migrated to a diner a few blocks away and sat over an egg bagel—the owner claimed never to have heard of a water bagel—and a bad facsimile of coffee. During the courtroom proceedings, when the questions and answers had begun to beat a repetitive tattoo and Jay's mind wandered, the word "current" kept surfacing in his head, until it lodged there like a splinter demanding attention. As he dunked his bagel in the virtually tasteless liquid, he suddenly remembered the context: Miss Astor saying, "My current gardener." Her use of the word "current" had to mean that the gardener now caring for her grounds had replaced someone else. How recently? He could hardly wait for the next day.

As Miss Astor passed down the aisle to take a seat next to her attorney, she again threw him a smile. Dressed in a simply tailored navy blue taffeta tunic dress, accented by a single diamond brooch, and a broad-brimmed matching hat, she lent a touch of relief to the severity of her outfit with white gloves and purse. Her shoes were of black suede and her sheer silken stockings of sunburn tan.

Jay smiled back and, before the judge arrived, leaned out of his first-row seat in the jury box and asked an attendant to hand Miss Astor a note. It read: "What is the name of your current gardener and when does he come to your house?" She took a small gold fountain pen from her purse, unscrewed the cap, scribbled on the paper, and handed it back to the attendant. She had written: "Piero Magliocco, every day."

Called to the stand and asked about the trip to New York when she first met Kaufman, Mary prefaced her answer with some comments about her marriage having begun at that period to fail. She dabbed her eyes with a lacy handkerchief and explained:

"I felt as though I had been in a foreign country and had suddenly found people who spoke my language. I met Edna Ferber and Moss Hart and Alec Woollcott and Oscar Levant. I went to a small gathering where people hung around the piano and listened to a new score that George Gershwin was playing for them; it was a new concept of opera and was to be known as *Porgy and Bess*. I felt that I was accepted easily and without question; I liked their ideas and opinions and points of view."

For nine days, the spectators hung avidly and silently on every detail that dealt with life as most of the spectators had never lived it—a Bohemian world of orchidaceous ladies and artistic gentlemen. Rumors circulated that, behind the scenes, pressure was building for Judge Knight to conclude the proceedings. Apparently, Will Hays and the Legion of Decency had appealed to studio executives to immediately stop further hearings of the case, with its "spicy testimony and scandalous mention of big film names." On the last day, Judge Knight summoned the lawyers to his chambers, where they deliberated on a settlement. When the judge and the lawyers emerged, their smiles betokened an agreement.

"Baby Marylyn Thorpe," the judge declared, "will remain with Miss Astor during the school months of the year, except for weekends, and with Dr. Franklyn Thorpe during the summer and vacation periods, except for Christmas and Easter, which she will share with both parents. The child's teachers, nurses, and governesses will be selected by mutual consent, and the cost of the child's upkeep will be shared as the court may direct. As for the diary, its final disposition will rest with the court, for the nonce to be placed in a vault assigned to County Treasurer Roger Byrum. By stipulation, it will be made available again only if the custody case is reopened at some future date."

Mary retreated at once to her Toluca Lake mansion, where numerous friends, including Jean Harlow and Jay, celebrated her self-declared victory. He had hoped to catch a glimpse of Mr. Magliocco, gardener, at Mary's house, but they arrived too late. At some point during the celebration, Jay asked her if he might stroll through her garden. She told him to feel free to "perambulate" wherever he wished. As he wandered toward the garden shed, he wondered where—in which safe-deposit box, in which hands, in which bonfire of the vanities—the million-dollar diary would end up.

The shed revealed nothing unusual, except a stack of torn papers in one corner that he assumed Mr. M. used for repotting and planting. All of them treated the same subject: the recent polio cases in the city. Her faithful gardener had collected information on recent advances in the treatment of the disease and on prevention; perhaps his training as a priest had left him with pastoral sympathies. At the house, Jay inquired discreetly of the maid which kind of vehicle Mr. M. drove.

"A ratty old truck."

Trying to appear indifferent, he laughed and said, "I suppose Miss Astor has him park it in the garage lest he offend the neighbors."

"Oh, no," she replied, "he leaves it on the street. Miss Astor's garage is always full up with cars."

Friday, around midafternoon, August 14, the day that he had decided to trail Mr. M. to his house, Jay left his hotel, leisurely drove west on Wilshire Boulevard, turned north on La Brea, passed Hollywood High School, and turned west on Sunset. The ritzy women with large brimmed beribboned straw hats mixed with vagrants scrounging through trash bins and picking up cigarette butts from the street: two separate worlds, living side by side, utterly oblivious to the other. Across the street from Schwab's Drugstore, he turned north into Laurel Canyon, the heat immediately abating as he drove under the canopy of sycamores and through the wooded retreat of the rich, whose homes, snuggled into the hillsides and twisted streets, looked like outcroppings of brilliant ore. The view of the San Fernando Valley from the top of the canyon had attracted a few painters sitting at easels. Across the valley floor, the fruit groves stretched north to the San Bernardino Mountains and as far east as the eye could see. He saw irrigation ditches and farmhouses, and at the foot of the canyon that ribbon of activity, Ventura Boulevard.

As he came down the north side of the canyon, he had to stop at one point for several deer crossing the road. The creek near the bottom, shielded by oak trees and heavy brush, still trickled water, even though the heat had sent thousands to the beaches. As he approached Ventura Boulevard, he noticed that on both sides of the canyon road large homes were being built, catering to the tastes of those in the movie colony who eschewed Beverly Hills and Bel Air for the sylvan and bucolic San Fernando Valley.

He took Laurel Canyon north to Riverside Drive and turned east to Toluca Lake. Mr. M.'s Ford truck stood outside Mary's house. Parking down the street, he glanced at his watch: four o'clock. He waited for over an hour before Mr. M. appeared, wearing overalls and a straw hat. Throwing some shrubs onto the flat bed, Piero drove off in a cloud of blue smoke that issued from his exhaust pipe, suggesting that the vehicle badly needed a ring job. Jay followed him north to Magnolia Boulevard and then west. Keeping another car between them, Jay more than once had to run a stop signal to keep him in sight. At the corner of Laurel and Magnolia, Mr. M. went into a pharmacy and disappeared for a few minutes, returning to drive south on Laurel just a few blocks to Hesby, then turning east for two blocks, and, halfway down the street, parking alongside another car in the driveway of a one-story, Spanish-looking house with red ceramic roof tiles. Jay gathered that most of the houses on the north side of Hesby had gardens that ran right through to the next street, Otsego. Continuing around the corner, he stopped at the boundary of the garden. Father and daughter had found themselves a nice place, and the garden, which Jay assumed Piero tended, had been planted with walnut and orange and lemon trees. Rows of yellow and pink rosebushes, gardenias, camellias, and a trellis of wisteria snaked across the landscape. A fountain with water continually seeping from a raised font proved an irresistible lure for birds, flapping their wings and happily chattering.

Coming back around the block, Jay discovered that the car had departed, leaving only Mr. M.'s Ford truck. All his instincts told him to see Arietta when Mr. M. was gone from the house; he therefore chose to wait through the weekend, until her father had returned to work on the Monday. In the meantime, he could entertain himself with Jean Harlow, who had suggested that he ring her on Sunday about noon. A voice, older than and different from Jean's, answered the phone. Her mother, as he quickly discovered, had come to the house to nurse her daughter, who had complained of a fever. Had Jay not lingered for a moment to ask if he could lend some assistance, Jean wouldn't have picked up the extension phone and recognized his voice.

"Come right over," she insisted.

"Jean's not well," said the older woman, clearly annoyed.

"Geez, Mom, leave Jean to run her own life."

Not wishing to get caught in the middle of a family spat, Jay said that he would drop by and leave if Jean did not feel well enough to receive guests. Picking up some flowers from a stand on Sunset Boulevard, he drove to her house and was met at the door by her redoubtable mother, who immediately made it clear that his presence was an imposition. When Jean materialized, they retreated to the upstairs sitting room and, as before, played poker.

Jean did seem ill. Shadows under her eyes and a lack of anima-
tion made her look not like Jean Harlow but like a washed-out
peroxided blonde who had spent too many hours on the town
the previous night. A certain heaviness in her manner belied the
dynamic woman he knew and admired. A year later, she would be
dead of uremic poisoning from malfunctioning kidneys impaired by
a childhood illness. That last day Jay saw her, with her mother hov-
ering nearby, he asked about the mysterious death of her husband,
studio executive Paul Bern. Her mother tried to interrupt, but Jean
asked her to leave.

"The Nazis would like to pin it on Longie," Jay said.

"Not a chance. Paul blew out his brains."

"The circumstances *were* suspicious."

"You tellin' Jean?" She looked around and whispered, "He passed
himself off as a lover, but, in fact, he was impotent! Couldn't get
it up."

Jay decided that with her mother in the next room, now was
not the time to pursue such a delicate subject. Excusing himself,
he kissed her on the forehead, thanked her for rescuing him at
the front door, and said "Cheery-o" to her mom and fluttered his
fingers.

Sunday he drove to Santa Barbara and hiked up to the mission.
As a way of remembering T-Bone, he looked past the foam-fringed
coastline to the breathtaking ocean, turning his back on the cel-
ebrants fingering their beads and crossing themselves, the faithful
who had trekked to the mission to celebrate—what?—and murmured a few lines from a Milton poem,

> And now the sun had stretched out all the hills,
> And now was dropped into the western bay;
> At last he rose, and twitched his mantle blue:
> Tomorrow to fresh woods, and pastures new.

For several minutes, he stood on the hill admiring the waves
breaking on the shore below and the sails fluttering in the distance;

he stood as if the winds from that first spinning place had carried him across the centuries to this high holy mount. And he looked upon his youthful life and wondered what it weighed: the college education, the marathon dance contests, the journalism, the law breaking, the love he felt for T and Arietta. What mattered any of it, unless he could say that his life before would meaningfully affect what came after?

Returning to L.A., he encountered a blistering sun baking the valley, which rarely enjoyed the ocean breezes that sometimes relieved the city. In the heavy air, he found it hard to breathe, a frightening sensation that brought back memories of his friends and him as children seeing how long they could hold their breath and thankfully gasping air at the end of their foolishness. The same car that he had seen on Friday, three days before, stood in the driveway, but not Mr. Magliocco's truck. He walked to the front door, shaded by an overhanging roof, rang the bell, and refrained from peeking in the curtained windows. A middle-aged woman greeted him at the door. She wore a nurse's uniform, and her gray hair was fixed behind her head in a bun. Her face vaguely resembled Arietta's.

"Is Arietta Magliocco at home? I'm an old friend."

The woman looked at him incredulously, as if he had just said something hugely stupid. After she readjusted her expression, she asked, "Your name?"

"Jay Klug."

She closed the door and left him standing on the ceramic-tiled walkway, which, he noticed, had decorative floral designs. Even if the woman denied him entry, he had established one fact: Arietta was, or had been, here. But no, that was inference; the woman might have gone merely to ask her mistress if she had ever heard of the name that he had given her. At her return, she introduced herself as Amalie Holz, Arietta's aunt. Her nurse's frock led him to entertain a thousand doleful thoughts. Aunt Amalie led him through a handsome living room containing four white upholstered chairs and two couches and several end tables and stately lamps with fringed shades, all of which looked as if they had just come from the furniture store, and into a spacious paneled den with a large picture window facing a pool. She asked him to wait a minute, disappeared, and then motioned for him to follow her. The bedrooms stood off to the side of the house, and Arietta occupied the back one. Aunt Amalie opened the door—and Jay nearly collapsed. Arietta lay in an iron lung, entombed to her neck, dependent on a mirror, mounted above her head, to see. Amalie explained that Arietta had bulbar and anterior polio, which inhibited swallowing and breathing. Aunt Amalie closed the door silently and left them. An easy chair rested next to the lung, no doubt for her aunt and, when she was absent, Mr. Magliocco. The only other furniture in the room was a bookcase topped by some framed photos, a stuffed giraffe, and a kachina doll.

Jay knew a little about iron lungs because a Newark friend had contracted polio, and he would occasionally see him at the hospital. Before the advent of the iron lung, patients drowned in their own secretions or choked to death. Some Harvard engineer, building on earlier designs, constructed an airtight tank that used electrically driven bellows to create alternate negative and positive pressures to contract and expand the person's diaphragm with an even rhythm. Jay wondered: What if the current failed? Perhaps that was why a battery-driven auxiliary pump stood nearby.

Arietta forced a smile and a breathy hello. The absence of despair in her face and voice caused Jay to break down and cry uncontrollably. He sobbed for several minutes and stopped only when he started to cover her face with kisses.

"My face is . . . all wet now," she said playfully.

Snorting back further sobs, he found a towel in an adjacent bathroom and mopped up his tears.

"Where . . . are you . . . living?" she inquired.

"The Franklin Arms off Wilshire. But I don't want to talk about me, I want to hear about you. Tell me everything." It took a moment before he realized that talking did not come easily to her, and added, "If you have the breath for it."

She asked him to spoon some water from a glass into her mouth, an action that took some deftness to avoid her choking. She frequently paused to save breath and nodded when she wanted more water.

"End of June . . . on a Saturday . . . swimming . . . the North Hollywood public pool . . . the next day . . . woke up . . . achy. Blamed it on . . . swimming forty laps. But as the day . . . went on . . . more and more tired. My neck stiff. I figured . . . probably strained it . . . swimming . . . and there was . . . nothing . . . seriously wrong. By evening . . . a fever . . . ten o'clock . . . that night . . . father . . . alarmed . . . called a doctor."

Her ordeal, which she disclosed laboriously, all the while gulping air, Jay subsequently rendered in her words but in his cadences for his unfinished novel:

The doctor examined me thoroughly, diagnosed a virus, and tried to allay my dad's fears. I passed a miserable night, getting up with great difficulty to use the bathroom, and by morning felt terribly dizzy. My father decided to take me to the hospital for tests and called an ambulance. I insisted on walking to the driveway. I haven't walked . . . since.

They did a spinal tap, which made my dizziness worse. The doctor said I had meningitis. In the evening they moved me to a makeshift room on the second floor, a sun parlor, where I had no buzzer to call for a nurse. I spent the most horrible night of my life, so dizzy that I thought at any moment I would fall out of bed.

The following day, the doctor did another spinal tap, in order to relieve the acute pressure on the brain and to check the diagnosis again. And again the verdict came back meningitis. My father hired a private nurse to stay with me because I was obviously not improving.

The next morning, Dad sat with me for several hours and managed to understand my mumblings: 'My legs are heavy. I can't move them.' He looked terrified because polio had been rampant. In fact, three weeks before, a neighbor's daughter had come down with it.

Another spinal tap convinced the doctors I too had polio. By that afternoon, my intercostal muscles were becoming involved and my breathing was deteriorating. The doctors frantically tried to find an iron lung because the hospital I had been brought to didn't have one.

An ambulance came, and as the orderlies carried me into it, my father's face appeared at the window. I heard him say, as the tears ran down his cheeks, "Why my lovely Arietta? God is punishing me." I felt certain I would die.

I barely remembered my trip to the other hospital. The minute I arrived, the staff put me into the iron lung and a priest gave me the last rites.

The next few days were a blur. I constantly ran a high fever, which meant the polio virus was still very active and doing more damage. I cried all the time. Can you possibly imagine finding yourself suddenly unable to move a muscle or breathe without a machine, and to think you have a whole life of this in front of you? The horrible doctors complained to my father I would never recover because my morale was so low. But they did absolutely nothing to help. I never had hot packs, which would have relieved the excruciating muscle spasms, because they could not be applied inside the lung. I was never given pain pills because the hospital felt I would become addicted. I don't even remember being washed. They never combed my long hair, which had become completely matted with the cotton batting around my neck.

At first, when they opened the lung to wash me, I couldn't even bear the weight of a sheet on my body. Fortunately, it was warm, so I wasn't cold. I lay on a wool blanket to prevent bed sores. How I itched! The nurses spent most of their time trying to scratch my back with back scratchers pushed through the portholes. After days of this misery, the doctors thought that my intercostal muscles were flickering, a good sign. Maybe, I would eventually be able to breathe on my own.

But I was receiving no treatment, so father spoke to his employer, the movie star Mary Astor. It was she who had found this house for my Aunt Amalie to rent. The next day, I was moved to a new hospital, with my dad at my bedside trying to raise my spirits and constantly repeating, "Arietta, one day you will never even think of this terrible time."

I was then moved to a ward in the company of other polio patients, ranging in age from five years to fifty, twenty-five men and twenty-five women. To my astonishment, they laughed. Overnight, I stopped crying, and I have not cried again because of the polio. To make up for the life I once had, I now live in memory. Although I feel certain that my store will never run out, I grieve that I cannot add to it with dances and boyfriends and . . .

She cast a lovely smile over Jay. "Lovemaking in the woods."

Rather than communicate through the mirror, Jay sat facing her and frequently stood to stroke her hair, or kiss her forehead or nose or cheeks, but not her mouth. It wouldn't be long before her father returned. His presence would make it harder to talk. But before he could ask her about the murders, she made the oddest request.

"Please dance . . . and pretend . . . you're dancing with me."

Positioning himself behind the iron lung in view of the mirror, he slowly broke into one step and then another, all the while extending his arms as if holding Arietta. And as he whirled his imaginary partner around, leading her by one hand and then the other, he actually began to believe that he and Arietta were dancing and that when she rested her hand on his shoulder, he would pull her close and kiss her mouth.

Fearful that his twists and turns would remind her of her paralysis, he began to slow down, but she sputtered:

"No, no . . . continue. After the fox-trot . . . the tango. Then the Charleston . . . and the black bottom."

And so he danced, wishing for a miracle to cast off the iron lung and lift Arietta to her feet to join him in a celebration of movement. While she laughed with joy, tears ran down his face.

At last he quit and sat beside this bodiless beauty, stroking her cheek. For the longest time they said nothing, providing a restorative peace. When he finally asked why she and Mr. M. had run away, she grew pensive. Even now he feared she wouldn't disclose the secrets that she and her father had taken such pains to hide.

Her silence began to torment him, and he told her that she had to dispel the dread darkening his life.

"Come back tomorrow, and I will tell you everything."

Now free of the fear that she'd again run away, he neglected to anticipate even worse.

As he pulled into the Magliocco driveway, next to Aunt Amalie's car, he noticed in the rearview mirror a black coupe parked two doors away across the street, and, at the corner, a yellow car. All the other visible autos on Hesby were parked in driveways. He reached under the front seat and removed his pistol. Aunt Amalie took him directly to Arietta's room. Lest he tax her, he did most of the talking, reminding her that she had promised to tell him why she was lamming it.

"I can't help but think that you and Heinz Diebel are somehow linked." She neither spoke nor nodded. "My guess is that since Zwillman had you watching other Nazi sympathizers, you were keeping tabs on Diebel as well."

He put his ear to her lips and told her to whisper. Finally, she did, saying she regarded disclosure as betrayal.

"You don't have to incriminate anyone, just tell me why you're a suspect in Heinz's murder."

In short breaths, she explained that Diebel rarely appeared in public, except in dance halls, and then under an assumed name. Few people outside the movement knew him. She had met him at a Friends picnic in Parsippany and found him vicious. She said that Longie wanted to scare him with a good thrashing. "I had no idea . . . he'd be shot."

"You moved away from your partner on the dance floor and took Diebel's hand. Was it to identify him for the killer?"

"For a thrashing."

Jay wiped her forehead. For several minutes they sat listening to the rhythmic pumping. Then he said, "The Friends eventually discovered what you'd done and put a price on your head, which explains why Longie wanted to find and protect you." She nodded. "But what about Axel Kuppler?"

The painful look that possessed her face spoke volumes and yet nothing.

At one time, Arietta had been seeing him. He played around. Margie worked for him; he was her pimp.

"Was it one of Longie's boys or a jealous lover who shot him?"

Jay waited. At last, she said, "Neither."

That left only one person who knew about her secret life, the very man whose name Jay had refused to utter.

"Your father?"

Her eyes misted.

"Don't . . . ask me . . . that question."

Suddenly it all made sense. The Friends were chasing not only Arietta but also Mr. Magliocco, an experienced hand with autos, who may well have driven the getaway car for Diebel's murder. Then Jay remembered the gauntlet gloves. Axel must have found out that Piero had abetted in the crime, and Axel must have shared this information with the Friends. Throw in the fact that Mr. M. did not approve of his wooing Arietta . . . curtains for Axel. By running away, she was loyally protecting her father. Of one thing Jay was sure: Arietta would never admit it.

"Can we talk about us—and what happened?"

She looked away and then back into the mirror, as if she had come to a decision. "In the other room . . . to the right side of the fireplace . . . you'll see a bookcase." Pause. "On the second shelf from the top . . . a black diary fringed in red." She told him to read her comments during the period they dated and, if he wished, the other days as well. She stopped to catch her breath. "I find it . . . hard to talk." She began to wheeze. "The passages touching on us . . . will make you understand better . . ."

Pressing his cheek to hers, he kissed her hair, and left the room with Arietta's shimmering face peering out of that ghoulish-looking machine thumping like a disembodied heartbeat. In the den, he found the diary and sank into a leather chair, immediately turning pages.

Arietta had dated some entries and not others, but he located the first entry bearing on him.

March 7, 1934. When Rico dropped out of the marathon, it looked as if Longie's plan was sunk. Luckily, I latched on to a handsome young fellow, Jay Klug. I thought him quite cute, a good dancer, a guy who had gone to college, someone I'd like to see again. But be careful, Arietta, that he, or anyone else, never finds out what you were doing at Dreamland.

March 13, 1934. Jay came to the studio. I was flattered and agreed to go out with him if father approved. Am I building sand castles again? Then, of course, there is father, who wants me to date Catholic boys, even though he left the church. I feel sorry for him. He once had a wife and a good job, and then . . . I love my dad dearly, but we have little in common. I listen to him talk about opera and rum-running and the Waterhouse and how he met mother and left the church. He tells the same stories over and over. It's really become terribly boring.

I like Jay because I can be myself with him. A part of me wants to be an intellectual and a professional dancer. Jay talks about books and plays and FDR and the New Deal. I like his ideas. We go to movies and discuss Jean Harlow, whom he once met. (One night we saw Mary Astor and George Kaufman!) We play the piano and sing. And Jay's open-minded. Although Jewish, he accepts me easily and without question.

Over the next several months, Arietta's diary exhibited a soul in torment over her affair with Jay.

Finally! Jay asked me to come to dinner at his parents' house. They live in a rented place that's small but comfortable. His father, like my dad, is very old world, but that's where the similarity ends. Dad's years in the church made him unbending; Jay's father is an open-minded socialist. I liked the passion of the man; he too cares about the welfare of people and the country. Jay's mom, who is quite a beauty, has the gentlest disposition and brings to mind my own mother. She deeply loves her son, and I feel sure her influence will affect him in later years, just as memories of my mother's kindness remain with me.

I do believe that Jay has fallen in love with me, and though I am not sure of my own feelings, I do enjoy being with him. He's kind and he's nice, and he does keep me on my toes, literally (when we go dancing) and figuratively (when we talk about "the world"). And then, of course, there's Axel. . . . I still can't believe that it's over. Or is it? From time to time, he calls. He was my first, and I matured in his company, even though I was young.

Jay is different from Axel. Axel dominated and taught me. He was the teacher and I the pupil. Jay's formal education is better than mine (his four years of college show), but in matters of love I am no novice. I wonder: Am I falling for Jay? I've been through it all before with Axel, feeling the same way, the same emotions. How come? Does this happen to everyone who falls in love? And if Jay is Mr. Right, what does right mean? I worry that my head and my heart are driving me in opposite directions. What's to be done?

I've come to realize that my indecision regarding Jay is because I don't know my own mind or what I want. Like so many other girls my age, I wish to be free of my father's house and start my own life. But I haven't the nerve to do it without someone else, a loyal man who will stand by me through thick and thin. To live without a husband—I can't bear to see Dad's loneliness—would scare me and probably drive me to marry just for the sake of getting married. And that would be a mistake.

Showing the effects of her flight from Newark, Arietta's diary became fragmentary—until Cape May.

May 12, 1936. Rolf Hahne, whom Axel and I had met at the boat, showed up in Cape May Township. I was shocked. Had Jay not appeared, things might have gone badly. Keeping my composure, I gave Jay a story that I think he believed. To put him off our track, I said I wanted to see my cousin in Chatsworth. Actually, I did want to go to the Pine Barrens, but I also knew that it would probably give me a chance to lose him. Though I had planned to seduce him, I didn't count on being seduced myself. Climaxes such as I had never known! What rapture! I could feel my eyes rolling up into my head and thinking that I never wanted his hard, furious lovemaking to end. Unfamiliar sensations, skin-tingling ones, swept over me, and, had it not been for my father's predicament, I would have returned to Newark with Jay. But whatever else happens, that day will always live in memory: the rivers of light, the dappled water, the golden pebbles, the shimmering trees and leaves. We were Eden's children just as it must have been in God's garden.

Hearing an altercation at the front door, Jay closed the diary and got up. Suddenly Rolf Hahne was standing in the room with a pistol in one hand, giving orders. "Show me the telephone!" Cauliflower cut the line with a knife and ordered Aunt Amalie to go to her room and stay there. A mistake!

Hahne pushed the gun into Jay's ribs and demanded to be taken to Arietta, shoving Jay along in front of him. On seeing the iron lung, Hahne exclaimed, "What's this?" The small lamp over Arietta's iron lung lit Rolf's face, making his grimaces all the more terrible.

"Polio," Jay replied.

Hahne ordered him to sit on the floor with his hands behind his head, and then turned to Arietta. "Axel told me that you know who killed Heinz Diebel. Now don't lie to me." Placing the gun against Arietta's head, Cauliflower virtually foamed at the mouth. "Heinz was a most important person in our movement. His death must not go unpunished!"

Arietta whispered, "I don't know. The person's face . . . was covered."

Rolf straightened his back and paced, as though trying to decide how to proceed. "You see how far our hand extends, from Germany to Los Angeles. Now you are in my hands." Without any transition, his manner suddenly changed into that of a slighted child. "When you and Axel picked me up at the ship and we all went to dinner, I felt buoyant. Here, I thought, are real friends. Now, tell me," Hahne pleaded, "who killed Heinz? And what about Axel?"

She shook her head to indicate ignorance.

Rolf went to the wall socket and pulled the electrical cord. The lung wheezed to a stop. The auxiliary pump started at once. Overcome with rage, Jay lunged at him, but Rolf, the stronger of the two, tossed Jay against the wall and struck him over the head with his gun. Rolf removed a knife, snarled, and disabled the auxiliary pump. "If you want me to restore the lung, tell me the names of the killers."

When Arietta began to wheeze badly, Rolf said, "All you have to do is give me names, and I will return the plug to the socket." Cauliflower laughed cruelly. "I would hate to see so beautiful a fräulein choke to death. But that need not happen. Just two words will save you."

Arietta's face was turning red, and she was now gasping loudly.

A ferocious barking and growling sounded in the hall behind Arietta's closed bedroom door. Then scratching. Rolf turned a bilious green, and his eyes exuded hate. Arietta was growing paler as Rolf tiptoed to the bedroom door. With Rolf's focus elsewhere, Jay removed his pistol from under his shirt. When Rolf swung the door open, three things occurred at once: a German shepherd sprang at Rolf's gun hand, a shot issued from the hall, and Jay discharged his own pistol. Slumping to his knees, Rolf managed to turn his head sideways, revealing a bullet wound to the forehead and one to the neck, slumped forward, and fell dead at Jay's feet.

Standing in the doorway, leashing the dog, and holstering her pistol was Francesca Bronzina. As much as Jay wanted to know about Francesca's miraculous appearance, he first restored electricity to the lung and revitalized the auxiliary motor. Rubbing Arietta's cheeks, he slowly restored her color. In the meantime, Aunt Amalie had gone next door to call the police and Mr. Magliocco, all of whom seemed to arrive at the same time. Two cops removed the body, and Mr. M. cried over his daughter. When the hubbub had subsided, Francesca answered their feverish questions.

"From wiretaps we knew that the Friends, fearing to appear weak, had directed Rolf not only to silence pro-boycotters, but also to avenge the murder of Heinz Diebel. Axel argued with Rolf once the latter discovered that his friend was a pimp. To save his own skin, Axel said that Arietta was involved in Diebel's death. The shooting of Leonora Wells in Norma . . . a terrible thing. Once our agents located him in L.A., I became his shadow. Finally, I approached him to learn what I could. He was persuaded that I shared his feelings for fascism. The rest you know."

Interrupting her explanation, Jay mentioned that he had seen a yellow car at the end of the street. Was it hers?

"Yes. Fortunately, I did not have to choose between following you or Rolf. He led me right to you. And from my several meetings with him, I knew he feared dogs. The rest was easy. A dog trainer let me work with his German shepherd for a few hours, and Aunt Amalie opened her bedroom window to admit me and Botsie."

When the others left, Arietta and Jay were wordless. Running a hand through her hair, he kissed her lips.

"I read the diary."

"You're not angry?"

"No, I'm in love."

Her words caught in her throat. But before he could fill the void, she pleaded, "Don't say anything."

Then they just sat and mutely stared at each other. How long that quiet lasted, two minutes, ten, more, he couldn't measure. Finally, he ended the indecision that had been torturing his sleep. "I want you to marry me."

It felt as if eons elapsed before she spoke.

"Is it because . . . of the polio?"

"No, it's because I love you. I'll pick out a ring tomorrow."

"Let's wait and see."

Arietta wanted to hear about his attempts to find her and her father, taking pleasure, he surmised, in the thought that he might have been running after her not just to satisfy Longie's wishes but also to ease his own heart's pain. She was silent through his recital, her face expressing a range of emotions. When he finished, she said:

"I am sorry about your friend T. I feel partly responsible."

Of what transpired between them after that, he had no memory. The language of fondness is fragmentary, a phrase, a word. When it came time for him to depart, he kissed Arietta's forehead, promised to see her the next day, and cried all the way back to the Franklin.

At last, he slept well, rising late in the morning, and, fortified by his wish to marry Arietta, nerved himself to telephone Longie, knowing full well that he would have to deceive him. If his odyssey in Abe's employ had taught him anything, it was the paradoxical truth of the Yiddish proverb, *Men ken makhn dem kholem gresser vi di nakht.* Abe had blown up a dream to be bigger than the night. Throwing caution to the winds, Longie had used his Third Ward Gang, ignoring the complaints of the ACLU, to break up Nazi meetings and to crack heads. The big guy had paid people to protest the Olympics and had sanctioned a murder or two. All for naught. The games were played, and Brundage profited.

"Did your boys ever find Arietta?" Jay asked disingenuously.

"No, the trail went cold. But we did discover that the day of Axel Kuppler's murder, a call was made from his apartment to the Magliocco house."

"And?"

"If the call was made before he was killed, he probably made it. If after . . ."

"Arietta or her father," Jay volunteered.

"You said it, I didn't."

Trying desperately to think like a cop, Jay said, "What if someone forced Axel to make the call . . . or the Maglioccos hired a hit man, who telephoned them once the job was done? You have to admit, there could be other explanations."

"It's all academic now, as they say. We're in the clear."

"Maybe someday I'll run into her."

"If you do, give her my best. By the way, you know a dame who calls herself Margie the Bop? The boys tell me she's been asking for you. She's dancing at Minsky's."

Her stage name amused Jay. "We used to be pals. I'll write her."

"My advice, kid, is buy a train ticket and come home. I'm sure your parents would love it."

The conclusion of Mary Astor's trial had brought an end to Jay's contract. Unless he wanted to return to Sierra Powder Puffs, he had no means to remain in California and see Arietta. The work that he most cared for, journalism, was in Newark.

"I'd really like to see Los Angeles before returning back east. Do you have any contacts who could fix me up with newspaper work in the city?"

"Listen, kid, I owe you a favor for sending you on a wild-goose chase. Come back east and I'll pay for you to go to law school."

The generosity of Longie's proposal overwhelmed him. He said thanks a million, but given his commitment to Arietta, he felt obliged to decline. "I know I've mentioned law school before, but I don't think I'm ready."

"Jay, you're older now, and wiser, at least I hope so. Think over my offer. It's good any time."

Jay repeated how much he appreciated Abe's kindness, asked him to give his regards to Puddy and the others, and said that he just might try to find work at the movie studios. Longie asked about T, but Jay decided to relate that story another time. They wished each other good luck and concluded the conversation warmly. The next time that he and Arietta were alone, he told her about Longie's generous offer.

"Did you mention . . . father and me?"

"He brought it up," Jay answered, fudging the truth.

"What did he say?"

"They found Axel's phone records. The day of the murder a call was made to your house. The cops don't think Axel made it." Screwing up his courage and risking all, he asked, "Who made it, Arietta?"

She looked away, but finally spoke, admitting that she had made the call. "I had gone to his trollop's apartment . . . to condemn his pimping." She explained that the door was partially open. "Axel was still alive, unconscious, lying on the floor, bleeding. I panicked, guessing who had killed him. Wildly searching his apartment . . . to find any incriminating evidence about me and Axel . . . I failed to call the police . . . or an ambulance." Her eyes pooled with tears. "I left him to die . . . unattended. Wasn't that hateful?"

"That's when you called your father?"

"Just before I left the apartment—to tell him what I suspected. He didn't deny it."

They sat in silent contemplation for a while, each of them no doubt trying to imagine the thoughts of the other. Whether out of genuine concern or simply to seek safe ground, Arietta changed the subject, though her voice quivered with fright.

"Will you really go to law school?"

"Arietta, you needn't worry. I'm not leaving, certainly not now . . . in fact, not ever."

Her anxiety seemed to melt away, and for a few minutes they chatted fondly. After less than an hour, Aunt Amalie came into the room, said it was time for Arietta's sponge bath, and sent Jay home.

The next day, Amalie called to say that Arietta did not feel up to a visit. Could he come tomorrow instead? She assured him that nothing was seriously wrong and that occasionally Arietta suffered from extreme fatigue, which made talking difficult. He spent the afternoon looking for an engagement ring but could find nothing tasteful. Most of them looked obscenely loud or painfully poor. He decided to heed Arietta's advice and wait.

Again he slept well and lazed about in the morning, fussing with his summer suit so that when he saw Arietta his clothes would be-speak his intentions. While he was admiring himself in the mirror, one of the hotel staff knocked at the door and handed him an en-velope stamped special delivery. Arietta's name was on the return address. But before savoring her words, he finished adjusting his tie, a token gesture of his desire to hold her presence dear.

My Beloved Jay,

My aunt is writing these words and has promised not to blush. Your wish to marry me has given me more joy than I deserve. I love your every movement, your every touch, your every word.

As you probably guessed, your last visit initially elated me, but then as I began to think of what you would be giving up to make a life with me, I could not convince myself that you would be happy with a cripple. Yes, I know that is a harsh word but an honest one. I suspect you must have felt it when you said, "I'm not leaving, particularly now." The "now" could refer only to my condition. When you quickly added "not ever," I knew that it was intended as an afterthought, because you sensed what you had actually implied. If you married me, you would feel trapped, even though you might want to leave. With this cloud over us, we would always be weighing our words, never free to live and love with abandon.

Although I don't want you ever to forget me, I want you to be brilliant with learning, married to a woman who is your equal, in every way. Longie has given you an incomparable opportunity. Take it, for my sake. I want to read about you in the years to come. Jay Klug, the famous lawyer—and novelist.

In breaking off our "engagement," I realize I am leaving behind someone I'll long for every moment of the day. I do so already.

Love,
Arietta.

Postscript

The sale of his father's business to Helena Rubinstein enabled Jay and his parents to limp along until he had graduated from an outstanding law school, at which time he went to work for Abe Zwillman, handling some of his more problematical business affairs. When Abe died in 1941—the authorities said he hanged himself, even though his hands were tied behind his back—his estate went principally to his wife, with a few gifts to friends, like a red Cadillac to Jay.

Shortly after Zwillman's funeral, Jay entered the army and fought with the Allies as they moved from North Africa into Sicily and through the boot of Italy. South of Rome, they camped in a small village. Mail from home, posted months before, finally caught up with them. Among his letters was one from Mr. Magliocco, written in Italian. Jay had a local priest, who spoke good English, translate it.

Dear Mr. Klug,

Forgive me for writing to you in Italian. It's easier for me. As you know, I've always felt protective about Arietta. She can now sleep outside the iron lung and, though she spends a few hours each morning in it, devotes most of each day to reading and to writing in her diary. I know how much she feels your absence and would love to correspond with you but feels that you would misunderstand her intentions. Let me assure you that her breaking off the engagement was not from a want of feeling but from an act of self-sacrifice. That she regrets it now, I have little doubt. However, as we say, the water that is fed to the plant can no longer be returned to the pail. I pen this brief note to beg a small favor: Write to her. Should you decide that my own flagrant sins, which I know from Arietta indirectly caused the death of your friend, prevent you from corresponding, I will surely understand.

Praying for your safe return and success, I am

Yours sincerely,

Piero Magliocco

In May 1945, Jay resumed his job as a journalist, fully intending to complete a book about his farraginous journey through the chronic angers of a hungry world. But he has been delayed by more important matters: a marriage and helping to raise the three children, two sons and a daughter, he has with Arietta. Now completely free of the iron lung, she can walk with the aid of braces, though she prefers that Jay push her in a wheelchair, which she calls her jaybird chariot, a better name, by far, than "jailbird," a tag that Jay might well have earned had the Kefauver crime committee been able to incriminate him in Longie's felonies. His appearance before the committee made headlines in Newark, because he told the investigators that the real crimes of the 1930s were committed not by gangsters but by bankers and industrialists who grew fat off the Depression, off the beggaring of millions. It was families robbed of their self-respect who joined "gangs." Asked whether he would be willing to put his thoughts into writing, he said, "I'm sure that I shall not rise to the level of inspiration, but perhaps in the book that I'm hoping to resume, I can achieve explanation."

FINI

Glossary

broost: brisket
benny: a man's overcoat
bupkis: nothing
chutzpah: nerve
ecco: lo, behold
es vet dir gornisht helfen: nothing will help
forshpiesers: hors d'oeuvres
gelt: money
Il uomo é un pavone: The man is a peacock
lansman: countryman
Men ken makhn dem kholem gresser vi di nakht: One can blow up a
   dream to be bigger than the night
mishuganah: crazy
mit vergnügung: with delight
non sono d'accordo: I disagree
noshes: snacks
putz: penis
Shabbas: Sabbath
shanda: scandal
shmattahs: rags or cheap dresses

schvarzes: blacks

tuchis: backside

volk: folk, common people

yahrzeit: the anniversary of someone's death, especially a parent's